Praise for Mary Kay McComas and
What Happened to Hannah

"Blending poignancy with humor, crafting characters as real and recognizable as your next-door neighbor, Mary Kay McComas weaves stories that brighten the heart."

—Nora Roberts

"I love Mary Kay McComas. Her books are honest and real, and transport you to a place that feels like home."

—Patricia Gaffney

"It is hard not to be moved by the tender love story that emerges from the depths of violence in this haunting and touching novel. You will never forget *What Happened to Hannah*."

—Jessica Anya Blau

"[An] inventive contribution . . . that steals the show. McComas focuses on the most important relationship of all—the relationship one has with oneself—and spins an introspective and irresistible story that, for some readers, may make this collection worthwhile."

—*Publishers Weekly* on "Melon Lemon Yellow" in *Bump in the Night*

Praise for Mary Kay McComas and What Happened to Hannah

"Blending poignancy with humor, crafting characters as real and recognizable as your next-door neighbor, Mary Kay McComas weaves stories that brighten the heart."
— Nora Roberts

"I love Mary Kay McComas. Her books are honest and real, and transport you to a place that feels like home."
— Francis Gulley

"It is hard not to be moved by the tender love story and energies from the desire of violence in this haunting and touching novel. You will never forget What Happened to Hannah."
— Jessica Anya Blau

"[An] inventive contribution . . . that steals the show. McComas focuses on the most important relationship of all—the relationship one has with oneself—and puts an introspective and irresistible story that, for some readers, may make this collection worthwhile."
— Publishers Weekly on "Makin' Ends Yellow" in Home for the Night

What Happened to Hannah

Mary Kay McComas

WILLIAM MORROW

An Imprint of HarperCollinsPublishers

This book is a work of fiction. The characters, incidents, and dialogue are drawn from the author's imagination and are not to be construed as real. Any resemblance to actual events or persons, living or dead, is entirely coincidental.

HarperCollins books may be purchased for educational, business, or sales promotional use. For information please write: Special Markets Department, HarperCollins Publishers, 10 East 53rd Street, New York, NY 10022.

FIRST EDITION

Designed by Diahann Sturge

Library of Congress Cataloging-in-Publication Data has been applied for.

ISBN 978-0-06-208478-1

12 13 14 15 16   OV/RRD   10 9 8 7 6 5 4 3 2

For my sisters, Karen Aris and Amy Perry.
More than sisters, better than friends.

What Happened to Hannah

Chapter One

He should have called her three years ago. Now he had no choice.

Opening the center drawer of the old oak desk in his office, Grady removed a folded piece of yellow notepaper and spread it out flat in front of him. He rubbed his damp palms on his khaki pants and sighed out loud.

The creases in the note were pliant and soft from frequent folding, the writing a bit faded. A name and two sets of numbers, nothing more. But how many times had he slipped them from the drawer, dialed all but the last digit and hung up?

She was twenty years and a phone call away, yet there were moments when he could feel her standing next to him, catch the scent of her hair, hear an echo of her voice.

How pathetic is that?

He blew out another long breath and picked up the receiver, trying to ignore the knot in his stomach.

If he thought about her long enough, a familiar guilt would bore holes through the memory; anger would trickle in, pool, and eventually congeal into a sense of hopelessness and failure.

Mostly he tried not to think about her—but he couldn't help being curious.

Leather creaked as he pushed himself straighter in the chair. He should make the call before he remembered too much, before he lost the tenuous hold on his professionalism. Changing his mind was no longer an option.

He dialed the numbers.

He stared at the phone and grappled with his doubts. Who was she now? Still the strong, brave, serious Hannah, so beautiful that a teenage boy would risk his friends and reputation—everything—to be with her? Or was she someone else entirely?

He didn't know if she'd married or if she had children. Both her business in Baltimore and the private number were listed under her name, but that didn't mean anything except that she had her own life and her own business.

Well, part of a business.

Insurance, for crissake.

He smiled and let loose a soft private chuckle. Insurance. The night she disappeared he'd feared for her life, prayed desperate prayers that she'd run away. He'd worried himself sick. Then slowly and gradually, as months piled up to years and no word of her returned to Clearfield one way or the other, he still refused to believe what everyone else assumed to be true. She simply couldn't be dead. She couldn't be. Bright summer days were still glorious, snowy nights with full moons were still magic, and rainbows still brought her to mind. He had fantasies of her popping up on television or a movie screen or in some magazine showing off her chateau and rich, handsome husband—Clearfield and Grady Steadman an empty lapse in her memory.

But never, not in his wildest imaginings or his simplest dreams, had he pictured her selling life insurance to Main Street, America.

It made perfect sense, of course, and he wasn't disappointed when he found out where she was and what she'd been doing. Aside from the relief that she was alive, he felt satisfaction, pride even, that she'd been smart enough to hide herself in plain sight. She was living a normal life out in the open, where those who might have hunted for her would never think to look.

A male voice answered, clear and crisp. "Benson Insurance & Investments."

"No Levitz?" The short response had thrown him.

"I'm sorry?"

"It's not Levitz and Benson Insurance anymore?"

"No. I'm sorry. Mr. Levitz retired a couple of years ago. My name's Jim Sauffle. Can I help you?"

"It's just Hannah now?"

"Hannah and three other full-time agents, but she owns the business. Is there something I can do for you today?"

"No. I need to speak with Hannah Benson."

"Of course, may I tell her who's calling?"

Better not. She might refuse to pick up. "It's a personal call."

Three years ago, when he'd felt compelled to track her down, he prepared a speech and never used it. Dozens of times since then he'd thought of calling, simply to say hello. Too late for that now. This wasn't a personal call, not really. He had three times the ground to cover with her, all of it rocky and full of potholes. He'd wing it, he decided. There was no telling how she'd react to any of it, so he'd handle her like he would any other stranger.

He held his breath and listened to the loud pulse in his ears over the soft Muzak on the other end of the line. He reminded himself, once again, that whoever answered next wouldn't be the same Hannah Benson he'd known so long ago. It would not be a sweet, beautiful young girl, but a grown woman who very likely wasn't going to be too thrilled to hear from him.

"Hannah Benson." Her voice soft and expectant, and so familiar. "Hello?"

"Hannah. Hi. You might not remember, it's been a long time. This is Grady Steadman. We went to school together in Clearfield. Virginia." He added the state as an extra nudge, in case it was amnesia that had kept her away for so long. A guy could hope.

If some silences were golden, this one was pure lead.

"We used to be friends, Hannah. My mother taught at the high school and—"

"Hello, Grady." Jesus. That hadn't changed—the warm chill that ran up his spine when she said his name, the way she dragged on the *r* and went light on the *y*. It rang the same, despite the lack of warmth and welcome.

"Hi. It's been a long time." He grimaced. He said that already.

"Yes."

"I know you're at work. I tried your home number a couple of times last night and couldn't reach you. How are you?" He was stalling.

After a brief pause came, "I'm fine. How are you?"

"I'm good. I . . . Okay, I wish I were calling under different circumstances. I wish . . ." What did he wish? That things had turned out different between them? That he'd called three years earlier? That he hadn't called her at all? He cleared his throat. "I wish a lot of things but, unfortunately, this isn't a personal call."

Like an idiot he waited half a second, holding his breath, wondering if she'd make some sound on the other end to convey her disappointment. He couldn't even hear her breathing.

"Hannah?"

"I'm listening."

"Hannah, your mother passed away yesterday. I'm sorry. There's just no easy way to say it."

He wanted to see her eyes. She had the truest, bluest eyes he'd ever seen—always frank and honest, if you took the time to look. He'd come to know and trust what he saw in those eyes. If he could look into them now, he'd know if she was in pain or indifferent; sorry or glad. The silence told him nothing.

"Doc Kolson says it was probably a heart attack. She died quietly in her sleep."

Quietly, like Ellen Benson had done everything else in her life. *Quietly* tolerating years of abuse and regular beatings at her husband's hand, then just as *quietly* she bashed his head in with a fry pan when she'd had enough. Hannah's mother had been a very quiet woman.

"Hannah?"

"Yes." He heard the hesitation in her voice as she gathered her thoughts. "Ah. If you'll give me an address, I'll send a check for the expenses."

As cold as that sounded, it was more than he had anticipated. As far as he knew she hadn't seen or spoken to her mother since she was sixteen years old, and things were . . . complicated between them before that.

"I wish it was that simple, Hannah. I truly do. But you have to come home."

"I don't think so."

"If it were simply a matter of burying your mother, I might not have called. There's more to it than that."

"Look, I appreciate the call. I do. It can't have been easy to track me down like this, but I'm afraid it's a waste of your time. I'm willing to pay to see that she has a decent burial and if she has debts I'll pay them if need be, but that's all. I can't go back there, Grady. I won't." He took a deep breath and opened his mouth to blurt out the rest of it, but she spoke again. "What about Ruth? If this has to do with half the farm being left to me or something like that, then send me the papers. I'll sign everything over to her. I don't want anything except to be left alone. No offense." She added the last as an afterthought. "It's nice of you to let me know."

"I'm not offended. I can't even blame you. I don't know what all happened that day or the night you left, but I know it was bad—bad enough for you to risk your life to get away from it and to stay away. But that was a long time ago, Hannah. And now there's another life on the line."

There was another short silence. Then in a softer, kinder but still tentative voice she asked, "Is Ruth ill?"

He held the phone to his ear with one hand and rubbed the other over his face then back through his short dark hair. What the hell was he doing? Why hadn't he given the number to Doc Kolson and asked him to call her? Pastor Barnes would have done it. The new priest at the Catholic church, Ellen Benson's priest, would have made this call. But no, he had to do it. He had to hear her voice.

He leaned back in his chair and swiveled a bit to the right to look out the large window in his office—through the blinds, across the street, beyond the sleeping March gardens and the leafless bushes and trees to the large white gazebo on the shallow knoll in the center of town . . . where he'd taught Hannah to kiss.

"No, not ill. Ruth died five years ago, Hannah." He heard her sharp intake and closed his eyes. "Jesus. I feel like I'm peeling this Band-Aid off so slow I'm taking skin with it. I'm sorry. I'm really sorry. I would have called you when it happened, but your mother never hinted that you might still be alive for another two years—after her first heart attack. Then when I tracked you through the DMV she asked me, begged me, not to call you. She said if you were happy somewhere she didn't want to ruin it for you; and if you weren't, why add to your troubles. Now I'm serving you a double dose of sad and . . . I should have called sooner. I'm sorry."

She sighed soft and sad over the line. "I am, too. I'm so sorry. Poor Ruthie. So young." She paused and was thoughtful. "I suppose I should be curious as to how she died or why but . . . I feel like they're both finally at peace and the rest of it doesn't matter. Not now. Not anymore. I suppose that makes me sound heartless and insensitive, doesn't it?"

"Not to me. But some of the rest of it does matter. I haven't gotten to my primary reason for calling."

There came a soft, humorless laugh at the other end. "I've run out of relatives, Grady. So, again, if it's about the farm . . ."

"It's not. And you haven't quite."

"I haven't quite what?"

"Run out of relatives." He waited for her to say something. "Hannah?"

"Don't say it."

"I have to. Ruth had a daughter. Fifteen years ago. And she needs you."

"She needs me." She didn't sound like she knew what that meant. He heard her moving around, the pattern of her breathing changed. "What, she needs a kidney or something?"

"She needs a home."

"Come on, Grady, get real. What the hell am I going to do with a fifteen-year-old girl I've never even met before?"

"Get to know her. Make her a part of your family."

"What family?" she exploded. "You just told me my whole damned family is dead."

"You never married?"

"No! I didn't." Christ, he was a total ass to feel so elated . . . wasn't he? Then she made a point to add, "On purpose! To avoid this very thing. I don't want to be responsible to or for anyone.

You got that? It's selfish, I know, but there you are. That's me. Selfish. Selfish, selfish Hannah."

This wasn't quite what he expected, but it didn't make any difference. Hannah was still the girl's only living relative. He'd envisioned a little initial resistance, but he'd been counting on some maternal instincts to kick in and save the day. A little empathy maybe, so she could put a child of her own in the same situation.

But all was not lost. In his experience people who were truly selfish didn't think about being selfish or call themselves selfish. They simply *were* selfish—the lack of thought and intent being part of the definition. He had a feeling Hannah wasn't as selfish as she was scared. And scared didn't cut it—her niece was scared, too.

"Don't you want to know about her? Aren't you curious?"

"No. I don't and I'm not. Now, if you've covered everything you called to tell me . . ."

"She looks like Ruth. A little taller, I think, but slim and blond. Her eyes are more like yours, though. A darker blue."

"Grady."

"She's a nice girl. Smart. She's a sophomore over at the high school. She runs. She's on the track team. I understand she writes poetry, too. And . . . Oh! One good thing—her hair's always the same color. I'm not sure if it's because she doesn't care for green or purple hair or because she didn't want to trigger her grandmother's heart attack prematurely, but it all works for me."

"Well, it's not working for me. I'm not going to change my mind. I'm not equipped to raise a child."

"She's not a toddler. Most of the messy stuff is done. She wants to go to college in two years. Things could get very screwed up if she's made a ward of the court. Two years, Hannah. It'll be over in a heartbeat. She'll be eighteen and legal. Her share of the farm will pay for most of her education. In the meantime, all you'd have to do is sort of . . . supervise her. Sign a couple of field-trip permission slips. Make sure she eats. Nothin' to it."

"Right. Nothing to it. For two years. In Clearfield. I'm sorry—"

"No! Not in Clearfield. Well, yes, but only for a couple of weeks. You'd have to come get her, sign a few custody papers, take care of things at the school, get things rolling on the sale of the farm, but that's it. Two weeks tops, I'd think."

"You'd think?"

"Two weeks tops." Now to drive the point home. "She needs you, Hannah."

He gave her moment. If a spark of the girl he once knew still existed in this woman, she'd do the right thing. If this was the right thing. For all he knew she could be a mild-mannered insurance saleswoman by day and a kinky-freaky sadomasochist by night—to whom he was delivering an innocent young girl.

He doubted it, but he'd sure as hell check her out as thoroughly as he could before she left town again. For now, he'd go with his gut instincts. And they were telling him that the mere fact that she was now silently contemplating the issue at the other end of the line meant that, deep down, the girl he knew survived.

"And this person's been living with my mother for the last five years, I take it?"

"A while longer than that. Ruth was pretty sick for a while."

"What about her father?"

"Never in the picture as far as I know. No name on the birth certificate."

There was a loud sigh and more silence. He rubbed the back

of his neck to ease some of the tension and impatience he felt, reminding himself that Hannah hadn't had three years to prepare for this phone call.

"What if we meet and hate each other?" she asked, keeping her tone stiff and uncommitted over the misgivings and trepidation in her voice. "She'd have to come and live here. I'd be taking her to a different state, aren't there laws against that?"

He grinned. Victory, satisfaction, anticipation. He felt them all and had to pull—hard—on years of practice to stay cool and professional. "Only if you're stealing her and crossing state lines, which you wouldn't be . . . And you knew that already. Let's not make this any harder than it has to be right now. Just come down and meet her and we'll take it from there. We'll see how it goes. If it doesn't work out, it doesn't. At least you will have tried. I can't ask for more than that."

"Even that is asking for a lot."

"I know."

She didn't speak again for several seconds. "You always were very persuasive."

He glanced out at the gazebo, memories tugged at him. He wouldn't pretend not to know what she meant. "Some things are worth a little extra effort."

Once upon a time *she* had been worth *a lot* of extra effort.

"Sometimes some things are best left alone."

"Sometimes some things need to change."

"It doesn't sound like you've changed. You're relentless." Her laugh was soft, but he could tell she wasn't amused. "You're not going to give up, are you?"

"I can't. It's important."

That importance clawed at him from within, for the girl, for Hannah, for him—and it went beyond his job, his civic duty, and his responsibilities as a decent human being. This was his chance at redemption, to attempt success where he failed before; to right a wrong in a convoluted, circular fashion. Because once, a long time ago, Hannah had come to him for help and he'd failed her. Miserably. Young and powerless, shocked and confused, no excuse, no amount of adult reasoning had ever been enough to abate the monstrous guilt, the ego-shattering self-doubt, or the tender pain of a first love lost.

Second chances didn't come along often enough to be ignored or taken lightly. It was too late to change things for Hannah, to be of any use to her, to change what happened so many years ago. But it wasn't too late for her sister's child.

He heard her shuffling papers and moving around.

"I need time," she said. "To think. And I can't just drop everything here and take off for two weeks. When would I have to be there?"

"Your mother's funeral is scheduled for Monday morning at ten."

"Christ, Grady, will you give me a break? I have a life. I can't possibly—"

He cut her off. He didn't want to give her *too much* time to think. And it wasn't only her life they were talking about. "This will be Anna's second funeral in five years. She shouldn't be alone."

"Who's—?"

"Anna. That's her name. It's short for Hannah."

The background noise ceased and she waited a beat. "Are you making that up?"

"Nope." He laughed silently. "Frankly, I never would have thought to . . . but I did save it for the very end. Just in case."

Chapter Two

Hannah turned down the car radio and drove straight through town. She didn't slow down to gawk at the changes or hark back to the good old days. There weren't any good old days as far as she was concerned, and she wasn't deceived by Clearfield's quaint country charms. No one knew better than she that the tree-lined streets and the pristine gazebo in the middle of the town square were a facade of downhome living and the American way. It could have been Any Small Town, USA, but it wasn't. It was Clearfield—home to a dark, festering truth for which she was now the final vessel.

She took her foot off the gas and slowed down for an unexpected red light at the intersection of Main and Merchant—an upgrade from the four-way yellow blinker that dangled there before. She closed her eyes and tried not to laugh, hysterically, at the sizzling anger bubbling up inside her. It was a testament to her wild, erratic emotions at the moment—pissed off at having to obey anyone or any-*thing* in this town and the giddy, unreal sensation of being there in the first place.

Using her thumb and index finger to push her sunglasses

up, she rubbed the sweaty impressions they left on the bridge of her nose and then let them slide back in place. She reached over and cut off the heat. It registered forty-two degrees out and was as bright as July; freezing cold winds blew tree limbs like whips and she was sweating. The March weather made as much sense to her as finding herself parked at a red light in Clearfield—in other words, none at all.

"Heavy traffic." The four o'clock rush hour got a sniff of disdain. She and an old man in a faded green pickup truck were stopped on opposite sides of the intersection for three other vehicles. Those now long gone, the two of them sat and stared at each other, waiting for the light to change again. Clenching her teeth, she darted a look to both sides of the road—at the full bumper-to-bumper parking along the sidewalk and the lone pedestrian entering an antique store called Granny's Attic—then back at the old man across from her.

Hannah blew out a deep breath to ease some of the tightness in her chest, and put a hand over the knot in her belly. With her elbow on the car door she jammed her fingers into her straight dark hair and rested her cheek in the palm. She wanted to scream.

The old man's wrist perched loose over the steering wheel—and he must have felt her looking at him from behind her glasses, because he suddenly lifted his hand in greeting. She startled and gasped, then just as quickly stomped down on the extra surge of paranoia.

This isn't a trick, she reminded herself. *People in small towns wave at strangers all the time. He doesn't recognize me. He isn't going to tell on me. There's no one to tell, remember? This isn't a trick. Grady wouldn't trick me.*

The light changed and she gunned the engine. The lumbering green truck rolled out from the opposite direction and she watched as the old man passed her by without a second look.

See? Simply a nice, friendly old gentleman. Not a trick. No one to tell, right? Grady wouldn't trick me.

At least she hoped he wouldn't. *People change . . . but not that much.* She'd keep the doors locked and the motor running until she was sure, of course, but she knew all too well that there were times when believing and taking a leap of faith were her only options. Besides, she'd taken a leap with Grady before and—

She shook her head and shuffled him to the back of her mind. She wasn't here for Grady. She came here to meet the girl. Her sister's daughter. Ruthie's baby girl. Why did that seem like such a strange concept?

Twenty years was a long time. Wasn't that what Grady said?—*It's been a long time . . .*

It was a long time—to run, to hide, to fear. To hate. She could have, would have, gladly lived another twenty or a hundred years without coming back to Clearfield, had it not been for the call from Grady Steadman.

Talk about a blast from the past. More like a nuclear meltdown. Out of the blue like that? *Foosh!* Four years of expensive psychotherapy down the toilet in a heartbeat.

She could still feel that horrible, sickening sensation as the blood drained from her face and her stomach roiled with the shock and terror of being found and caught—like a fugitive—as if she'd been hiding under a rock all this time. The past rolling up on her like a tidal wave, crashing down on her, washing her back into the past as if the last twenty years had never happened.

But they had happened. Every single month, day, hour, and second of them had transpired with her blessing, she assured herself, then flipped the left-hand turn signal when she spotted the neat little red brick church up ahead. She was not, in any way, the same Hannah Benson who left this miserable, dinky, white-picket-fenced town so long ago. She *had* changed; she'd made a point of it.

Truth told, after the first six months, she'd stopped running and she didn't bother to hide anymore. She was young, a few weeks shy of her seventeenth birthday when she woke up one morning, close to dawn, curled up tight to stay warm under a pew in the Sixth Baptist Church of Our Lord in Baltimore. She lay there, *so cold,* listening to the silence, to the occasional creak of wood contracting, and realized, as if God had whispered in her ear, it was over. She could stop running, stop hiding, because there was no one chasing her, no one coming after her, no one looking for her . . . and there never would be. She had survived, escaped, and was free.

After that, only the hate and mistrust remained, growing up inside her—growing up *with* her, she supposed. Like two massive twin sentries guarding and protecting her as they faced the unknown together.

And love? Well, she'd buried that with her decision to run. Even then she knew there was no going back to it. What she hadn't realized was that she'd never find it again, either.

She slowed to make the turn with barely a glance at the Catholic church where she and her mama and sister had gone to eight o'clock mass every Sunday—in modest hand-me-down dresses that were always too long, but long enough to hide the scrapes and bruises. She felt again the insane urge to laugh, but didn't. What a paradox that was, huh?—listening to sermons about a good and benevolent God on Sunday morning . . . after a Saturday night at home with her daddy.

Of course, the occasional limp or black eye that often elicited a Monday-morning call from the school nurse—Nosey Bitch was her name at their house—were grounds to remain in the truck, in blessed peace, during the service. Sort of a special, well-deserved treat, she always thought.

The closer she got to her destination, the tighter she gripped the steering wheel. The faster her stomach rolled, the louder it growled. The back of her throat swamped with salty saliva and the metallic taste of bile.

It didn't seem to matter how often or forcefully her mind registered that she was being foolish and behaving irrationally, she couldn't shake the overwhelming need for positive, tangible proof of her safety. *It would be foolish and irrational to stray too far from the car without proof,* came a countering logic from deep inside her where instinct or intuition or . . . whatever it was that she relied on so heavily to keep her alive and well dwelt.

Hannah took the next right, and because there was no one she trusted more than herself, her hand didn't go anywhere near the key in the ignition after she stopped and put the car in park.

Amazed, she found a certain comfort in the leafless trees and bushes surrounding the rolling field of tan and brown grass in front of her. The whole place looked dead, or at least sleeping—harmless, in any case. One of two squirrels searching for food, scampered up a tree while the other sat on his hind legs, picking at something it had found in the grass, ignoring her. Peaceful was a word some dark corner of her mind seemed to recognize.

She wasn't sure if it was a bad or good thing that there wasn't another human in sight.

Detached and robotic, her fingers pulled on the door handle and she got out. The exhaust from the car's engine curled at her ankles. She debated against closing the door, but the constant *ping-ping-ping* alert that the keys were still in the ignition ate at her last raw nerve. She silenced it with a gentle thump of the door. Then all she heard was the constant, well-tuned hum of the car's engine and the barely there sound of the wind wafting through the empty trees—like background music almost.

Walking straight ahead, she knew where to go—covering the same territory she'd prowled a thousand times in her dreams. She took straight lines and sharp angles like strolling through neighborhoods, one after another, staying off the lawns, head down, not looking at the houses or reading the addresses until she came to her block where all the Bensons laid together for all eternity.

She knew grandparents and uncles and aunts, though her visits had been few in the past. Intuitively, she sought out the newer flat markers, rather than those that were upright or leaning at odd angles. His was the third she came to.

Karl Aaron Benson
June 11, 1936—November 23, 1992

That's all it took. Her throat closed. Her heart went wild. She tried to suck in air and heard herself wheezing. She pulled her sunglasses off as her vision blurred. She couldn't swallow. Panic and adrenaline chased through her arteries, sent everything careening out of control. Her mind, her body, the rotation of the earth. It was as if his hand—strong, practiced, and vicious—shot out from his grave to grab at her throat again.

The last of her courage gave way to the old fears. Memories glutted her senses. She gagged and sobbed at the same time, reached out for something to hold on to and found nothing.

She moaned as screams from the past pierced her ears again . . . and her vision dimmed to gray. Over and over, the shrieking tore at her. It *would not* stop. Her hands shook violently. The cries bounced in her brain like ricocheting lightning, sharp and burning. Her right hand fisted around something cold and hard and heavy, but when she looked down both hands were empty . . . and covered with *blood*.

Blood everywhere. So much blood. She covered her ears with them and sank to her knees, and with a heave that came from the center of the universe, she vomited.

She heard herself gasping and gagging, sobbed as the screams grew distant. Coughing and spitting. The blood turned to tears. Her heart hammered in her chest and her lungs worked hard to feed her more oxygen. When she could trust her eyes again she opened them to find herself on all fours, staring down at her father's headstone.

He was truly dead. Dead and vomited on.

The symbolism didn't escape her as she pushed back to sit on her legs. The landscape settled to its previous state of rolling, sloping terrain. The adrenaline drained away slowly as she sat there numb and staring.

"I'm back, you son of a bitch," she said, her voice a bare whisper in her ears. "I win."

Chapter Three

Hannah wasn't one to linger too long where she knew she wasn't welcome—or near foul deposits of vomit, for that matter. It was a culmination of raw nerves and high anxiety, and there was no denying the release gave her some relief. Granted, she was now disappointed in her lack of control. Sorry, too, that she'd given into her darkest fears and the wild imaginings of the paranoia she'd worked so hard to conquer but . . . she was also human. And every day it got easier and easier to admit it. She slipped. She made a mistake. She needed to move on.

After a few more minutes, she brushed her tears away and searched the pockets of her jacket for a tissue. Pulled together, she picked up her glasses, got to her feet and walked away. It was just that simple, wasn't it?

He was dead and she was safe. Everything else she could handle.

Despite the sour taste in her mouth the air blustered clean and crisp, cool against her skin. Her black jeans were wet from the knees down and that felt good as well. The cemetery bolstered an energetic sense of life inside her. Life and strength and youth.

She passed the graves of two stillborn children—both named Boy Benson, four years apart—born three and seven years before her. Mama used to pick the last chrysanthemums of the season and deliver half to each on All Soul's Day—which is how she'd come to know where to find the dead Bensons.

She'd never attended a funeral until several years ago when her partner and truest friend Joe Levitz lost his wife—which could be thought of as odd by some, considering all the dead relatives she had. But if all funerals were as sad as Julie Levitz's, she couldn't believe she'd missed much.

It took her several minutes to find Ruth—as far from Karl as the Benson plot allowed. Mama's work, no doubt, as there was a new, fresh-dug grave laid out and draped under a canopy nearby.

She avoided looking into it, keeping her eyes directed elsewhere.

And wasn't it just like her mama to think that she and Ruth would find more peace this way? As if Karl could continue to torment them in the hereafter if they were laid too close to him?

One side of her mouth curled upward. The last forty-eight hours demonstrated that that sort of thinking ran in the family, she supposed.

Ruth Ann Benson
Daughter and Mother
April 20, 1975——December 2, 2007

Short. To the point. Sadly, too few people carved epitaphs on gravestones anymore. What would Ruthie's have said? She was fourteen when Hannah left town, still a child in truth. What sort of woman had she been? A woman too young to die, obviously—but had there been time for her to pull her life out of the hellhole they grew up in? Was she happy? Productive . . . aside from having the baby?

Buried with the Benson name, did she never marry? For the same reasons Hannah hadn't? Were hers not too long, not too complicated nowhere relationships with impossible men, too? Did they at least have that in common? Who *was* Ruth?

Hannah tried to remember her and kept pulling up images of blond baby dolls with vacant blue eyes and frilly pink dresses. Quiet. She couldn't recall Ruth ever speaking in anything but a whisper—in the dark, from across the room—it was always a strain to hear her. Even when she cried.

But then, none of them cried very loudly back then.

She sighed and tried to feel sadder but the plain fact was, she hardly knew her sister; and if she felt anything at all for her, it was guilt.

Ah, guilt! *Oh, that pang, where more than madness lies, the worm that will not sleep and never dies.* A quote from Byron that her therapist, Dr. Fry, had engraved on a small smooth metal disk for her to carry around in her pocket; a gift that came in the mail months after their sessions ended. Even now it floated around on the bottom of her purse somewhere. Though they'd done their best to work through parts of Hannah's guilt, Dr. Fry must have known it would worm its way back to bite her on the butt from time to time. Like now.

Of course, there were things you could tell your therapist and also things you didn't dare tell anyone.

Staring at Ruth's name carved deep into cold rose marble, she found it hard to keep telling herself that she wasn't responsible for anyone's actions but her own; that she couldn't control the choices other people made. She'd come to terms with the choices she'd made, learned to live with them on a day-to-day basis. But there were always those nebulous queries as to how *her* choices had affected others—Ruth and Mama . . . and Grady. What would their lives have been like now if she'd made different choices?

And this girl, this niece of hers? Well, if her choices didn't mess up the girl's life, the girl was indeed going to mess up hers. She wanted to see that thirty-six-year-old woman with the near-perfect life she'd designed to suit herself who willingly takes a teenager into her home without having a psychiatric disorder named after her. Where *was* she?

Like a deer with her ears to the wind her head lifted at a sudden noise . . . actually a sudden lack of noise as she realized the engine in her car had gone quiet.

Swinging around, she saw a large brown SUV parked near the rear of her car—a blue and red bar of light across the top and a yellow-gold county sheriff's emblem painted on the door. A man in khaki brown pants and a thick, darker brown jacket—also bearing a yellow-gold county sheriff's emblem— straightened up out of her car and stood to face her.

"Ho-ly shit," she muttered once the knee-jerk–cop-sighting alarm quit tripping her fight-or-flirt responses.

She couldn't say she would have known him anywhere, but here in Clearfield and with the memory of him so close to the surface of her mind she not only recognized him, but she enjoyed an intense ripple of glad relief as it passed through her.

At the very bottom of her emotional barrel lingered a little unfinished business between her and Grady Steadman—a first love for both of them, with no chance for it to come to a dramatic, upsetting teenage resolution on its own. No chance at all really. Ever. A mistake, but still one of the more exciting, sweeter memories of her youth . . . and it wasn't like she had so many of those that she would easily forget him.

He put his right forearm on the hood of her car and held the open door with the other hand. And, *damn*, if he didn't shift his weight to an easy stance and look up across the slanting hillside at her with that same cocky confidence he'd had as a kid. Always so sure of himself—like he had a book with all the answers to all the mysteries of the universe in it. Like he'd written the stupid thing.

She used to watch him, stare at him, marvel at him, and wonder how people like him came be. People who assumed they were liked and welcome wherever they went; people so sure that what they wanted, everyone else wanted, too . . . and they *did*! Was he born like that or was it in the vitamins his mother fed him? And why couldn't every mother buy the same brand?

His body was different. He'd always been tall and well proportioned—as those special people tend to be—but it was a man's body now, not a boy's. It was as if someone had blown into the end of his thumb and his body ballooned out to perfection, with more meat everywhere and broader shoulders. Even from a higher elevation she could see that his stomach was still youthfully flat, and she'd have bet dollars to donuts he was ripped.

Disgusting. Truly. She ought to resent someone who looked hunkier now than he had twenty years ago. Someone who was doubtless married with a litter of children, living a sweet little life in a postcard-pretty town like Clearfield . . . and who had, in all probability, come to know more about the unstable insanity of her childhood than she had ever wanted him to. But this was Grady.

Grady, who once slowed his pace to hers and tangled their fingers together, who used a gentle fist to tip her chin up merely to look into her eyes. Grady, the first person to ever say she was wanted, the first to say *I love you*. Out loud. The first to give her hope.

No, as much as she was inclined to wish she could, she

would never, could never desire anything for Grady that wasn't good and true and wonderful. It was what he'd always seemed to expect *and,* in her opinion, what he always deserved.

She started down the hill toward him, watched the wind touch his hair. Dark but not black—it was more the color of bark on a maple tree, clipped short and wavy. He was in full uniform, right down to the dark cop glasses. Behind them she knew his eyes were mossy green, quick and sharp, bright with humor . . . and the aforementioned confidence, of course.

She matched his closed-lip smile of recognition and prayed she wouldn't trip and slip down the shallow hill . . . because she could feel him checking her out as well. Uncomfortably aware of it. So much so, she resisted the urge to stick her tongue out at him to break the tension between them.

But then he reached up and took off his glasses. His gaze came back to her warm and receptive. His smile grew wide and white and out they popped . . . two of the most incredible, ridiculous. and undeniably naughty dimples she'd ever seen in her life.

She'd forgotten about those.

"Welcome home, Hannah."

Grady could have picked her out of a crowd at three hundred feet. It was in the way she stood . . . and it was hard to describe.

A scrapper's stance, straight and strong and ready, but more graceful, more subtle than a man would be—more guarded as well. He'd seen a similar attitude in the army, in some of the older, better Rangers who were scary-as-hell tough but didn't really look it—in fact, they went out of their way to conceal it. It used to remind him so much of the way Hannah would try to blend in until she was near invisible, but once detected she was prepared and entirely capable of defending herself. And, of course, once you finally noticed *that,* it was way too late.

His body automatically responded to it. It stirred, braced itself, anticipated whatever she might throw at him. As a teenager he'd responded to the challenge . . . and not because it was simply there. Not like a mountain climber who scales the peaks to boastfully say he's done it; not just for a notch on his belt. The challenge of Hannah was never to conquer her, never to have her and brag about it—never to change her. The goal was to win her acceptance, and her trust—and there was a time in his life when he would have died for it. Gladly.

She started down the hill toward him. Still tall and trim there was a feminine softness to her figure now, real curves where only a promise had been before. But she walked the same, grace with purpose, he once called it. Restrained, controlled, no motion wasted. She was like a self-contained energy source, and the closer she got the stronger became the electro-magnetic field that emanated from her. His skin prickled with it.

He took a deep breath and put a smile on his face.

The long, thick black braid she'd always worn down the middle of her back no longer existed. Her hair was shorn short to her chin and stylish, the word wispy came to mind, but his daughter would call it something else.

Phat, perhaps, but he was always two or three words behind the times with her vocabulary. He wasn't sure what *nice* was anymore. And he had no idea what language his son spoke these days, they so rarely talked—although hello, goodbye, and may-I-have-my-allowance had stayed the same.

Halfway down the hill, Hannah's lips curved upward in response to his smile.

What he most wanted to see were her eyes. No blue Crayola in the box matched them. Not even in the giant-sized box. He'd checked.

As if she'd somehow read his mind, she reached up to remove the dark sunglasses that hid them.

He bent his head and removed his own and looking back up, there they were, not three feet away . . . true clear blue, sparkling like fine-cut Sri Lankan sapphires.

He opened his mouth to breathe, his throat collapsed. His brain scrambled for one of the lines he'd prepared to greet her with. Regrettably, the only one that came to him was the one he knew she would least want to hear.

"Welcome home, Hannah."

Though she'd been looking at him the whole time during her descent, she made a point of raking her gaze down the front of his uniform, and up again. He held his breath. Her lips twitched.

"Hey, Andy." She startled a half-laugh out of him. He hadn't known what to expect but teasing humor never made the list. "How's Opie'n yer Aunt Bea doin'? And Barney?"

"Great. Twenty years and all I get is a rash of shit about the job?"

She laughed, and the sound quavered inside him.

"Grady, Grady." She shook her head, sad and sympathetic. "What's become of you? I turn my back for a lifetime and look what happens to you. What was it? An epiphany? Did the clouds part and the angels sing to you?"

"Not exactly. I needed a job. Since I knew all the tricks to this one, I figured I'd be good at it."

Something new. She was deliberately teasing him. The old Hannah might have asked similar questions, but she'd have been dead serious about them. It intrigued him. What else was different about her?

"I get it. Like the devil's child growing up to become a minister."

"I wasn't that bad."

"Yes. You were. But it's still good to see you." She held out her hand in friendship.

Her hand! Okay, so he'd been hoping for a hug, a kiss on the cheek, something—anything that told him she hadn't forgotten what they once had together. But the sinking feeling in his chest told him she was right. They were all but strangers now.

He stepped around the open car door, flipped it closed, and slipped his hand around hers. Cold like the weather, their palms warmed instantly.

"It's good to see you, too, Hannah. I wish the circumstances were different."

"It was these circumstances or none at all." She spoke, blunt and honest—a Hannah Benson hallmark that he knew well. Her gaze wavered and she pulled her hand away, stuffed both in the pockets of her bright red jacket. "But I'm here now so what do I do next? First."

The *next* was a slip and his eyes darted over her shoulder, not directly behind her from where she'd come but at a right angle where he guessed she'd gone first. It struck him as odd that he hadn't, until that moment, thought it strange that the cemetery would be her first stop. It was she who asked the question when his eyes came back to hers.

"How did you know to come find me here?"

"I didn't. I thought I saw you when you passed through town." In fact, he'd been keeping an eye out for her. "I thought you were going straight out to your place . . . . out to the farm, so I followed. When you weren't there, I backtracked. Simple cop stuff. I told you, I'm good at it."

She appreciated the levity and tried to hold on to the lighter mood. "This is so strange and I've had so little time to think about it. Can you tell I'm a nervous wreck? How do you talk to kids? What do you say to them?"

"Hell if I know. I've got two of my own I can barely communicate with."

"Two. Wow." She didn't seem surprised. "How old are they?"

"One's a few months younger than Anna, the other is almost two years older."

"Teenagers. So this is old stuff for you."

"Teenagers are never old stuff. They change their minds every seven seconds. You never know what they're thinking or what they'll do next and . . . I'm scaring you, aren't I?" He gave a weak laugh and couldn't keep from reaching out and putting his hands on her shoulders. She felt solid and real. "Sorry. Just be yourself. And don't expect too much at first. It's going to take time for both of you to warm up to each other. If it makes you feel any better, Anna isn't like my kids. She likes them, they're friends, but she isn't *like* them. She's different." Hannah's eyes scrunched as if wincing with pain. She knew what it was to grow up *different*. "Not weird different, just . . . Well, she seems more mature than both my kids put together. She's been through a lot. She grew up fast but she's still a kid. Does that help?"

She looked at him for a second, didn't seem to mind that he still held her.

"I don't know if it does or not. It's all happening so fast and I'm totally unprepared. My head is bulging with questions." She lifted her hands, palms up. "I don't know where to start. Her, I guess. Is she banking on this? I'm pretty set in my ways, you know? Does she know this might not work out? She won't go around touching all my things, will she? Does she know she doesn't have to go with me if she doesn't want to? She's a teenager, that's at least a second phone line, right? Er, no, they all have cell phones now, don't they? I don't know anything about kids except that I hate rap music. I don't think this is going to work, Grady. I don't think it's a good idea and— What are you staring at?"

"You. You're really worried."

She threw up her hands, turned out of his loose hold and walked a few feet away. She took a deep breath and turned back. "I need your help, Grady. I don't know the first thing about being a mother."

Which is why it will probably work, he thought. Anna wouldn't know the first thing about *having* a mother.

"You don't have to. It's not like she needs to be spoon-fed or have her diapers changed. You take one thing at a time, play it by ear and do what feels right. Mostly she just needs somebody. Someone to be there, to care about her. A friend."

"What if she hates me?"

"Are you kidding?" He looked her over. "What's there to hate?"

"You want a list?"

He was tempted. "Maybe later. Right now, since my going out to the farm alerted them to your arrival, I think we should go out and see how it goes."

"Them?"

"We've had her at our house the past couple nights, but they all went out to the farm today to straighten things up for you. And to cook. You know my mother—there isn't anything a good meal can't fix."

"Your mother's there, too?"

"Yes. And she's dying to see you again. C'mon. Let's go."

"Wait. Wait a second. Shouldn't we have some sort of plan or something?"

He liked the concerned expression on her face. She wouldn't be concerned if it wasn't important, if she didn't care about the outcome.

"Okay. I think a straightforward, frontal attack is our best bet. They're expecting us. They have youth and enthusiasm on their side, but we have experience and we control all the money. It'll be a fair match."

She scowled at him as she bit the right side of her lower lip to keep from smiling. "I'm serious."

"I remember." Did she? "But she's just one little girl who needs you a hell of lot more than you need her right now. All you have to do is treat her like a human being and expect her to treat you the same. Everything will turn out fine. I promise." When she still looked doubtful, he added, "If she turns on you and her head starts spinning, I've got your back."

For a fraction of a second she looked appalled, but then she laughed, and it was so worth the extra time and effort to make it happen.

"There you go, that's better. I'll follow you back out to the farm and introduce you."

"You're still kidding, right?" She gave him a strange look.

"No. Why?"

"Have you forgotten how horrible it feels to look up and see a cop in your rearview mirror?" Teasing him again. He liked this new vein of sassy in her.

He raised a brow and gave her his best cop glower. "Only for someone who's feeling guilty about something."

She grinned and shook her head. "Only for everyone, pal. I'm following you."

"Fine. I'll go slow."

She blinked and exposed a flash of memory that sent his heart wild an instant before her defenses came down like the shields on the Batmobile.

Please, Hannah. Aren't you ever going to let me kiss you? Don't you want me to?

I do. More than anything. But . . . I don't know what to do. I don't know how.

Yes, you do. It's easy.

No. I don't. And you'll laugh at me.

I won't. I never will. I'll teach you. And I'll go slow.

She hadn't forgotten. But that didn't make him entirely happy, either.

"Good," she said, and walked brisk and sure around him to her car door. He turned with her—hoping, for what he wasn't sure. But the moment was gone. "And don't kick up a lot of dust. I had my car detailed last week."

"Yes, ma'am," he said, putting a hand on the door as she slipped inside. She settled herself in, tossed the sunglasses on the rider's seat and picked up the keys from where he'd put them. She fastened her seat belt; glanced up at him with her hand on the key in the ignition. She looked tired. Wary and emotionally overloaded. He couldn't resist the urge to make her smile again.

"So you know . . ." he said stern and coplike, then waited and watched as she braced herself. "I'm tough on tailgaters."

The slow grin came all the way into her eyes. "Thanks, Sheriff. I'll remember that."

She was going to remember a whole lot more than that, he decided, walking around the front of his truck and getting in. There were questions he needed answers to, for Anna's sake—for his own sake—and these two weeks might well be his only opportunity to get them.

He needed to keep a bead on the fact that a few hours earlier she'd crossed the Mason-Dixon into what she considered enemy territory because he'd asked her to come. She traveled here under his flag of protection. At least for a few days, until she could see for herself and get used to the idea that the war zone she'd grown up in was gone.

Chapter Four

Grady put the truck in gear and pulled out, watching her back out and follow in the rearview.

He would get his answers, he vowed. She was . . . the unfinished overpass in the movie *Speed*. Except in his story, he was a kid who wasn't prepared for it, wasn't trained to deal with impossible situations, wasn't used to having no time to think things through. He'd stopped the bus, hard and abrupt, on the very edge of falling, but it didn't explode. He'd wanted it to—God, how he'd wanted it to—but it didn't. And the passengers stayed inside, they wouldn't get off, and he couldn't leave them. He couldn't move forward. Eventually, he'd had to back the bus up, rebuild speed and momentum, then jump the gap she'd left in his life and go on.

And he made it. He circled the airport for a while, got the passengers off, slid from the bottom of the bus with a different heroine—who in the end took a cruise with someone else and left him with two kids to raise—but that was a different story, though he'd managed to get through that one, too.

He slowed the truck to a stop at the intersection in front of St. John's Catholic Church and turned left.

The point: The gap was still in his road. Oh, he knew now why she ran that night and there was no way he could fault her for it. What he didn't understand was why she'd let everyone, more importantly him, believe she was dead this whole time. All those years without so much as a peep from her, no phone call, no letter, no message in a bottle. He needed to finish his freeway, make it whole.

Hannah had the answers. She was the only one with all the materials to make it right but he hardly knew her anymore. It would be nice if she freely bared her soul to him, which he didn't at all see happening—but if she didn't . . .

His gaze took another pass at the rearview mirror. He used his left hand to pull on his tense, aching neck muscles. *Well, he'd simply have to wrestle her to the ground and pin her there until she talked,* he thought, and not without some interest. Though, he didn't relish the idea of making her angry. He'd seen her angry before.

As a young boy, in grade school still, he'd heard about her fighting—girls and boys alike—but he only witnessed it once. A stupid kid thing really, but he'd never forgotten it . . .

Turchen County was the second smallest county in the state, and Clearfield was the county seat. It boasted one school building for every level. Some kids rode the buses for an hour and a half every morning to get to school, then an hour and a half back home in the afternoon.

The high school kids had their own buses. But for three hours a day the middle school kids ruled the back of Bus 19 that transported the two lower levels back and forth along the rural roads west of town as far as Ashville Flats. It was their territory.

Early in the school year, he and the nine other sixth graders he'd ridden in the front of the bus with since kindergarten were still trying to find their place, and seats, among the seventh and eighth graders. They were all a little nervous. Even then they knew that this sort of thing could make or break your chances of being one of the cool kids at the middle school, and after that the high school.

Josh Greenborn was desperate to be cool. He wasn't a particular friend of Grady's, but he was tolerable if you didn't mind his loud voice and remembered to put salt on almost everything he said. He didn't lie exactly, but he blew things up, a lot. That fall he was particularly obnoxious—and he wasn't fooling anyone. Looking back, it was pretty pathetic.

Unfortunately, before any of the eighth graders got around to assigning Josh his seat—mid-bus directly behind the grade schoolers—the Benson sisters got on the bus to go home.

Not that anyone noticed.

The Benson family was an insular unit that for years seemed resolute in the effort to stay cut off from the rest of the community. Little was known about them. The father was a surly sort who spoke to few and often hung out in the seedier establishments around town. A pious woman, the mother never missed church, avoided eye contact, and rarely said a word. And the two little girls—they could have been imaginary.

From time to time the Bensons were whispered about in adult circles. They were *those* people. Words like *deplorable* and *shameful* often slipped out to fall on young ears, but who paid attention to what adults talked about when you were a kid? Most of them, apparently.

It was no sin to be poor in Turchen County. Still, among those whose income fell below the Gross National Average there were poor people and poorer people, and the Bensons fell into the latter category. Which isn't to say the girls wouldn't have been reasonably acceptable kids if they'd been, say, funny or athletic or remarkably pretty . . . or they might have found a place for themselves with the kids who played in the band. But the Benson sisters weren't anything.

That thought made him cringe now. But all it ever meant was that neither of them stood out as anything special. Just two little girls who got on and off the bus most days when it stopped at the end of the long gravel drive to their house. One, a contrast of black hair and white skin, the other smaller and . . . golden, with hair the color of a buttercup. Both were as faded as the hand-me-down clothes they wore and so quiet the wind seemed to pass straight through them.

Truth? Grady couldn't swear that either sister registered on his radar as anything more than a phantom blip before Hannah Benson beat the holy living crap out of Josh Greenborn on the bus that warm, sunny autumn afternoon.

It wasn't something one could overlook, even if Josh hadn't first leaned over the seat in front of Grady to whisper, "Watch this."

Absently, he watched Josh sneak up the aisle and into an empty seat three rows forward on the other side. He looked back to make sure he had an audience, smirked, then snatched the loose pink hair ribbon off the curly yellow ponytail of the little girl sitting in the seat directly in front of him.

The little girl's hand shot out and up when her head jerked backed from the tug on her hair, but it was too late to catch the ribbon. She turned in her seat and saw it dangling from Josh's fingers invitingly. She looked into his face with an almost blank expression, her pale blues wide and unblinking, skin pale; her little pink rosebud mouth solemn and set. Her gaze lowered to the ribbon, grew worried and fearful; the temptation to snatch it back drew a small pucker between her brows before she glanced at Josh again, then turned around and did nothing.

Josh turned and gave those watching a how-lame-is-that look. Stretching his arm forward, he wiggled the pink ribbon in the girl's peripheral vision but she ignored him. The top half of her blond head above the seat didn't budge. But the taller, black-haired girl beside her took note, turned her head, and looked back at Josh.

Hot blue. That was the impression Grady had of her eyes that afternoon. Like the blue flame on his mother's gas stove—like laser beams maybe, and just as direct. The thrill of trouble brewing zipped through his muscles. *Now* Josh had his full attention. Though when Grady looked around in anticipation, he saw that most of the other kids had lost interest, had looked away or were talking among themselves. He nudged Max Bayan, sitting next to him on the aisle, and directed his attention back to Josh. He didn't want to be the only one watching when the older Benson girl, with all that rage and fire in her eyes, tried to hand Josh his ass on a tray.

Not that there was much of a chance of that happening. Josh wasn't that much bigger than she, but he was a whole year older and a boy. Hardly a contest, but it would likely be a while before they had this sort of entertainment on the bus again.

When he looked back, Hannah was sitting forward, the blond head of her sister bounced along the back of the seat toward the window, and then Hannah took her sister's place on the aisle. Unfortunately, Hannah was as good at ignoring Josh as Ruth was. And while Grady might have tormented Hannah a little longer, knowing her to be the easier target, the one more likely to respond, Josh once again turned his attention to Ruth.

With his arm over the hand bar along the top of the seat, he dangled the pink ribbon *on* her face, it looked like, pulling it up slow and enticing, then dipping it again. Nothing. Minutes went by and neither girl responded. As Grady started to swallow his disappointment, Josh said something to them. He couldn't hear what, but the older girl turned her head and looked at her sister. Then everything happened at once.

Hannah had Josh by the arm and with one ruthless jerk

crashed his face into the metal bar on the back of the bench, turning in her seat and grabbing him by the hair with both hands. Girls screamed; boys shouted and whooped and started to laugh. Grady stared in awe as Hannah's lips parted to show her straight white teeth and Josh's head blurred with blinding quick movement as she drove and smashed his face against the metal frame of the seat and hand bar—again and again. Fluid sprayed and little red dots landed on the kids nearby. More screaming and yelling and everyone started leaving their seats.

Grady was vaguely aware of the bus pulling over to the side of the road and he couldn't seem to do anything but sit there. Mesmerized. Shocked. He couldn't see her eyes, her lids were lowered, her attention focused on her work. He'd never seen anything like it. He'd never been in a fight himself and the few he'd seen at school . . . well, they weren't nearly as intense. And there was never any blood.

After what felt like several long minutes, but could only have been seconds in fact, she stopped. Josh's head had gone heavy, hanging from her hands by his hair. Grady saw Hannah's lips move and her sister reached up and slipped the pink ribbon that hung loose and tangled around Josh's limp fingers into her lap. Hannah then tossed Josh back against his seat. He slid slowly to the left, toward the hysterical girl in the window seat. Hannah turned and sat back down.

Maybe more than the fight itself, it was Hannah's cold reaction to what she'd done that was entrenched in his memory most deeply. While the bus driver screamed at her—before, during, and after she ascertained the extent of Josh's injuries—Hannah sat in apparent calm, facing straight ahead. Grady thought she looked righteous, like she hadn't done anything wrong. As if she'd given Josh the beating he deserved—and part of him agreed with her. Of course, she'd gone way overboard—and who would have thought she could?—but more than a small part of him thought it wrong when the driver forced Hannah to get off the bus, on the right road but still three or four miles from home.

He admired the way she refused to let her little sister get down with her and a few minutes later he was impressed as hell, actually, to discover that her bravery was all an act.

After the driver closed the door on Hannah, she used the radio in the bus to report what had happened and that she'd be turning the bus around to take Josh back to town to the emergency room, and then she drove off.

Hannah stood alone, grasping the front straps of her backpack, head bowed as road dust lifted from under the big tires. He couldn't take his eyes off her. She looked so small and vulnerable. He turned his head and kept watching as the bus left her behind.

In the final second before the high cloud of grit and grime engulfed her, she looked up.

Even now he could see that dirty tear-streaked face in his mind; felt stunned and overwhelmed by the emotions exposed in it. Remorse and resentment—and fear. It made him feel sick inside, knowing she'd probably be in as much trouble at home as he would have been in if he'd been fighting on the bus. And it hadn't been her fault, not entirely. Josh was a pain in the ass and she was defending her younger sister. Would her parents give her a chance to explain? He watched her until she disappeared in the veil of dust.

Only Ruth got on the bus the next morning. And two days later, if she noticed Josh's two black eyes and the discoloration of his broken nose under the layers of tape, she gave no sign of it. She sat alone in the seat that she and her sister always shared. Weeks went by before Grady noticed Hannah getting on the bus with her sister again . . . and he noticed because she wore a royal blue sweater that reminded him of the color of her eyes that day, a sweater so big on her that it no doubt belonged to her mother—but it hid the cast on her left arm almost completely.

It didn't occur to him to even speculate as to how she'd come to break her arm during her suspension from school that fall, but he didn't have to guess now.

He glanced back in the rearview mirror a lifetime later. To his knowledge few people messed with Hannah or her sister after that . . . and she'd seemed as gentle as she was strong when they were together. But that lightning quick temper was something else he planned to check out before she left town with her niece.

"I can do this. I can. How hard can it be? I'm not signing any papers, I'm meeting her. That's all."

She turned left at the stop sign behind Grady and followed at a more than legal distance—in no hurry to get where they were going.

"Call Joe," she said into the earpiece of her Bluetooth, worrying her lower lip as she waited.

Despite the amusing irony of Grady's chosen profession, it made coming back to Clearfield more of a threat to her. She couldn't afford to underestimate anyone. She'd gotten this far by telling herself that if she could keep certain things hidden for twenty years, she could certainly do it for two more weeks. But cops were trained observers. What good old Grady might have taken in stride, Sheriff Steadman was more than capable of stumbling onto and getting curious about.

She'd have to be careful.

She was always a fast learner, quick on the uptake of a situation—survival skills. Grady's voice on the phone two days ago was a crash course in false assumptions, namely, that the past she believed to be long dead and buried wasn't. It was alive and well and going to high school. If a young, unknown girl could innocently breach the barrier between Hannah and the life she'd run away from, anything could.

She'd have to be very careful.

"Are you trying to undermine my confidence?" The soft tenor voice of Joe Levitz was a balm to her soul. "I'm old, but I can still sell insurance, you know."

"What. No hello, how are you doing?"

"How could you be doing anything? You haven't been gone ten hours yet."

"I need you to remind me why I'm here."

He made the soft, familiar scoffing noise she loved. "I should have written it down for you."

"Just tell me. Again."

"All right. You are there because you are a fine, good young woman with a wealth of love to give, and you are pouring some of it back into your family where it belongs. You have a deep sense of responsibility. And it is what you are meant to do."

"How come that doesn't make as much sense now as it did Friday or yesterday or even this morning?"

"Because the closer you get to your true destiny, and to what is real and vital in your life, the harder the devil tries to tempt you from your path."

Hannah wasn't a religious person, but Joe was—and he and his life were the best things she'd ever known. Even second hand, his faith was an encouraging comfort.

"Could the devil disguise himself as a county sheriff?"

"He could. But with all the self-doubt you have already, why would he bother?" Good point. "Were you speeding again?"

"No. I ran into Grady. He's a sheriff now."

"Grady . . . the boy. He arrested you?"

"This would be a whole different call if he had. And he's not a boy. He's a big, tall man."

"You like big, tall men. Many big, tall men."

And Joe would be delighted to see her pick one and settled down like the classic Jewish princess she wasn't.

"Yeah, well, this one makes me nervous."

"Nervous is good."

"Not that kind of nervous." Not altogether. "What if he starts asking questions?"

He paused. "Then tell him the truth, Hannah. Make yourself free. It's time."

"I . . . had an attack. Like before."

"The panic again?"

"Yes. But worse."

"That makes sense, doesn't it? First you face your fears, then you conquer them. A minor setback. Are you better now?"

"Yes." But for how long? What else would sneak up and grab her unexpected? Could she fight it off again, or would it drag her into the madness forever?

"This is all good, Hannah. It's time. Truth and peace, they are sisters."

She shook her head, slow and doubtful. "I'll do what I can for the girl because you think it's important, but I can't promise anything else."

"*Not* because I think it's important but because—"

"Yeah, yeah. It's my responsibility. Because it's what I'm meant to do."

"And because *you* want to do it."

"I do?"

"Deep down, yes. And because it will save me a great deal of time, in what few years I have left, not to have to listen to you whine about the regrets you would have if you stood by and did nothing."

"So, once again, this is all about you?"

"Of course."

"And you know me so well.".

"Also true."

Hannah sighed and wished he had come with her. "In that case, wish me luck because I am about to meet her."

"You don't need luck, Hannah, you need faith," he said, then he made it a wish. "Have faith."

He disconnected and she flipped the cell and the earpiece back in her purse.

The most frustrating thing about Joe Levitz was that in all the years she'd known him, he hadn't once ill-advised or misdirected her. That made telling him to stuff his opinions extremely difficult. To make it worse, he never offered them unsolicited. Oh, she knew the trick was to not ask him what he thought in the first place, but she couldn't seem to help herself. Joe was more than simply her former boss and business partner; her mentor and her dearest friend. He was her savior, her confessor, the father she should have had . . . and he was always right—about everything.

Except maybe now. *Hell of a time to start being wrong, Joe.*

Have faith, he'd said.

Okay. So how hard could this be? Most people have families, and most of those involve children. She'd spent the better part of her life professing the importance of and selling the means for sound financial futures for them. She knew about kids. She'd heard all the boastful stories and seen the joy that most people share with their children. She knew they weren't impossible to live with.

Living with a fifteen-year-old girl could not be worse than *being* a sixteen-year-old girl living alone . . . and somehow the thought comforted her.

"I can do this."

But children were famous for their intuitive judgments of adult character. What if this kid sensed that Hannah wasn't the

purest soul on the planet and ran off screaming? Another rumor: They could sense fear like horses and dogs, in which case
this . . . Anna would definitely have the upper hand.

"Be calm. Have faith."

Caravanning behind Grady, they soon left tarmac for gravel
and rumbled four more miles down the road before the house
came into view. The sky was growing dark, but there were
no dark billowing clouds hovering overhead, no lightning, no
ominous thunderclaps from a B-rated horror movie.

It was just an old silver-gray farmhouse with a dull red roof
and a wide front porch, left to weather and ruin by years of neglect. Smaller than she remembered. A matching barn stood off
to the left at a distance, but barely. Hannah estimated that the
next stiff wind would provide the new owners with enough
firewood for the next thirty years. Two of the three smaller
outbuildings were heading that way as well. There were three
cows in the four-acre field west of the house and the rest had
gone to grass, for hay perhaps.

Hannah caught herself holding her breath, anticipating
memories that would launch up to stun and overwhelm her,
memories to be filled to the gills with toxic emotions, but . . .
Well, perhaps she was maxed-out emotionally and the house
was the least of her worries. The strange fact was, all she felt
as they turned into the drive was a detached curiosity—and
nervous about meeting the girl.

The sound of their tires crunching across the gravel toward
the house alerted those inside to their arrival. A light came
on, bathing the porch in a soft welcoming bug-light yellow as
a woman in a black skirt and sweater pushed open the screen
door and stepped out. She stuck her head back in briefly, then
let the screen door swing shut, and started down the steps to
meet them.

Grady pulled up on the grass in the front yard and Hannah

did the same as there were already two vehicles parked in the space along the side of the house where her parents used to park, closer to the back entrance. Tonight she was a guest being received at the front door.

Her fingers shook when she reached for the keys in the ignition. She grabbed that hand with her other and held them in her lap for a second, taking a deep bracing breath. She might have taken several more—and hyperventilated—if she hadn't glanced up through the windshield to see Grady waiting for her. He winked and flashed his dimples at her. He had her back.

Right. She turned the engine off and pulled the keys out.

". . . and I've been on pins and needles all day. I can't believe it," Mrs. Steadman was saying when Hannah opened the car door. "All this time and you're back. Look at you, all grown up. And so beautiful. You always were such a pretty girl and now look at you . . ."

Mrs. Steadman taught freshman algebra at the high school and talked faster than a speeding bullet. Blessed with this knowledge she repeatedly invited her students to ask her to slow down if they needed her to, but neglected the offer during her less complicated social discourses—which tended to run on. She was very kind, Hannah recalled, from the few times she'd gone to her after class for extra help. And trustworthy . . . if she'd never told Grady about the night before she left town.

She dressed in the same skirt, blouse, and cardigan sweater– a style she'd favored years ago—perhaps a size or two larger— in a tasteful shade of dark plum, not black. Time had taken its toll gently on her face; her curly cap of dark brown hair had turned to white, but the generous smile remained the same.

"A grown woman. My stars, it's like a miracle that you've returned to us."

Hannah stood beside the open car door as Mrs. Steadman reached her, then reached *for* her, pinning her arms to her sides in a smothering hug. Bending her arms at the elbows—for balance mostly—Hannah patted the woman's hips in greeting.

"Hi, Mrs. Steadman. It's good to see you, too."

"Let her get out of the car first, Mom."

"Oh. Yes. Of course." She captured Hannah's face in her hands. There were tears in the hazel eyes behind the thin pink plastic-rimmed glasses. "It's you, isn't it? I can't believe it."

"Yes, ma'am."

"I'm so glad to see you safe, dear." She searched Hannah's face thoroughly, and when she was satisfied that all was as it should be, she lowered her hands. "Now, where are your things? In the trunk? Grady. Get her things, dear, and bring them into the house. Let's get you in out of this cold. March is always so unpredictable. Last Wednesday the children went to school without coats. Can you believe it? How was . . ."

Grady circled them, stopped beside Hannah with his hand out for the keys. She looked up, met the merriment in his eyes. Obviously she looked as uncomfortable as she felt and this wasn't the part where he would come to her rescue. She was on her own with his mother.

But before she could glare at him, the screen door squeaked, drawing their attention to the porch.

A stocky young man dressed all in black—jeans, T-shirt, and boots—and silver—chains, rings, earrings, and eyebrow stud—stepped to the edge of the porch. He tilted his head—and the jet black shag of hair thereon—to one side and stared down at them.

Someone gasped, soft and incredulous. Hannah could feel herself staring. *My God. A Goth in Clearfield.* Some things *had* changed—a lot.

"How was your trip?" Mrs. Steadman drew a second breath. "You must be tired. Oh, here they are now. They've been so busy. The children are very excited, you know. They worked like troopers today, getting things ready. They're eager to meet you and they've been asking questions for two days solid. Since Grady told us you were coming, and . . ."

"Careful," Grady whispered. He had to reach in front of her to get the keys still dangling from her right hand while she remained rapt by the boy in black. "He's a visiting dignitary. This is a test, and *you* are the United Nations."

The nylon of his jacket grazed the wool of hers; his shoulder blocked her view all too briefly. The impulse to hide her face against his chest until this whole nightmare ended was almost more than she could bear.

She turned to look at him, hoping for more of an explanation, but he'd turned to the rear of her car. She started to follow but the screen door opened again—for a girl wearing what Hannah could only describe as fairy-clown clothes.

Starting from the bottom up, she had on black high-topped army-type boots with thick red tights or leggings, a yellow floral-print silk or nylon skirt with multiple handkerchief hems, and a purple cable-knit sweater. She didn't appear to be pierced anywhere but her earlobes, and her hair was short and straight . . . and pink and orange, if the yellow bug light on the porch wasn't affecting it.

Following her, a relatively bland couple: a tall, lean youth in jeans and a Clearfield High School hoodie with short, soft brown curls and Grady's mouth set mutinous and grim on his face. The girl wore jeans as well, with a yellow-and-white striped V-neck T-shirt and red tennis shoes. She had thick, long wavy blond hair, like her mother—and an oval-shaped face with a straight narrow nose set between Hannah's eyes, and a wide, full mouth. She was disarmingly pretty.

"Of course, we didn't know what all to tell them about you, we've been out of touch for so long. In . . . in fact, some people thought you were dead, dear. At first . . . But we'll get caught up in no time, you'll see. Come down everyone, don't be shy now. Hannah's come a long way to meet you."

"Come help me here," Grady called out with his head in the trunk.

The boy in black skipped down the steps, loped toward them, chains clinking, loose and graceful despite his size. The girls followed at a slower pace. The other boy remained on the porch, leaning against a support post, his arms folded defensively across his chest. Did that mean he didn't want to meet her?

Already she could feel the young people communicating in a language she didn't understand—and they had yet to speak. Or was she overreacting again? It made perfect sense that they would understand one another's moods and nuances better than she did. *One step at a time, Hannah.*

Grady hung the strap of her garment bag on the boy's shoulder and gave him her small tote bag and briefcase, going back for the larger, heavier suitcase himself. He pulled it out of the truck like she'd packed two weeks of feathers and set it on the ground. By the time he'd tapped the lid of the trunk down, the girls had joined them on the dry brown lawn.

"Hannah, let me introduce you to everyone," he said. She pulled her gaze from her niece's face and looked at Grady. He picked up her bag and motioned with his head to the Goth. "That's Biscuit."

"Oh, for pity's sake," Grady's mother interrupted. "That's Bobby Walker. I don't know why you people insist on calling him Biscuit."

"We told you, Gramma," the fairy-clown said, even as she watched Hannah like a carnival attraction. "His head's shaped like a biscuit."

"Why, it is not. His head's shaped like a . . . ah . . . the business end of a dust mop today."

"Not his hair, his head . . ."

And while the two debated the shape of Bobby Walker's head, he smiled at Hannah and said, "My mom calls me Sweetie-pie and my dad calls me Mr. Lippy."

There was a warm, intelligent look about his eyes that led Hannah to believe his mother understood him best.

"What would you like me to call you?"

"Biscuit is okay."

"Just don't call him to dinner," Grady said. "He'll eat your cupboards bare."

"Man, Sheriff, do you have to spoil all my fun?"

"It's my job, son." He walked by them to stand near the girls. "This is my little Lucy."

"Dad." The girl with the pink and orange hair had his eyes . . . and gave them a practiced roll.

"Colorful, don't you think?" He nodded his head at her as if he was indeed pleased with her creativity. She didn't seem to be embarrassed by the introduction. Or maybe she was simply too busy checking Hannah out to notice.

The boy, Biscuit, looked interested in her quietly elegant Volvo—one of the top three safest cars in the world, the insurance agent in her was always willing to point out . . . just not today.

"Hi, Lucy, it's nice to meet you."

"Hello." Her smile polite, but cautious.

"My son, Calvin." Grady motioned with the suitcase to the boy on the porch.

"Named after my husband, you know," his mother injected. "He passed, too, while you've been away."

"I'm sorry to hear it, Mrs. Steadman." She waited a moment, then called, "Hi, Calvin."

He gave her a short nod as his sister said, "Cal, unless you're mad at him." She slid a disapproving glance at her father, which he ignored.

So it was Grady's fault the boy stayed on the porch—the relief amazed her.

"And this stunner is your niece." He put his free hand on the girl's shoulder and gave it a reassuring squeeze. "Anna, this is your Aunt Hannah."

Their tentative, hello-stranger smiles were all but identical. Never much of a hugger, Hannah made a supreme effort and stepped forward with both arms out for a hug—at the same time the girl stepped up with her hand held out for a friendly shake. Hannah lowered her left arm for the shake as Anna brought hers up for the hug. They laughed, as awkward as the moment.

Hannah held out her right hand again. "How about we start with this and work our way up."

Anna took her hand and smiled, relief in her eyes. Hannah could look straight into them. They were the same height. Grady said she was small and blond like Ruth, didn't he? But she wasn't as small as she was thin. Eating-disorder-thin came first to mind, but the smooth lean muscles of her thighs under the denim and in her arms, and a respectable bustline, dispelled the idea. She was simply tall and young and mostly muscle.

"That's one thing I never made you kids do . . . hug strange relatives." Mrs. Steadman motioned everyone back toward the house with her arms. "When your Aunt Kathy, my own sister, came to visit I didn't force you to hug her, because she came so rarely I knew she was like a stranger to you, though she'd been here years before and we talked about her all the time. You were always more comfortable meeting strange relatives when you knew you weren't going to have to hug them . . ."

With the Steadmans leading the way to the house, Hannah leaned toward her niece and murmured in a low voice, "Just so you know, I'm not a strange relative. I'm a relative who's been a stran-*ger*."

Anna's shy smile widened and her eyes lit with amusement for a second or two.

"Besides, there were always hugs all around by the time Aunt Kathy had to leave. It never failed. There's a reason why people say that blood's thicker than water and that's because it's true . . ."

Lucy's smile, however, was not shy . . . and neither was she. Dropping back two paces she slipped into the space between Hannah and her niece and whispered, "Gramma's a little wound up right now, but when she runs out of steam we have, like, a million and a half questions we need to ask you."

"Great." Hannah appreciated the warning. "I'll look forward to answering any I can. I have a few of my own." She hesitated. "Nothing too tough though, right?"

Lucy scrunched her face and shrugged ambiguously.

They followed Mrs. Steadman up the steps. Cal opened the door for his father who carried the greater load, let Biscuit follow, and stood waiting for his grandmother and the girls.

"I've seen it a hundred times or more," Mrs. Steadman rushed on. "People always bond faster to their own flesh and blood than they do to people who are not related. And that makes sense, doesn't it? Go ahead and take those up, please, boys. The girls made up the bed in the last room on the left for Hannah."

From his place several feet inside the door, at the bottom of the stairs, Grady caught her attention as she stepped up onto the porch. He was merely checking on her, making sure she was still all right, and for that he got a grateful smile.

"And we made a nice Sunday supper. Grady wanted to have you over to the house, Hannah, but the girls thought you'd be more comfortable here, and after driving all day it would be a shame for you to have to get back in the car and drive all the way out here with your stomach full. That's how accidents happen. You're tired, you get a full stomach and there you are, asleep at the wheel. Grady's seen it a hundred times or more, haven't you, dear?" He hummed something in the stairwell. "And we all decided that on this first night you and Anna wouldn't mind a little company, what with the newness of everything, and the funeral tomorrow and whatnot. And it's pot roast, you know, so we can clean up quick and leave early if you're tired from the drive."

"It smells wonderful. This is all . . . very thoughtful of you, Mrs. Steadman. I appreciate it."

"Oh Lord, call me Janice, dear. I'm not your teacher anymore. I retired several years ago, you know. How many now . . . ? Let's see . . ."

Chapter Five

As there were more of them than would fit around the small Formica table in the kitchen, someone had cleared away the boxes of . . . *stuff* that had covered the dining table for as long as Hannah could recall, and piled them in two corners of the room.

Possibly, they were not the same exact boxes of stuff that had been there before, but boxes of the same *sort* of junk that crammed every nook and cranny and cupboard and drawer; that was stacked in layers around the edges of every room and piled high on every flat surface of furniture in the house.

Stuff. Like trash bags of clothing coming from or going to Goodwill; stacks of newspapers and magazines someone may or may not get around to reading someday; thirty-year-old lamps that are perfectly good except for a short in the wiring; ancient broken toasters kept for just-in-case; bags of knitting yarn and oil cans and hats, a few books, picture frames . . . *stuff*.

And it wasn't like her mother had been a terrible house-keeper. She'd done her best. Level II hoarding was a gene in the Benson DNA and her mother had acquired the habit by marriage. She couldn't bring herself to throw anything away.

But Hannah knew as well as she knew her own name that most of the junk got dusted off on a routine basis up until the day her mother died.

To tell the truth, Hannah wouldn't have recognized the place if it had been any other way.

And she did recognize it—from the scratched and scarred dark-pine floors and trim to the faded pastel paint on the walls . . . though the color might be different, so it could have been painted at least once since she left. Or not.

She recognized it but that was all she allowed herself. She sensed the memories crouching in the dark corners and shadows everywhere she looked, but that's all they were, right? Just memories as old and worn as the living room couch—which was also new to the job since her time, but shabby and frayed nonetheless. At the moment there was no lingering sense of evil or danger—or joy, for that matter. It was only a tired, old rundown house . . . full of stuff. No more.

Mrs. Steadman gave everyone but Hannah a chore to do before dinner—the boys setting the table, the girls helping with the meal. Grady made a brief call on his cell phone from the kitchen, then came looking for her. He found her in the hall outside the living room, looking in.

"Are you okay?"

"I'm fine," she said, turning to him, leaning back with her hands between her and the wall. It was a whole new jolt of strangeness to see him without the brown jacket, wearing the khaki-tan uniform with the brown epaulets and insignia and the shiny gold star on his chest. Not that he didn't look good in it . . . and it wasn't purely that thing about a man in a uniform. Grady wore the uniform like a comfortable second skin, and there was something about *that* she found . . . . well, arresting. "Don't you wear a gun?"

"My mom won't let me wear it or my hat at the dinner

table." His tone was grievous and childlike for a second before he sobered to ask, "Is this too much? Did you want to be alone with her?"

"God, no." She put her head back against the wall. He smelled good, like soap and starch. "This is . . . awful but much nicer than I anticipated. Thank you for thinking of it, and for going to all the trouble." She skipped a beat. "Will your wife be joining us? I'd like to meet her."

"No. She doesn't eat with us anymore. She left when Lucy was four."

"Oh. Sorry."

He shrugged and looked away. "It happens. Lucky for me she left the best parts of herself behind."

"So it's you and your mother raising your kids."

Nodding and frowning absently, he rested his hands on the top of his belt as he surveyed the living room in the low lamplight. "They had that in common. Lucy and Anna, back in kindergarten. They were both being raised by their grand-mothers essentially, so they ended up friends. Jesus. Will you look at all this shit. Your mother really was a pack rat, wasn't she?" He shook his head. "You've got your work cut out for you here."

Denial muddled Hannah's mind. Her gaze roamed, slow and befuddled around the room, over the heaps of clutter, then up to his face. "What?"

"Well, if you and Anna plan to sell this place, you'll need to clear it out first."

"Get real. There's no way to get a backhoe in here without widening the front door first . . . or removing one side of the house." He laughed. "I'm serious. I'm not going through all this stuff by hand."

"It's the only way you'll know what to keep."

"Job done. I don't want to keep any of it."

"Anna might."

The sudden picture of hauling all this back to Baltimore rocked her. She envisioned her three-bedroom condominium bulging with junk *and* a teenager. Suddenly she wanted to weep.

He looked at her, chuckled, then used one finger under her chin to close her mouth.

"The girl is one thing, Grady. Maybe. But all this . . . this is . . . too much."

"Obviously. But there might be a thing or two she'll want to keep to help her remember her mom or her grandmother. You might, too, once you've had a chance to go through some of it. There's no way to tell what's here until you go through it."

She didn't care what was here. She had her own stuff. Nice, fairly new stuff—she didn't need or want what was here.

She thought she heard Grady say, "We'll all pitch in and help." But that couldn't be right . . . they'd be pitching until the kids turned fifty.

Mad laughter bubbled in her chest again, and she couldn't make herself blink. She heard an odd calmness in her voice when she asked, "Do you have any idea what you're saying? There's an attic . . . and a cellar. Do you know how long there have been Bensons living in this house?"

"A good long while." He took her by the shoulders and helped her turn away. His hands were big and strong and warm through the thin knit of her cashmere sweater. They were capable hands—her hands felt more like fins. She caught herself leaning back into them for comfort and direction as he coaxed her down the hall, then stepped to one side.

"Come on," he said, shoving his hands in his pockets but looking straight into her eyes. "It's time to eat. You'll feel better after you've had some food. Tomorrow after the funeral, we'll get organized. You've got eight, ten, probably a dozen extra hands to help you. It won't be as bad as you think. We had to do it at our old place when my mother moved into town with us. Of course, it wasn't quite this . . . well, like this, but we'll manage. It's all about getting organized."

"You don't live down the road anymore?"

"No. I moved into town when I got married. Then Mom moved in with us. It was never more than a hobby farm anyway, and I don't have the time to work it. So, now there's a commuter from Charlottesville playing gentleman farmer on the weekends. The rent pays the land taxes and gives my mom an extra income. Why don't you sit here at the end." In a softer voice he added, "So we can all keep an eye on you," like she might run away. Again.

And so the evening began, with Janice Steadman's friendly chirping now an incessant buzz in Hannah's shell-shocked ears and the rest of them making furtive eye contact with each other, sending messages back and forth and around the table. And she wasn't being paranoid. Anna and Lucy sat on her left, Grady and the two boys across from them, and Janice faced her from the other end. Hannah couldn't count the times she sensed that the cutting of her meat held them riveted, only to look up and have them discover that their own plates were more fascinating.

However, the food did help. The more she ate of the ordinary meat-and-potatoes meal the stronger she felt and the clearer her inner voice became. She might have come back to her childhood home but that didn't mean she had to revert back to the weak, frightened girl she was when she lived there. She was not the sort of woman who allowed things to simply happen to her anymore. She had choices. She was in charge. When she got handed a problem she dealt with it.

She had two weeks to decide the best thing to do for the girl . . . and to ready the farm for sale. Both tasks were doable.

Daunting but doable. Mentally, she rolled up her sleeves and prepared to dig in.

"Grady says you sell insurance, Hannah," Mrs. Steadman said from her end of the table, after an all too brief moment of silence. She was clearly determined to keep the conversation flowing. "That must be interesting work."

"No, not really," she said. Seeing that Janice was taken aback, she added, "It's more challenging than it is interesting. Insurance, the basic idea of it and the way it works, is cut-and-dry. The challenge is to decide if you want to work for one company or for several different companies. I'm an independent broker, so I need to know which companies are easiest to work with, which ones serve the general public the best, which ones an individual client can afford and still get adequate coverage with. Then there are the claims and the rest of the business end of it. It's not fascinating but it serves a need. And sometimes it's the difference between right and ruin, as my former partner puts it."

"How did you end up selling insurance in the first place?" Grady asked, looking enthralled, but only because he couldn't connect the dots between the sixteen-year-old girl he'd known and the thirty-six-year-old insurance agency owner he looked at now.

The dots were numbered and easy to follow, taken as a whole. However, she didn't think it the time or the place . . . or the best company in which to recount the first few steps she'd taken.

She smiled at him, hoping he'd understand. "Actually, I didn't get to sell insurance in the first place. Not at first. My . . . well, my ex-partner, my partner before that, my friend before that, his name is Joe Levitz and he hired me when I was seventeen to work part-time handling claims at his agency. Filing, at first—that was a short time before everything went to computers. After that I processed simple claims—fender benders, dented garage doors, things like that. I took training classes and a few courses from the community college—accounting, economics, business law—and eventually got licensed to sell insurance when I was twenty-three. I built my own client base . . . which was hard at first, but I got better at it. Then Joe—whose sons became a lawyer and a museum curator—made me his partner. He showed me how to run things, then a few years later, agreed to let me buy him out, gradually, when he retired."

She started to say something else, then looked down at her food for a moment. "It doesn't feel right to tell you everything Joe did for me in one paragraph. There's so much more. Volumes more." Her eyes met Grady's, perceptive and inquiring. She wanted to tell him all about Joe, about all he'd done for her—an amazing story really. But as she glanced around at the others, mostly children, she backed down. "But that's pretty much the gist of it."

Once or twice since the meal started, she caught Anna staring at her with unveiled curiosity—and once or twice Anna caught her doing the same. Their strained smiles screamed of the tension between them, and now that the opportunity presented itself, Hannah made her move.

"I understand you're a runner, Anna." She took a bite to make the question seem casual, then put the fork on the plate and gave the girl her full attention.

Unfortunately, Anna had a mouth full of carrots. She nodded as she hurried to finish chewing. By the time she was ready to speak, however, Lucy had lost patience and blurted out, "Anna's going to break the school record this year. It's thirty-seven years old. Do you know how long it's been since we had anyone as fast as Anna in this county?"

Hannah took a guess. "Thirty-seven years?"

"That's right. She might finally get a little competition at regionals, but there won't be anything there she can't handle, and then she'll go to state. And she's only a sophomore, you know."

"I know. That's wonderful." She smiled at Anna who looked like she wanted to crawl under the table and hide from the spotlight. Hannah prepared to ask how long she'd been running and what she liked about it, but Lucy wasn't finished.

"For the next two years she's going to have college scouts watching every move she makes. She'll be able to pick and chose a scholarship from at least fifty different schools. She's that good."

"I had no idea." Peripherally, she caught Anna frowning and shaking her head at Lucy. But when she looked directly at her, Anna shrugged like it no big deal. "That's wonderful, and very impressive. What an accomplishment. You must—"

"Yeah, well, she's worked hard for it," Lucy broke in, seeming to be angry. "She's been training since the seventh grade. She runs all year long and . . . *Ow!*" She glared across the table at her brother who had kicked her under the table. Cal slanted Hannah a wary look, extended it to his father, then gave his sister an insistent stare.

"I don't care." She all but shouted at him. "Hannah needs to know. If we don't tell her now, there's no telling what she'll do. She could ruin everything."

"Luce," whispered Biscuit, to get her attention and shake his head—at the same time her father said, "That's enough, Lucy. Stay out of it."

"Oh! Sure. Of course, I have to stay out of it." Now she shouted, clearly angry. "Anna's only *my* best friend so it doesn't actually involve *me-e*. I don't get to say anything about anything. The only one who gets any say in this at all is *her.*" Hannah's brows froze mid-forehead when the teen frosted her with a cold green stare. "And *she* doesn't know anything about it.

It's not fair that some stranger gets to walk in here and decide everything. Especially since . . ."

"That's enough." Grady's loud, stern voice brought instant silence. Even Hannah blinked and swallowed. With a halting glance around the table she found that no one, except Lucy, could look her in the eye for more than a millisecond. "Quietly finish your meal, or leave the table."

"No." This time Hannah startled Grady, who looked as if he wasn't used to having his orders countermanded. She turned to Lucy. "I mean, please don't decide to leave the table. I think Anna is very lucky to have such a good friend. It might take a little time, but I hope you'll come to understand that I want what's best for her, too. And obviously, her running is very important. I can see that. And I'm glad you brought it to my attention right away. I . . . . I haven't had much time to prepare for all this. There's a lot to do. My friend, Joe Levitz? He offered to scout out a high school this week. You know, just in case. There are dozens of very good schools in Baltimore. I'll call him tonight and tell him that a great track program is mandatory."

She hadn't gotten the last word out when Lucy's chair started to scrape across the floor, then fell over backward as she jumped up from the table.

"Oh my," Janice said in distress—not that Lucy noticed.

"You don't get it," she said, loud and impassioned. "You don't understand anything. The records she needs to break are *here*. The county she wants to represent is *this one*. The state she deserves to take first place in is *Vir-gin-ya,* where she's from. Not Bodymore, Murdaland," she shouted, using Baltimore's nickname because of its high-crime rates.

Stunned by the girl's reaction to what she believed to be a reasonable and accommodating plan of action, Hannah watched in dumbfounded silence as the girl stormed from the room.

"Ah, God." Grady groaned and let loose a long-suffering sigh. He was put out and embarrassed and concerned at the same time. "That was . . . There's no excuse for her behavior. I'm sorry. This has been . . . hard on her. Hard on everyone."

Hannah shook her head and lifted a helpless hand. What happened? One second she's the welcome benevolent aunt come to help out and the next she's Cruella De Vil looking for new coat material. How did she end up the bad guy?

And if Lucy's taking the move this hard, then it followed that Anna was, too. Looking at her, Hannah watched one corner of the girl's mouth bend into a regretful smile.

"I should go talk to her," she said, quietly—and Hannah realized it was the first time she'd spoken since they met. "May I be excused?"

There was so much to say, so much to talk about, but she was anxious about her friend, so Hannah nodded and watched her leave the room. Sighing heavily, she leaned back in her chair, her appetite gone. Her gaze caught on Cal's.

He waved his fork over his plate and told her, "Lucy's a drama queen."

"And mouthy," his father added.

"And afraid she'll never see Anna again," said Biscuit, who seemed incredibly sensible despite his hair. Hannah found she liked him. Very much. "She'll be able to visit, won't she?"

"Of course." They could all visit—*if* she and Anna decided to adopt each other.

"Would anyone like more gravy? I did a good job on it this time, I think. Nice and thick and I strained out all the lumps. Biscuit, dear, you haven't asked for seconds and I know your hollow leg isn't full yet. Here Cal, pass him . . ."

The problem was, she and Anna both had to decide that staying together was best for both of them. Hannah had a pyramid of doubts, the very tip of which was the basic desire to take on the responsibility; plus the potential dramatics of living with a teenager. Then, on the off chance they wanted to work something out, could she honestly say she was the best person for the job? Emotionally, she had a long fuse but on occasion her explosions were catastrophic. And while she'd only lost control of herself twice in her life, she couldn't guarantee there wouldn't be a third time.

And Anna . . . God only knew what Anna was thinking.

Time. There was time to decide. Time to get to know each other better, she reminded herself. Time to look at all the facts and choices. No life-altering plans needed to be made before the dinner dishes were done.

"We'll see you at the church tomorrow, then," Grady said, shrugging into his brown jacket, getting ready to leave once the last dish was stowed away. The boys were already out the door and the girls had been called down from Anna's room. She could hear their footsteps in the hall above. "Everything's been taken care of so there's nothing for you to do but show up."

"And the alter-society ladies, friends of your mother's from her church, have planned a nice little lunch for afterward," Janice said with a pat on Hannah's forearm. "They're hoping you'll come, but they told me to tell you that they would understand if you weren't up to it." She turned in the doorway to leave. "Cal? Are you waiting for your sister or is she coming home with me? You both have school tomorrow afternoon, you know. I hope your homework is done. Biscuit, you wash that gunk out of your hair before I see you next. Church is no place for self-expression."

Watching his mother, Grady let out a long, loud breath, like he might at the end of a tiring day. He looked like he could use a hug . . . but she wasn't the one to give it to him. Not if she planned to slide through the next two weeks without reopening that particular bag-o-bugs. She had her life, he had his; they were different people now and she liked it that way.

He turned, studied Hannah's expression, and gave her a resigned smile—made sweet and boyish by the dimples.

"Sorry about that spinning head at the dinner table. I can promise you it won't happen again."

"Please don't say anything to her. I can handle honest opinions."

"There's still the little matter of respectful delivery."

"Let me try to earn that— What?" she asked when he grinned.

"You really don't know much about kids, do you?"

"I told you that."

"Yes, you did." Looking up, she saw his gaze had dropped to her mouth. Instinctively she pressed her lips together and curled them inward, they were tingling. He inhaled and looked up when he heard the girls on the stairs. "You'll learn fast enough. Get some rest. I'd tell you that everything will look different tomorrow, but that would be a lie."

She laughed—what else could she do?—and glanced up as the girls hit the landing and started down toward them. They exchanged a look and said goodbye. Anna stayed on the bottom step as Lucy crossed the small foyer to exit in front of her father.

But she stopped in front of Hannah first.

"Sorry about before," she said, quick and stiff. She met Hannah's eyes and while the apology sounded sincere enough, she wasn't entirely sorry for her outburst—and neither was Hannah.

"I'm glad you said something, Lucy. I can't solve a problem until I know what it is, right?"

Her expression guarded, she lifted one shoulder in a most expressive shrug. "Whatever."

Whatever? Such an indeterminate word, yet the way she said it removed most of the ambiguity and left Hannah feeling like a failed diplomat.

"Good night, ladies." Grady gave both aunt and niece an encouraging nod before he followed Lucy out, pulling the door behind him.

Hannah followed the door closed, her hand inches from the knob until it latched. She was suddenly alone with the lion. Automatically, she reached up to lock it. The dead bolt was tight and hard to turn.

"I forgot. You don't lock your doors here."

"Yes, we do. That one, we do. Gran's always afraid someone will wander in off the road." She stalled, realized she'd used the wrong tense, and swallowed the emotion that it evoked. "It's probably stiff because we never use that door. We always left the back one unlocked."

"Okay." That one word seemed to finalize the discussion. She scrambled. "Look, I meant what I said to Lucy, just now and at dinner. I want to be honest with you. I have no idea what I'm doing here. I'm flying blind and feeling my way through this. Like you are, I imagine. The last thing I want to do is make things harder on you. So, please, don't leave it to me to guess at what you need or what you want. Chances are it might not even cross my mind. I don't even know what time to have your breakfast ready in the morning. Or what to cook for that matter."

Anna looked a little worried, and desperate to take Hannah at her word. "I don't . . . actually, eat a regular breakfast."

"You don't. Well, see there? Problem solved. *And* we have something in common. It's a twofer." She grinned and watched the first thin layer of ice melt away from Anna's protective coating—felt a layer of her own thawing as well. "I'm coffee and a piece of toast till noon."

"I'm toast and juice before I run and then I'm an apple and a protein shake on the bus. I make the shake."

"Great. I'll make the apple." She wondered if she should write things like this in a notebook. "Let's try that again. I'm early to bed, early to rise."

"Makes a girl healthy, wealthy, and wise." Anna grinned, and Hannah heard the rhyme echo in her mother's voice.

"You and I were clearly raised by the same woman."

"I like to read at night but I'm dead by ten, usually before,"

"I'm right behind you, after the ten o'clock news. Except maybe tonight. I feel like it's been a really long day. How about you?"

She nodded. "Do you want me to lock up?"

"Maybe you could show me the routine."

She bounced off the last step and headed for the kitchen. "Do you want to lock the back door?"

"No. That's all right." Was it too much to hope for a burglar in the market for stuff? Lots and lots of stuff?

"That's about it," she said, after checking on the coffee-pot, turning out the lights in the kitchen and living room, and turning the heat down for the night as she'd been taught to do. "When Lucy stays over, Gran leaves this lamp on so she doesn't kill herself coming down to the bathroom . . . she used to, leave it on."

"That's a good idea. I'll do it, too, for the first few nights at least." She paused. "Anything else I should do?"

Humor quirked the girl's mouth and twinkled in her blue eyes. "Like reminding me to brush my teeth?" Hannah gave her head a feeble wag. "No. I'm good. Good night."

"Good night." She watched the tops of the girl's slim, muscled legs disappear from view as she hurried up the stairs, then remembered. "Anna?"

"Yes, ma'am?" She stopped on the landing and Hannah went to the bottom of the steps to look up at her.

"I meant to tell you earlier . . . I'm sorry about your grandmother. And I'm very sad about your mom."

Tears sprang to her eyes but they didn't spill. She blinked them away as she shifted her weight uncomfortably from one foot to the other. Her expression solemn and circumspect, she nodded, looked away after a moment and came back. "I'm sorry for you, too. But I'm glad I finally got to meet you."

What a sweet, selfless thing to say.

"I am, too."

And she was, but she still wasn't convinced she was the right person to finish raising her. A teenager in her life would wreak pure havoc on the nice orderly little life she'd created for herself. And, yes, she knew how selfish that sounded, but it was a valid point that needed to be considered.

Still, beyond that, a bigger concern nagged at her: Would the girl continue to be a portal to the past? Would she always remind her of Ruth and mama and the life she'd work so hard to forget?

Yet, if all the stars in the sky aligned perfectly right and she and the girl were a bread-and-butter fit . . . who in their right mind, if they knew the truth about her, would leave a child in her care?

Chapter Six

When Hannah opened her eyes the next morning she barely recognized the room. Her gaze roamed to where bags and boxes of junk had been rearranged and moved aside to accommodate a twin bed, a half-empty chest of drawers, a 4 x 6-foot space in the center of the room, and access to a closet door on which hung her garment bag—the closet being stuffed.

She shuddered, hunkering deeper under the blankets, but she was too stiff to stay in bed much longer. It hadn't taken her long to discover that she had to sort of spin in the same warm spot between the sheets all night because moving an inch in any direction exposed her body to frozen linen, so cold it would jolt her awake with shock and chills.

All the junk, and it didn't even provide good insulation.

She wanted to call Joe—from bed—for a motivational speech, but she already knew what he'd say. She couldn't even call him to report in as she had nothing to report as yet.

She wasn't in the habit of going to him with every little thing that came along, but he was an excellent sounding board when life tossed her a tangle. From time to time she would gather together a list of several small things to take to him, so sweet elderly Joe would still feel loved and needed. Or so she told him.

At the moment, she just wanted to hear his voice. She could dog-paddle well enough for the deep end of the pool, but this was an ocean: bottomless, rimless, immense. She felt alone, and she was scared and—she knew what he'd say about that, too.

She listened to the rain on the roof for a few more seconds, then flung back the covers and started to swear. "Shit. Shit. Shit," she whispered, as she hadn't yet heard Anna stirring.

Rather than mosey down to the kitchen in her robe and slippers to make coffee, she danced in place on the frigid floor and scrambled into jeans, a long-sleeved T-shirt, a thick wool-blend sweater, two pairs of socks, and her slippers, then scurried out into the hall, "Shit, shit, shit," and down the stairs to the thermostat, cranking it up until she heard the furnace rumble to life beneath her.

Stiff and shivering, she shuffled to the bathroom, then to the kitchen, and almost wept when she found the coffee on a timer, already made and steaming hot. Pouring a cup, she warmed her hands on the outside of the mug, used them to heat her cheeks and the frozen tip of her nose. Taking it over to the kitchen table, she pulled a chair out and remembered from rote the exact right place to position it, over the floor vent to wait for the heat.

Thankful that it was already blowing warm air, she rubbed her toes together over it.

First decision of the day: no more being thrifty, leave the damn heat on at night.

Her coffee cooled rapidly, yet she hadn't finished the first cup when she heard the screen on the back porch creak open. She glanced at the clock on the wall, the cord trailing down the wall to the electrical socket, and saw that it was 6:15. She barely formed the question in her mind as to who could be visiting so early, when Anna appeared on the porch and smiled at her through the window in the door.

"Hi," she said entering on a short blast of cold air, her cheeks and nose rosy, her eyes brilliant with health and energy. She wore gray hooded sweats with a bright yellow safety vest. She looked glad to see her. "Good morning."

"Where the hell have you been?" The question popped out of Hannah's mouth before she could stop it—as she simultaneously realized there was no timer on the coffee and why she'd gotten such a quick response from the furnace. Anna had been up, made *her* coffee, turned up the heat and gone running before Hannah could think straight. Some caretaker *she* was! In addition, even to her ears, the question suggested more anger than surprise.

And sure enough the girl's smile drooped. The alarm and confusion in her bright blue eyes made Hannah feel like . . . shit, shit, shit.

She held up both hands. "That's not what I meant to say. I'm sorry. I can see where you've been. I can't believe you've been out running already, in the rain. What time did you get up?"

"Four-thirty," she said, but her bubble of high spirits had already popped. She pulled the hood off her head. She'd scooped her thick hair back in a looped ponytail and a fine sheen of perspiration mixed with rain covered her skin.

Decision two of the day: Don't assume anything about this girl. And think harder before speaking to her—decision three.

"You're soaked."

"Yes, ma'am. I'll shower in a bit."

"You run every morning?"

"Most mornings." She opened the refrigerator door and took out a plastic pitcher. "Unless there's ice or snow on the road. In the summer I train for cross-country and it's cooler early in the morning." She filled a tall glass full of orange juice. "In the winter, I cut back because I don't like to run in the dark. And Gran wouldn't let me. There's less daylight before *and* after school so I start getting serious again for the track team about the middle of February." She chugged the OJ in one lift, filled the glass again, and set it on the counter. "I run with the team after school once track starts. Except on weekends."

"When is that?" She watched as Anna started removing things from the refrigerator and setting them on the counter beside her juice. A large container of yogurt, whole milk, two bananas, frozen strawberries . . .

"It started two weeks ago." She took honey from the cupboard as well and two tall cylinders of powdered additives—one said *protein* and the other said *fuel*. She turned to face Hannah. "I ran early today because I wasn't sure what you wanted me to do about track . . . because we haven't had time to talk about it."

Hannah leaned back in her chair and crossed her arms over her stomach. *This is one amazing kid,* she thought. Losing her grandmother aside, it had to be horrible for her to have to wait and wonder on how much her life was going to change because of some aunt she'd never met before; to have to ask permission of a complete stranger to continue doing what she loved best. Looking back, she would have hated it, resented the hell out of it. Yet Anna seemed willing, if not quite eager, to bow to Hannah's potential authority over her, even when her eyes expressed deep concerns and urgent hopes that went unspoken.

"Tell me what *you* want to do about track, Anna."

"Oh. Well. I talked to coach. He called when he heard about Gran," she said, turning to drop the banana she peeled into an industrial-looking blender she'd pulled to the center of the counter. "He said I could keep training with the team if I wanted to. Until I leave. He'll have to pick someone else for the relays, I guess, but I'd like to run with my friends for as long as I can. And Cal said he'd give me rides home if that was going to be a hassle for you." She added the last bit hastily and glanced over her shoulder to get Hannah's reaction.

"I think that's an excellent plan. And if Cal is going to be there anyway and it's okay with his dad, maybe we can work something out with the gas, since we're a little out of his way."

She poured and measured her ingredients into the blender—it was very nearly full. "No, um, Cal doesn't do track. He plays football and basketball. He only said he'd give me a ride . . . if it was a hassle for you. To be nice."

In case the horrible, wicked aunt made a stink.

"I see. Well, I can't imagine why it would be a hassle for me."

"Oh." She sounded disappointed. "Good."

"And I'd love to see you run. Would it be all right if I came early to watch?"

"Sure." She might have imagined a lack of enthusiasm in the girl's voice as Anna chose that moment to turn the blender on. She let it run for as long as it took her to drink the rest of her juice. All part of the girl's routine, Hannah realized.

Hitting the off button and reaching into the cupboard directly above for three tall water bottles with large straws, she poured from the blender into two of them and filled the third with water. One shake and the water went in the frig, and she started sucking on the other as she cleaned up her mess.

Hannah found she enjoyed watching her. She had long, slender, graceful fingers—her body fluid and efficient. Her hair was a wildflower yellow, like her mother's had been, and shiny. She caught Hannah looking and started to fidget.

"Um, I usually take my shower now but I can wait if you want to go first."

"Thank you, but you go ahead. You stick to your schedule and I'll work around you. In Baltimore if . . . if things work out you can have your own bathroom."

"Cool." She had a nice polite smile.

"By the way, thank you for the coffee . . . and for the extra blankets last night. I forgot how cold and drafty this old place is."

"No problem."

The funeral home was sending someone to drive them to and from St. John's at nine thirty.

It was still raining.

Hannah wore a black wool pantsuit with a silver gray blouse and flat shoes—having learned the hazards of heels in a cemetery at Julie Levitz's funeral.

Pacing in the hall at the bottom of the stairs, waiting, Hannah tried not to think of the hypocrisy she felt in attending the funeral of the woman she hadn't made contact with in twenty years. She'd mourned the loss of her mother years ago, cried for her, missed her, reconciled herself to never seeing her again. She still had an aching sadness, but she couldn't truly call it grief—not like she'd grieved then.

Not like Anna grieved now, she thought. Ellen Benson was a different person to Anna—a different kind of mother, as well as a grandmother. She needed to remember that. Hopefully, she'd been a better mother to Anna—and the pang of resentment she experienced at the thought of it was unfair. She knew that.

She rubbed at the dull, ache throbbing in her temples. She'd been through all this, she reminded herself. She'd come to terms with the fact that the woman had done the best she could but . . . she hadn't managed to forget, not at all.

She stopped at the door to the living room, her attention stuck on an object she knew though she'd rarely seen it uncovered. A dim light filtered through the large front window and gave luster to the lacquer finish on the rear curved portion of a rocker, concealed beneath a striped-yellow-to-tan-to-brown-knit afghan.

Hannah's heart chugged sluggish and painful in her chest as she walked closer to it. She noticed a distinct lack of clutter on and around it—as if it sat in a place of honor amid the chaos.

She stood for several seconds, her hands in fists against her chest before she gave way to temptation and carefully pulled the blanket off, unveiling a small armless bentwood rocker. It looked fragile and she knew it to be old; she couldn't keep from gliding a hand over the floral tapestry on the cushioned back. Roses, faded to a unique shade of red, buds and blooms on a royal blue background.

The pattern on the seat matched. She smiled at the lovely little chair and let the discomfort around her heart yield to a strange sense of triumph and joy. Was this the feeling of peace Joe had been telling her about?

She turned when she heard Anna on the steps behind her. She wore a pair of those thick-soled chunky black shoes kids wore, a long straight black skirt, a black turtleneck sweater, and a black winter coat that buttoned up the front—she'd also painted her nails black.

"You look very nice," Hannah told her.

"Thanks. You, too."

"This chair," she said, looking back at the rocker. "I hardly ever saw it growing up. Mama . . . your grandmother always kept it buried, over there in the corner. She used to have her sewing machine there, near the window for the light. She kept this little chair beside it, covered with boxes of patterns and remnants and whatever else she could find. She said it belonged to her grandmother and that she would give it to whichever one of us got married first." She gave a soft laugh. "An incentive program, I guess. Like your mom and I would race one another to the altar after . . ." She touched the soft tapestry with the tips of her fingers. "She'd tell us stories about her grandmother, and about her mama and her daddy and her two brothers who lived in Ohio. Then we had to promise not to talk about it—this chair. She was always so afraid that . . ." She hesitated. "She was afraid something would happen to it."

Anna made a soft noise and when Hannah turned to look at her, she offered a thoughtful expression. "Do you want to hear something strange?"

"Sure."

"The first time my mom came back here, when she first brought me here to live, I was, like, five, I think . . . She stood there, like you are now, and she told me almost the exact same story. Only she told me what Gran was really afraid of."

"She did?" Scratches, dust . . . but not the truth. It would be too wrong to tell someone so innocent about something so evil.

"Mom called him Gran's husband. I didn't even know he was her father until after she died. Sheriff Steadman explained it to me."

"He shouldn't have."

"Why not? Because of how he died? Because of what he did? Gran never talked about it, but my mom did. She thought it was important for me to know about people like him. So I could avoid them. So I'd know what to do if it happened to me."

"What would you do?" She had to ask.

"My mom said to call the cops and run like hell . . . like you did."

"Like . . . She told you?" Hannah, the blood draining from her face, heard the distant shouting in the back of her head and felt dizzy. She lowered herself onto the little rocker, barely noted the creak of the wood as it took her weight. "What did she tell you exactly?"

"That you were never afraid of him." She glanced at the floor. "She told me how you used to try to help Gran . . . and her when you could. She said you were smart and brave and that's why she named me after you. So maybe I'd be like you."

Her throat tight, her eyes were stinging with tears, she started to shake her head slowly. She couldn't look at the girl; she had the story all wrong. "I wasn't brave. I wasn't smart. And I was always afraid of him."

She pressed her fingers to her lips trying not to cry—not so much for the past itself, but because her sister, who suffered agonies of her own in ways Hannah could only imagine, had gone to her grave with such misplaced beliefs—had named her daughter after a delusion.

"You all were," Anna said, her voice soft with compassion. "He was a terrible man. My mom said that you running away to save your own life that night gave Gran the courage she needed to kill him."

Hannah looked up. She could tell by her expression that she didn't know any more of the story than that. She didn't know the truth. Maybe Ruth hadn't known the truth . . .

"And Gran used it like a time line," Anna went on. "She'd say: a long time ago, before Hannah left. Or a while back, a few months or years or whatever, after Hannah left home. But it was never before or after he died."

She smoothed the creases of her slacks and took a deep breath, trying to tug herself together. The less they talked about the past the safer she would be.

"She probably wanted to forget all about him. I'd like to."

Anna pressed her lips together and nodded, but then she said, "My mom used to tell me that . . . that Gran wanted to forget. But she couldn't because of me. Gran was afraid it might have been passed on to me, you know, all the anger and the bad temper but Mom said it wasn't hereditary. You don't think it is, do you?"

"No, I don't." But she once did. And sometimes, in weaker moments, she still worried about it. "Your grandmother was from a different time, she didn't know. She didn't know about leaving an abusive husband. She didn't know that it was a learned behavior, that his father was probably exactly like him. She . . ." *thought I had it, that I was the spawn of the devil himself,* she almost said. "She did the best she could." Then when it occurred to her, she grew concerned. "She didn't accuse you . . . or say something that . . . she never . . ."

"No. She didn't talk about it and we got along okay, so . . . I don't have that kind of temper anyway. I guess she thought I got mostly her genes or something."

"What about your mom?"

"My mom's temper? No, she was more . . ." She hesitated. "She didn't have much of a temper, either."

They both heard tires in the gravel drive. Hannah took a deep breath and stood up.

"I'm glad your mom was better informed. I think she was very wise to tell you about it. I didn't at first. I tend not to talk about it much, but she was right. You do need to know how to take care of yourself."

Chapter Seven

Turns out she was a pillar in the St. John's Altar Society. The ladies couldn't say enough about her," she told Joe later that afternoon as she drove to the high school to pick up Anna after track. "They maintain the altar and the interior of the church, raise funds for flowers and candles and vestments, you know, all the stuff used at the altar."

"Hence their name, I suspect."

"Well, yeah. But then the priest—he's young, a different one than I told you about—he comes over to us after the grave-side service, practically in tears, and tells us how much he's going to miss her. She was the rectory housekeeper, can you believe it? For most of the last twenty years. That was her *job*."

"Many people turn to their church in times of crisis."

"Well, yeah. But the weird thing is I never pictured her as having a job. Or as being an active member of . . . anything. Or as anyone other than who she was the night I left—this sort of beaten spirit who couldn't lift a finger to help herself, much less someone else. I don't know." She slowed at the stop sign. "It's like it's finally, genuinely sinking in that time didn't stop here once I was gone. I mean, I knew it didn't but . . . I never thought of my mother actually getting up off the floor and making a real life for herself . . . and for Ruth, and then Anna. I never thought of her as . . . being a real person, you know?"

"I believe that's a common childhood ailment. My younger son didn't think I could spell my own name until he was almost thirty."

"But you were always real to him. He loved you, cared about you, *worried* about you. They both did. I didn't worry about her, Joe. If I thought about her at all, I simply assumed she stayed locked up in the house and on welfare like before. I was so wrapped up in myself, so busy worrying about *me* that—"

"No, no, no," he broke in, his voice stern. "You don't get to do this to yourself, my friend. You're not there to add to your guilt list. That's all in the past. It's good that you're getting to know who your mother was. Try to feel proud of her achievements, happy that you were mistaken, glad that she found a purpose in her life. But you have suffered enough for the past. You have tried to forgive her, now you must also forgive yourself."

"I know." Her voice came out as weak as her resolve. "It wasn't her fault, or mine." Four years of therapy and the final outcome was that her family was a no-fault accident, an act of Nature beyond the control of those involved. Theoretically, even her father wasn't responsible due to ignorance or mental defect—although *her* nature wasn't that theoretical. Her more practical mind told her that right or wrong, at one point or another, they had all made choices.

"Tell me what else happened." He always knew when she needed to talk, and not about anything in particular.

"Um, two young brothers, a little younger than Anna, and their mother came up to us after the priest left and asked if we wanted them to move their cows." She smiled at the silence on the other end. "Did I mention there are three cows in a fenced field next to the house?"

"Aromatic cows?"

"Not really, plain brown cows pretty much. Apparently they're 4-H projects for these two boys and Mama let them use the field in exchange for chores. Anna knows them pretty well. She and I sort of talked it over real fast and decided they could leave the cows for now and maybe work out something with the new owners, and we'd use the boys to help us clean out the house."

"Always thinking, aren't you? By the way, I've been look-ing over this list you e-mailed me and I can't think of anything to add. You seem to have thought of everything. Two antique dealers there at the same time is good business, and having them and the used furniture buyers doing a preliminary walk-through will save you some time, I believe. Was that a car horn?"

"Yes." She sighed and rolled her eyes. Joe disapproved of talking on the phone while driving—even with a handless earpiece. "They do that here. Honk and wave. I have no idea who they are. And I'm pretty sure they don't know who I am. I think they just like to honk and wave—like it's the friendly thing to do. But it's also annoying, and very distracting."

"Especially when you're on the phone."

"I knew you were going to say that."

"I know you knew. So, where are you going?"

"To pick Anna up from school."

"This late?"

"She has track until five thirty. I'm a little early. I'm hoping to see her run."

"How is she doing?"

"Dealing with Mama's death or dealing with me?"

"Yes."

"She cried a little during the service. Not hysterically. A

few loose tears . . . Oh! That's something else I found out. Mama had heart problems for several years. She'd been in the hospital a couple of times, so this wasn't unexpected." Not that it would be any less painful for Anna. "Anna let me hold her hand for a few minutes."

"That's something."

"Yeah, but then she hemmed and hawed when the Steadman kids came over to ask if she wanted a ride to school. It took me forever to realize that she wanted to go, but she didn't want me to feel abandoned if she did." She paused. "She's a nice girl, Joe. I like her."

"Why do you make this sound like a bad thing?"

"It's not but . . . I don't want to make a mistake. I don't want to do anything that might hurt her. She's gone through so much already."

"Then you won't. You'll bend over backward to do the opposite, you'll see. Listen to your heart, Hannah. It has all the best answers."

"Mmm." If she asked the right questions—maybe. "So, anyway, I wrote my first official note to the school to excuse her absence and she left with them. Then I went back to the house to call junk dealers and antique collectors and work out a plan to evacuate the house. Joe, you wouldn't believe the stuff in that house."

"So you've said." He chuckled. "And what about the boy?"

"What boy?"

"The sheriff."

"Oh. Him." Her heart picked up some nervous speed. "He's going to be trouble. He keeps looking at me."

"Oh? And what do you keep doing to cause this?"

"Nothing. I swear. Every time I looked up, he was staring at me like he's trying to figure me out."

"Have him call me. I'll straighten him out on impossible puzzles."

"He doesn't know me," she said, ignoring his comment. "He remembers this . . . this sad, frightened, pathetic little girl he somehow managed to think he was in love with for two or three seconds in high school and I'm not her."

"Two or three seconds," he said shrewdly. "Sometimes that's all the time it takes."

"For what?"

"To know someone better than we know ourselves. But if you're no longer attracted to him, then I can't see why this would be upsetting. Let him look. You're a pretty woman. You don't have to look back, you know."

"And I can do anything for two weeks, right?"

"Right. Longer if need be."

"You're not having fun there, are you?" she asked, eager to change the subject. "It took me so long to get you to retire, maybe I shouldn't have asked you to watch things for me. Maybe all this is a bigger mistake than I thought."

"Don't you worry. At this moment I recall perfectly why I decided to retire. Your boy, Jim Sauffle, is making my backside ache."

She cringed. Joe had the patience of Job when it came to new agents starting out—when it came to most everything, actually. His backside didn't ache often enough to be ignored.

"Talk to me," she said, slowing to turn into the parking lot at the high school, close to the football field where track events were also held. In short terms Joe described her new associate's faulty handling of a group health policy for a Precision Auto Parts franchise and then a term life package for a newly married couple with young children from previous marriages. Apparently, he'd quoted a set of terms to both clients, went back a few days later saying he'd found better policies for them, then only the Friday before had reversed his decision once again.

Hannah worried the stitching on the leather-covered steering wheel as she pulled into a parking space overlooking the field below and turned off the engine. "Friday I got Grady's call, Joe. I'm trying to remember if Jim tried to talk this over with me or if he . . . well, if this is the new Precision place out on Fredrick Avenue near Catonsville. Larry Watts already has a policy on his other franchise. With me. I'm sure Larry would have told him. Why didn't he just attach them?"

"That's what Mr. Watts asked me first thing this morning. And since he's worked with you for so many years, he's willing to let me get to the bottom of the problem and get back to him. Young Jim and I had a discussion. That's when I found out about the term life clients as well."

While her mind tried to wrap itself around the idea that her new associate might be trying to steal from her, issuing new policies to her preexisting clients . . . she became aware of a group of runners taking off around the track.

"Mixed with the multiple quotes, I want to believe all this was a stupid mistake but—" She broke off when a solitary runner broke from the pack, her long legs eating up the track with ease and confidence.

"I'll keep an eye on him. He did seem confused about—"

"Oh, God, Joe. I wish you could see this."

"What?"

"Anna. She's running. She's . . . beautiful. She's . . . Joe, she's so graceful. She's almost a quarter of a track ahead of the others, and she doesn't look like she's straining at all."

"It's a quarter mile track?"

"I don't know. It's around the football field."

"Has she gone around more than once?"

"She just started the second loop around."

"Then she might be a long-distance runner. Sixteen hundred meters maybe."

"How many laps is that?"

"Four. You said she runs cross-country in the fall?"

"Yeah. I think so. I gotta go, Joe. Do whatever you think best with Jim. I'll call you back later."

Hannah couldn't take her eyes off the tall, lanky girl on the track. Running looked as effortless and natural to her as walking was for most people. Gradually, she'd taken close to a half-track lead ahead of the others and still didn't seem to be fatiguing. She ran with her knees up, her arms bent, her blond ponytail swishing back and forth in a relaxed rhythm.

She watched Anna through the wire fencing as she made her way to the gate, heading for the bleachers. Being that this was only a practice, there wasn't a large crowd of spectators. One or two adults, parents she imagined, watching from the stands and a few younger onlookers leaning against a low wire fence around the track—Biscuit and Lucy were among them.

Though their coiffures were somewhat dull due to the funeral that morning, they had gone to great lengths to make up for it with their wardrobes. Hannah now found it endearing in a strange way—perhaps because of the deference they'd both shown to her mother at the service that morning. Both had dressed in severe conservative black clothing, their hair devoid of all but their natural colors. Biscuit served as a pallbearer, along with Grady and his son, and three other gentlemen she hadn't recognized but later found out were members of the church who knew and were fond of her mother—the parish gardener and two CCD students from many years past.

Lucy had glued herself to her best friend's side for support and was nothing but caring and concerned. Even on such short acquaintance, all in all Hannah found herself impressed with Anna's choice in friends—they were certainly her defenders.

During Anna's third pass around the field, they noticed Hannah's presence in the bleachers; and while Lucy didn't seem to care one way or the other, Biscuit started climbing the seats toward her.

"You don't have to sit up here alone, you know."

"I don't want to interrupt . . . or distract her."

He laughed as he sat down beside her. "Fat chance of that. She gets into a zone and can't hear or see anything except the sound of her feet and her breathing, and the track about eighty feet ahead of her. Not the whole track. That's too much. This reporter interviewed her last fall, and he wanted to know what she thought about while she was running. She said she mostly thought about putting one foot in front of the other, and breathing."

"She makes it look so easy."

He nodded, watching Anna. "This fourth lap she'll push it a little harder, to shave off a couple more seconds."

As if he'd whispered in her ear, Anna picked up her tempo on the far side of the field and while she still looked uncommonly graceful, there was no doubt that she was working harder.

"Does she try to break the record every time she runs?"

"Just her record. It's always nice to break someone else's record but that's not really what it's all about. If it was, you'd go nuts. There's always going to be someone faster than you are. After a while you'd have to give up. It's more fun to beat your own personal best. You get to know yourself pretty well. You test yourself over and over again. And you amaze yourself over and over again by what you can do. It's a great feeling."

"You're speaking from experience." She waited for Anna to cross the finish line, slow down, circle back halfway toward a man holding a stop watch and a clipboard, then bend with her hands on her knees to catch her breath, before she looked at Biscuit.

"I ran junior varsity three years ago when I was a freshman, then I wrecked my knee in a car accident. It wasn't the same after that. I can still play basketball, though. I'm a pretty good forward." He wiggled his fingers at her and grinned. "I have good hands."

"Do you miss the running?" she asked, ignoring his youthful innuendo. Looking back at Anna, she watched the girl straighten up and look directly at the tall wire fencing on the scoreboard end of the field. Following her gaze, Hannah spotted Cal Steadman leaning against the front of an old light-blue pickup truck, his arms crossed over his chest.

"Nah. Not anymore. It's more fun to watch Anna do all that work." Catching her glancing between Anna and Cal, he added, "We all like watching her."

"Cal comes to watch every day?"

He shrugged. "And to pick up Lucy. And to hang with me."

She had a sinking feeling in her chest. "I think I messed up again. I'm supposed to let her ride home with Cal, aren't I? That's what she wanted to do, right? What she usually does? I'm screwing up her routine."

"It's already screwed up. Coach is letting her practice with the relay team for now, but once he decides who to replace her with, it'll be screwed up even more. Then there's the move to Baltimore. You picking her up today is pretty minor in the overall screwed-upness of things. Besides, she's glad that you wanted to see her run."

"And Cal?" she asked on a hunch. "Is there something . . . going on, between the two of them?"

He scrunched his face and looked like he either didn't want to or wasn't supposed to speak on this issue.

"No," he said at last, and she sensed he was lying—or at least not telling the whole truth. "Not really. They're friends, is all."

"Good friends?"

"Pretty good." He looked at her, made a quick assessment, then lowered his eyes to concentrate on his black nail polish. "Lucy says Anna's had this thing for him since like sixth grade. I'm pretty sure she was just his little sister's best friend until like last summer because he was way hot on Cassie Jordan for a long time. Cal and Cassie, they were a pair. Until last summer. I don't know what happened. I don't think he knows what happened, but suddenly he wasn't so hot on Cassie anymore and they broke up." He glanced over at his friend, leaning against the pickup truck, then tilted back on the bleacher behind them, his arms stretched out wide. "He's been smart about it, though. He didn't make some big, huge move on someone else right away—Cassie would have made her life a hell. But I know my boy and I've seen the way he looks at Anna and . . ." His soft laugh was relaxed and philosophical. "His old man knows him, too."

"Grady?"

"That's the one."

"He knows there's something going on between them?"

"No, but he, like me, saw the potential for something to begin, and he told Cal to back off."

"Why?"

He bobbed his head. "Because Anna's leaving town. He said there was no point in starting something that can't be finished."

Wise advice stemming from Grady's firsthand experience. "So this was recent?"

He nodded. "And it was Lucy's fault . . . again. Seems Cal said something to her about maybe taking Anna to the prom, *maybe*, and I think Lucy may have said something to Anna about it, of course. But then old Mrs. Benson . . . well, your mom, she died. So when the sheriff told them about you coming, Lucy went off about how unfair it all was . . . including Anna having this thing for Cal for so long and not being able to go to the prom with him now. Cal said it was the nicest nightmare he'd ever had."

Hannah looked at him askance and he went on. "Cal likes to keep his dad in the dark about his life as much as possible—you would too, if your dad was the sheriff. It's hard enough to find any privacy in this town. Living with the sheriff, or the high school principal, makes it close to impossible."

"Your father is the high school principal?" He gave her a droll look and nodded. She clamped down on her molars and tried not to laugh . . . or to reexamine his attire. "So Cal's embarrassed to have his dad find out that he likes Anna?"

"Not embarrassed exactly, just . . ." His expression soured, but he still had no word for the feeling. "It's easier when they don't know."

"If that was the nightmare part, what's nice about it?"

"Finding out for sure that Anna's hot for him." He frowned. "I don't think he's all that surprised to hear it. I mean, a guy can sense these things, you know. But confirmation is always cool. But then the sheriff told him to back off, so then they had to fight about it."

Ah. The fight. "Why are you telling me all this?" she asked, when it occurred to her that she'd gotten more information in the last ten minutes than she had in the previous seventy-two hours. "I thought Goths, in particular, were sort of reticent and tight-lipped."

"That depends."

"On what?"

"On the point we're trying to make." He stretched his long legs out in front of him. "If it's to be as weird as everyone seems to think we are, then why bother talking at all? If it's to embarrass our families, then our attire is usually enough said, more than enough—and, of course, if your father is the principal of a high school, then it's a particularly satisfying statement. But to the people who know us best, how we dress and how much or how little we talk doesn't matter."

"I see."

"And to answer your question, I felt sorry for you last night. At dinner. I got the feeling you were walking into this blindfolded and that's not fair, for anyone. The sheriff wants everything to go smooth for Anna, and for you, but . . . you can't just say make the road smooth and expect it to be that way."

"No. You can't." *Smart young man,* she thought, looking at him. He had fine dark brown eyes that were keen and perceptive. She wondered if he'd be in any trouble for talking to her. "Thank you. Biscuit."

He smiled when she said his name. "You'll get used to it." Then he hesitated and grew sober again. "There's something else I think you should know about. I mean, not that you have to do anything about it or anything, but you should at least know."

"Please. What?" He looked very reluctant to tell her. "Please."

"It probably doesn't make any difference. I don't know that it *should* make any difference. I mean, putting things off doesn't make them any easier and quick breaks are better anyway and . . . the sooner it happens, the sooner everyone can start adjusting and all that stuff, but . . ."

"What?"

He took a deep breath. "April's a huge month around here. Well, not always. I mean, it's the normal stuff, but with Anna leaving and all . . . things seem bigger. Like for one thing, Anna's birthday is in April. Sheriff already said if it's okay, he'll drive us all up to Baltimore the weekend after but . . . well, we also have two big meets and one's with Ripley." The way he spoke the name of the rival county told her the animosity between the two schools hadn't lessened in twenty years. "Anna was a major part in wiping the floor with them last year, but then there's the prom the first weekend in May and, well, I don't know if that's such a good idea, but . . ."

"Now I know."

"Right." His expression brightened. "Informed decisions, right?"

She nodded and looked down at Anna, deep in discussion with a man Hannah presumed was her coach. "Did she ask you to talk to me?"

"No," he said quickly and, she suspected, honestly. "We talked about it, of course, but it's, like . . . well, the sheriff said you were dead set on two weeks, so . . . I thought you should know, is all. So you'd know why Lucy's so mad and why Anna might be sad and why Cal's standing over there, instead of down here with us."

"I appreciate it. I can't say that it changes anything but maybe I won't step on as many feelings as I did last night."

"Yeah, well, it's not like most of us aren't dying to get out of this bass-ackward town as soon as possible anyway. It's just that we want to do it our way, in our own time. And in the middle of high school, we sort of figure that's after graduation. We make plans, you know? We want to finish school and graduate with our friends, not a bunch of strangers. We want to head out of here to . . . wherever, at the same time; come back every few years to see the parental units and the kids who didn't make it out. It's tough on everyone to have to leave something in the middle of it but, well, I moved here five years ago. I'm living proof that you can leave everyone you know and survive."

So am I, she thought. Yet the look they exchanged told a

more accurate story—survival came after the pain and the sorrow, when you couldn't live with the misery and loneliness any longer.

"You seem very protective of Lucy. Are the two of you . . . you know?"

He leaned forward as a barrier and hid whatever he was feeling with humor. "What. I look stupid enough to want to date the sheriff's *little Lucy*? Besides the drama queen stuff, and the bossy stuff, and the telegraph, telephone, tele-Lucy stuff, *and* the fact that she's too young to do anything but *group* date? I look that masochistic to you?" His eyes dared her to give an honest answer.

She couldn't stop her gaze from bouncing around to the multiple piercings on his face. A snort-laugh escaped her and he grinned.

"Certainly not." And before the smile in her eyes faded, they met his. "I appreciate the information, Biscuit.

Chapter Eight

There's enough funeral food at the house to last us six months but Joe says runners need protein and carbs especially," Hannah said in the car on the way home. "I should get a book if . . . Do they have cookbooks for runners? I don't cook a lot at home. I have a nice lunch, usually, and a sandwich or something in the evening. It might be fun having someone to cook for—not that I'm a great cook or anything; I haven't had a lot of practice but this'll *be* good practice for me." *Take a breath!* "Anyway, we should go through the food and keep what's best for you—you'll have to tell me—and donate the rest to . . . what? A nursing home? Is there a women's shelter here?" *Finally. Years and years too late.* "Maybe Father Scott can help. Then we can make a list of what's still missing, whatever you need and . . ." She glanced from the road to the silent girl beside her. "Well, I thought I'd go in to see the principal tomorrow, get him started on your paperwork. Just in case. I can hit the grocery store after that. In the morning you can ride in with me or ride the bus like always, whichever, but I have the antique dealers coming in the afternoon, so do you think, would you mind asking Cal and Lucy for that ride home they offered?"

Such a very bad idea. Not wise at all and fraught with future disappointment and heartache for the girl—and, okay, a clear pitch for aunt-of-the-year on her part. But the moment the words bubbled from her lips and she caught the elated little fidget that passed through Anna until her fingers twitched in her lap, she knew it was out of her hands anyway. No one knew better than Hannah about falling in love with the most impossible person at the most inopportune time—or how hopeless it was to prevent.

What had Grady been thinking, trying to keep them apart? Had he forgotten? Had it been so long that he couldn't recall what it was to be a meteor caught in the pull of earth's gravity; to feel sucked into the eye of a hurricane? Or was that solely her memory of it?

When the senior class graduated from Turchen County High School in late May of 1990 the underclassmen still had another two weeks of school left before summer break. She'd turned fourteen in January and would be heading for high school in the fall—a thought that both thrilled and terrified her.

To think she had only four years left before she could legally liberate herself from her family with enough of an education— more than both her parents put together—to do something with her life . . . away from them . . . far away, was like the sunshine she got out of bed for every morning.

And yet, four years is a long time. The previous three she'd spent as the weirdest, creepiest, most socially dysfunctional outcast in all the histories of all the middle schools in America was proof of that. Not that she cared. Truly. Who cared what those stupid kids thought? They *were* stupid after all. Most of them wouldn't know their own butt if they sat on it. And she was a straight-A student, even though it irritated her father sometimes—in fact, *because* it irritated him *most* of the time.

She'd be riding a whole different bus next year and Ruth would be alone on the one Hannah was riding that very early June afternoon. She wasn't too worried about it, though. By now most everyone knew that if they messed with Ruth, they'd answer to Hannah, so she'd be safe enough. But the rides to and from the high school were long and boring and she dreaded sitting all by herself in a seat with no one to talk to . . . or worse yet, having to share the seat and having no one to talk to.

She startled when a long boy-body slipped into the seat beside her on the bus. She instinctively put her back to the window to assess her exposure and evaluate the danger she was in.

"Where's your little sister today?"

Grady Steadman. A member of the Turchen County High School pantheon best known for his athleticism, rowdy weekends, and for the occasional clever and daring feat of illegal vandalism. Less famous, she was sure, for being one of few who would glance at her kindly, who would sneak her a faltering smile from time to time, and who never, that she could recall, said a mean thing to her.

"Sick." She settled back in her seat but didn't relax. She never relaxed.

"That's too bad." He waited a moment. "But then if she was here I couldn't sit down and we couldn't talk, so maybe it's a good thing, if she isn't *too* sick, I mean."

"No." Ruth was two years younger but started her monthly curse the same year Hannah had, the first thirty-six hours of which were a sharp cramping misery for her. "She'll be better tomorrow."

So don't get too comfortable in her seat.

"Good. Then today we can talk."

Talk? That was twice he'd said it, like they had one single thing in the whole entire universe in common.

"Talk about what?"

"Well, I don't know. Anything." He looked around the bus for a good topic. "Um. You're coming up to the high school next fall, right?" She gave him one nod and looked out the bus window. "Are you excited?" She shrugged one shoulder. "Looking forward to it?" Another shrug. "Want me to get lost again and leave you alone?"

She turned her head to look at him. He grinned at her—but not in the malicious or mischievous way that most of the kids did—benevolently, his green eyes gentle and soft with humor. He had no intention of getting lost again or of leaving her alone. On the contrary, he liked where he was and who he was with—for the moment anyway. And he had those stupid dimples . . . *ah, jeeze.*

"You're on the wrong bus."

"Yes, I am." Her astute observation and comment pleased him. "I had a dentist appointment this afternoon. My mom dropped me off earlier but now I'm taking this bus home so she doesn't have to drive all the way back into town to pick me up, then take me back to school in time to ride the high school bus home."

She'd never been to a dentist—couldn't imagine why a smile like his would need one.

She'd also run out of plain-as-the-nose-on-your-face things to say to him. The silence grew awkward and oppressive, a familiar full-body cringe started deep inside.

"Wa-why don't you just ride home with your mother?"

"Sometimes I do. Depends on if she's staying late to tutor or check papers and I'm staying late to practice or if I'm between sports and going home early, and she decides she wants to go home right after school to cook something special for my dad or something like that. Depends."

Cringe. Cringe. Her stomach started to hurt.

"What do you do for fun? What do you like to do?" he asked, like he genuinely wanted to know.

A tough question. She had to think about it; no one had ever asked before.

"I like to read." She waited for him to laugh but he simply nodded and hung on for more, like there was more. "I . . . I like to work in Mama's garden." Because she had recently and it was the only thing she could think of that sounded halfway interesting. "Also I have a book of state birds. When I see one I mark it off in the book. I like to do that, sometimes."

A rush of hot blood shot up her neck and into her cheeks as she lowered her gaze to her lap. He may not have thought she was anything special or bright before, but now that he'd actually spoken to her and knew *for sure* she wasn't, she wanted to curl up and die—not that she didn't wish to curl up and die on a regular basis but this was different. This time she felt it but didn't truly want to . . .

"Your parents are pretty strict, aren't they?"

She nodded. *Strict.* Is that what people called it? She reckoned it was one word they could use for it, but it wasn't the most descriptive.

"Do you think next year, in high school, they'll let you go out some? To the football games maybe? Or to some of the parties?"

"Not *your* high school football parties." His personal pronoun and the four words her mind singled out from his last three sentences spilled from her lips with a snippy resentment that surprised her, and him.

It didn't matter that she was, at present, too young to be invited to the high school parties; nor was it especially important that once old enough she likely wouldn't be included by her peers. What she resented was knowing that if all conditions were equal with her classmates—physical beauty, nice clothes, good grades, social finesse . . . all of it—her father still wouldn't allow her to go. She resented the hopelessness of it, the emptiness of her future, at least for the next four years.

Though that's not how Grady Steadman interpreted it.

"First off, they aren't my parties. Other people throw them, I just show up when I can get a ride after the games. And second, there are other kinds of parties. Not so rowdy. Sometimes the parents are home even."

She kept her gaze fixed on the back of the seat in front of her, wondering where he planned to go with all this useless information.

"Me and my dad are rebuilding the engine of his old truck for me to drive, now that I have my license. It's going to be so great. I hate having to depend on other people to get around, don't you?"

She nodded, but she never would have guessed Grady Steadman could be so strange. Why was he talking to her?

"You know, once it's finished, in a few more weeks or so, if you needed to go to town for something and if I'm going that way anyway, I could give you a lift— *What?*"

She wasn't sure what the expression on her face was like but at least half of it was skeptical because he responded to it.

"What?" he said again sounding annoyed. "I could. I would. You don't believe me, do you?"

"No."

"No *what?* No, you *do* believe me; or, no, I'm right, you don't believe me?"

She looked straight into his fine green-hazel eyes. "No, I don't believe you. I don't believe you'd give me lift, I don't believe you're interested in what I do for fun or how I feel about going to high school, and I don't believe you're sitting there talking to me like we're friends when I know for sure that you wouldn't be if all *your* friends were here."

He sat there and stared into her eyes with the oddest expression on his face. Staring as if hypnotized, staring like he couldn't stop. No longer upset, giving no indication he'd heard a single word she'd said, he looked sort of . . . sappy, if you asked her.

She might have tried to stare him down but this time . . . well, she looked away first.

"You're wrong," he said in a sure, low tone. "The only thing that could have kept me out of this seat today is your sister. And the rest I'll prove to you."

Then he left, went back to the back of the bus and the fresh flock of cool kids he'd be reigning over the next two years, before she could think of a snappy retort to send him off with. She didn't want him to prove anything to her . . . didn't *want to want* him to, that's for sure. The only way she'd make it safely through the next four years is if she remained invisible— invisible at school but more importantly invisible at home, and Grady was nothing if not . . . VISIBLE in a big, big way.

Her lips curl in a lopsided smile now, remembering, looking back in speculation as to how one passed through a major pivotal moment in their life with barely a blink of their eye and without noticing the sudden ninety-degree angle in the direction their life was heading. How did that happen? How could it?

"I'll ask." Anna's soft voice was a gentle reminder that the past was the past for a reason—it didn't exist anymore. "And what I eat is pretty basic, all the food groups, more protein and carbs like your friend said. Gran kept a list of stuff . . . and I can teach you."

"Good." She smiled and did a double take at her niece while she watched the road ahead. "What?"

"I do eat a lot, though. At least twenty-five hundred calories a day, at least that . . . and way more in the fall when I run longer distances. I eat a lot. I always feel hungry."

She looked so worried Hannah couldn't help herself. "Oh my, that is problematic. Do you think we'll make enough off selling the farm to cover your grocery bill?"

Not knowing how much a farm sold for or how much of that money would go to her for food—the concern in Anna's eyes escalated and Hannah felt like a heel.

"Oh, Anna. I'm sorry. Honestly." She gave a soft laugh as her expression asked forgiveness. "I'm kind of a . . . smartass sometimes. There will be plenty of money for anything you want. Food, school, travel. Oh! I have the best idea. What if I take you to Europe as a graduation gift? Would you like that?" She glanced at a confused Anna. Did that sound like a bribe to her, too? It did, didn't it?

Okay, so scrape away the fear and uncertainty, vanquish the memories, throw ice on the anger and pain, and deep down under it all somewhere, struggling to stay alive, burgeoned the tiny hope of family. She was stunned to discover it still existed. She was. At first she wanted to laugh at the absurdity of it—and it was daunting to realize that her heart hadn't turned to stone after all. But it thrived as true and real as the frightened and hopeful girl beside her . . . this girl who could well be Hannah's last chance at ever having a family.

Like she knew anything about family in the first place . . .

Plus, Hannah was lonely. There, she could admit that, too. She had Joe. She had a few other friends, good friends, caring friends that she cherished but . . . well, it wasn't the same. It wasn't what she hoped to find in this girl.

It was worth a try, wasn't it?

"Well, it's only a thought. We have time. You can think about it." She hesitated, taking the left at the church toward the farm. "You know, Anna, for the record I want you to know that I think I want this to work. I'll be honest and tell you I wasn't sure at first. In fact, I told Grady no a dozen times before I agreed to come down here but . . . I don't know. Being here, being with you . . . well, I'd like to keep what's left of our family together.

"It won't be easy. I'm old and set in my ways; I'm used to doing and having things a certain way . . . and I'm not used to having someone else around. I could very likely drive you nuts. But I think we should give it a try anyway.

"So I'm going to leave it up to you to decide. And while I think it would be less complicated for you to come live with me in Baltimore I don't want you to feel like that's your only option. It's not. I'd have to be your legal guardian, I think, to keep you out of the foster system, but there are boarding schools or we might be able to board you with someone here in Clearfield for a couple of years. You seem to have your head screwed on straight. We could go to court and have you declared an emancipated minor, if that's what you want, and you wouldn't have to send me Christmas cards if you didn't want to. But you do have choices, Anna. There's nothing worse in the world than thinking you don't have choices, so it's important to know that you do. You can even make a choice and change your mind if you want. It's up to you."

God. Was she bungling this—giving the girl too much freedom, too many options? Where was that fool Grady when you needed him for parental advice? She should have kept her mouth shut until she conferred with a responsible adult who knew something about children.

Joe. He said be yourself and go with your gut. Grady had as well. Yet she couldn't help thinking that logically one's gut, hers in particular, would be predisposed to be as dysfunctional as one's dysfunctional life experiences, hers being particularly so.

Have faith, Joe said. So perhaps a queasy gut would be her natural state from now on.

Instincts on high, she peeked at the girl as they pulled onto the gravel drive to the house. Eyes downcast as she considered the black polish that looked so unnatural on her nails, her lips curved in a light smile, the swell of her cheek drawing hope into Hannah's heart when Anna nodded the understanding of her freedom.

Chapter Nine

It was that sort of day.

It started early. Shortly after Anna left for school, the three antique dealers (one from Clearfield and the others from nearby towns) that she'd invited for the initial walk-through arrived with clipboards and colorful stickers to mark those things they found valuable and wished to bid on later . . . after Anna had a chance to see what they were taking. They would return in a week or ten days to do it all over again on whatever they uncovered under all the *stuff*.

They were surprisingly methodical. One started at the top of the house working his way down from the attic; one from the bottom up—the cellar being the truest test of a man's tenacity and gumption in her opinion. And the third dispatched himself to the wobbly barn and out-buildings saying it was quite possible that this first pass-through would take more than one day.

Truthfully, this calculation figured far more realistic than her own, so she called the two used-furniture dealers she'd scheduled for Wednesday and asked them to come Thursday instead. Neither was thrilled or very gracious about the change to *their* schedule, but what could she do?

She, on the other hand, had no idea where to start. At random, from whatever room she happened to be in, she took a box or a bag or an old cookie tin to fret over the contents. *How old are these buttons? Should I set them aside for the dealers? Toss them? Jesus, a whole box of yellowed crocheted doilies—did Mama crochet? Grandmother Benson? Dealers? Keep one for Anna? Recycle these old newspapers . . . from 1984! Good Lord. Were they on microfilm or would someone be happy to see them?* And so the day went, one ineffectual but seemingly dire decision after another with barely a dent made in the actual tonnage of stuff in the house. By lunchtime, she had a headache and felt so frustrated and discouraged, she hid herself amid the junk in her room and called Joe.

"I'm drowning in this stuff."

"And making everything harder on yourself than need be." He sounded distracted. "Let the professionals do their work. Don't worry. If the ancient newspapers have any value, they'll know and take them off your hands. That's why they're there."

Oh, yeah. "I knew calling you was the right thing to do. How's everything at the office?"

"To be honest, I'm not sure." This un-Joelike ambiguity made the muscles in her shoulders and neck bunch and twist like rope. "Nothing to be alarmed about yet, but apparently young Jim didn't understand that your clientele were to be routed to me in your absence and not simply added to his own small kettle of fish."

"You think he's trying to steal my clients from me?"

"I answered a call while Jim was at lunch, a simple claim for damages done to a neighbor's boat—a can of yellow house paint dropped on it while it was parked in the drive—and you'll never guess who it was."

"Who?"

"Clive Morrison. Remember him?"

"How could I forget? He bought that homeowner's policy from me thinking he was buttering me up for a date. He all but stalked me for months and then suddenly he fell in love with one of the girls from my exercise class . . . and just so there weren't any hard feelings, he came back and bought life insurance policies for both of them after they got married." Her soft laugh was incredulous. "A very weird guy."

"Indeed. But the reason he called back after reporting the incident to Jim, who said he'd happily handle it for him, was his curiosity as to whatever happened to you." She heard his reluctant sigh over the line. "Any one of the three incidents I've counseled him on in the last couple of days would be nothing, but taken as a whole, I admit, I'm concerned."

Selling insurance is a *business,* meaning the whole point is to accumulate as many customers as possible to make more and more money; concurrently it is equally as important to keep those customers satisfied to prevent them from wandering off and taking their business to another broker who might offer them a better deal—or more often, since most companies were pretty competitive with their prices, to another broker who is friendlier to them, remembered their children's birthdays with bright-colored company cards or, and—this is the big one—is consistently *there* when they are needed. It's a part of the *business* to look for, bait, and reel in new customers but in the broker biz there is no greater sin than stealing clients from other brokers in your own office. Generally, if detected, it's a signal that the thief is preparing to break off on his own and had no qualms in taking your livelihood with him. But also, generally, if the company owner is wise, a noncompete clause is part of the standard employment contract—and Joe taught her to be very wise.

And so aside from their unwillingness to accuse Jim Sauffle of cheating or stealing or of being just plain too stupid to see the lawsuit they'd slap him with, they had to wonder what he was thinking and if his actions were simply ill considered or deliberate.

"And you say you spoke to him again yesterday about channeling my clients on to you?"

"I did. I made myself very clear."

"I guess he needs to hear it again from my lips."

"Perhaps that would be helpful," he said, stiff and rightly riled at having his instructions, his words, questioned. "Meanwhile, I will arrange to have Gwen and Caroline organize their schedules to be in the office whenever he is, and to answer the phones."

"Okay. Tell them I'll be home as soon as I can be."

A few hours later she sat on the front porch steps in her coat, hunched over the thin county phone book with her cell phone in hand when Sheriff Steadman's SUV rumbled up the drive, dust drifting under the wheels.

It was bright but chilly out. The breeze had a sweetness to it that she was 98-percent sure was all in her head, because it blew so clean and refreshing and so the opposite of the inside of an old farmhouse stuffed with stuff.

The truck stopped and Grady spent a few more seconds talking on his cell phone before flipping it closed and getting out. His eyes were hidden behind his menacing cop shades again, but she didn't need to see them to know they were trained on her. She could feel them.

"Hey."

"Hi." He took long lazy strides to the porch and stopped at the bottom. "What are you doing? It's cold out here."

"Promise not to laugh?"

"Sure."

She leaned forward to whisper loudly. "I'm pretending that I'm not waiting for Anna to get home." He smiled but he didn't laugh. She held up the phone book and her cell. "I brought these out with me so I'd look busy trying to track down a sanitation department or something to have one of those big Dumpster things brought out here, but mostly I'm watching the road."

He took off his glasses and made a to-do of glancing at his watch. "I'd say you've got at least another hour or more."

She nodded. "That's the laughable part. Who does this? I'm like a kid with a new toy. I'm going to end up suffocating her, aren't I? Or I'll overcompensate and she'll think I'm ignoring her like she doesn't matter." He kept his head down and took two steps up before sitting on the step below hers, his thick leather belt with all his police accessories rubbing with an indissoluble sound. He blocked most of the bite in the air with his shoulders—and didn't bother to hide his smirk. "See? I knew you'd laugh."

"I'm not. I don't think it's funny. I think this is normal and I'm glad to see it."

"Normal." She scoffed at the word. "You're not obsessive with your kids, I've seen you."

"Obsessive would be lurking in the halls at the high school or riding the bus home *with* her. This is only normal parental worry, which I do constantly, by the way. It's my job. When they're out at night I wait, awake, until I hear them come in. If they're not home after school when they're supposed to be, I wait and depend on my mother to let me know immediately. I wait and watch and pray that I'm making the right decisions for their futures, for their psyches, for . . . everything until they're old enough to make their own decisions—and even then I know it won't be over. I wait to see them all the time, to see if they're okay. It's what I signed on for."

Something he said before niggled at her. "You said you were glad to see it. What were you expecting? Did you think I wouldn't feel anything for her?"

"I didn't know what to expect," he said honestly, looking to see how she'd take it. "My hopes were high, I admit, but, well, we don't really know each other anymore, do we?"

Oh, he's good, she thought as she shook her head and silently tiptoed around her inner stronghold to make sure all the windows and doors were locked against him. That might well be the nicest, smoothest preface to an interrogation she'd ever hear.

"People can change a lot in twenty years. I'm still trying to hurdle this cop issue." She wagged her head ingeniously. "A little track allusion there in case you missed it."

He chuckled and turned to her more fully. "That's a nice change. The humor. You used to be so serious and grave about everything."

"As opposed to now, when I'm obsessed and neurotic about everything?"

He tilted his head. "Okay, so maybe that's just another form of serious and grave only now it's coated in humor and not so obvious."

"Maybe."

"That would mean that somewhere along the way you've learned the art of camouflaging your thoughts and feelings. That would be new, too."

"They taught you all this fascinating psychology at cop school, did they?"

"No. In fact, I learned more about reading people in the army, before cop school. I tried college for a couple of semesters after high school, but sitting at a desk preparing for a future that would take *place* at a desk made every bone in my body ache. So I quit school and joined the army—learned all my best lessons there. I even married an army brat. I was very gung-ho army." He gave her a lopsided, one-dimpled smile. "Unfortunately, it took my wife another seven years to figure out that she'd actually hated the army all of her life, that she hated me more than the army, and that she wasn't too keen on kids, either.

"She went off to find the life we'd robbed her of, and I brought a four- and a six-year-old back here to live with my mom, who was already worn pretty thin caring for my dad, who'd had his second stroke in four years." He gave a derisive chuckle. "It occurred to me then that someone was, maybe, trying to tell me something. So I took a hardship discharge and spent a little time over in Ashburn at the police academy. Of course, I was only a deputy at first but that worked out well, too. It gave me a little more time with the kids, helping them to settle in and get used to the new way things would be. It was tough on Cal—all of us, but especially Cal. It changed something in him."

She knew about those kinds of changes, the kind that occur when the innocent hardwiring of a child's mind, or even worse his heart, is painfully and cruelly ripped out and left to reconnect in any way it can . . . or not.

"Anyway, three or four years later when old Charlie Barton decided to retire, the good people of Turchen County elected a local boy to take his place. That was eight years ago."

"Did you resent having to redirect your life like that?"

"No. Well, maybe a little at first. I was a Ranger. I had plans. But I had bigger responsibilities here." He paused. "Much bigger. Eventually I realized I could do more direct good for more people here. I don't regret the redirection I chose."

Of course, he didn't. He was one of those people, wasn't he? The kind who assumes things will work out, and they do. The kind who is always so sure that the ice he's standing on is frozen solid and it never once, ever, cracks under his weight.

She'd seen it coming; could have put it off a little longer if she
hadn't been distracted by how easily he narrated his rendition
of the last twenty years.

No, that wasn't completely true. It came to her that she
wanted to tell him her story, at least some of it. She'd suffered
hardships, like him. She'd made something of herself, like him.
She was proud of her decisions—most of them—like him. She
was proud of herself.

Pride goeth before the fall. Loose lips sink ships. But *Keep your
friends close and your enemies closer* was the maxim she aimed for.

"Joe Levitz." Her answer to so many questions. "I owe him
everything. I was sixteen when I left here. Sixteen. Barely a
year older than Anna." He nodded but let the aperture go by.
The night she left was, apparently, another story for another
time. "I read about homeless, runaway, throwaway kids now
and wonder how I didn't end up drug addicted or dead or . . .
worse than dead that first year but . . ." She looked at him and
gave him a reticent smile. "Joe says I just ran out of the bad luck
I grew up with. It was time for my luck to change. And maybe
growing up the way I did, did give me an edge on the streets.
I knew to keep my head down, my defenses up, and to blend
in wherever I went."

She didn't think it important or necessary to describe the terror of living on the streets to him. If he didn't know or couldn't
imagine, then nothing she said would faze him anyway.

"I traveled light and washed up in restrooms; I avoided
other homeless people, thinking I could mix better without
them; and I rarely slept in the same place twice. I slept best in
churches; no guards and they were locked up tight at night.
Some of the smaller, neighborhood libraries were good, too.
Lots of good hiding places." She took a deep breath.

"I was panhandling when I met Joe, a few blocks from his office. That's Joe's word, by the way, "panhandling." A nice way of saying I was begging strangers for the change in their pockets. It was January, I'd just turned seventeen, and it was so cold I had to keep stomping my feet to keep them from freezing. His wife, Julie, had him drinking decaf coffee at home for his blood pressure, so he stopped at the coffee shop every morning to get his motor running." Her laugh was soft as she recalled that morning like it was yesterday. "That's what he told me, right there on the street, like I'd asked him. He told me how he'd met Julie on a blind date and loved her the minute he saw her, and about his two boys. It was very weird. I thought he was a sweet, lonely old guy who liked to talk . . . talked so much no one wanted to listen to him anymore. And I didn't mind. It had been a long time, months and months, since anyone spoke to me like a real human being."

You being one of only a few in my life who ever had, to begin with. She glanced at him but didn't skip a beat.

"After a while he got around to telling me that he was too tightfisted to simply give money away, but if I could show up at his office every Tuesday and Thursday afternoon he'd pay me a fair wage to file insurance policies. He didn't ask any questions. Not at first. Not about where I slept or what I did when I wasn't at the office. In time, though, he offered me a furnished room over his garage for more work. I was his Handy Hannah, he'd say. I mowed his lawn, poked around in his gardens, and shoveled the walks in the winter. I filed and filled in answering phones sometimes. Everything I did for him had value. Worth. He'd say things like that, and I was so starved for a little appreciation that I soaked it right up." She slipped Grady another fleeting look. He didn't look at her, thank God; his eyes were downcast as he listened intently. "Pretty sad, huh?"

After a moment he shook his head. "I was thinking more *amazing* or . . . *miraculous*. I was thinking he had a good eye for character."

He looked at her then but didn't hold the gaze, thinking, she supposed, that she'd loosen up and say more if he wasn't drilling her with his eyes. He was right.

"I started finding brochures lying around in odd places advertising GED-study programs for high school dropouts, and then articles about obscure government and private grants that went untapped and were easier to get because too few people knew about them. Joe's idea of subtle is dropping an anvil on your head, but he didn't have to drop that one on me more than once. I missed school; I wanted to go back. I got the results of the equivalency tests on my nineteenth birthday. Joe and Julie bought me a dress and took me to this fancy restaurant to celebrate. I thought I was so grown up and free . . . almost like—"

She caught herself, she'd said enough. Until that time, she'd been too busy surviving to give her past more than a few cursory thoughts, which she immediately tamped down, solid and sure. But the happier she became with her life—the more secure, the less afraid—it came to pass that she could no longer contain the memories.

They haunted her dreams, plagued her like so many flies on a cat carcass. They triggered panic attacks that left her weeping; every muscle and bone in her body aching from her efforts to keep her mind intact and clinging to the here and now. And again it was Joe Levitz who caught her before she went under for the third time.

These fragile moments of her life were none of Grady Steadman's business—not as a sheriff, not as a man. Not anymore. Twenty years of steadily digging herself out of the hole she'd grown up in and four years of therapy with Dr. Fry made her, at the very least, as normal as anyone else. She had a few problems and a leviathan secret no one could ever know about. But everybody has problems, everyone has secrets—hers were just darker than most and punishable under the law.

At least her mama said they were. Gradually, over the years, she'd allowed herself to speculate, to consider the circumstances and to hope, briefly. But she always came around to the same conclusion: better to be safe than sorry.

"Well, I still wanted my own apartment, of course, and a better car and all those things you want when you think you have the world by the tail, but I was still a few years off. Like I told you the other night at dinner, I started out small at the agency and took classes at the community college. Of course, nowadays we do a little bit of everything . . . sell mutual funds, annuities, and securities . . . we offer comprehensive financial planning services like retirement and estate planning. The more we offer the more the agency is worth.

"Joe didn't push, but I knew that he hoped I'd like the business enough to stay and make it mine . . . which I did actually, but I was so afraid I wouldn't pass the broker exam and he'd be disappointed—"

"Not possible," Grady said, looking up in surprise as if he hadn't meant to speak out loud. "He made you his daughter, adopted you as his own. You could never disappoint him. I hope I get to meet him someday."

"If you bring the kids up to see Anna on her birthday, you will. He's going to love having someone young around again. Her especially . . ." She was thoughtful. "There's something about her, don't you think? Something special. Or is it my limited experience with people her age showing again?"

"No. She may look and sound and act gentle, but she's the toughest kid I've ever known, aside from you." Their eyes met and if she had the tiniest hope that those years in her father's house had remained a secret, it was crushed—and wasn't it . . .

well, *something* that she still burned with the shame and humiliation of it? So many years and so many hours of therapy later? "Ruth brought her here when she was four, almost five, and was in and out of her life—mostly out—until that last year." He paused. "She came home sick. AIDS. Drugs and prostitution. Anna and your mother nursed her to the end. Anna was ten."

It wasn't solely the wind stinging her eyes and making them water. Poor Ruth. She pictured the pretty, fragile blond babydoll, and while she knew in her heart that it was she who'd given Ruth the only chance she'd ever get at anything resembling a normal life, every fiber in her being regretted not being there to protect her, as she always had.

They looked at each other and she shook her head—no, she didn't need to be reminded that there were two ways to handle what she and Ruth lived through; and, no, she didn't know why she'd chosen her path and Ruth the other. She suspected luck had a great deal to do with it.

And while it seemed absurd that Ruth's idea of taking Anna out of harm's way was to bring her back to Clearfield . . . things had changed by then, hadn't they? Anna was safe—though Ruth's life choices made it clear that she hadn't grasped the same security in her mind for herself. Had the misery of their childhood remained with Ruth until the very end or was there peace at last for her in death's embrace? A true and physical ache in Hannah's chest threatened her composure.

The familiar sound of vehicle-on-dirt-road caught their attention. The car drove by; they had a little more time. "It must have been horrible for Anna watching her mother slip away like that . . . . and then Mama getting older and older. I've wondered a couple of times, if you'd called me earlier, if I'd have come."

"And . . . ?"

She shook her head. It had been her mother's idea . . . her command in fact that she run. *Go! Take your tainted soul and run, Hannah. You are cut of the same cloth, you and him . . . They'll come for you, arrest you. Darkness possesses you both and now you've shown your hand, girl. Go! Go and beg God's forgiveness!*

"I don't know. Joe says there is a time for all things under heaven . . . things happen when they're supposed to happen, I guess, but I'd like to think I would have come. If I'd known they needed me." She laughed. "Though considering the song and dance routine you had to do to get me down here now, that doesn't seem very likely, does it?"

He smiled and stood as if to leave. "You're here, aren't you? You came when you were needed most."

"Well, you never did take no for an answer, Grady. I suppose being a pain in the ass is another attribute that made you perfect for the job?"

"Absolutely. That's the part I excel at."

Apparently they'd come to the end of Phase One of the cross-examination because he turned the conversation to the plans she'd made for the cleanup of the farm and which day would be best for him to rally the troops for Hazmat training. She laughed at his joke but she wasn't fooled. She'd gotten off easy this time, but she knew he'd be back, and his questions would get much harder . . . and closer to the night she'd run away.

She knew this by the way he made sure to mention that he was making a *simple* background check as part of the legal guardianship process. But simple wasn't a word that applied to anything Grady was or did. It hadn't as a teenager and she couldn't imagine that he'd changed that much since then.

He must have passed the kids bringing Anna home because they arrived mere minutes after he left. She got a nod and small flick-of-a-wrist wave from Cal, a cool silent stare from Lucy, and a smile as warm as the day was cold from Anna before she unbuckled her seat belt and stepped down.

"Thanks for the ride," she said into the cab, and for the first time Hannah saw Cal smile. She'd noticed before the similarity of his mouth to Grady's, but no evidence that he'd also inherited his father's preposterous dimples—noting now that compared to those in Cal's fresh young face, Grady's had aged some, matured, elongated and melted into the other lines life had etched on his face over the years.

Poor Anna. No wonder she had a thing for Cal. Who could resist that easy, generous Steadman smile . . . and those silly, sexy little hollows?

Hannah stood at the bottom of the steps waiting for her niece to join her, watching the truck back out and head down the lane.

"Where's Biscuit?"

"Home. He's got his own car. Besides, there're only three seat belts in Cal's truck, and the sheriff's really strict about them. I heard him say once that he'd rather have his kids out robbing banks than riding around without seat belts." They walked up the front steps in unison to the porch.

"He's pretty tough on them, huh?"

Anna's brow creased as she thought about it. "Not as tough as you might think for a sheriff. Look at Lucy. Gran never would have let me go to school like that. It's not my style but still . . . I always thought Gran was way harder on me most of the time." Hannah closed the front door as Anna unbuttoned her coat. "Sheriff Steadman has rules, though. Everyone at school knows them and most everyone is afraid to break them because . . . well, he tells us all the time that he *does* take prisoners. And he does. But his rules are mostly common sense, stuff that we shouldn't do anyway. He's the same with Lucy and

Cal. They have some pretty loose boundaries, but he doesn't tolerate them stepping over the lines."

"So these prisoners he takes . . . these are the kids he puts in jail, I'm assuming."

Anna chuckled on her way back to the kitchen. "Depends. Sometimes he has to put them in jail, but most of the time he just makes them *wish* he'd put them in jail. This kid in Cal's class, Ronny Templer, got caught driving drunk last year. He had to go to court and pay a fee, and the DMV suspended his license for six months; and then the judge said that for those six months plus three more after that he had to do community service for Sheriff Steadman." She bent and sent her upper torso into the fridge to retrieve the smoked salmon, broccoli, and penne pasta casserole someone left them, and set it on the counter. "He made Ronny ride with Tony Owen's Towin' every afternoon after school and weekends, too, and be on call for night runs if Tony needed him. Most of it was dumb stuff like fender benders and people backing into ditches and getting stuck in the mud." She frowned at the top of the casserole. "Does this say heat at three fifty for twenty or thirty minutes?"

"Thirty." Hannah reached out and turned the oven on to preheat.

She enjoyed Chatty Anna immeasurably; felt bonded, related, and was already wondering how to keep the flow moving. It was like a corny mother/daughter scene from an after-school special—unlike anything in her experience. She was awestruck. And loving it.

"One night there was a real bad accident out on I–81. No one died, no one was drunk or anything like that, but people were hurt. Bad. A couple of kids. A mom. This little old man who they think fell asleep at the wheel or maybe had a heart attack or something. The sheriff told Ronny that he'd kept a cool head in an emergency and that that was a real talent." She slid a plate of brownies up beside the casserole waiting for the oven. "Dessert."

"Pre-ssert." Hannah peeled back the plastic wrap. "We should both have one while we're waiting for dinner to cook. So we don't get weak."

Anna tried to look appalled. "Well, only because I'm starving."

Eyes twinkling, she nodded gravely. "Only because."

They both chuckled and snatched up a brownie.

"So Ronny got permission from his parents to take the EMS First Responder course. He's all about becoming an EMT or a paramedic now. I think he could go to medical school if he wanted, he's a pretty smart guy."

"So Sheriff Steadman cured him of his drinking problem." She didn't mean to sound so demoralized but, honestly, the whole thing sounded so . . . Mayberry that she felt a little nauseous. "And the rest of the kids at the high school are rethinking theirs? Their drinking habits, I mean."

Anna tilted her head as she chewed her brownie then gave her aunt a measured glanced and answered, "Not really. I can't imagine that things for us kids have changed much since you lived here. There's not much to do on weekends but drink and get stupid, but we have to be more careful than kids used to be because of all the new laws—and that isn't all Sheriff Steadman's doing. So we go out in groups. We have designated drivers. We spend the night at a friend's house. Ronny sleeps where he falls now. At least that's how it was with Lucy and a few of our friends last summer. I went a couple of times," she said, bravely testing the waters.

"Oh, jeeze." Hannah cringed, covered her face with one hand, and held the other one up all at once. "Wait. Wait a second. I get that you're trying to be open and honest with me, but maybe, in this case, maybe you shouldn't. I mean, in the back of my mind somewhere I understand it. I do. I know kids do it; there's peer pressure and all that. But I sell insurance, for God's sake. I know the carnage of underage drinking . . . any-age drinking, actually. And . . . and I like to think of myself as a responsible adult . . . and now I'm thinking of becoming *your* responsible adult, so I'm sure I can't approve of this kind of behavior. No matter how responsible you are, it's still illegal. "

She wanted to grab the girl and shake her. Hard. Hadn't they had enough booze in their lives? Instead she offered Anna a second brownie, and when she declined took another for herself. It was a brownie moment—she needed to be comforting, indulgent, and . . . chewy. "Do you drink a lot?"

Anna smiled before picking up the casserole dish and opening the oven door. "No. I tried a sip of Lucy's beer last summer. I didn't like the flat, icky taste of it. I could have tried hard liquor or pot, too, I guess, but aside from it throwing my hydration levels off when I'm training, I've decided not to risk having to live with that kind of insanity in my life anymore. Children who have addicted parents have a higher rate of suicide, lower self-esteem, an increased incidence of de-pression; on average total health-care costs 32-percent higher than children who don't, and they have a greater likelihood of becoming addicted themselves. I don't need that." She turned and gripped the counter behind her with both hands. "Do *you* drink a lot?"

At first Hannah thought the girl was joking. But the flame blue eyes looking back at her were not simply a reflection of her own genetically, they mirrored a steely strength and deter-mination that she knew as well . . . well, as well as she knew her own name.

"No. I don't. And I tend not to tolerate people who do drink, which is hard on my social life sometimes." Alcoholism was not a favorite subject for her—too many questions without scientific answers, outnumbered by memories that were as clear as HDTV. To keep her hands busy, she took a head of red leaf lettuce from the crisper and started washing it for salad. "It's not like it used to be, though . . . in other people's minds. Now that so many movie stars belong to AA or Al-Anon, society is more open-minded about it. They consider it a disease or an addiction and not a character flaw."

"Do you truly believe that? Or are you saying that so I won't hate my mom?"

Stopping mid-lettuce-rip, Hannah looked up. "Do you hate your mom?"

Anna shook her head, her eyes softened and her lips bowed in a tender smile. "I loved my mom but she was seriously damaged, inside, you know? She was sweet and gentle and weak. She couldn't figure out how to live in the world. The drugs and alcohol made her think she was hard. Like you. She told me I could grow up to be the perfect person because I was part her and part you—I could be gentle and tough."

"She thought I was hard and tough?" Oddly, that hurt.

"She thought . . . you were her hero. I never heard her say one bad thing about you. Ever. Not even . . ."

"What?" Anna shrugged and looked away for a moment. "Not even what, Anna?"

"Not even when you ran off and left her behind. I mean, she never put it like that. I did . . . sometimes. Because you never came back. You never wrote. You never called her. You just disappeared on her. But she explained that."

"She did?" Panic and bile rose in her throat. Anna knew? No. She knew and could still look Hannah in the eye? No, no. She knew and hadn't told anyone?

Anna gave a grave nod. "You and your father had a horrible fight over a boy. Sheriff Steadman, right?" Hannah nodded. So far, so right. "Gran was afraid he'd kill you and told you to run.

She told you to hide and to never come back. Then the next day when you didn't come home, he started in on Gran again, hitting her, saying it was her fault that you'd left, that she was a terrible mother and when my mom worked up the courage to step in like you always had, he knocked her clear across the room, she said. Knocked her out cold and when she came to, Gran stood over him with the frying pan in her hand and he was dead. Self-defense."

Well. That was a nice tidy version of what *could* have happened. Told by a third party with no experience of the fear and horror one powerfully built man could reign down on a woman and two small girls with his fists and a bottle of Ten High. It came off as rational and straightforward. An open-and-shut case. And maybe it had been for her mother. Heaven knew, she deserved it. But it wasn't so simple for Hannah.

The truth was far from out in the open, but the case would remain shut if she could avoid all the traps inherent in returning to the scene of the crime. And get her butt out of town again. Soon.

And so she picked at the smoked salmon, broccoli, and penne pasta casserole in some sort of rich creamy sauce as her niece went back for seconds and helped herself to more salad and a second dinner roll. They talked about school—Anna's favorite subject was History. They went over the packing process. Anna didn't want to take much, thank heavens—some of the stuff in her room, a small box of mementos; her clothes and the computer she'd earned half the money to buy working at the Tastee-Freez last summer. And a short while later Hannah wolfed down five brownies while Anna wrapped two in a paper towel to eat in bed while she read.

Jackie Sprat and her aunt, she thought, amending the nursery rhyme to suit. It had been that sort of day.

It appeared that Anna's thoughts and views were as lean as

her legs. Her memories were sad but nothing that couldn't be washed away with fresh, clean water. She was trim and healthy in every way possible—unlike her aunt whose solid layer of adipose tissue, no matter how hard she worked on it, wasn't just for insulation; it didn't just surround and protect her vital organs—it was heavy and greasy inside. Foul and poisonous. The monsters that lurked in the shadows of her mind were plump with secrets and fleshy with painful scars.

Anna knew what she wanted—in her life and from the house she'd grown up in. Hannah hid in an insurance office and couldn't bring herself to throw anything away from her childhood. Anna was sweetly in love with the Steadman boy, and Hannah was running from his father.

Hannah savored what she was determined would be her last brownie for the night and listened to her niece's steps as she walked down the hall toward the stairs. They were so un-alike and had so little in common and yet it was their handful of similarities and the few commonalities that were touching, opening avenues of understanding and binding them together.

And it felt good.

She grinned, sighed, and slouched back in the kitchen chair, extending her legs out in front of her, crossing them at the ankles. So *THIS* is the feeling most people know when they thought of family. Not fear, not resentment, not the burden of responsibility beyond their years. This is what it was like to have your heart bloom with gladness and pride for some-one . . . not you, but close—if that made any sense at all. And maybe real families didn't . . . make any sense, that is.

God knew, and she knew, that living in a house with people related to you by blood didn't make you a real family. Not really. But individual, unique people trussed together on a visceral level, who were kind to and considerate of one another, who taught and learned from each other, who cared and looked after one another . . .

Hannah jerked straight up in her chair hearing . . . first a soft muffled cry and then a clattering thud coming from the bathroom down the hall from the kitchen. After that silence, and then a gut-wrenching sensation that something was terribly wrong as she dashed from the room.

"Anna?" She couldn't recall the last time she'd used her voice to shout out loud. It made a queer noise. *"Anna?"*

A peculiar/familiar odor in the air filled her with dread as she reached the door below the stairs. The bathroom door was closed and the instincts she'd honed in that very house so many years ago came tearing back. *Run. Hide.* Curling her fingers into fists as she always had, she whispered, "Anna?"

She picked up a sad little moaning noise on the other side of the door.

"Anna? Are you all right?" She waited a breath. "May I come in?"

Hannah wasn't sure why she knocked on the door—to preserve the girl's privacy or to prolong her entrance, but then she didn't hesitate any longer to grip the doorknob firmly and twist.

Anna groaned again and Hannah pushed the door open wide. It wasn't the stench of the vomit on the floor and in the toilet that had her stomach roiling; it wasn't the confusion and misery on the girl's face that pulled at her heart. It was the sight of the blood in the sink and dripping from Anna's mouth and nose that had her tamping down the shriek in her throat and reaching for her phone.

Chapter Ten

Her complexion was as white as the petals on a daisy when he entered the emergency room through the sliding glass doors. She paced in front of a treatment room—her hair disheveled; the look in her eyes a little wild. Hugging her coat in her arms, she looked like a baby with a security blanket, but the relief in her expression when she looked up and saw him was anything but infantile.

At first, anyway. At first she looked like any other powerless parent of a vulnerable child—terrified, dazed, a little crazy. At first, but then . . .

"Where the hell have you been? Is this what you call an emergency response time? What if she'd set herself on fire?"

"I came as soon as I could. I called ahead; they said she was stable. I'm here now." He reached out to support her but she wasn't in the mood yet. She swung out and whacked him on the arm, *then* took a step toward him to rest her forehead on his chest. Both responses were so normal, so natural, he smiled. "She's going to be fine."

"You said permissions slips and food and sell the farm. You didn't say anything about vomiting blood and ulcers. She was so pale and she looked so frightened." He began to see the problem with her hair when she sent her fingers straight into the crown, then straight up from the top saying, "Then when I looked back from calling 911 for the ambulance, she was on her hands and knees, crying, trying to clean up the bathroom, saying she felt much better, that it was probably just food poisoning."

"Was it?"

"Not unless the casserole had razor blades in it. You should have seen all the blood." She held out her hands and used her own health as proof. "And I'm fine. She has an ulcer and she was afraid, very afraid, I wouldn't want her if she was sick."

"They're pretty sure it's an ulcer, then?" She nodded. "Poor kid. The stress got to her. Is she inside here?"

He moved to enter the treatment room, tucking away for later a decided disappointment, and no little annoyance, that Hannah wasn't at the girl's bedside. He couldn't think about that now. It wasn't as if she'd kept her lack of child care experience a secret—though common compassion and sympathy were paramount if she planned to be the girl's guardian.

"No. They took her to surgery."

"What?" It was more an exclamation than a question, but he wanted answers, too.

"Not, not for surgery, precisely." Perhaps she wasn't as insensitive as he thought—she'd picked up on his anger. "Just to look. Into her stomach with a tube. An endoscope, they said. And it's not necessarily stress, either. I mean, I thought that, too, that it was my fault, the stress and all, but the doctor said no, they don't think that way anymore. There's a bacteria. Here, I wrote it down so I could look it up."

She handed him a slip of paper with *Helicobacter pylori* (or *H. pylori,* for short) written on it.

"Apparently it's a bacteria that can simply be there, in the stomach, without making trouble most of the time, but it thrives when there's extra gastric acid produced like when you're constantly hungry, like she is . . . and stressed, of course, but he thinks the bacteria had already weakened the stomach lining long before Mama died and I entered the picture. He said it's very common and relatively easy to fix, and that it might have been caught earlier if she hadn't been feeding the pain in her stomach, thinking it was simply hunger."

He kept staring at the notepaper, feeling foolish and not wanting her to see it until Tom Kelsey, the ER doctor, called out to him and reiterated most everything Hannah had just told him. He'd been very quick to condemn her for being thoughtless and unfeeling toward Anna when, in fact, it was clear she'd taken full responsibility and that the whole ordeal had been harrowing for her.

A nurse emerged from the treatment room with Anna's purse; her clothes and shoes were stuffed in a plastic bag, all for Hannah to transport to a room on the second floor, where Anna would sleep overnight for observation before going home in the morning.

"I'll go up with you," he said, following when she turned in a circle to look for the elevators.

"That's not necessary, but thanks. I was—" She broke off, embarrassed. "I was a wreck before, and I appreciate you dropping everything to come to my aid but . . ." She looked back down the hall. "But I feel so much better after listening to the doctor say the same thing to you that he said to me. It's ludicrous, I know, but—"

"But what?"

She shook her head, planning not to answer before she suddenly did. "I don't trust doctors. I was ready to hijack the ambulance and head for Charlottesville if the ER doctor who used to treat me was still here."

"Dr. Pageant? He'd be, what, a hundred and forty years old by now?"

She looked up at him and saw what he wanted her to see—that he wasn't making light of her feelings, merely putting them in perspective. Also, that he knew what she was talking about. That the fine physician had tended her injuries—her mother's and her sister's wounds—over and over again without ever actually helping them. If she was bitter, she had the right to be; and if she wanted to talk about it, he wanted her to know he'd listen.

"Really, I'm fine." She pushed the up button to call the elevator—she was blowing him off. "The nurse said Anna would be sleepy. They'll start her on an antibiotic and two different acid blockers tonight and send her home in the morning. But, do you think your mother might be willing to pick us up and take us home? I came in the ambulance—"

"I'll come."

"No. I don't want to take you away from your work any more than I already have. Please, ask your mother for me." He sighed and agreed as the elevator doors opened. She stepped in and turned back to him smiling—still blowing. "Besides, I need you to make sure that Lucy understands that none of this is my fault. I don't want her gunning for me." She gave a soft laugh. "Maybe she could visit Anna after school tomorrow."

The doors had begun to close when he saw it in her eyes, the relief, the satisfaction that she had once again made a clean getaway from him—leaving no trace of her true self behind. He'd seen it at the cemetery and earlier in the day when they spoke while they waited for Anna to return from school. Hannah was hiding something from him—and it was starting to annoy the hell out of him.

Plus, it was probably why he'd been so ready to believe she'd been derelict with Anna. Maybe. Maybe believing the worst of her was better than not knowing what to believe . . .

He shoved his hands deep into his jacket pockets once she was out of sight and the elevator was lifting her up and away from him. He wasn't surprised by how tempted he was to take the stairs two at a time and meet her when she got off; wrap his fingers around her throat and choke her secret out of her, but, as he recalled, fighting Hannah was never as effective or as expedient as . . . finessing her.

He turned on the heel of his boot, and headed for the door, deep in thought.

He'd tried overhauling an old pickup truck with Cal a couple summers ago, but kids were different today. When Cal turned sixteen, he wasn't interested in waiting while the two of them gave an old Ford a face-lift, he just wanted to go.

He laughed at himself as he pushed through to the parking lot, the midnight chill refreshing on his face. Come to think of it, that's all *he'd* wanted at sixteen—a set of wheels, freedom. His parents each had a car for work and it was—help his Dad with the abandoned '62 Ford truck from the farm, or borrow theirs every time he wanted to go somewhere.

The remains of the teenage Grady shuddered inside at the thought of dating girls in his mother's car. But in a fully restored tomato red pickup-*mobile,* he'd perfected the art of finessing girls. Well, the one girl he'd ever needed to finesse, anyway . . . the one he'd wanted enough to bother with finessing.

He hadn't been driving it long—a week, maybe two—still grimacing every time he turned onto the dirt road that led him home because the dust was so hard on his new paint job. Even driving less than the speed limit kicked up a fine film he'd feel compelled to sham off before going into the house.

However, that morning, that first morning of his Finesse 101 class, he was hungover from having passed out beside the campfire he and a bunch of kids from school had been partying around the night before. His mission: to get home and into bed before the sun was fully up in the sky to avoid detection by his parents . . . and the extra chores they'd pass on to him when they discovered he'd been out all night again.

So he was speeding a little, furious about all the damn dust and bracing himself for the extra pain in his head on the down side of the short rise in the road he was taking when he saw her—halfway down the next rise, on foot, coming toward him.

Hannah Benson.

"Fuck!" He lost his concentration and the jolt to his head from the gravel road made it feel like a bell clapper on Sunday morning. His eyes blurred a little, but he didn't lose sight of her and his mind, despite the ringing in his head—or perhaps because of it—was at a total loss to imagine why she was out walking the road barely after dawn.

Always modestly dressed, it was summer and she had succumbed to black shorts that hit her just above the knee and a pressed white cotton shirt that might have been one of his—the tail out, sleeves rolled up above her elbows. While there had always been catty rumors of the Bensons' getting last pick from the charitable donations at their church, he'd always thought Hannah's choices were classic and tasteful if not particularly hip. That day she looked as tidy and fresh as he felt hung over and stale.

He slowed the truck down, leaning his aching body over the seat to roll the rider's side window down, then came to a complete stop when he rolled up beside her.

"Hey. Good morning, Hannah. What are you doing out here?"

She'd stopped and turned toward him, but stayed near the side of the road instead of approaching his truck—unlike any other girl in town would have, considering who sat inside. And if the other girls didn't want to flirt with him, they'd at least have expected him to take them up and deliver them to wherever they were going. But not her. She didn't approach, she didn't care, she didn't want or expect anything of him. And, God, it was maddening.

"I'm going to work."

"Now?"

She nodded. "Mrs. Phillips hired me to help out Old Mrs. Phillips for a while this summer. She needs help bathing and cleaning and cooking, things like that."

"Old Mrs. Phillips? Who lives on this end of Dempsey?" She nodded again. "Every day?" Another nod. "And you walk every morning." No nod necessary. "How long does it take you?"

She shrugged. "Hour and a half or so."

"So you get there by what, seven?"

"Yeah, about." That reminded her not to dawdle and she turned to walk away.

"Wait a second." Patiently, she stopped and turned again. He kept his foot on the clutch and let up on the brake so the truck rolled backward to frame her face in the window again. "Do you want a ride?"

He regretted the offer instantly. Every second he wasted here with her was a second closer to his father's alarm clock ringing at six thirty; to his mother rolling out of bed; to her pulling on her robe and scuffing out of the bathroom and down the back stairs to start breakfast. Being summer they let him sleep until eight, sometimes nine, but his mother was unpredictable. Sometimes the sound of her slippers would simply pass by his door. More often they would slow down. The handle on his door would rattle when she carefully opened it; she'd stand for several loving seconds watching him sleep and then close it again. If she stopped there today, there'd be hell to pay.

What was he doing?

He asked himself the question, then watched as Hannah's telling eyes asked it as well. Her gaze roamed over his beloved tomato red Ford but gave nothing of what she was feeling away—no envy or scorn or admiration. Just confusion and distrust . . . of him.

"No, thank you."

"Why not? Are you afraid?"

"No." She began walking and he started rolling backward again.

"Wait a second, will ya? Why don't you want a ride? I can get you there in fifteen minutes."

"Then what would I do until seven?"

He stopped the truck to consider her point, then let it start rolling again. "We could talk for a few minutes."

There. He'd finally lost his mind. And it was all her fault.

"Talk about what?"

Normally that question would have made his head explode because she'd used it on him before, a couple of times, and the tone of it always made it seem like they had nothing to talk about. Which they didn't. But he was ready for it this time.

"Well, I saw a bird in our barn last week and I wondered what kind it was. You said you knew about birds."

Whatever punishment his parents doled out wasn't worth mentioning in light of the look of surprise on her face. Suddenly, he knew that every tiny little crack he made in Hannah's shell would make him feel extraordinary things inside his chest. Suddenly, Hannah Benson made some sense to him.

Push and she'd push back. Pry and she'd close up tighter. Attention confused and flustered her. Interest surprised her. Kindness was never expected.

"It's all blue," he went on, dreaming up the bird as he went. "Top and bottom but not like a blue jay or a bluebird, with a little black on its wings, I think. It flew by pretty fast but I don't remember ever seeing—"

"I . . . I said I had a book of birds. I didn't say I knew anything about them . . . only if I happen to see one that's not familiar . . . I . . . I look it up and mark it in the book."

"Oh." It was imperative that he not sound disappointed, he had a feeling disappointment was an everyday thing in her life. "Good. So you're not one of those people who sit in the weeds all day or hang out of trees in safari suits with a camera and binoculars around their necks waiting to see double-billed, tri-eyed, single-winged, chartreuse doodas?"

The twitch of her lips in each corner of her mouth shot hope through his veins like adrenaline—but even better was the tiny light of amusement far and deep within her eyes.

She's alive! Alive! He heard Colin Clive's voice from Frankenstein's laboratory in his head.

"No. Just if I happen to see one I don't recognize."

He heard a period on the end of her sentence so he had to think quick.

"I'm guessing that having you over to check out the birds in our barn is out of the question, but maybe you'd loan me your book sometime?" Her expression was quizzical. "Well, I like knowing what's flying around my farm, too. And you know how it is when you don't know something, it starts to bug you a little and then after a while it makes you crazy, right?" She looked at him a full ten seconds and was completely unreadable. "Really."

She wore her backpack loose and near empty but slipped it around to her chest, unzipped it, and reached inside. She withdrew a small 4x8-inch hardbound book and held it out to him through the open window.

"If it's not one I've seen already, will you mark it?"

"Sure." He took the shiny bird-covered book in his hand

and almost flinched with feelings he wasn't sure he could identify. Feelings he'd heard about in church like *humility* and *honored* and *blessed*; *compassion* and *gratitude*. Sharing a book was not a big deal, he knew that, but sharing anything with Hannah Benson was a rare thing for anyone.

She gave him a satisfied nod and started slipping the straps of her pack back in place.

"Bye."

"Wait. Damn." He took his foot off the brake again. "Wait a second. You loan me your book, but you won't let me give you a lift into town?"

"No."

"Why not?"

Without stopping she looked at him, then at his truck and back again. "Well, for one thing you're driving backward."

There it was again, that infinitesimal spark of humor that came and went so fast it might have just as easily been a play of the early morning light. Still, he was so dumbfounded by it, he could think of nothing to say so he pulled away from her slow and easy not wanting to cover her in road dust, drove to the top of the hill, and made a tight U-turn.

This time he pulled up beside her with only the driver's side door and a foot of air between them.

"Is this better?"

"I'm sorry, I shouldn't have said that. I didn't think you'd turn it around. And I still can't ride with you. My parents wouldn't like it."

"Oh," he said, and yet in spite of all the brain cells he'd destroyed drinking the night before, he came up with, "You mean riding with me or getting a ride, period. That's two different things there."

Again she stopped to look at him and again he'd have given anything to know what she was thinking.

"With you, yes. Riding with anyone, I guess."

"But there's riding up here *with* me and *just* riding, say, on the tailgate, which is as far from actually riding with me as you can get and still be riding. See the difference?"

She searched his face for deception, for the slightest trace of trickery, then looked over her left shoulder for the first time since he'd come upon her. He hadn't thought about her still being visible from her house and whether or not her parents might be watching her—so he followed the direction of her gaze and nearly went limp with relief to see that none of the house was visible from this point on the road.

With one last considering look, she turned and walked to the back of his truck. He put it in neutral, set the brake, and jumped out.

"Wait a second. I'll put the tailgate down for you. Unless you want to ride in the bed."

She put up a hand to stop him. "The bed's fine. Thanks."

And she was up over the end before he could lend her a hand. Of course.

"Okay then. Hold on to your hat." Her eyes widened with fear and immediately she started to struggle to get up. "I'm kidding. I promise." He waited for her to settle down again. "And don't try to talk to me a lot because you'll get bugs in your teeth."

Caught off guard, she laughed out loud, a quick, sharp hoot of pure merriment that she tried to cover, too late, with one hand over her mouth.

He wanted to call her on it, tell her that her laugh was the nicest sound he'd ever heard, but he knew instinctively she'd hate it and never laugh for him again.

He cursed the dust again as he maneuvered around potholes and drove barely fast enough to hide the fact that he was stalling for more time.

Glancing back in the rearview mirror it was like watching something private and forbidden when she closed her eyes, tipped her head back, breathed in deep, and sighed. In that moment of peace with tiny wisps of black hair dancing around her face, the healthy hue of her skin looking warm and soft, she was about the prettiest thing he'd seen in all his life.

It was . . . magic, maybe, the way her features changed when she let her guard down; when the sharp edges of caution and distrust drained away, smoothing out and softening her fine features.

A careful glimpse at the road, and when he looked back—their eyes met and held for a long second.

"You okay back there?" he hollered out the window, wanting to seem casual and relaxed. She nodded and he kept his rearview mirror watching a little more furtive after that.

It took eleven minutes to drive to the old Phillips house on Dempsey Street. Pulling up at the curb in front of the sidewalk, he knew better than to make an effort to help her out. Instead he waited, watching in his side mirror to see what she'd do next—smiled to himself when he saw her approaching his window.

"Thank you for the ride."

"You're welcome." He was desperate for something else to say. "Doesn't look like it turned your hair gray or anything."

"No." In a very self-conscious, un-Hannah Benson moment, she looked down at her shoes and the grass she stood on. "No, it didn't. It was a fine ride. Thank you."

"You're welcome," he said—*once more!*—back at square one. The sun was getting higher and higher in the morning sky and his head was starting to feel thick again. "I have to go. I'll return your book."

She nodded.

"I'll see ya."

"Bye."

Needless to say he watched her as he drove away, so quiet and self-contained with no idea of the influences she'd had on his life over the years. What a puzzle she was to him. She stepped into the street and sat down on the curb as he turned the corner at the end of the block. And she'd sit there until seven thinking God knew what in that head of hers . . .

The temptation to circle the block and sit with her nearly overwhelmed him—and if he could have thought of ten different things to say to her that he thought she might respond to with more than a nod or a shake of her head, he would have—his parents and his chores notwithstanding . . .

Letting the memory go as he released the auto-lock on his cruiser and opened the door, he had to remind himself that things for Cal were different. His grandmother didn't sleep as sound as she once did, for one thing; and he was the son of a cop, for another. Cal was well aware that there was no slack in his rope, that if anything it was shorter than everyone else's because of who he was.

Their father-son-clunker revival was a bust because there hadn't been a lot of free father-son time to work on it; Cal hadn't been interested in it, *and* the whole family depended on him to run errands, taxi Lucy, and to generally fill in for a dad who was, it must have seemed like sometimes, everyone's dad.

The car hadn't had time to cool off since he'd gone inside. He sat for a moment with the keys in his lap thinking two things: One, he needed to give Cal some recognition this week for being the kid he was—he knew for a fact that there weren't many parents who had fewer complaints about their kids than he did. And two, were the secrets to finessing Hannah different than they used to be?

* * *

Hannah stood in a corner of the room until they got Anna off the stretcher and into bed, took her vital signs, adjusted her IV monitor, and started her antibiotics. By then, she'd fallen asleep again and looked so young and pale and . . . so defenseless, it brought tears to her aunt's eyes.

She approached the bed in silence and sat in the chair provided. She was nervous. Frightened, if truth be told. The last time she'd gone beyond the emergency room of a hospital was the night after she'd retrieved Ruth's hair ribbon from Josh Greenborn; after the police and Principal Samms from Turchen County Elementary School had come to talk with her parents and after her daddy had blackened her eye, cracked three ribs, broke her arm and her wrist, and then told the doctor she'd fallen down the cellar steps. She'd been admitted for observation of a possible concussion and released the next day—though recalling it now, that one night of feeling safe while she slept was hardly worth the verbal beating she got when the hospital bill came in the mail a month later.

She sighed, blowing air out like it was smoke from old memories best left burning to ash and then into oblivion.

"I'm so sorry, Aunt Hannah."

The sigh had aroused her. The girl looked exhausted. And worried. More worried than any child ever should look.

"Don't be silly, Anna. This isn't your fault. And, I must tell you that much to my relief, it isn't mine, either. I was seriously worried that I might have to go out and buy some sort of protection for myself against Lucy when she found out it was an ulcer and that my coming here might have caused it." This didn't produce the levity she'd hoped for. "Did the doctor tell you about the bacteria and that you'll only need to be out of school a couple of days. And maybe start running again in a week or so, if all goes well?"

She nodded. "I saw your face."

"*My* face? What. When I walked into the bathroom?" She tried to think back. "Did I look horrified?"

"Pretty much."

"You would, too. I mean, you don't get to see people vomit blood very often."

"And you haven't known me four whole days yet."

"Oh. I see." She was still apologizing. "That's true but you and I . . ." She reached through the bed rails to take the girl's hand. "We don't have the luxury of taking our time to get to know each other. We have to get acquainted on the run, as we go along. This was terrible for both of us at first, but not as bad as it could have been. And I learned a lot about you in the process. Like . . . you're allergic to bee stings and you've had your tonsils out; you have a fairly high tolerance for pain if you've been running around with that burning in your belly for a while like the doctor said; and, best of all, you're not a whiner." Anna smiled at that. "Now, I am a bit of a whiner myself, I have to warn you, but *other* people who whine make me crazy." She paused a moment because the next part was gravely serious. "I hope that if nothing else you've learned that I can dial 911 faster than anyone else you know."

"And you're a good hand holder." Anna held up the evidence between them. "You can hold tears in your eyes without crying, and I especially liked it when you told the ambulance driver to shut up and drive or you would, when he told you to follow us in your car. I didn't want to be alone."

Hannah nodded. "Me neither. And I talked to the sheriff downstairs. Either he or Mrs. Steadman will come for us in the morning after you've been released."

"You're going to stay here all night?"

"Of course. There's nothing like a night in a straight-backed chair to help you appreciate sleeping in a very narrow twin bed."

"I think it reclines a little."

"Even better. I'll get a pillow and blanket from one of the nurses and we'll sleep like a couple of lumberjacks in here. I'm pooped, aren't you?"

Anna nodded and grinned and wiggled into the pillows until she was comfortable. She was sound asleep when Hannah returned; and as she stood there looking down at her, one thing as simple and real as anything she'd ever known became clear to her. It may have been a sense of obligation or responsibility . . . or even a guilty conscience that had gotten her there, but it was Anna, the girl, who was keeping her here. It was Anna who was subtly moving into her dreams of the future and making it look . . . not so isolated, not so lonely.

Maybe, if everything worked out, next winter on Christmas Eve they could dress up in pretty dresses and go somewhere amazing—a play maybe or a Nutcracker ballet—come home and open one special gift in front of a fire in their pajamas; wake up the next morning and open some more; invite Joe and a few others to Christmas dinner . . .

Slipping off to sleep she started a list. She was going to need to buy a new, larger set of dishes . . . and get a new apartment or a house with a fireplace . . .

Chapter Eleven

As March sprouted into April, watching the pallor in Anna's cheeks dissipate was as gradual and lovely as watching spring arrive.

The day after Hannah brought Anna home from the hospital, Thursday, Grady showed up in the afternoon, backing a small U-Haul up into the front yard, opening the back and lowering a ramp to the ground.

"Relax. You don't have to fill it. I just want to make sure you have plenty of room for the things the two of you want to take with you." His eyes twinkled at the horror on her face.

"I was thinking the trunk and backseat of my car." She put her hands on her hips. "Who's going to drive that thing back to Baltimore?"

"Cal offered, but I think it might be wise if we both went. I feel obligated to make sure I'm delivering Anna into a good home environment—as a family friend and as sheriff." She turned to him with a look of outrage on her face, but he didn't give her a chance to speak. "And if Cal and I both go, Lucy will claim a greater right to the trip than either of us so I suspect she'll come; and if all three of us go I'm sure my mom won't want to feel left out—"

"Good home environment?" she sputtered.

"Well, yeah. You didn't expect me to dump your niece on just anybody, did you?"

"Dump her?" His stupid dimples dipped briefly as he enjoyed her loss of composure. He was teasing her about a very serious subject. "You ass."

"You said yourself you didn't have any experience with children."

"You said I didn't need any. *You* said she wasn't a child."

Backed into a corner he grinned. "So I did. But I also promised my kids we could drive up and see your place. Lucy says she needs a place smaller than all of Baltimore to picture Anna in when they e-mail each other."

"IM," she said, turning to go inside, then coming about when she heard a car on the gravel road. "They'll probably instant message each other. And text. It's faster. Who's that driving your patrol car? Cal? Is that legal?"

"It is today." He shrugged. "He and Lucy stopped to get boxes at the Food Lion. I'll come back for them—the kids, that is—before supper. I wasn't sure how much arm wrestling I'd have to do to get you to accept the truck. It's on the county, by the way."

"That's not necessary."

"Part of the adoption package."

"The one that hasn't been decided on yet?"

"Of course."

"Hm." Now what was he up to, she wondered, watching the kids park and get out.

"Anyway, I thought Lucy could help Anna pack while she's got these few days off from school, but as I understand it she isn't supposed to lift anything heavy for a while yet."

"We go back for a checkup in a week. Everything is on hold until then." She reconsidered the *everything*. "For her anyway. I feel so bad for her. She misses her running and she's afraid she'll lose her edge. Can that happen in a week?"

"Maybe. A little. But she's a strong, usually healthy girl, she'll get it back."

She nodded and smiled at Cal and Lucy as they came across the still brown grass with awkward stacks of boxes in their arms.

"Anna's going to be so happy to see the two of you. She's been bored silly all day."

"Daddy, I left Anna's homework in Cal's truck. Could you swing home and bring it with you when you come back for us?"

"Sure."

"Also we brought milk shakes." Her glance at Hannah only slightly defiant. "That's okay, right? She likes strawberry, but we brought her vanilla just in case."

"She's avoiding acidic and spicy foods for a while. Milk shakes are perfect."

"Did you happen to think Hannah might like one, too?" Grady asked his kids, as a reminder to be respectful, she suspected. They looked hesitant.

"Oh, God. I hope not." She stepped in to put them at ease, still hoping to win their favor her way. "Stuff like that goes straight to my hips, so don't you worry about me. Go on up to Anna now. I'm sure she heard you drive up."

She watched them push and jostle through the door with their boxes and was already frowning when she turned back to Grady only to catch him lifting his gaze upward from her hips. He smirked his appreciation of the confectionary sacrifices she'd made over the years.

"Oh, please," she said, her voice full of exasperation, her face filling with heat. "Go arrest someone."

He laughed out loud and it was just as infectious as she remembered. She lost control of her scowl but biting down on her lower lip kept her smile at bay as she turned to go inside.

"Use Cal to help you move things; it's his excuse for hanging out with the girls."

She hesitated with the screen door in hand, glanced over her shoulder to see him bound off the front porch and stride with purpose toward his cruiser. He needed to get back to work, clearly. But stepping into the house she wondered if reminding him that telling Cal to steer clear of Anna was, at this age, essentially the same as telling him to *try harder* to be with her for whatever time they had left.

Even she knew that.

Would it ring a bell to tell him that any adversity, be it her move to Baltimore or his disapproval of the relationship, would only increase the romantic notions between the two young sweethearts? Couldn't he recall that it was the danger, the physical and emotional danger that had made their own love so much an adventure—that it heightened the excitement . . . and that it was fundamental to the trust and confidence that slowly formed between them?

She watched through the screen as he drove away. Wiser to stay out of it, she decided. The fewer references she made to the past the better the chances the past stayed buried. And Anna and Cal? She closed the door and glanced up the stairwell to the second floor. Wiser to stay out of that, as well, perhaps.

She started up the steps to make sure the young people had everything they needed—to check on Anna again, if truth be told. She'd slept away most of the day and hadn't complained of any pain when she woke during one of Hannah's frequent visits—too frequent probably, unnecessarily frequent perhaps, but she couldn't seem to help herself. Something inside her required constant reassurance of the girl's well-being.

"Have you told her yet?" she heard Lucy asking. She stopped four steps from the top not meaning to eavesdrop exactly—but only to discover what she may or may not have been told yet and if not, why not.

And okay, she had a feeling it was the same thing as eavesdropping but, still, she listened.

"No," came Anna's soft, disheartened voice. "And I'm not going to."

"Why not? It's *your* life."

"I told you, it doesn't matter."

"Your dreams, your future, everything you want, everything you've worked for doesn't matter because what she wants matters more?"

"No. But I'm the one messing up her life. She didn't ask for me, you know. I'm not sure she wants to take me yet, and I have nowhere else—"

"So what if she doesn't. You don't need her, you have us."

"I know but . . . Lucy, she's the last real family I have. Your Dad and Gramma and you and . . . and Cal are great but . . . that's your family. She's mine . . . whether she takes me or not, she's all I've got. And I'm . . . I'm scared. She doesn't seem to mind that I got sick, but I'm not taking any more chances. If she wants to leave here a week from Saturday and if she wants to take me with her, then I'm going."

"And you're willing to give up everything for her?"

After a long silence, Anna's voice came again. "Everything but you."

"I can't believe you. At least tell her you want to stay till the end of the year. What's the worst she—"

"Shut it, Lucy," Cal snapped. "You're making her feel worse."

And, once again, she'd proven that listening in on other people's conversations led to no good.

Not that any of it was news to her.

Slinking one step at a time back down the stairs to avoid any creaking, she knew the fear and desperation in Anna's voice would linger in her mind. Part of her was thrilled that she thought of her as family, and she wanted to be *that person* for her, but another part was terrified.

She sighed when she reached the bottom—in both relief and resignation. There came a time in all things new and different and frightening when one simply had to bully through to the other side or turn and run in defeat. In the past she'd done both: She'd run from her home and from love, and she'd bullied her way through to a new life. She knew the heartache and rewards of both; knew both were monumentally difficult. But not so monumental as her motivations—fear, anger, survival.

And now? Well, the situation was similar, wasn't it? Run in fear for her own comfort and survival or face and defeat her doubts about the future with the love and compassion she had for Anna.

She sat on the bottom step and let her body slump against the wall. The friends laughed about something above and she smiled at the happy noise. If she were a praying person this would be the moment when she asked for enlightenment or at the very least a good clue as to what to do. As it was, she was tired of thinking about it. It gave her a headache. And she had enough on her plate for the moment.

In fact, her plate was beginning to tip and things were falling off . . .

"I wasn't aware we could load things up today. Or have you settled with someone for the entire lot?" Jacob Grover from Yesteryears Antique Emporium asked in a testy tone when he spotted the U-Haul on the front lawn. She sipped on a much-needed late-afternoon cup of coffee. "I hate to think I've been wasting my time here the last couple of days."

"Well, to tell you the truth, Mr. Grover, I feel like you and your colleagues have been wasting *my* time the past couple of days, and my time is limited. I mean, I know there's a lot of junk here, but there has to be a better way of assessing the value of it other than by wandering around looking at it for days on end.

"So to answer your questions, the truck on the lawn is mine for the things my niece and I will be taking to Baltimore with us. I have not settled with anyone for the entire lot and you may begin loading up the things you want tomorrow. There will be a procedure to follow, which I will explain to all three of you in the morning, that I think will make the entire process as fair as possible."

He took a curt leave of her, making it clear that people with no knowledge and no real interest in the value of antiques were the bane of his existence.

Like she cared.

"It's simple," she told Joe over the phone the next morning. "Anna and I are sitting here on the couch with a bag of snicker doodles and a couple of glasses of milk. Almost everything is marked at least twice with their different-colored stickers. Their assistants bring it all by us a piece or two, or a boxful, at a time. If Anna doesn't want to keep it, they make written bids for it once and then it goes out the door and into the truck of the highest bidder. We've been sitting here since eight thirty this morning and I have to tell you, we're getting pretty sick of these snicker doodles."

She laughed when Anna looked at her and grinned. It was good to see the healthy light in her eyes again. She had acquiesced to staying home another day and returning to school on Monday with no heavy lifting or running until after her follow-up with the doctor on Wednesday. Hannah could tell she was restless and cramped up and missing her daily runs, but she never once complained about it. Instead she leaned over and whispered, "Tell him how much they're going to pay for that rusty old cast-iron kettle."

She related several items both she and Anna would have labeled as trash that got very high bids and drew some very unexpected poor sportsmanship from the dealers who lost them.

"And they've hardly made a dent in it, Joe. I swear, if it were up to me I'd take Anna by the hand, toss a lit match at it, and walk out the door."

Her peripheral vision caught the girl turning her head to look at her, so Hannah gave her a wink and smile in an attempt to assure her that she'd squeeze every cent she could out of the place for her—even if it took years. But the girl stood and hurried from the room.

"Oh, God, Joe, I think I may have said something wrong. I'll call you back later." She cut her cell phone off and jumped to her feet, only to meet Anna in the hallway returning with a metal box a little smaller than a milk crate in her arms.

"That better be full of hot air, young lady," she scolded despite the enormous relief she felt to see the girl smiling. She held out her arms to receive the box. "What's all this?"

"What you said to your friend Joe, it reminded me. Gran used to say almost the exact same thing. She'd say 'If we had anywhere else to go, I'd burn this place to the ground.' Then after she had her first heart attack she made this box. I should have given it to you right away, I guess. I forgot."

The box was cold to the touch; condensation was forming on the outside. A key attached to the handle by a long black shoelace dangled loose on one side. A lockbox stowed away in the freezer for safekeeping, not by the fearful, ineffectual mother she knew but by the grandmother Anna knew—a very different woman.

The lid popped up with a turn of the key and displayed a series of marked files and folders inside.

"Gran said if anything ever did happen, like a fire, these would be safe in the freezer. She said her and I and this box were the only important things in the house and that everything else could be replaced. I wasn't supposed to try to save anything else. She made me promise."

A very *different woman indeed,* she thought, skimming through insurance documents and birth and death records . . . and a copy of a proper, legal will that most Bensons wouldn't have thought to bother with. And because it was a very different woman, closer to her granddaughter than she'd ever been to her eldest daughter, Hannah asked, "Mind if I read this? Do you know what's in it?"

Anna shook her head, no, to both questions.

A simple, straightforward declaration that the farm and everything on it was to be divided equally between her children if any survived her and/or their descendants; that temporary custody and guardianship of the minor child Anna Ellen Benson went to Grady Steadman until such time as a suitable and caring home could be found for the girl.

Huh. Surely her mother had asked Grady to take on the responsibility of Anna should anything happen to her rather than simply assigning it to him. And Grady would have taken that commitment very seriously when he agreed to it—which meant he'd have taken Anna into his own home before he let her become a ward of the state, as he'd mentioned in his original call.

She considered being annoyed that he'd gotten her to come under some . . . minor, but still false, pretenses; but glancing over at Anna while she refolded the document to put it back in the box, she suffered no animosity toward him at all. How could she? Overnight Anna had redefined the concept of family for her.

Sliding the will into its designated folder, her fingers brushed against an envelope at the bottom of the file. Slipping from one document to the other, she lifted it out. In her mother's scrawling script the name Hannah Benson was written in the lower right-hand corner and under that the word *Private*.

She almost laughed out loud at the strange buzz that rippled across her shoulders as she realized that this woman . . . this very different woman her mother had become, was trying to speak to her from the grave. That's how it seemed anyway. Just as she'd almost reconciled herself to the fact that her mother had sent her away, that she'd become a stronger person to take care of Ruth and Anna for all those years and had completely forgotten about her first child, here was a letter from her.

"So are we going to have to do this every day," Anna asked, startling Hannah. "I mean, how are we going to do it when I go back to school Monday? Do you need me for this? I don't mind helping if you do but—"

"No." She let the letter fall back to the bottom of the file and closed the lid on the lockbox. No telling what her mother's last written words to her would be, but if they were as stunning and hurtful as her last spoken words, Anna didn't need to know about them . . . and Hannah sure didn't want to read them. "As far as I could tell there wasn't one thing they carried out of here today that either of us wanted, so I think it's time for a new plan—especially now that we have the truck the sheriff brought us." Anna raised her brows to show she was all ears. "If there's anything outside your room that you want, you tell me. We'll move it straight into the truck so it'll be safe. You pack up what you want from your room, which is still off limits to the dealers, and we'll move it box by box into the truck until it's time to leave." She decided to go first. "I think we should take the little rocker and . . . maybe Mama's sewing machine, too. Anything else?"

"I'd like . . . there's a pin she used to wear to church all the time. Would it be okay if I kept that?"

"You can keep anything you want, Anna. Even if you're not sure you'll want it forever, take it now anyway. We can always get rid of it later." She once again envisioned her three-bedroom condominium bulging with junk . . . no, Anna's life-treasures. She shrugged. "Worse comes to worst, we can buy a bigger house."

Suddenly, amazingly, it was that easy now.

Hannah woke up suffocating, crying, and gasping into her pillow until she rolled onto her back, covering her face with both hands as the screaming faded into the distance—or had it? She came more alert, straining her senses to separate nightmare from nighttime, hoping she hadn't done anything to disturb Anna.

Her BlackBerry read 2:36 A.M. and she scrunched back into her warm spot between the sheets—for soul-comfort more than the threat of frostbite now that they were leaving the furnace on at night. Still the wet spots on her pillowcase from the tears were cold against her cheek, and she couldn't find the courage to close her eyes again.

She lay awake in the dark unable to keep her thoughts from spinning around like a top. Her mind was fragile and weary but she couldn't turn it off. For days now she'd been thinking and rethinking—second-guessing her assessments; fighting off memories—hoping and fretting and so unsure she was making the right decisions for Anna, much less herself, pulled between the desire to make it work and the possibility of utter emotional disaster . . . for both of them.

Two episodes in a week. She knew what was happening.

Being here. In Clearfield. On the farm. Allowing everything from a rocking chair to the county sheriff to stir up memories she'd fought long and hard to come to grips with; to lay to rest and forget.

She couldn't let it happen again. That's all there was to it. She'd have to be more vigilant, less susceptible to the memories that were becoming as thick and plentiful as the dust motes under her mother's furniture.

In the days that followed, Hannah hosted an array of dealers and experts who combed through piles of magazines and newspapers. Antiques and thingiewajigettes left the house in tonnage proportions. The Dumpster she ordered arrived, and over the weekend and then every day after school Cal, Biscuit, Lucy, and the two 4-H boys, Sam and Jeremy Long, hauled armloads of trash out the back door and threw them in. It was decided they'd recycle as much as they could—paper, glass, aluminum, and some of the plastics. The young people's idea, not hers. To her, dropping a bomb on the house was more the way to go.

Meanwhile, the metal lockbox lay on the hall table between a picture of Ruth and Anna as a baby and the lamp Hannah still left on at night to guide her to the bathroom.

She walked by the box fifty or maybe a hundred times a day and thought about the letter inside, yet her curiosity still couldn't overcome the dread she suffered at what it might have to say—her greatest fear stemming from the fact that her mother had left Anna to the care and custody of Grady, not her. And not once had Grady mentioned that the idea of Hannah taking custody of Anna had been anyone's idea but his.

Not that Hannah cared what her mother wanted now. She planned to make a family with Anna and that's all there was to it. Still if her mother's letter was disparaging or discouraging in any way . . . well, she didn't need or want to know it.

"Man, I thought my mom had some canning jars, but compared to your mom she don't have hardly any at all," young Jeremy Long stated when he spotted Hannah standing at the top of the basement steps. And this observation came *after* the antique dealers had taken most of the blue Ball Mason jars, many in a darker green or amber as well as a few in cobalt blue, coddling them in bubble wrap and packing them light and loose in boxes.

Jeremy was maybe eleven. He had a wiry frame with thick sandy blond hair in a bowl cut that hid his eyebrows but let his mischievous mud-colored eyes shine through. He looked too scrawny for the load but Hannah was sure she was younger when she started bringing the Mason jars up from the cellar every summer to help her mama can everything from strawberry jam to apricots and zucchini.

She could almost feel the sweat break out on her forehead and neck as she remembered those long hot summer afternoons in her mama's kitchen. Kettles of water boiled from dawn until suppertime, a stationary black fan blowing air up off the floor. Scalding and cooling peaches and tomatoes to peel them; coring pears by the dozens, picking through crates of cherries and snapping millions of beans.

Ruth particularly liked the sweet watermelon-rind pickles Mama used to make, and it was Hannah's particular job to skim the crock of sauerkraut in the backyard every morning after breakfast because the smell didn't upset her stomach like it did Ruth's.

Looking back, she knew the elephant's load of the work had been her mother's, particularly when she and Ruth were young—and yet she always gave them a lion's share of what little praise came their way from their daddy.

And, of course, it became a way for her to keep all three of them safe and out of the way, hidden in the kitchen . . .

★ ★ ★

"Hi, Mama." Hannah hung her backpack on the hook just inside the back door, noting the tiny scratches on the back of her hands that she'd gotten from Old Mrs. Phillip's rose garden. When she had her own garden there would be no roses in it. The last place anyone should feel any kind of pain was in their flower garden, and she didn't care how good they smelled. "Sorry, I'm late."

"You're late?" Her mother turned a frantic eye to the clock on the wall. The air in the small kitchen was thick with the steam from canning and summer humidity. It smelled of at least one batch of burnt sugar, Mama's sweat, and the Ivory soap she used to wash the jars.

"Only a few minutes." She'd planned it that way so her parents wouldn't guess that she'd taken another ride home with Grady Steadman.

A strange boy—Grady. She wanted to like him but she knew better. She hadn't spent the last ten years growing up a weed in the lush garden of Turchen County children without having been picked at, teased, attacked, and in general made the brunt of every trick in the book—including false friendships. He didn't seem like the sort of boy who would be so unkind as to pretend to be her friend, but how could she tell? How could she test him?

And did he really think he was making her life easier by getting her home an hour and fifteen minutes before she was expected?

Still, somehow she hadn't been able to refuse him, climbing into the cab of his cherry red truck like most any girl in Clearfield might.

The bird he'd wondered about in his barn turned out to be a common indigo bunting and he'd feigned disappointment that she'd already marked the specimen in the book he returned to her. He asked if they were nesting in her barn as well;

and when she said she didn't think so, that she'd spotted her buntings in the scrub field on the other side of the cow pond, he set about making up a ridiculous—and sort of amusing—story about the probability of their sightings being of the exact same buntings—Sherry and Jerry Bunting, maybe; and that perhaps flying around in his barn made them hot so they flew the short distance across their family farms to her cow pond to cool off. He emphasized the *short distance* between their farms and planted a seed about the size of an avocado pit as to how easy it would be for *them* to meet at the pond sometimes, too. To talk. About other birds.

A bemused smile softened the line of her lips. Really. She couldn't believe he expected her to fall for that kind of nonsense. It wasn't like she was known for her quirky sense of humor. What was he up to? Why was she so eager to find out? And what if—

"I'm going to slap that stupid look straight off your face if you don't snap out of it, girl." Her mother's angry voice startled her. Anger in her house came in varying degrees and disguises and it wasn't always what it might seem to be at first. This particular irritation was fear based—she could tell, and should have noticed sooner her mother's sudden frenzied awareness of the time. "You picked a fine day to dawdle. Your Daddy's been with Buzz Weims all day. They're up in the barn and they're both spittin' mad about somethin' or other, and if you don't help me clean this mess up and get dinner on the table he's gonna take it out on me." She took the time to look pointedly at her daughter. "And it'll be your fault this time."

Hannah was always hard-pressed to see the connection between her mother's beatings and it being her fault but it didn't matter, they were a team—Mama, Ruth, and her. They shared the beatings and the pain and the fear and the fault and that was the way it was, the way it had always been. Besides, she knew from experience that blaming someone else was all you could do when there was simply no more room to blame yourself for anything else.

"I'm sorry, Mama." She went for the large kettle of boiling water first—more heat and nervous sweat was the last thing they needed in the room. "What are we having? You can start it while I clean up. Where's Ruthie?"

"Cramped up again. We'll be lucky if we can get her to the table." Hannah set a half-empty crate of peaches on top of a full crate and looked up in time to see her mother's stricken gaze and the blood draining out of her flushed face. "I don't think I got anything out for supper."

To most everyone else in America the answer to that would have been a call for pizza or Chinese takeout or at the very least frozen dinners. In the Benson house it was enough to make your mother's hands tremble before she could get a good grasp on the counter to keep herself from tumbling to the floor. It was enough to make the thoughts in your head whirl, to hurl every notion of Grady Steadman into the wind and every theory of peace, happiness, and normalcy into cosmic nothingness.

They stood staring at each other—paralyzed, petrified—her mother's eyes already welling with tears.

"What . . . what about eggs?" Mama scowled but before she could speak Hannah went on. "Not breakfast eggs, not fried. An omelet. Old Mrs. Phillips taught me how to make them for her lunch because she likes oatmeal for her breakfast and she needs the protein and . . . well, there's lots of different ways to make them, with cheese or vegetables or a little breakfast ham mixed in. I . . . I could make one for each of us with just the things we like in them. Something special for everyone. I'll make a little one for Ruth with only eggs and cheese so she can leave the table sooner. And you can make the toast—"

"How many eggs?"

"I use two for Old Mrs. Phillips, I'll use the same for Ruth. Three for us and four for Daddy to make it look more like a supper. A dozen?"

The look they exchanged was not mother to daughter or vice versa—it was prisoner to prisoner on the verge of escape, telling each other that from this point on they were each on their own.

"Do it and pray, girl. Do it and pray."

"There's like a hundred-batrillion jars left down there." Jeremy Long's young and uncommonly sarcastic voice brought her back to the here and now. "Plus those there on the shelf that she did last summer. Anna said to empty those."

"Ah, no. Let's not. I'll pack those up myself and take some of them with us." She had a sudden hankering for her mama's canned peaches . . . and watermelon-rind pickles, if she still made them. And she knew for a fact there were just two shelves of jars left. "Is your brother down there with you?"

He arrived at the top of the stairs. "No, ma'am. He's up in the barn smashin' cans which'll be *my* job tomorrow 'less he smashed 'em all today, which'd be just like him cuz he always gets all the good jobs."

"I didn't realize there were good and bad jobs in this nightmare."

"Oh, yeah," he said, leaning the box of canning jars on the counter for a moment so he could take his time talking. "If I don't get to smash cans tomorrow I wanna ride with Cal when he takes them to the recycling place so we can throw them all in this big container, and then when there's enough they smash 'em again into one big square of smashed cans. It's awesome. They collect all sorts of things there. Copper, steel, bikes. Metal ladders. They have a place that's just for batteries, some are gigantic, man . . . and wire, too. Tons of it."

Why had she never before noticed how cute eleven-year-old boys could be? His brother Sam was a year older but likewise as chatty and friendly, with lighter-colored hair and a wiser, more experienced elder-brother look in his eyes. She could have gobbled them both up with a spoon, and wondered how on earth their mother had manage to raise *two* such pleasant children.

Granted, she didn't have much experience with families, but she had the impression that in the event of there being more than one child, that one of them had to be . . . a problem, at the very least. Even in Grady's fairly normal-looking family, Cal appeared the calmer, less rash child. And God knew in her own family, Ruth had been the kind, sweet natured, tolerant Benson sister.

Nature or nurture? She'd heard people debate the question before . . . they always had good arguments for both theories— good exceptions to both, too. Her mother believed, and had taught Hannah to believe, that anger and violence were her nature, part of her DNA and inescapable, though Joe and Dr. Fry alleged that, barring any physical anomalies—namely a brain tumor or a severe chemical imbalance—it was purely nurture, a pattern passed from one generation to the next *like* a gene. But without the intrinsic character to back it up, it was unwelcome and easily broken. Who to believe?

She'd long ago decided to err on the side of caution with her genetic makeup and take it to her grave untapped. Fortunately, she'd been spared the sort of wild longings to procreate she'd heard some women get and, of course, had never started a relationship with any man with the intent of making it a permanent affiliation. Too many traps on that path—power, trust, truth. Love. The potential for life as horrific as her mother's? No, overall it was safer, less worrisome to keep her genes to herself, shun serious relationships and protect the life she'd created for herself.

But who knew kids could be so . . . fun?

She gave Jeremy a smile and nod not knowing how to respond to his obvious delight with the recycling center except to
enjoy it. "You're still stacking those on the front porch, right?"
She motioned with her head to the jars.

"Yes, ma'am."

"Good. Your mother's here to pick you up. I'll go up to the
barn. Tell her Sam's on his way, okay?"

"Okay."

"Hey, Jeremy?" She turned to him from the doorway—he
did the same from the hall. "Thanks for your help today."

His grin was big and bright and easy. "Well, don't tell my
mom but it is kinda fun. I never seen so much junk in my life."

She laughed. "Me either."

She stepped out into the early evening air thinking of what
little time she'd spent out of doors that day. She inhaled deeply,
closing her eyes, picking out the scents of new moist earth and
something sweet from the woods—bloodroot or Virginia blue-
bells maybe—and freshness.

She'd spent most of her day with a Mr. Clayson from Charlottesville, who specialized in vintage magazines, the appeal
there being not only the age but who was on the cover. His eyes
twinkled over her mother's cardboard boxes of nonsequential
copies of *TV Guide* and the occasional *McCall's, Time,* and *Life*
taken, Hannah suspected, from some waiting room. He was
less enthusiastic by the time he got to her father's ancient hunting and fishing periodicals—also pinched, no doubt—that were
not only dull and faded but falling apart, yet he took them, too,
leaving a room full of dust with much less to settle on.

The odd thing was, neither of her parents had been big on
reading. Mama didn't have the time and Daddy found it frustrating.

She followed the stepping-stone path through the backyard

that ran parallel to the rotary clothesline that still stood like the skeleton of an umbrella waiting to be draped with clothes in every season of the year, thanks to the stepping stones. Her mind flashed once more on her mama rubbing Corn Huskers Lotion into her red, cracking fingers and hands like a body balm from Saks. Hannah's lips curved in an ironic smile as she wondered how long it had taken her to buy a dryer after daddy's funeral.

The barn loomed ahead of her, its familiar lines seen in a hundred million other barns across America; the big sliding doors still closed against the winter cold. Where the old farmhouse had weathered from white to gray, the barn had bled from red to brown to the same shade of dirt surrounding it.

She approached the smaller, hinged door closer to the house, thinking of those omelets she'd made so long ago— light, fluffy, colorful with diced tomatoes, bell peppers, and cheddar cheese—sweat beading on her forehead, hands shaking, her stomach so nervous she was terrified she'd throw every tasteless mouthful right back up.

Until her daddy finished, leaned back in his chair, and nodded.

His voice always echoed in a room, filled it to the corners, but it wasn't half as unnerving as having him look straight at her . . . which he did, his pale, icy blue eyes narrowed and speculating. "She says this meal was your doing."

She glanced at her mama, who kept her eyes on her plate. "Yes, sir. Old Mrs. Phillips taught me."

His gaze slid toward his wife and back again. "I suspect someone should be teaching you something in the kitchen by now."

"Oh, but she's very helpful in the kitchen, Karl, I've taught her everything my mama—"

"Shut up, woman!" Hannah watched her mama cringe and brace herself for a slap that didn't come.

When she looked back at her father, he was staring at her again. "Didn't I say you could learn a thing or two from that old woman? She ain't as weak and feeble as she lets on, is she?"

"No, sir. Not feeble but she is—"

"She pay you for the week?"

"Yes, sir," she said, reaching into the front pocket of her shorts to retrieve the crisp bills that totaled the seventy-five dollars a week wage agreed upon by her daddy and the younger Mrs. Phillips, which didn't—according to her and her dear old mother-in-law—have anything to do with the extra twenty-five dollars in her back pocket. She slid from her chair, careful not to scrape the chair on the floor as the sound had a tendency to scrape on his nerves as well, and walked the money behind her mother's chair to hand it to him.

He took it without a word and counted it while she returned to her seat.

"Tight-fisted old bitch, but she pays on time and she beats the alternative." That being having to sign an underage work waiver for Hannah to work almost anywhere else, leaving him open, once again, to the scrutiny of Social Services—a branch of the government that he despised even more than the IRS, for which he had nothing but loathing and contempt. "Also appears she can teach a mule-headed girl like you to cook a decent meal. Not a bad bargain, I'd say. Not bad at all."

Looking back, Hannah couldn't help but wonder: Had her father known how delighted she was to get away from the farm every day; if he were aware of how kind and sweet Old Mrs. Phillips and her daughter-in-law were to her; if he knew what a thrill it was to see a cherry red truck bumping down the road toward her most every morning, and eventually every afternoon, too . . . would he still have thought he'd made such a grand bargain that summer?

Of course not, she thought, yanking the barn door open with a fury she hadn't realized she was feeling.

Sam Long startled and turned to her still bent over the small disks of compacted cans he'd been retrieving from the old plank floor and stuffing into plastic bags. The weak light from a single bald lightbulb affixed to the wall behind him was enough to show his relief that the place wasn't falling down around his ears after all.

"Sorry about that." She smiled at him then started looking around. "Your mom's here to pick you up. I'll finish this. We don't want to keep her waiting." She glanced into the large cardboard box that had been brimming with aluminum cans two days earlier to see it was all but empty. "Ten more minutes and you would have had this job all wrapped up."

Sam handed her the plastic bag. "Nah. I'm leavin' those for Jeremy. He likes smashin' cans." Despite the sudden dull ache in her abdomen, she marveled again at Mrs. Long's amazing child-rearing skills. Not perfect Stepford sort of boys, surely, but remarkably caring and giving. "Tomorrow while he's smashin' what's left of 'em, I'll go with Cal to the Recycling Center in Charlottesville. They have these big, awesome crushin' machines there. They're the best but they have cranes and backhoes and everythin'. It's a really cool place." He stood at the door nodding, and when she continued to gape at him, he grinned—big, bright, and easy. "Well, okay. See ya tomorrow after school, then. Bye."

And he ran off.

And before she could recover from her disappointment that the Long boys were just your average, normal, goose-'em-every-chance-you-get brothers, the door slammed closed and left her standing in the dimly lit barn.

All but the corner she stood in went black with shadow; the

sagging loft overhead creaked ominous and oppressive under the fading light of evening that could be seen through the holes in the roof. She began to scoop up smashed cans . . . one, two . . . and to count to keep her mind occupied. Three, four, five . . .

A cool breeze brushed across the back of her neck and she shivered. She thought she heard her father's voice, calling her, and shook her head in denial.

"One, two," she started again, out loud.

She groaned and covered her ears as the first shrill scream in her head threatened to blow out her eardrums. She flinched when it came again, her eyesight blurring from the pain. The palms of her hands were hot and damp and sticky.

There was a cracking sound like lightning and the screams. Over and over.

"Oh, God," she whimpered as the pain buckled her knees and she sank to the floor, pressing her hands against her head to keep it from exploding. "Please, please stop. It's not real." Something wet on her face. She looked at her hands. Blood. Sticky, dripping from her fingers. "I can't do it. I can't. Please, please stop," she whispered as she rocked her body to dislodge the panic rising up inside her, threatening to steal her sanity altogether. "Shhh. Shhh. Ruthie. Shhh. Please. Please stop."

"Ms. Benson? Hannah?" A strange, young, frightened male voice came out of nowhere. Somewhere in her mind she knew she needed to pull herself together, reassure him, pretend that whatever *he* was seeing was somehow normal behavior while her muscles quivered in horror. "Are you sick? Are you hurt? Hannah? Should I call—" The expletive he uttered wasn't unfamiliar just powerful and wrong for someone young to say, and then he started to shout. "Help! Someone help me! Hannah? Help! We're in the barn."

"No. No, please." It took a conscious effort to unclench her fists and clamp them to his arm and the front of his shirt, hoping the blood wouldn't terrify him. She gulped air and tried to ignore the queer galloping of her heart. "Please. Don't." She peeked to see who . . . Grady. No, Cal. Oh, God. He looked terrified . . . despite the lack of blood on his shirt. No blood anywhere. It was all in her mind. "Please. I'll be fine. I'm sorry. I—"

"My dad's here. Wait here. I'll be right back."

"No! Cal, please." With no little effort she pushed the sights and sounds back into the mental coffer they'd escaped from— something she'd done thousands of times before with no less labor. Her hands shook as she removed them, put them on the floor, and tried to push herself to stand up. "Please. I'm sorry you had to see this. I—" She tried to sound calm when she felt anything but. "I know how this must look." She attempted a laugh. "You must think I'm crazy. I—"

"No, ma'am. I don't. Are you okay?"

"Of course, I—"

"Want me to call my dad?" Clearly, *he* wanted to call his dad.

"I wish you wouldn't." Her breathing started to slow down and she couldn't feel her heart battering against her chest anymore. "In fact, I'm going to ask you not to mention this to him at all. Beg you, actually."

She saw fear and concern in his face but also intelligence and understanding—another facial expression he'd inherited from his father. She found herself wanting to pour her whole heart out to him as she had his father in the past but . . . well, she wasn't quite that far gone. Yet.

"I . . . I have panic attacks. I used to. They're rare now. I'm not on medication or anything anymore and I'm not a danger to Anna, of course. I promise. I was . . . It's strange for me to be back here, is all. I believed I'd left it all behind."

Perception came quickly to him and softened to something like sympathy as he looked around the old barn. God knew what he was thinking, but when he looked back at her, his smile was gentle and dimpled and secretive. "When I was a kid I thought this was the creepiest barn in Turchen County. Old lady Ben— your mom, used to get me to haul stuff up here for her if I was with my dad when he came to pick up Lucy. Which was like all the time back then. Like those bundles of old newspapers back there. And for a long time she used to keep her emergency firewood up here." He stood and stretched a hand out to Hannah. "She'd find a couple good-sized branches the wind knocked down, and she'd get me to 'run 'em on up' here . . . you know how she was."

"I do," she said, falling in love with this tall, quiet teenage boy as he prattled on for her comfort.

"Well, between you and me, I never came in here alone. If my dad didn't come up here with his own bundle of junk, I stood at the door and threw it in. And you know what else?"

"No, what."

"She never said anything about finding the bundles or the sticks or whatever other stuff she used to ask me to bring up here on the floor, just inside door. I think this place creeped her out, too." She smiled at him and his brow furrowed. "You're okay now?"

"I am. Thank you." But she needed to be sure. "It's wrong, I know, to ask you to keep things from your father but—"

He laughed out loud. "But he's bossy and he overreacts to everything." He finished her sentence on a note of intimate acquaintance and common capitulation.

"I don't know about that but—"

"Trust me. The longer you keep him in the dark, the safer your secrets are."

She nodded. She'd already figured that one out. He pulled on the string to turn out the light while she started to slide one of the big barn doors open with barely a glance at the drooping loft. And she left it open—whether to let the rancid memories out or the fresh air in was a toss up.

They started back to the house together.

"Do me another favor?"

"What's that?"

"Do you think you could handle both of the Long boys at the recycling center tomorrow? I'll call their mother tonight and make sure it's okay, but I wanted to make sure it was okay with you first."

He nodded, shrugged, and smiled—and looked at her as if *now* he thought she was talking a little crazy.

Grady brought pizza for the young cleaning crew and stayed to have a few pieces on his dinner break.

Did she look shaken to her core? Did she look afraid to let her thoughts wander further than the three large-sized pizza boxes Grady balanced on one hand when he strode into the kitchen? Would he be able to see in her eyes that she'd been to hell and back that afternoon without ever leaving the farm? Would he be able to tell by the tremors in her hands that every muscle in her body was programmed and set to run?

She hurried to take the boxes from him, to give herself something to do—something normal—to keep her hands and mind busy.

"Here, let me take those. I'm not sure Anna can eat pizza but I'm famished and the other kids, I'm sure, are starving, and I can fix Anna— Oh." She opened the top pizza box and froze. Her stomach flipped and her emotions ping-ponged between anger and fear at his spying on her. "How did you find out that I like white pizza?"

He unzipped his jacket and started to take it off. He hadn't missed the accusation in her voice and his eyes were watchful.

"I didn't. I didn't know what kind you'd like, so I got one that's half plain cheese, the other half with everything; a whole pepperoni because I know my kids like it, and the white one for Anna. You said nothing too spicy for a while." He slipped his coat over the back of a chair without looking away. "I figured something would be close to what you preferred, but if it's the white you like, so much the better. Is something wrong?"

"No." She answered too fast and too sharp so she smiled. "Of course not. I'm tired and testy and I . . ."

"What?"

"I hate it here. I hate being here." He wanted answers and explanations, why not give him a couple to keep him busy? More to the point, distract him, she decided impulsively. "I'm having a terrible time sleeping. I keep waking up. I bought sleeping pills over the counter, but if I stay here much longer I'll need a prescription." *For something industrial strength,* she thought. "I'm having a little trouble with my business. I can handle some of it by phone and the Internet—when I can find the time. But I need to be there for the rest. Joe's helping all he can." She reached up high to remove a stack of paper plates from the cupboard beside the refrigerator, fished napkins from the drawer below and set them next to the pizzas on the table. Overhead she heard heavy footsteps hurrying toward the stairs, like a small herd of starving caribou heading for the first patch of spring grass. Fine, so she wasn't familiar with caribou, but it sure sounded like more than four sets of feet up there. "But Joe's not *me* and my clients expect *me.* I'm tired and on edge and I have a lot on my mind. Okay?"

"Okay." He acted satisfied for the moment—but he didn't have a choice to be otherwise as the young people swarmed the food, laughing and chatting and pushing them further away from each other.

Hannah sighed with relief and covered it with a hum of pleasure as she took her first bite of pizza—Alfredo-flavored cardboard that stuck to the roof of her mouth.

Running away would be smart. Wise. If only for a few days—to refortify her defenses, to remind her that the past was in the past and it couldn't hurt her anymore . . . unless she let it; unless she let the secret out.

She could talk with Joe, make an appointment with Dr. Fry . . . but there was still so much to be done before they could put the farm up for sale. And leaving Anna here to finish up alone was unthinkable, of course. *Not that she couldn't handle it*, she debated, nodding and smiling when the girl wordlessly offered her a second piece of the white pizza. Anna was amazingly independent. She could—

Hannah pulled up short. What was she thinking? She put the slice she'd been about to take a bite of back on her paper plate and her shoulders drooped. She was a coward. She'd been braver twenty years ago, tougher. Anna was counting on her. And Grady, blast him, watched her like she might sprout horns. She couldn't run now. Not yet.

No more memories. No matter how benign or ordinary, they were a danger to her here where everything reminded her of *something*. She couldn't afford another breakdown or chance being caught in such a weakened state ever again.

Another one of those things that are easier said than done. Just turn the memories off. She would if she could.

She glanced at Cal, busy helping Biscuit tease his sister about the mouse that had chased her around one of the bedrooms upstairs. She felt reasonably confident that he'd already forgotten what he'd seen in the barn less than an hour ago.

But her muscles still quivered in the aftermath. Part of her mind strained to hear the screams again thinking she could hide herself before they reached full pitch and she did something stupid to frighten Anna—or attract Grady's already suspicious concerns.

Still, more than anything she wanted to run, to go back to Baltimore where she belonged, where she was safe and nothing haunted the peace she'd created there. Her gaze gravitated toward Anna and her friends; and while she expected to feel some sort of shame in wanting to make a break for it, she didn't.

She was becoming very fond of Anna, but Anna didn't know—no one knew. She was the last. And every day she was here she could feel the burden bearing down on her; her fear and guilt swelling, the strain threatening to shatter her sanity.

Chapter Twelve

Maybe he should have been an actor, Grady thought as he gave her two full minutes before following her oh-so nonchalantly from the kitchen—a slice of pizza in one hand and two more on a paper plate in the other. Another Pacino, perhaps, as he took a blasé glance into the dining room and then the living room to see that not quite half the stuff had been removed—and that had been the furniture. Or what about a Hugh Jackman, whose smile he'd heard was irresistible—not unlike his own, he hoped, when he used it to ask permission to sit below her on the steps, facing her.

"You'd think they'd never eaten before."

Her smile was small but it did reach her eyes. "Well, I never would have dreamed that I'd enjoy their noise so much. I love listening to them talk among themselves." She caught herself. "Not what they're saying in particular, I don't eavesdrop on them, but the happy, comfortable buzz they make when they're together. The sound of their friendship."

He nodded his understanding and wondered which famous actor he should impersonate now, which one had the most charm and subtlety to slip by her defenses.

She took a bite, chewed and swallowed—and to his surprise spoke first.

"Ruth was afraid of mice. She thought rats and mice were the same thing . . . and spiders. She hated spiders. Anything she could hear or feel but not see in the dark terrified her." He realized the story was being prompted by Lucy's antics earlier in the day, standing on a chair, hollering for Biscuit and her brother to come save her from a small gray mouse. He saw, too, that her expression was amused for the moment, recalling a fond memory of her sister. "Spiderwebs that pulled at her hair or brushed across her cheek would send her into hysterics. And it was our secret for years and years." She looked away and frowned. "I guess I'll never know how he figured it out . . . that if he put us both in the cellar and removed the lightbulb at the top of the stairs, she'd scream and cry—but only for the few minutes it took for me to wrap her in my arms and convince her I'd protect her from everything that crawled down there." Her eyelids took a long blink. "God, she was little."

"How old were you?"

She shook her head vaguely. "Six maybe. Nine when he finally figured out he had to separate us to get the best results. I got sent to the attic. It was cold up there but there was an electrical socket in the overhead light fixture. He took out the bulb, but as you know, there's more stuff in that attic than you can shake a stick at—and a window. Sometimes I had daylight. When I didn't I had a small lamp that I covered with a piece of soft carpet that warmed and lit the little space I made for myself . . . and for which I got the third worst beating of my life because it was also a cozy little fire hazard up there." An odd little smile rippled across her lips. "After that he strapped me to a chair up there to keep me out of trouble. For my own good."

He could tell by the mocking look in her eyes that those had been her father's words and she hadn't believed them then any more than she did now.

"And Ruth?"

She looked away and shook her head like she might not answer. He watched her force the wedge of pizza in her mouth and bite down, chew, and do it again. As he was about to give up on the answer, starting to debate if he should ask the question again, her voice came soft and wispy.

"We all had our own special kind of hell here and the cellar was Ruth's. If she wouldn't go down on her own when he told her to, he'd simply pick her up—kicking and screaming—and take her down." She started a new piece of pizza, like keeping her mouth full and the story coming in parts made it easier to tell. "I used to wonder why he didn't just shove her off the top step when she cried and begged him not to make her go down there, but as I got older I realized that a fall could kill her and then all his fun would be over."

She looked into Grady's eyes, but he wasn't sure what he was seeing. Her shields were up, protecting her as if she were merely telling a story—about someone else, someone she knew but not intimately anymore. "That's what it was for him, you know. Fun. He loved hurting us and scaring us and controlling us. It made him feel important and powerful. Plus, it was just plain amusing, I guess. Ruth would cry and scream and shriek in terror for hours on end—beg him to let her out. He especially liked it when we begged. She'd find her way up the stairs to the door, and when he figured out she felt slightly safer there, up off the floor, he'd open the door and take her back down to the bottom . . . though he never tied her up that I know of . . ." She closed her eyes and leaned her head back, resting it between two railings. She shook her head. "I won-der why he didn't. Maybe he was afraid she'd lose her mind and stop screaming, huh?" She shook her head again, dropped what was left of her pizza on the plate, and tossed it on the step above hers before looking at him again. "Is this the kind of information you keep following me around to find out? For your good-home-environment file on me? Think I'll take Anna back to Baltimore and lock her in a closet now?"

"No." He made his answer as clear and firm as he could make it. "But don't try to tell me that growing up in this house didn't affect you."

"Of course it did." She gave a soft, mirthless laugh and brought both arms up between them to display her naked wrists. "I can't wear watches or bracelets . . . or cotton socks that are too tight around my ankles. And I wouldn't recommend grabbing me by the wrists for any reason, because I fight dirty."

"So noted." His keen eyes caught a spark of evasion in her eyes as if he was a guard dog and she was tossing a bone in one direction while she escaped in another. "But that wasn't your hell . . . being isolated, being tied up wasn't . . ." Her blue eyes flashed. Surprise. Fear. A warning to back off before they looked away. But that wasn't going to happen. He may not know this grown-up woman, Hannah, but the Hannah they were talking about he knew very well. "Your hell was having to listen."

She sighed and closed her eyes, but she didn't deny it. After a second or two she squeezed her eyes shut tighter and used both her hands to push her short, shiny hair away from her face. Then she laughed, sort of.

"He used to get so pissed at me." Suddenly the threads on the worn stair runner needed plucking. "And I could never do anything right. I couldn't cry when he hit me so he'd hit my mother instead. I came defective from the factory, you see. All I ever felt was anger and defiance. It made him *crazy*. That first night Ruth spent in the cellar alone I called to her. I figured if I could hear her, she could hear me. I told her to be brave. I told her the longer she cried the longer he'd leave her there. I told her that the mice were more afraid of her than she was of them. I told her to find something to beat the floor with like I showed her to keep the mice away. I told her she was a big girl, that she needed to be . . ." The loose thread on the rug broke free and startled her. "He wrapped duct tape across my mouth and around my head at least a dozen times and told me if I touched it before morning he'd leave Ruth in the cellar for a week." She shrugged. "Mama pulled out half my hair trying to get it all out before school the next day. But I would have gone bald if I'd thought it would keep Ruthie out of the cellar."

She dropped the thread on her uneaten pizza and sat up straighter, indicating she was preparing to get up—that what she'd told him was just an old story and he could take it or leave it.

"I believe you, Hannah." His throat was tight so the words came out in a whisper. He wanted to shout it, to keep her there and talking to him, but she just nodded and asked if he wanted a cup of coffee for the road.

"No, thanks. Keeps me awake and I have a board meeting tomorrow." He moved his legs and let her step by. Though she held on to the railing with her free hand, he automatically put a supporting hand under her forearm to assist; and despite the fact that he detected no overt shaking of her hands or arms, there was a distinct trembling within. The story had cost her. And the gift had been given to him.

Part of him was grateful, the other part wanted to dismantle something with his fists. An hour ago he'd thought he knew about her childhood. Horrible, shocking, unspeakably appalling and other such words that indicated he didn't—couldn't actually—comprehend the magnitude of it. Those few details made his blood run so cold it burned like fire, and still he couldn't wrap his head around it. He was a man of the world. He'd seen things and he knew humans could be more vicious than animals. But how anyone could look into the face of a child and inflict that kind of cruelty was beyond him. So was the sort of strength required to survive it . . .

And whether Hannah told him professionally for his *home environment assessment* or personally because they'd once been good friends, it didn't matter to him. She was talking and all he wanted to do was listen.

"I didn't realize the sheriff's department was run like a company with a Board of Directors," she said on her way back to the kitchen. He hurried to catch up with her.

"Well, I hadn't thought about it before, but I guess it is. We all have to answer to someone, I suppose. My board is the County Board of Supervisors and the County Administrator. They approve my budgets; keep me on the up and up—"

"Bitch him out when the deputies aren't writing enough speeding tickets or fining people for being one minute late on their parking meter," Lucy chimed in as they filed into the kitchen. "Or my favorite: running down jaywalkers on Main Street where the crosswalks are four blocks apart. And they refuse to even think about painting in two more to make it convenient for people. They *want* you to jaywalk, risk your own life, basically, if you were anywhere but here, just so they can make Daddy catch you and write you a ten-dollar ticket.

"He hates his job," she announced. Hannah turned her head to look at him and he held out his hands—he couldn't deny it. "He'd much rather be on patrol or even in investigations than pushing papers and fighting with the Board of Supervisors but a sheriff makes the big bucks, and he has mouths to feed." She opened hers and then batted her eyes at him.

He took this opportunity to snap her lips closed with a single knuckle under her chin. "Remind me not to put you on my reelection committee." He flipped open the pizza box to see if any remained—scowled at his offspring when he found it empty. "And I don't hate my job. It's not as . . . rewarding as when I worked chiefly with the public, is all. I *liked* chasing down the jaywalkers."

The young people groaned and made disparaging remarks with teasing laughter in their eyes. And Hannah smiled when she began to appreciate that even in families where tensions ran high from time to time, there were also calm, close, comical moments that outweighed the others a hundred to one.

That night she lay awake in the faint moonlight, straining to make familiar shapes of the objects in the shadows of her room. She didn't dare close her eyes.

She told herself it was the wind whistling through the hundreds of tiny fissures in the siding, not whispering voices that roused her whenever she started to doze off.

She needed to keep her mind in the here and now.

She started a mental list of things to go over with Joe in the morning, then worked on a plan for her favorite and fairest of the three antique dealers to return for another, hopefully final, viewing of some questionable items they'd uncovered in the last few days. It made her feel diligent.

Of course, her favorite catalog was the one she kept on Anna—who didn't care for the color pink but preferred greens and then blues instead. She loved milk more than any other drink she'd had so far. Her taste in music was eclectic, her one requirement being lyrics she could sing along to. She would listen to but wasn't fond of heavy metal . . . to which Biscuit rolled his eyes in a belabored fashion and said, "It ain't for little girls anyway." She was a staunch defender of her sex, and her humor was easy and generous.

She spoke with some consideration of becoming a nurse in the future, her stomach for the profession having already been tested, but she had qualms at the prospect of facing death every day for the rest of her life. Her next best choice was teacher of small children, kindergarten or first grade, when their eyes were bright and their teeth went missing. But her deepest, darkest wish—told to her aunt alone in front of a repeat episode of *Law and Order: Criminal Intent* with Vincent D'Onofrio, the only episodes worth watching they'd agreed—was a family, with lots of kids.

"Not the Olympics? The way you love to run?"

"I'll always love to run. And it's nice that people around here think I'm something special, but if you look at bigger towns like Richmond or Charlottesville, I'm barely competitive. There are lots of kids as fast or faster than me out there."

"But you're a sophomore . . . fifteen years old. And Lucy says you're going to clean up at the regional races and then again at the state competitions."

"We'll see." She shrugged. "And the big family thing is my long range plan, so don't worry. Gran made me promise I'd finish college, and I want to travel a little before all that."

"With the Olympics maybe . . ." The suggestion was made softly, and with hardly any pressure at all.

Anna smiled tolerantly. "We'll see."

Though Anna never said a word about it, Hannah hadn't forgotten her discussion with Biscuit that afternoon at the track. She had a birthday—a big one, her sixteenth—two track meets and a senior prom with an almost guaranteed date with someone she cared for if she were still around to participate. And in Baltimore? She'd be the *new kid* for the last two months of the school year, an outsider. There might be enough time to make a new friend and meet her new track coach but . . . well, wouldn't it be better to get a fresh new start with everything in the fall?

It was two months . . . not forever.

However, two months was plenty long enough for Jim Sauffle to rob her blind . . . *if* that was what he was doing. On the other hand, it might be way too long to spend with a lonely teenager overtly trying to make the best of things. And, on an extraordinary third hand, it was definitely too long for her to stay in Clearfield if she wanted to keep her mind intact and her secret buried.

She'd taken Anna out of school for the one-week checkup with Dr. Kolson. The written excuse had taken close to thirty minutes to compose, and she'd laughed at herself when she realized how responsible and, well, legal she was trying to make it sound.

They were parking in the lot outside his office before she decided to simply ask Anna if she wanted her to go with her when she saw the doctor.

She wanted to be included, to hear the prognosis and precautions and whatever else Anna and the doctor would say to each other, but the fact was Anna was closer to being a grown woman than she was to being a child and she deserved the choice of privacy.

Anna's practice was to see the doctor alone before he spoke to her grandmother, but after a second look at her aunt's anxious expression she invited her to join them.

"I won't say a word. I promise. And if you have to undress or something, I'll leave. I only want to hear what he has to say." She couldn't believe how grateful she was.

Dr. Kolson was Ellen and Anna's family physician, a young man trained at Penn State and the University of Virginia who never met old Dr. Pageant, but had heard his name from some of his more elderly patients. Hannah quizzed him on these facts when he expressed his condolences on Ellen's death.

"Your mother was very kind to us when my wife and I first moved here. Over the years as I got to know her better, her dry wit became something I looked forward to dueling with during our appointments. I enjoyed her very much."

Dry wit? Her mother had a wit—wet, dry, or otherwise? She was tempted to reidentify herself as being *Ellen Benson's* daughter and to ask Anna to show him the picture of the old woman that she carried in her wallet. But he didn't look as confused as she felt, so maybe he wasn't.

Plus, he displayed a real concern for Anna's health and seemed to be trustworthy enough—for a doctor.

"She should finish up the antibiotic for the total ten days, of course, and the acid suppressant and the antacid for a good six weeks to make sure that ulcer has time to heal completely, and then I'd say she should be good as new." This he decided after he'd asked Anna to lie back and palpated her abdomen through her T-shirt.

"What about food restrictions?" Hannah found it a hard buy that such a shocking episode was going to have such a simple ending.

"Nope. She can eat anything she likes. However, I would recommend, as a precaution, that any time she takes any kind of medication, even if it's just an aspirin—actually especially if it's an aspirin—she should eat something with it unless otherwise instructed. That's a good idea in general and certainly a good idea with a history of ulcers."

She nodded and glanced at Anna, then stood and crossed the small exam room to stand beside her. "And what about her running?"

He grinned and his eyes twinkled at Anna as if they were

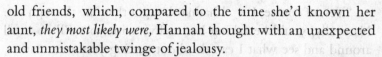

old friends, which, compared to the time she'd known her aunt, *they most likely were,* Hannah thought with an unexpected and unmistakable twinge of jealousy.

"I am not looking to be tarred and feathered and run out of town by Coach Duncan and the rest of the track team, so I'll say she can start running again if she starts out slow and works her way back up to speed." He held up his index finger. "And stop immediately if you experience any pain or dizziness or anything else out of the ordinary. I'm serious." He put a hand on Anna's shoulder and got very sober. "I'm trusting you to use your head, young lady. The next couple of weeks are important, to give yourself time to heal. After that you'll feel better than you have in quite a while."

"I already do."

"Good. But don't push it. I want to see you back in two weeks and then we'll decide if you can run at the meet against Ripley, where I fully expect you and the rest of the team to crush them like the bugs they are." He laughed, becoming somber when he noticed that Anna wasn't . . . exactly.

Though her smile was large and exuberant, both the doctor and her aunt could see that it didn't reach her eyes.

"I won't be here in two weeks, Dr. Kolson," she said, her voice thick in her throat as she looked to Hannah to help her explain. She smoothed her hand across the girl's shoulders and gave her a soft reassuring hug.

"I was going to bring that up next. I'm going to need copies of Anna's health records. I'm taking her back to Baltimore with me in a few days . . . if I ever get my mother's house cleaned out. And if you could recommend a good family practice sort of doctor like yourself, that would be great. All I have is my gynecologist and I'm not sure he knows anything about running, much less runn-ers."

The doctor was visibly taken aback.

"Yes, of course, I . . . I hadn't thought that one through yet. Naturally, you'll be taking her to live with you. I'll . . . call around and see what I can do about getting you some names, and I can have her records ready by tomorrow afternoon." He looked at Anna, clearly shaken and confused as to what to do next. "Well. That sucks."

His declaration startled Anna and she laughed as tears welled in her eyes. "Yes, sir. And I wanted to thank—"

"We've been through a lot together, you and I," he said, cutting her off, taking her hand and tugging to get her off the examination table. "First your mom, then your Gran. I didn't lose one night's sleep knowing you were there watching over them. I couldn't have asked for a better nurse. I'm going to miss you." He pulled her into his arms and gave her a warm hug, then held her away from him by her shoulders to deliver his orders. "I want you to keep in touch, now. I want to hear about Baltimore and your new school and the track team there; where you decide to go to college, all of it."

"Yes, sir." Anna blinked several times and swiped at a tear that got away. "I will. And I want to thank you—"

"People are going to want to know how you're doing— and, frankly, your pal Lucy makes most of them a little nervous because they never know what she's going to do or say."

Anna grinned. "She says that's why we're friends, because opposites attract."

"In this case I believe she's right. She can't be taking this well." He released Anna and opened the door, stepping back to let them exit. "I imagine Sheriff Steadman has his SWAT team on standby."

"No, I don't think he's going to need one," Anna defended her friend. "We're working things out. We have phones and computers, and it's only a six and a half hour drive and we'll both be sixteen soon. We're going to be okay."

The doctor met Hannah's eyes as she passed through the door in front of him. She couldn't tell what he was trying to ask her—*Is taking her away from everything she knows and loves the right thing? Can you handle this? Are you sure you know what you're doing? Who are you?*—so she lowered her eyes and looked away, not knowing how to answer him. Not knowing the answers, period.

Maybe this wasn't the doctor, or the time, to ask for a sleeping script, she decided.

"I have no doubt of it. Now if you . . . either of you, need me or have questions, don't hesitate to call. I'm just a phone call away."

They both promised and thanked him and Hannah asked after outstanding medical bills on their way out. But aside from those accrued from her final, fatal heart attack, her mother had kept her bills up to date and paid. Another interesting and disquieting variance from her childhood, when the Benson family owed money to half the town and the other half knew it.

They were both quiet on the ride home, casting furtive glances at each other, the tension of their unspoken thoughts a growing, palpable thing despite the affectionate smiles they gifted to each other when their eyes met.

Biscuit and the Steadmans, all the Steadmans, were at the house ready to work when they got back to the farm. The Long boys had other after-school activities that afternoon.

Hannah had made up her mind, but her plan was only half cooked as she watched them approaching her car, eager to hear Anna's prognosis. That they loved her was undeniable; that she loved them back was indisputable. Right or wrong Hannah knew in her heart what she needed to do.

"So what did the doctor say?" Grady asked, holding her door open for her, lowering his head a bit when she couldn't quite meet his eyes. "She's right as rain again, right?"

"Why don't you ask her?" She waved a hand to the other side of the car where the rest of the Steadmans hovered around her niece. "Better yet, listen."

His gaze lifted and his features softened with humor and joy as he watched Anna and his family respond with silliness to the relief they felt. Hannah ducked around him to the front of the car. She had something to say and she didn't want him too nearby when she said it. He might try to change her mind, but for Anna's sake—and her own mental stability—she couldn't let him.

"Anna? Come here a second, will you?" The girl broke away from the others and came to her, smiling. Hannah palmed her face, then watched her fingers twirl a small thatch of pale wavy hair so like her sister's. She glanced at the Steadmans, who'd come together as the unit they were on the rider's side of the car, watching and waiting to see what was happening.

She looked back at her niece thinking she could have made this announcement with a little more tact and . . . privacy but it was her experience that once a decision was made, it was best to carry it out promptly and get it over with.

She reached out and took both of Anna's hands, looked her straight in the eye and said, "When I go back to Baltimore, I think you should stay here."

Chapter Thirteen

The silence that followed Hannah's announcement dropped loud and heavy, and it was Mrs. Steadman who broke it first.

"Oh, my." In her distress she turned to Grady, whose expression had turned to stone; not even his eyes revealed his reaction to her words. It still took the young people several more seconds before they took action.

"Yes!" Lucy squealed, jumping up and down in place until her brother elbowed her off balance and she bumped into Biscuit. "What? This is great. Let her go back to where she came from. Anna doesn't need her. She has us."

"Lucy." Grady's voice, low and lethal, had Lucy's attention immediately. "Keep your mouth closed and stay out of this."

Right away Hannah could see that Lucy had gotten the wrong impression and that Grady's anger wasn't directed at Lucy but at her. *Oh, them of little faith!* So easy to jump to all sorts of wrong conclusions when you don't know someone; when all you hear was what you want to hear, isn't it?

But she and Anna were family. They were getting to know each other and bonding . . .

Hannah looked to her niece, expecting to see wonderment and excitement at the prospect of staying, but instead she found confusion and concern and clear, true-blue eyes blinking back tears. Anna shook her hands loose from her aunt's and turned them to fists at her sides.

"Why? Why don't you want me? What did I do?"

"What?" In shock she watched the tears spill over onto the girl's cheeks. Anna looked first to Grady in disbelief and then at her friends, utterly mortified, before she turned back to Hannah. Heartbroken, she did what she did best—she ran. "Oh, God! Anna, stop. Please. You don't understand."

No way could she catch up with her, but she broke free of the hold Grady suddenly had on her arm and ignored whatever he was saying and followed the girl as fast as she could. They all did. Hannah, though, was only marginally aware of the others.

She chased Anna and Grady chased her; the three teens jogged along behind him as Janice Steadman took the rear, huffing and puffing and shouting, "Let's all sit down and talk about this." They were a gaggle of awkward, honking geese chasing a lovely, graceful swan.

Anna went around the side of the house and slipped in the back door, off the porch, through the kitchen, down the hall and up the stairs to her room—no doubt in record time. She didn't slam the door in Hannah's face, but it closed as she arrived seconds later, out of breath and trying to swallow her thrashing heart.

"Anna," she gasped. "Please, can I come in? Or will you come out and talk with me? Anna?" She tapped on the door as the others gathered at the bottom of the stairs. Janice kept the teens at bay as Grady moved halfway up the steps toward her. She held up her hand to stop him. "Anna?"

"I thought we were becoming friends," the girl called

through the door, her voice hoarse with emotion. "I thought you liked me. What have I done?"

"Nothing."

"I'll change. I'll do whatever you say."

"Anna—"

"Please. Please don't leave me. I know you don't want me, but I won't be any trouble, I promise. I'll . . . I'll . . . Everybody leaves me."

"Oh, Anna." Enough is enough. She opened the door and marched in, went straight to the bed, drew the girl into her arms, and held her tight. "Enough now. Listen to me. Let me explain."

She let the girl cry a few seconds longer because she hadn't held anyone in her arms like this since Ruth; no one had needed her in years. Nor had she known the desire to give so much of herself to someone—an overwhelming, instinctive, almost animalistic necessity to comfort and protect the child in her arms.

"Anna." She spoke near the girl's ear, holding her with one arm, caressing her hair with the other—aware of others packed in the doorjamb. "I can't think of any other way to work this out for the both of us. I have to go back to Baltimore this weekend. I have a business that I can't neglect. Depending on how things go there, I could come back in a few days or maybe the next weekend for a few days."

"But I—" Anna started, her voice cracked.

"I know you're willing to come with me and I can't tell you how grateful I am that you're not being a little, well . . . that you're being such a good sport about it, but the more I think about it the less this all makes sense."

She stopped abruptly when her left shoulder began to rise up toward her ear and the grip on her left upper arm became painful. Grady mumbled from behind her. "Can I talk to you for a minute?"

"No." She looked pointedly at his hand on her arm. "And let go of me. I've made up my mind. I know you're the authority on parenting here and I know I was the one who asked you for help, but pulling her out of school less than three months before the end of the school year would, I think, do her more harm than good. And then there's the track meet with Ripley . . . they *need* to be brought to their knees. And, of course, the prom . . ."

Grady backed away as she peeked at Anna again. And there was the amazement and joy she'd hoped for; her lips bowing, eyes sparkling through her tears with hope. "Really?" she whispered, swiping at a final tear that got away.

"It makes sense, doesn't it?" she asked adult to adult, and the girl nodded emphatically. "You finish up your work here, I finish up mine—and we make our big move in the summer when school's over, when the farm's ready for sale and I've had time to clean out my spare bedroom. I even thought you could stop in at Silverman's Hardware Store and pick out new paint for the walls . . . if you promise not to let Lucy help," she leaned in to whisper. "It can be all fresh and clean and newly painted for you when you get there."

"You don't need to go to all that trouble."

She reached out and stroked the girl's cheek. "I know I don't, but I very much want to. I know what you're giving up to come live with me in Baltimore and I want you to be as happy and as comfortable as possible under the circumstances."

"You're giving up a lot, too, though."

She smiled. "Yes, but oddly enough it doesn't feel like it. It feels like I'm getting a lot more than I'm giving up." She hesitated but only for a moment. It *wasn't* too early to declare where she stood. "And for the record: We are friends. Even better, we're family. I do want you, Anna. I love you. And I'm not leaving . . . well, except to go to Baltimore, but I'll be back as fast as I can."

The girl nodded, sniffed in acknowledgment.

Finally, she could look at Grady. Anna liked the plan and now that she'd heard it out loud, it made more sense than before. "However, I still can't figure out where to leave her while I'm gone."

"We'll take her." Lucy was quick to volunteer.

"I don't think that's the greatest idea right now."

"Because of Cal?" asked Lucy, and he jabbed her hard from behind. "*Ou!* Stop it."

"I would imagine the last thing your grandmother needs right now is another teenager to worry about." *And I don't need any additional reasons to run into the sheriff.*

"Oh my heavens, that wouldn't be the problem. I'm worried more about where we'd put her. Weekend overnights are one thing, but when there's school the next day these girls need their sleep, and I don't think there's enough room in Lucy's room for another single bed unless we borrow Milly Albright's. It has a little trundle bed that they could pull out every night and—"

"Mom. Mom. Hannah's right. They spend nearly every waking moment together as it is. They need time for homework and . . . whatever else they do alone, if anything. And I can already think of at least a half dozen people from Ellen and Anna's church, Altar Society ladies, with spare rooms who'd love to do this for Anna."

While the Steadmans settled Anna's future living arrangement among themselves, Hannah thumbed away the wetness on the girl's cheeks and gave her one more hug for good measure. She stood, flipped a tissue from the box on the bedside table, and held it out to her niece with a smile coming from someplace deep inside.

It was a strange sensation but she identified it instantly—a sense of belonging to or with someone that she'd never, to her recollection, known before. Not even with Ruth. Naturally, she'd always longed to feel it but she'd spent most of her life refusing to. Yet with Anna it came as something so natural, no court in the land could deny it. They belonged to each other . . . at least that's how she felt and hopefully, someday, Anna would feel it—and trust in it—too.

"Oh, that's a wonderful idea," Janice Steadman announced. "Frances Houser's son, Simon, graduated from William and Mary last spring and he's moved up into one of those towns outside of D.C. to be close to his—"

"Gramma, she can't stay with the Housers," Lucy interrupted. "Burt'll eat everything she owns."

"That's right." The old lady's eyes grew wide. She shook her head and brought Hannah up to date. "Two years ago Simon volunteered to be assistant coach for one of the little league teams and one evening he came home with all the equipment in the trunk of his car. Well, he opened the trunk for some reason and went into the house to get something and when he came back out, the equipment was gone. He thought someone had driven by and stolen it so he called Grady. Pretty soon he had the whole neighborhood out looking for this big bag of bats and balls and mitts, and sure enough, a couple hours later, Simon walks out to Burt's doghouse in the backyard and there's the ripped up canvas bag, slivers of bats, and cotton tufts out of the mitts all snarled in the string from the balls." She laughed heartily and it was hard not to do likewise. "Frances said it was because Burt was jealous of all the time Simon was spending with the little children in the park. But if you ask me I think he's just a big dumb dog who likes to chew. Frances had to buy stone planters for her yard because he eats the plastic ones and she's afraid the ceramic ones will cut up his innards." She drew a breath. "No, you're right. Anna can't stay there. *But . . .*" she stepped further into the room, the kids following, "what about the Sullivans."

"Too far out of town," Lucy stated. "Someone close so we can walk back and forth."

"The McManns?"

For some good reason the McManns weren't right either, but Hannah missed it as she slipped out of the now-crowded little room with one final glance back at Anna sitting Indian style on the bed among her friends. On cue the girl looked up and they traded smiles—like two people who belonged. Hannah's cockles were toasty warm.

She started down the stairs very aware that she wasn't alone and that he watched her intently.

"What?" She heard the defensiveness in her voice and sighed. She was feeling particularly wonderful at the moment and didn't want to fight with him. She didn't want to defend her decision but she would if she had to. "It makes sense. And she's happier than I've seen her since I got here."

"Yes, she is."

She looked back at him then. "So?"

"So you did good." He shrugged. "You might have warned me ahead of time."

"I wasn't sure ahead of time." She gave the front door a couple of good hard jerks before it opened and she pushed out through the screen door.

He nodded his understanding, following her, fighting a smile. "I thought I was going to have to duke it out with you right there in front of the kids."

"And that would have been funny?"

"Not really. But I think I was looking forward to it."

"And now you're disappointed?"

He grinned at her and she looked away, not wanting to see

the look in eyes that had crawled under her skin so often before. She started down the porch steps.

"You never fought fair." It wasn't an accusation as much as a recollection that came with a hundred little pings, like being hit over and over with soft cotton bullets. It compelled her to move away from him, but the sensation didn't abate. The consequences of losing so many of their disagreements in the past were never disagreeable. All too often it had been a matter of her fears holding out against his cajoling, wheedling, enticing, and flat-out sweet-talking to get what he wanted, which invariably involved something that thrilled her, pleased her, or touched her in places she didn't know existed.

Back then, fighting with Grady, and letting him win, was like watching the slow unfurling of a world she'd only dreamt of visiting—a small, enchanted place where two special people could simply be—then eventually it became something worth living and fighting and almost dying for.

"I always fought fair," he said, ambling along behind her, keeping his distance but staying within her personal space to keep her on edge. "You were just a genuinely bad loser."

That made her laugh and turn her head to look at him. He was teasing her. He knew as well as she did that every time she'd given in to him she'd won more than she lost.

She glanced at the cows in the four-acre field; noted that the front lawn remained brown with tufts of bright green grass shooting up here and there and that the forsythia bush some long-ago Benson had planted by the tool shed had begun to bloom. There didn't seem to be anything around for them to talk about . . . aside from the elephant standing between them.

She took a deep breath. "Please. Let's not do this."

"Let's not do what?"

"Let's not pretend that what we had in the past has anything to do with today . . . with who we are today and . . . and what

we want out of our lives. We're different people now in different situations with different goals. Pretending we have things
in common anymore is . . ."

He stepped up close and furnished the word. "Pretending."

"Exactly."

"But we didn't have anything in common to begin with . . .
except how we felt about each other."

"We were kids. We were—"

"Pretending?"

"Yes."

He gave a soft casual laugh and looked away; saw she was
walking him to his vehicle, but he gave no sign he was about
to take her hint to leave. "Trust me. Kids that age are all about
their feelings and none of it is pretense. It's getting them to use
their heads and think things through that's a challenge, and
they don't seem to be able to learn that until after they've been
hurt or get in trouble a couple of times. That's strictly adult
stuff . . . all the caution and distrust, the building walls to protect ourselves—*pretending* we don't feel anything."

"But I *don't* feel anything."

"Who said I was talking about you?" She looked to her
right, off toward the barn and the small stand of trees beyond
it as he watched a pink flush creep up her neck. "Well, it was
always about you, wasn't it?"

"What's that supposed to mean?"

"Doesn't *mean* anything. It's an observation. For instance,
we couldn't go to parties or movies because you weren't allowed. We had to sneak around so your parents wouldn't find
out. I had to tell you ahead of time if I was going to touch
you or you'd jump out of your skin and back away like a skit-
tish colt." The tone of his voice brought her eyes back to him.
"You never told me how bad it was—then left me to feel like a
naive fool for believing your stories of being the clumsiest girl

in the county. You even got to decide how it would end. You just disappeared. No phone call. No letter. No explanation as to why you wanted me to think you were dead all those years."

Though he sounded testy she could tell it was only a sound, and it was over—an emotional burp from the past, there and gone, said because it had once been something extremely hard to digest.

"I'm so sorry, Grady."

He shook his head. "I'm sorry." His half-smile was brief. "I've wanted to tell you that for a long, long time. I'm sorry. Sorry it happened to you. Sorry I missed it when all the signs were there."

"You were young. You weren't a cop then."

"I was stupid then. I didn't see it. I didn't even think to tie it all together." The guilt in his eyes was solid as steel, so it took a second or two to see the rust on the edges that still ate at him. "Worse, I couldn't make you trust me enough to tell me the truth."

"I never meant to hurt you. Ever. But I couldn't. It was . . . humiliating, I was so ashamed. I didn't want you to know. I didn't want you to think of me like that. I wanted you to think of me as someone normal, from a normal family. I didn't know what you'd think. I would have told you that night."

He sighed, stuffed his hands in his pants pockets, and leaned back against the door of his cruiser. "I know. Mom told me."

Her blood chilled and drained from her face, leaving behind a cold sweat and the dizzy, nauseous feeling of someone caught in deception. "Oh."

"She tried to keep your secret, not an easy thing for her in the first place, but when you didn't come back for me the next afternoon like you said you would, and she eventually heard you'd gone missing, she knew she needed to say something."

Hannah had no idea what she looked like that Friday night.

It wasn't until early Monday morning, before dawn, that she'd found the opportunity to wash up with the frigid water from somebody's garden hose, and it was several more days before she caught a reflection of herself in a car window. Mrs. Steadman must have been horrified.

"My first thought . . . everyone's first thought was that you'd gone home that night after seeing my mother and he'd finished you off. I wanted to kill him—and I might have if my dad hadn't gone with me to your house Saturday night. We met the cops there. Both your parents swore up and down that they hadn't seen you since the night before. Your father denied that he'd beaten you so bad you couldn't open one eye. My mother said you looked *ghastly*—bruised and bloody everywhere, your lips split and swollen. She'd start to cry every time she thought about it and how she hadn't insisted on taking you to the hospital. She said you ran off into the dark so fast and she was afraid of getting you into more trouble with your parents. And they, naturally, said they thought you'd run off with me that night. No one believed a word they said. The cops were threatening to take Ruth into protective custody when she walked across the yard to tell me it was true. You'd run off the night before after you and your father argued about you seeing me. In a softer voice, so no one else could hear, she said she thought you were hurt pretty bad this time and that if you were going to ask for help you'd ask it of me—and if you did, and if I loved you like you told her, I shouldn't let you come home again. Ever. Then the cops asked her if your father ever hit her. She said no and walked back into the house."

Hannah shook her head once. "He didn't. He tormented Ruth's mind but he didn't hit her. She was his beautiful *golden child* . . . though I think he might have hurt her in other ways."

They exchanged a meaningful look but neither of them wanted to discuss it. Not then. "Well, we know that arrangement didn't last much longer. The cops asked your mother if she wanted to press charges for the bruises healing on her cheeks, and when she said no they left. They told me there was nothing else they could do unless one of them pressed charges and testified against him . . . or without some sort of proof that he'd taken your life, an eyewitness, or your body. But they suspected the worst, too. I could tell by the look in their eyes. To get me off their backs they promised to list you as a runaway teen. That was the best they could do back then.

"I huddled in a blanket on my back porch all night hoping, praying you'd come back. I couldn't imagine, didn't want to think about all you'd been through. I just wanted to hold you, make it all go away. I heard the police and the ambulance sirens at dawn . . . and I knew for sure you were dead."

"Grady."

Again he shook his head. She didn't need to say anything.

"All the way over here I made deals with God. Let her be alive and I'll never drink again. Let her be alive and I'll never lie again. Let her be alive and I'll leave her alone so she can finish high school and leave this place like she planned. Just let her be alive." He looked up from the toe of his boot and gave her a one-dimpled, lopsided smile—the memory of the pain lingering in his eyes. "I guess I should have been grateful that He didn't smite me dumb for laughing when I heard that your mother had bashed your dad's head in with a frying pan."

And there it was again, that perfectly imperfect lie that provided her with the perfect alibi.

"I sat right over there in my truck." He motioned with his head to the four-acre field and the outbuildings. "I watched them drive your mom and sister off in an ambulance. Derringer's Funeral Home took your dad away in a plastic bag. The cops left. I waited." He shrugged. "I couldn't, didn't want to believe you were dead, and I knew you wouldn't just leave

without saying goodbye. I thought maybe you'd hide somewhere until you knew for sure I was home from that overnight
camping trip and then you'd come to me. For a little while I
thought maybe it was you who . . . lost your temper. I hoped
that you were still in the house waiting for the cops to leave;
that you'd look out a window and see me there, come down
and we'd run away together. That's the last time I remember
actually crying, driving home in the dark that night."

"Oh, Grady." She couldn't help it. She took a step forward
and placed the palm of her hand on his chest above his heart.
He took his left hand out of his pocket and covered hers, warm
and strong. "You have to know I didn't mean to hurt you. I
was so scared. I was a mess. I hurt. I didn't know what else to
do. And once I started running I kept going until I couldn't
take another step." She hung her head. "That doesn't excuse
me from not calling you and letting you know I was okay. I
know that. But I didn't know what things were like here . . .
if anyone was looking for me, if I would endanger you, if you
even cared anymore. It was years before I felt safe in my own
skin again. And by then I'd created this nice, quiet little life for
myself. And I, well, I assumed, I guess, that you'd gone on with
your life and married someone pretty and smart and funny and
could barely remember me."

"I did. I went on. I had to," he said, searching her face as his
hand left hers on his chest and came to cradle her face, tender
and comforting. "But I never forgot. I tried. But I never forgot. And the worst of it was, I knew. In my gut, all that time, I
knew you were out there somewhere. With all evidence to the
contrary, I knew . . . I just didn't have any proof."

It felt familiar and natural to rest her face in the palm of
his hand, to close her eyes for a moment and to feel peace. She
opened them to a face she'd once trusted more than any other
in the world—in truth, the first and only face she'd ever truly

trusted. He glanced at her mouth and she knew he was going to kiss her. She held her breath in anticipation remembering their first kiss . . . and their second . . . their third and . . .

Her heart slammed against her ribs in sudden panic.

Pulling his hand from her face she took a step back and shook her head. This man was still the kind, honest, trustworthy boy she'd fallen in love with. She was sure of it. That's why he'd been voted into his job. Everyone trusted him. They believed in him and relied on him to know and do what was lawful and right. They depended on him to find the bad guys and throw them in jail.

Her crime, her sin—her mother had been so adamant it was a punishable offense, and she'd believed it for so long that when she finally thought to question it, she couldn't bring herself to risk substantiating it—it was safer as a secret. And by then, of course, she'd kept it hidden so long that she was sure that would weigh as well. She couldn't risk going to jail. Especially not now.

"Grady. Please. I'm sorry. It never would have worked back then . . . and it's more complicated now."

Nothing in his demeanor changed as he asked, "Because of what you're hiding?"

"What makes you think I'm hiding something?" Unconsciously she took another, more telling step backward. "I'm not hiding anything. I've told you. My life is all about my business . . . and now Anna. There isn't anything else to tell."

He nodded, unbelieving. "Try not to forget who you're talking to, Hannah. I know you. And I know when I'm being lied to. I can see it in your eyes. I'll give you a little while longer to remember that I'm not the bad guy here and to figure out that no matter how many obstacles you throw up between us, I will have the truth."

With that he covered her two steps backward with one forward, took her firmly by the upper arms and kissed her smartly on the lips. "That's for being as stubborn and pigheaded as ever."

He turned and opened the door to his truck. She was flustered and frustrated . . . and some other things, too.

"Yeah, well, some cop you are, Grady Steadman. Punishing someone with a kiss sends mixed signals, you know. I wouldn't recommend that you make a practice of it."

He grinned at her, enjoying that fact that she was upset and sounding like a petulant child.

"Who said I was punishing anyone?" He got in, took his time getting comfortable and buckling up. He closed the door, rolled down the window, and looked her straight in the eye. "And you got the signal straight."

They scrutinized each other as he pulled off the front lawn onto the gravel and dirt—calculating and challenging each other like a couple of sumo wrestlers circling face-to-face on the mat. She shook her head to tell him there was nothing to win, nothing worth fighting for between them. His smile broadened, then he winked at her and drove away.

Chapter Fourteen

The female Steadmans declared May James to be the most qualified candidate to board Anna with for the last two months of school. Along with her husband, she owned a big yellow square-framed house with green shutters and a wide white porch that wrapped around three sides of it just two blocks from the Steadmans. Not only was she a notable member of the Altar Society, but she proctored the study hall in the high school library and knew Anna very well.

Best of all, in Hannah's opinion, she and her husband were relatively new to the area. Once military retirees looking for a quiet life in Little Town, USA, they'd discovered Clearfield on a holiday drive while stationed in Portsmouth at the Norfolk Naval Shipyard twenty-five years earlier. Another ten years passed before they moved to town permanently, long after the Benson murder/disappearance incident. There was no doubt they'd heard of it, of course—small towns being what they were—but they didn't unconsciously stare at her as if she'd returned from the dead and they were polite enough not to bring it up.

"And you wouldn't believe how many people do," Hannah

told Joe on Sunday evening over dinner. She swirled several strands of pasta in marinara sauce around her fork, then waved it over her plate. "'We thought you were dead,' they say, and some of them actually sound angry that I'm not. Like I pulled a fast one on them and now they're embarrassed about it. Like it ever made any difference to them if I lived or died in the first place."

"Maybe they are embarrassed." He set his fork down and took a sip of his red wine. When she looked up in disbelief he smiled tolerantly. "Maybe they don't know why. Maybe when they thought you were dead, they were ashamed for doing nothing to help you. And now that they know you're alive, they still feel the shame plus the humiliation of knowing what you went through to save yourself while they stood by and did nothing." He made it sound inconsequential. "In any case, how they feel now has nothing to do with you, does it?"

She smiled. "No. And I happen to be head over heels crazy about my niece. Wait till you meet her, Joe. She's a great kid. She's smart. She's pretty. She runs like a gazelle. She's got everything going for her. So much potential. I can't wait to get her out of that Podunk town and let her see what the rest of the world has to offer her."

"And knowing what you do of her fears of being left alone again, you still think it wise to bring her away from this town where she has spent so much of her life?"

She nodded. "I've thought about that. Especially after her meltdown last week." She sighed and pushed at the pasta on her plate, her appetite waning. "I'll talk to Grady, I guess. I know I can't live there again, but maybe we can work something out . . . shuffle the girls back and forth more often than I'd hoped, at least until she makes some new friends here . . . and gets to know me better. And trust me."

"It may take time."

"I know."

"It may never happen if life before coming to live with her grandmother was as sketchy as you say, and after it was one loss and then another. A child's psyche is a tender thing, as you well know."

She nodded. "I've thought about that, too. Maybe after we're settled in and she's feeling comfortable I might broach the subject of Dr. Fry or someone like him. She might like somebody to talk to."

She looked up at her friend to find his savvy dark-brown eyes twinkling under his bushy white eyebrows; the lines in his aged face etched by uncountable smiles almost invisible as he grinned at her. "I think you'll make this girl a fine mother."

She shook her head once. "I'm only her aunt."

"With the instincts of a good mother. Now, don't argue with me or I'll be forced to tell you I told you so, once again. Going after the girl was the best thing to do. You know how I hate being right all the time."

"Yeah right."

They laughed.

"I don't know why you left that old man in charge in the first place." Jim Sauffle was indignant. "He's damn near as old as God. It takes him forty-five minutes just to cross the parking lot and come in the front door. I was trying to help him out, make his life a little easier while you were gone. All he did was bitch."

Hannah leaned back in her office chair and took a deep, calming breath. Everything Jim said was absolutely true, and yet her first impulse was to throw her phone at him. Her second impulse: to tell him to pack up his desk and get out before she got out of her chair, crossed the room, and beat him stupid . . . if it were possible for him to be more stupid.

"First off, Jim, that old man's already forgotten more about the insurance industry than you'll ever know. In fact, this would have been a fine opportunity for you to work *with* him, pick his brain, and learn a lot. Secondly, I asked Joe Levitz to take over for me while I was gone because I trust him more than anyone else to do as I ask, which is clearly an issue for you as I had to ask you, more than once, to route my clients through to Joe."

"I was trying to help out. I want. . . ." He looked frustrated.

"What?"

"Well, I want . . . not right away, of course . . . I know I have to earn it and I have a long way to go . . . . a lot to learn and all that, but I'm hoping you'll at least consider me, eventually, for more than an associate position here."

"What. You want to be my partner?"

"Well, yeah." He said it like it made perfect sense. "I mean, I know it's your deal to give raises and bonuses instead of promotions; that you aren't looking for a partner right now, but I've been thinking that with your niece coming to live with you and you, you know, having . . . you know. . . ."

"What, Jim? More to live for now than just this agency?"

"Well yeah." At last, he looked uncomfortable. "You're going to want more time off now. You'll want to go home and cook dinner at night instead of taking evening appointments. You'll need more time for shopping and helping with homework and . . . and whatever else women with children do. You're a single parent now, and there's only so much time in a day. Believe me, my wife can tell you . . . she has a simple job, she puts in her eight hours at a 7-Eleven near our house and then goes home to do her *real* work. There's no place or time in her life for a serious career. And soon enough you'll see that, too, and either your young niece or this agency will begin to suffer. My bet's on this agency."

Everything Jim said was absolutely true and yet her first

impulse was, again, to throw her phone at him. She was beginning to wonder why she'd hired him the first place. Had he always been such a chauvinistic, age-bigoted jerk? Did he sincerely believe his sex alone made him a better candidate for advancement over Gwen and Caroline, both of whom had children and had been with the agency longer . . . *and* knew how to follow instructions?

"Thank you for that, Jim. Having never mothered anything before, I take it as a real vote of confidence from a man with, what, three children and a wife who obviously has two full-time jobs that I would choose my niece over this agency. I hope you're right and I'll take everything you said under advisement." She sat up and put her arms on her desk, laddering her fingers in front of her. "However, I should tell you that I would never take on a partner who couldn't or wouldn't follow my simple requests. I'm not going to ask you to leave right now because, frankly, I'm going shopping for my niece's birthday gift and I don't have the time to hire someone new to replace you. So, you have the next couple of months to turn yourself around, maybe check in with your wife for some sensitivity advice, learn to respect and get along with Joe Levitz, hustle your ass off to earn your pay and a few nice commissions and we'll talk again. Okay?"

As it happened, Anna wasn't emotionally attached to her bedroom furniture—which consisted of a box spring and mattress on a wheeled frame with no headboard, a battered side table with matching desk, a living room lamp and a scarred five-drawer chest with one handle missing—and had no objections to Hannah replacing it as a surprise for her birthday.

And so, later that afternoon, she met with the interior designer she'd hired to look at furniture, hand over the paint chip Anna had given her, and to discuss the girl for whom the room was being redecorated.

"I don't know her all that well. Yet. She's my niece. She's . . . ah, well, she's tall and beautiful and smart and athletic—she runs. She'll be sixteen a week from Thursday so that's why we have to rush this. She's kind of quiet so I don't know how she came up with that emergency orange color for her room, because she swore she didn't take Lucy, who's more of an orange person, to pick out the paint. But she says I'll be amazed at how many cool colors it'll go with . . . not that it matters to me. If she wanted the room painted polka-dot, we'd be painting it polka-dot but . . . do girls nowadays still have, like, those sweet sixteen parties, do you know?"

In the evening she called Anna.

"Hi. It's me again. Hannah."

"I know. I remember your voice from last night." There was humor in hers.

"You do? Am I calling too often?" She smiled, teasing back as she leaned against the doorjamb of her spare bedroom and wondered if the designer would toss the desk and recliner it held . . . and what she was going to do with all the books and boxes of . . . *stuff.*

Jesus!

"No. I can handle it. In fact I was going to call you. I have your number on speed dial in my new phone. I wanted to see if it worked."

"Okay. Call me back." She turned her BlackBerry off and waited, her smile unfaltering. When it rang she answered. "Hello?"

"It works. From now on you're just one button away."

"Well, that's nice but . . . who is this?"

Anna laughed and Hannah cherished the sound.

A couple nights later Anna called to check in. "Ask me what happened at school today."

"Anna? What happened at school today?" she asked obediently, smiling, her excitement level shooting through the roof—that's all it took these days it seemed, a thrill in Anna's voice.

"Cal asked me to prom."

"Oh. Wow. Shock and awe here. Shock. And awe. Although, I have to tell you, I was sort of expecting this . . . weren't you?"

"Hoping. I was hoping. His dad . . ."

"Right. I forgot." Her smile widened. She was liking Cal more and more all the time—he reminded her of someone. "He decided to walk over burning coals and cross his dad for you, huh?"

"Do you think he'll be in much trouble? Because I'd rather not go than—"

Hannah laughed. "Don't you worry about Grady Steadman, sweetie. Not about this anyway. If he gives Cal any trouble at all, you let me know."

And while Anna related the memory permanently engraved in her heart that day, Hannah too had a burst of recollection— of standing near her locker in the hall at the high school, spring of her sophomore year, and smiling up at Grady when he leaned against the locker next to hers, whispered *"hey,"* and grinned into her eyes . . . and of Jake Wilson, one of Grady's oldest and best pals, laughing and acting confused about the hold up to wherever they going. He asked why he was speaking to Goodwill Hannah about his friend's mental stability, and then asked about something she either didn't hear correctly or didn't understand at the time regarding her underpants.

Mostly she remembered the flash of Grady's fist as it flew passed her face on its way to the middle of Jake's and the three of them staring at one another—Jake from the floor, in appalled surprise—and the way Grady trembled when he closed her locker, took her hand, and walked away from his friend.

She didn't know if or how much more flack Grady took for caring about her—and she refused to let the recall endear him more now—it was eons ago—but if he didn't empathize with Cal's defiance, she was going to remind him.

She popped into the office Friday morning to hug Joe goodbye and to tell the others she'd see them bright and early a week from Monday morning.

She drove straight through to Ripley and arrived in time to buy a hot dog and a Coke at the concession stand before the first heat began.

She easily spied Anna standing with her teammates and coach and wanted to whoop and holler and dance a jig when the girl sensed her staring at her and looked up with a smile. Instead, she waved decorously and flipped her a thumbs-up for good luck.

"That means 'good to go' or 'well done'." Grady's voice from behind startled her, and she jerked like an eel out of water. "That's for after her race."

"What are you doing here?" She sounded as cross as she felt all at once—and he was out of uniform.

"Supporting our youth. As you can see, track isn't one of our big-money sports."

It was true. There weren't many spectators. Less than half of the bleachers on either side were occupied, but there were also small groups of people—mostly adults—wandering the outer rim of the fenced track.

"So what do I do, Sheriff? Whack at my leg with the side of my hand for 'break a leg' . . . which sounds like the worst possible thing you could wish on a runner, by the way."

He led her down the cement steps between the bleachers and stopped at a row that was high up and midfield. "How about crossing your fingers for good luck? But just two fingers. If you cross them all it's bad luck."

"Army Rangers again?"

He snorted a surprised chuckle and grinned at her. "My Book of Dad. I'm not sure all kids are, but mine were very superstitious and distrustful. Their mother leaving left them . . . unsure of things for a while. And they knew my job could be hazardous once in a while, so Lucy explained how crossing her fingers for good luck and wishing me to come home safe worked."

Anna happened to look up again just then, so she smiled and waved her single set of crossed fingers at her. The girl nodded and grinned and she mouthed, *"Thanks."*

"Protect and serve. Want another hot dog?"

"No, thanks. I'm too nervous to eat. I only ate that so I wouldn't pass out."

"I'll be right back, then. I see my kids over there looking like they're waiting for my wallet to show up."

She watched Lucy, Biscuit, and Cal move to the back of a short line the moment they saw him stand and head up the steps toward them—they knew him so well.

Glancing back at Anna, stretching her leg muscles, her focus solely on what she was doing, Hannah wondered if she was hungry, too, then stopped herself. If she knew nothing else about Anna, she *did* know the girl knew how to take care of a runner's body . . . the exceptional bleeding ulcer notwithstanding. If her own stomach was in knots, she knew Anna's was not so full as to give her cramps but full enough to give her plenty of fuel to win—she knew her that well.

She squirmed in her seat feeling ridiculously like a parent. Like Grady knowing his kids were hungry and surely short on funds.

Simply knowing, without being told. It wasn't a big deal certainly, mostly a lot of common sense, she supposed, but the fact that she had someone other than herself to think about, to apply her vast scope of common sense to, well, that was un-questionably satisfying.

Trying not to make Anna any more uncomfortable she tried not to stare at her alone and waited for the others to take their seats—Biscuit between her and Lucy with Grady and Cal behind them, making a tighter group—before launching into her list of questions.

"Should we go down by the fence like those parents over there?"

"You can," Biscuit answered, taking the role of tour guide around his mouthful of cheeseburger. "But you can see the track events better from up here. Those other people are watch-ing the long jumpers and discus and shot putters. We don't have anyone who pole vaults or a javelin thrower this year, or they'd be in the middle of the field and down there by the goalpost."

"She's never said anything about jumping over things."

"Hurdles. She doesn't." He popped a French fry in his mouth. "With those long legs she'd be really good at it, though." Cal darted a wary look at his friend and chewed his food with more aggression, but Biscuit didn't notice. "In track-and-field, you focus on what you can do best unless you want to get into multiple-event competitions and that can get to be crazy . . . and really exhausting. There are some kids in high school who try, like, two things at a time. They'll combine maybe one short or medium running event with one throwing event or a jumping event. But everything takes time for train-ing, if you want to be good enough to be competitive in it. So the more you do the more time you need for training, and in high school you don't have a lot of that kind of time."

"I see. And Anna focuses on the longer runs and the relays."

He nodded and finished chewing. "The 1600 meter run and 3200 meter relay . . . sometimes they call it the 4x800 meter relay because four runners run around the track twice each, which is 800 meters each, before they pass off the baton. That's 3200 meters total. But there are shorter relays . . . 4x100, 4x200, 4x400." He shrugged. "Anna's always run like there's something chasing her, she's fast, but the shorter sprints were never enough. Endurance and long distances are what she needs, and she's trained her body to give them to her."

"Oh, what do you know about it?" Lucy bumped him with her shoulder as Cal once again scowled at his buddy in a most unfriendly way. "You are so full of it." She leaned around him to look and speak to Hannah. "His mom's a psychologist so he spouts that weird psycho-babble stuff whenever he wants to show off. Anna runs because she's good at it. It makes her feel good. It makes her happy. Everyone has something they're good at and Anna's something is running."

"And what are you good at, Lucy?" She wasn't often in the girl's good graces, so she wanted to make the most of it.

She shrugged and leaned back so Biscuit's body hid her. "Not much, I guess."

"Well, that's not true."

"Yes, it is. Oh. You mean the way I dress."

"Not particularly."

"Other than that I don't do anything different or special. I'm just . . . average."

Hannah leaned far forward to look at her deliberately, then leaned back "I hope you don't mind my saying so, but I think you're good at telling the truth. And better than that, I think you're a good friend. I think that makes you special. Sometimes it can be very hard to be a good friend. You may not know it yet, but loyalty like yours is rare in the world."

Lucy made no comment and this time Hannah leaned back a little to look at the girl on the other side of Biscuit. Her eyes were downcast; her expression thoughtful and not disagreeable.

Grady's hand came to rest on her shoulder, grateful, warm and intimate. She didn't mind *grateful,* though it wasn't at all necessary. But *warm* and *intimate*? She tipped her shoulder and shifted her torso until his hand slipped away. She simply couldn't risk it.

"Why are they lined up like that? Why do some of them get a little head start like that? Because they're slower? Where is she going?"

This time Grady answered, leaning on his knees and talking over her shoulder. "They're staggered like that because the track is an oval and it's measured so that each of the six lanes is a quarter of a mile or 400 meters. They flip a coin before each race to see which team takes the even or odd lanes, but the distance for each lane is the same. Looks like they're doing the relay first. See the girl with the short reddish hair? That's Trudy Meyers. She's not quite as fast as Anna, but she's got the endurance for the 3200 meter run. Anna can and has run it, too, but only at all-day meets when one event is scheduled in the morning and the other in the late afternoon, so the runners have time to recoup. In these after-school meets there isn't time, so they focus on their best bet to win. Anna's faster but Trudy's good and very consistent.

"She'll start the relay because 800 meters is a nice warm-up for her; she'll barely be out of breath at the end, so she can push ahead a little and give the team a nice, safe distance to defend. If one of the two girls in the middle can't maintain, or if they fumble a pass-off, they've put Anna at the end of the relay to make up the difference. And, of course, to smash the Ripley school record."

"Of course." She clenched her fists in her lap and tried to remember the last time she'd been this excited about anything, or more confident of an outcome. Aside from Joe, when had she ever believed so wholeheartedly in anyone?

"Please go." She finished pushing her arms into the sleeves of a wool jacket that was getting too small for her and picked up her backpack.

"Not without you," Grady said, shaking his head. They were crossing Main Street toward the two-acre circular town square.

Once the older Mrs. Phillips was settled in an assisted-living facility in Ripley and once school started again in the fall, her father found her a new after-school job working for his friend Mr. Dimmit, who owned the local pawnshop. And she used the term friend very loosely here, as Mr. Dimmit didn't seem to like her father very much—which she might have considered a virtue had Mr. Dimmit been anything but a gruff, short-tempered old geezer who let it be known that it hadn't been his idea to have her underfoot from four in the afternoon until he closed at nine every night—and all day Saturday—but if that was his only way of getting half of what her father owed him, he'd take it.

It wasn't a hard job: sweeping and mopping the floors, washing windows, dusting off at least one example of everything under the sun that people valued—but not enough to keep, or couldn't keep because they needed money more.

It was quiet in Clearfield at 9:15. With most of the other shops closed as well, there was little traffic. The streets were wet with rain and they could hear their own footsteps on the asphalt. Cool but not cold, there was a restless breeze pushing the fall leaves around on the trees. It made the air so sweet and clean, she felt a little dizzy.

Or it might have been Grady. He made her a little dizzy, too, sometimes.

"I'll be fine. You have to go. I'll be in trouble if he sees you here."

"*If* he comes to pick you up, you mean?" Grady had begun to sound like everyone else when he spoke of her father—an edge of anger coated in disrespect and distrust—and he barely knew the man.

"He comes."

"I'm not talking two A.M. when the bars close, Hannah. You can't sit here in the dark all night again."

"I don't sit in the dark. I sit under the streetlamp." So her father could see her, recognize her, and maybe remember to stop and pick her up. "Right here on this bench." She plunked herself down firmly.

He stood looking down at her, his hands in the pockets of his thick barn jacket. "Man, you're stubborn."

"Well, you're annoying." She didn't make it sound like a bad thing.

"You're frustrating."

"So are you."

"You're also beautiful."

That caught her off guard and she squirmed on her bench. Her cheeks scorched as she looked away and fought her smile, then muttered, "So are you."

"What's that?" He sat beside her. Too close. "I didn't quite hear that."

She flipped her hand back and smacked him on the chest. "Yes, you did. Stop teasing me."

He grinned and leaned forward, his knee to her thigh. "But, Hannah, you're so easy to tease." He squinted and leaned closer. "Jesus, what'd you do to your face? Does it hurt?"

She touched the tender bruise above her ear, mostly hidden by her hair. "Not anymore, but it sure did smart when I did it . . . falling off a ladder." *After daddy hit me.* "I hit something on the way down, I guess."

"You're gonna kill yourself, you know that?"

She nodded; it was likely—one way or another. "So is . . . is that why you keep hanging around, then?" She looked over his shoulder for on-coming traffic then glanced back over her own, just to be safe. "Because I'm easy to mock and make fun of?"

He laughed and got to his feet. "Deliberately misunderstanding me isn't going to get me to leave either, so don't even try it. I tease to get a rise out you and you always take the bait."

She watched him amble across the wide sidewalk, out of the pool of light cast by the streetlamp to one of the thick maple trees that circled the town square. Under the wet branches, close to the trunk, she could barely detect him in the shadows.

"And I keep hanging around because I like you." His hesitation was brief. "I love you."

She turned more fully on the bench and strained to see him. She could spell the word *love*. She'd read about it in books, heard it preached in church, she knew there was a whole day dedicated to it in February—and yet it wasn't a word she'd had a lot of personal contact with.

"Don't."

"Don't what? Love you?" His voice was amused.

"Don't say it."

"I know. I thought saying it out loud would sound weird, too, but it's not so bad. I love you. See? And if that's how I feel I should say so, right? So should you, if you happen to feel the same way."

"I don't." Her answer was quick and firm because she wanted him to stop talking about it. *Jeeze*. "How can you tell?"

"That I love you? Well, let's see," he said, as if he were patiently talking to a child. "That's easy. There isn't anyone else that I'd stand way over here in the dark for because she's afraid of being seen with me and still think it was worth every second of it to be this close to her."

She didn't realize she was smiling until her cheeks tightened and rose up under her eyes adding to the pressure of the tears that were building up behind them. Cool drops of rain fairly sizzled on her brow and cheeks and chin, though she hardly noticed that either. She was aware of her heart beating in odd places—her ears, her throat, wild and erratic in her chest, slow and disturbing lower in her pelvis. She opened her mouth to speak but nothing came out—he'd blown a hole in her mind.

"Why me?" It wasn't a new question. She'd been asking herself why he kept coming around for months—first, with suspicion, and then curiosity and flat out bewilderment. Why anyone like Grady would spend two minutes with someone like her was like a rock star spending time with a river rock.

"Why not you?" He stepped forward but not quite into the light. "Once you get passed all your thorns, you're as easy to be around as anyone else. You're pretty and you're smart . . . and funny in a weird way. Please tell me we aren't going to sit out here in the rain. Let's move up to the gazebo, just until it stops."

Water fell from the sky—and not in random drops anymore. She looked down the street in the direction from which she expected her father to come. Grady was right. If her Daddy was drunk, it could be a while before he showed up; and if he wasn't, the scenario would end in one of two ways: He'd box her ears for being so stupid as to sit soaking in the rain or he'd honk his horn impatiently and box her ears for making him wait while she ran from the gazebo to the truck. There was no winning with her father, so the best she could do would be to get Grady in out of the rain.

She stood, he held out a warm, dry hand to her and they ran together to the gazebo at the top of the small knoll. A lot of good it did them—they were both dripping wet and shivering cold; out of breath, alone, and sexually aroused.

Grady started hunting for something on the ground, dashing out into the rain again to circle the porch until he found it, and then reentered on the other side.

"What are you doing?"

"You'll see. Come stand over here by me." She did. And when she was safe behind him, he took aim and threw a fist-sized rock at the single, pale spotlight in the peak of the roof.

"No!" she said when she realized what he was doing, but too late to stop him. "We can't do that. What if we get caught? That's vandalism." Her bones ached at the thought of her father's reaction.

"Shh." He turned to face her. Enough light from the streetlamps below enabled her to make out his features. He was smiling. "First off, we didn't do it. I did it. Second, I know what it's called. And third, I'm a kid. I'm supposed to vandalize things."

She gasped and rose up indignant. "Are you kidding me? Do you know how much trouble you'll be in if anyone finds out? And I *know* your parents won't be happy about it. Your daddy will have you cleaning your barn with a toothbrush, he'll be so mad."

"Are you worried about me?"

"Of course, I'm . . . no. I'm . . . What if some little kid comes up here and cuts himself on it?"

"I'll sweep it up before school tomorrow."

"And replace the bulb?"

"Um, probably not. If you keep your job at the pawnshop, which you most likely will, I could go broke breaking and replacing the lightbulbs up here."

A half-startled, half-bemused laugh escaped her. "You're going to come every night?"

"Yep."

"You're crazy, Grady Steadman."

"I am, Hannah Benson. About you."

She shook her head. She didn't get it. She couldn't help the way she felt about him—Grady could charm paint off walls. But why he'd pick her out of all the girls in Clearfield was a mystery he'd no doubt take to his grave.

She walked back to the gazebo's entrance that was closest to Main Street, looked down through the rain at the bench under the streetlamp where she should have been sitting. It looked like a lonely place in the drizzle and dark, and yet for her, every night, she knew it would become a warm and magical place that would also become the focal point of her days. She'd never been this excited about anything or more confidant of an outcome because she'd never believed in anyone as whole-heartedly as she did Grady Steadman.

He moved up behind her. He spoke soft and breathy in her ear. "Please, Hannah. Aren't you ever going to let me kiss you? Don't you want me to?"

"I do. More than anything." She turned to face him. "But . . . I don't know what to do. I don't know how."

"Yes, you do. It's easy."

"No. I don't. And you'll laugh at me."

"I won't. I never will. I'll teach you. And I'll go slow."

She swallowed hard and hoped he couldn't hear how frightened it made her sound. He carefully slipped her backpack off her shoulders and placed it lightly on the floor. He stood tall, several inches taller than she, and slipped his fingers around hers at their sides. He shook them a little.

"Relax. It doesn't hurt and I'll stop whenever you say."

She took a deep breath and let it out, shifted her weight and nodded.

"Ready?" Another nod. She'd come to know his expressions over the past few months—the subtle difference in his grin when he was teasing her and when he was simply enjoying something funny. The smiles he used when he was content and happy or glad to see her—and this one, which appeared to be filled with restrained emotions that tore at her to give in to him.

He released her left hand and used his fingers to smooth back wet tendrils of hair from her face; to thumb rain from her cheek and chin and to tip her head back, then cradle it in his palm.

Her heart beat so hard and so fast, she felt faint. The gazebo began to weave and spin.

"Close your eyes," he murmured . . . then a breath from a mere brush of his lips and he stopped, waited, then set them warm and soft on hers. Sweet and tingly. "Now you do it."

She got heady when his lips quivered under the sweep of hers; their fingers clenched tighter between them when she pulled her lips from his. He sipped at her lower lip and his body grew tense when she returned the favor, slow and deliberate.

"Are you sure you've never done this before?" His voice was thick as he tried to pepper his reaction to her with humor.

She came up on her toes to practice on his upper lip, then both, and then his lower lip again. She thrilled at the soft moan in his throat as he drew their entwined fingers up behind her back and held her head steady. "Open your mouth for me, Hannah."

She did, to ask why, but he swooped in and covered her mouth with his, his tongue darting in and out, sweeping as he drained the air from her lungs. She went reeling—mind and body—using her left arm to cling to him as his right hand reached out to grab a support post on the gazebo. He freed her hands to hold her tighter against him—she was inclined to help him out. She wrapped her arms around his neck and traced the shape of his lips with the tip of her tongue. She felt his fingers form fists in her wool coat.

Falling back against the support post when her legs grew weak she delighted in the feel of his weight against her to keep her upright, to keep him near, to give them more time to torment each other this way. She loved kissing him—loved his smell and taste, the feel of his lips and his tongue and his skin. And she was good at it. She could tell by his reactions—his breathing, his tense trembling, his hunger for more.

"Okay." The abrupt stop left her confused and throbbing inside, though he continued to hold her and didn't move away. They were both breathless and weak. "That's . . . some first lesson."

"Yeah," she said, her cheek just below his shoulder. "I think I'm a natural born kisser."

His chest vibrated with soft laughter. "I think we've finally found something we can agree on."

"Don't you agree? . . . Hannah?" Biscuit's voice yanked her back to the present.

"What?" She glanced from the boy to Grady to see if he'd noticed that she'd checked out for a couple seconds, but he was busy looking . . . she peeked back at the track . . . at the *third* runner in Anna's relay. Her gaze moved back to Biscuit. "What? Sorry, I was . . . watching."

"I said that it looks like Ripley's whole strategy is based on beating Anna in the last leg. They put both their fastest runners in the back, but I don't think either one of them will catch up with the head start she's got."

"Trudy and the girls set her up beautifully," Grady said, with no little pride for all four.

They all watched in silence as Anna took her place on the track, waited, ran a second or two with her teammate to receive the baton and took off at a steady pace less than a quarter of a track ahead of the runner from Ripley. The first lap was uneventful; Ripley lagged behind as expected. But soon after their second and final lap started, the Ripley runner started to surge ahead and the distance between them shortened, but only for a second or two. As if she had eyes in the back of her head Anna stepped up her pace as well, made up the original distance and crossed the finish line more than half a track ahead.

Their whooping and cheering filled the stands—who needed more spectators?

The runners and their friends stood, looking anxious and waiting.

"What's happening?" She got to her feet and stood with them. "What are we waiting for? We did win, didn't we?"

"We sure did." Grady stayed calm and remained seated. "Now we wait to see the times. Each girl's time for her laps, and the overall time to see if we broke Ripley's relay record."

The four girls presented different reactions that were easy to read—a satisfied nod, a victorious fist in the air, a happy dance, and Anna's wide grin.

"Yes!" Lucy squealed, while Cal laughed and his friend used his thumb and index finger to make a loud piercing whistle.

"They broke the record?"

"Yes. Yes."

Almost in unison they stepped down to the next bleacher, heading for the track.

"Wait. Wait a second." They turned to Hannah impatiently. "I might not see you again without Anna around. I wanted to invite you all over to May and Don James's house for a little surprise birthday party for Anna tomorrow evening. They turned their whole house over to me and said, Have at it . . . so I have." Her laugh was nervous; their expressions dubious. What did she know about birthday parties except for what the caterer told her? "If it doesn't rain we'll barbecue outside, if it does we'll do something else inside." Or so said the event planner from Anytime Party.

"Sounds great," Grady said, nodding at his kids enthusiastically. They wagged their heads in passive agreement.

"Don't forget it's a surprise. Maybe you could invite a few of her other friends? The whole track team if you think she'd want that. Her birthday isn't until Thursday, of course, but I thought we could celebrate here with her friends this week-end, and then if it's okay with you"—she looked at Grady and then at Lucy—"and if you'd like to, the three of us can go to Baltimore next weekend. See her new room. Eat out. Do some shopping. What do you think?"

Lucy gave her now famous whatever shrug and turned to go. It was hard to tell by the modicum of anticipation displayed by the teens if the party was a good idea or not, but they were polite and said they'd help with invitations.

She looked to Grady for reassurance after they'd hopped down off the bleachers to stand beside the fence that circled the field.

"They're screaming inside they're so excited."

"Amazing. Such control."

"They do it for us. So that every time we actually do make them happy or do something right, it doesn't go to our head. This way it's all a mystery and we're kept busy guessing."

"Your Book of Dad again?"

"Absolutely."

He kept her amused for the next forty-five minutes to an hour with wise and humorous lessons he'd compiled over the years—and then it was time for Anna to run her 1600 meters. The whole thing took less than five minutes, starting out as she expected—Anna running with the four other runners until af-ter the first lap when her legs began to devour the track a little faster and faster until she was so far ahead of the others that the race was almost boring.

Almost.

Anna had clearly *mopped the floor* with the Ripley runners as she—and everyone else from Clearfield—had planned. From above, Hannah watched Cal push restless hands into his back pockets and his sister fidget anxiously while Biscuit yelled, "Time. Time. What's her time?" at the keeper.

However, both teams cheered when the results were announced.

"4:39.58"

"Well, what the hell does that mean?"

Truly. She needed to get a book on this sport. It was frustrating to know nothing about it and have to depend on others to explain it before she could cheer or commiserate. She clapped and tried to look as happy and proud as Grady was.

"Well, she shaved a little time off her personal best of 4:40.68, but she didn't break Ripley's record of 4:38.15. She did a fantastic job."

Chapter Fifteen

So maybe *Have at it* were not the best three words to pass on to the caterer for Anna's birthday party.

The open-ended invitation might not have been wise, either.

Perhaps it was an omen when the cute, bouncy, cheerleaderlike woman was thirty-eight minutes late that morning to be let into the house and shown around—before aunt left to join niece, et al., at the farm to see if she could get any work done before it was time to come back, dress up, and greet guests just as the sun began to set.

Possibly a fast-food dinner and a bakery cake would have been the way to go as Anna was, so far, a girl of simple tastes . . .

But Hannah was excited. This was the beginning of all the wonderful things she could give Anna, all the fun things they would share, all the memories they'd make together. It was her time to shine as a new *parental unit,* as Biscuit would say, and she wanted everything to be special—she wanted it to be momentous, something they'd never forget . . .

"What the holy hell is going on here?" she asked when she could make her way past the tables and stage under all the colorful paper lanterns, around the Polynesian torches and Tiki poles to the raffia-skirted tables covered with strange-looking food to the chirpy blond caterer—already dressed in a colorful yellow-and-white-tank muumuu and white orchid lei.

She clapped and smiled fanatically. "Oh, I'm so happy you're back on time. Everything is nearly ready—"

"Are you out of your mind?" Lyndsey Makel from Anytime Party and Catering had come with two excellent references from personal business associates of Joe's in Charlottesville, and her boss swore that if he were throwing a party for his own daughter, she's the one he would ask. But Hannah still had to ask—"Are you nuts? This is a birthday party for a sixteen-year-old, not a . . . ah . . ."

Her attention hooked on and was reeled in by a very large brown-skinned, shirtless man in a blue hibiscus-print pareo and flip-flops holding a large bag of water in each hand—in which fat gold-and-red koi floated. Open-mouthed, she watched as he lumbered to the side of the house where she noticed—now—water cascading over a stack of smooth river rocks that reached as high as the end of the front porch and flowed into a gurgling stone basin that spilled into a ground-level pond big enough to block off access to the backyard. Once there, the man stooped and carefully freed the fish into the pool.

At the other end of the house, the path to the small grassy backyard was obstructed by a mound of dirt.

"Both are incredibly realistic plastic," Lyndsey said with a casual wave of her hand after noting her expression—*aghast,* if it were a true reflection of her thoughts—"Not to worry."

"What . . . what happened to the *little backyard celebration* we discussed?"

"I tried to call you," she said, still smiling. "Twice, but I went straight to voice mail."

Automatically, Hannah reached into the front pocket of her

jeans for her cell. "We had a little problem with our *imu* and—"

"Your what?" Her phone was dead . . . or off. For some reason she shook it to see if it was broken. Something, somewhere was definitely broken.

" . . . and even a midsized pig takes six to eight hours to steam cook properly, so we had to go ahead and make the decision to move everything to the front yard or it wouldn't be done on time for the party. But don't you worry about a thing now because we are fully insured for exactly this sort of thing."

"What sort of thing?" Dread filled her chest like a rain cloud.

"Careless accidents. They happen all the time, you know."

"Careless accident." Her temples started to throb.

"Oh." She laughed. "My moving crew accidentally knocked our makeshift imu into one of the smaller windows in back. Cracked it, nothing serious, and we'll have it repaired first thing Monday morning."

"Makeshift imu . . . a big plastic bird?"

Lyndsey's laughter was nerve piercing. "No, no. That's *emu* with an *e*. This is *imu* with an *i*." No discernible difference in pronunciation was detected. She pointed to the mound of plastic dirt to their left. "There. A Hawaiian underground oven? To steam the pig? But of course we can't just dig holes in people's yards so we were fortunate enough to find this oven and with a little creative thinking . . . Voilà! Our imu. It works fabulously. And I've had other planners ask where we got it, but you couldn't pry that out of me with a dozen cheese knives. And most people don't know the difference anyway unless they've actually been to Hawaii . . . or maybe if they read a lot . . .

"But anyway, the window? Not attractive. And you know, we don't always have a second site to set up like we did here. And to tell you the truth"—she finally took a breath and cast a satisfied glance around at her work—"I think this is a much

better venue anyway. It's bigger. There's more permanent veg-
etation to back up what I brought with me . . ."

That's when Hannah noticed the palm trees—twelve feet
tall if they were an inch—in huge decorative pots set about
the James's front lawn. Shocking yellow Birds of Paradise
nested artfully in May's pink and white azalea bushes; hibiscus
bloomed in various bright colors in small trees and floated in
bowls on the tables.

The blood in her head began to drain from her face as she
realized what she was hearing and seeing. A broken window.
A steaming pig. Real koi in a plastic waterfall/pool. The little
backyard celebration she'd ordered for Anna's birthday was going to cost her a fortune in flowers alone . . . and there was
a giant blue-and-yellow macaw sidling across the front porch
banister, bobbing its head and picking at the island grass and
seashell garland hanging thereon.

Her knees went a little weak so she slid into one of the
bamboo folding chairs at the closest table. She was afraid to
ask, "Inside?"

"Well, I didn't do much in there since we lucked out with
such nice weather for an April party, and we want to keep the
guests . . . especially the teenagers . . . outside and watching the
entertainment, so we've barricaded the entrance to the second
floor with a tasteful screen that we've found most people respect quite well and made the downstairs restroom available on
a first-come, first-serve basis. The kitchen is a little dream, and
with this side entrance it's made everything so convenient for
us. So all we needed after that was a place to put the costumes."

"Costumes?"

"Not mandatory, of course, but for the guests who come
and didn't realize there was a Hawaiian theme . . ." *Or a small
backyard celebration theme?* she wanted to ask as the space beside her left eyebrow began to twitch. *With paper BBQ bibs,*

perhaps? . . . "So many of them will want to join the festivities with a bright shirt or a lovely muumuu. For those who are interested, one of the dancers gives a short demonstration on the many ways to tie a pareo . . . or a sarong, if you will, but for you I've—"

"Dancers?"

She laughed—gaily. "What's a luau without dancers? And not just any dancers. I learned the hard way that hula dancing is a complex art form and even minor errors in the movements could invalidate the performance, bring bad luck, or even have dire consequences to the person being honored."

"You're kidding me." And she wasn't in a mood to be kidded.

So it was a good thing Lyndsey answered, "No. I'm serious. I'd rather skip the dancers altogether than use even one that's trained poorly." Her eyes grew large and sparkled with joy. "Lucky for us, I got three of the best for tonight. They will honor your niece and wish her great happiness, plus we have the five koi there for strength, power, and good luck. So much of what the Hawaiians do is symbolic and filled with traditions, which is why it's so much more fun than, say, a Hannah Montana– or Jonas Brothers–themed party . . . and yet so less complicated than a Jurassic Park or a December 21, 2012, theme—I've had to do both."

"For sixteen-year-olds?"

"Oh sure, though we do focus primarily on the college kids, of course, Charlottesville being the home of the Mighty Wahoo's and UVA having some of the best sorority and frat houses in the country. I'm a Lambda Kappa Gamma myself," she confided. "Great kids. Which reminds me, where's yours? She needs to get ready." She took a closer look at Hannah and winced. "You both do."

"She's at her friend Lucy's house. This is supposed to be a surprise and Lucy said it's lame anyway to be standing around waiting to see if people show up at your party if you don't have to, so I was sent ahead to be lame alone since the party was my idea. They'll come a little later . . . but I—I think they're going to clean up at Lucy's because the last time I saw her she was as filthy as I am." She stood and took yet another look around. The only parties she'd ever been to were Christmas parties, where the theme was, traditionally, Christmas. Besides, her niece would only turn sixteen once, right? "I came back a little earlier than I planned to. I was eager to see everything and make sure it was perfect, which . . . which you seemed to have done, um, quite nicely . . . and see the look on Anna's face; take pictures, that sort of thing."

Isn't that what a real parent would do? She felt so out of it already, she couldn't bring herself to ask Lyndsey the question. Instead she let herself get swept up in the last-minute bustle and was hustled off to clean up and change clothes. Lyndsey's orders.

Lyndsey, who apparently thought her too dumbstruck to follow her simple instructions, was waiting in the hall when she came out of the bathroom in her terry robe.

"I would give at least one of my limbs to be able to wear my hair in that short, feathery style around my face like that, but my eyes are too close together and my chin is too pointed to pull it off the way you do. Best of all it only takes a second to dry, I bet. Now I hope you don't mind that I took the liberty of picking out a dress for you." She picked up the long red cotton dress Hannah had seen on the bed earlier—a simple ruffled shoulder dress she thought she could handle for one night. "I guessed at your size, but I have a couple others we can choose from if we need to—but this is the prettiest if you ask me, and with your coloring . . . well, it never hurts to be beautiful, right? And there's a similar dress in your niece's room in a fabulous blue, but she may want to go with a sarong with her friends . . . or another style muumuu she's more comfortable with." She paused to breathe. "What are you waiting for? Time is passing and I still have things to do."

"I can dress myself."

"Of course you can, but I want everything and everyone to be as perfect as you. Now, it's still a little early in the season to be going barefoot, so unless you have some sort of shoes that are appropriate we provide little scuffs, or flip-flops if you prefer them, though I think the scuff would go better with the dress. And while I usually recommend to my friends that they moisturize, moisturize, moisturize, tonight you should skip your throat and décolletage until later so you don't ruin the flowers in your lei before the night is over."

Caught in the eye of Hurricane Lyndsey, Hannah flipped on her hair dryer, hoping for a little peace in which to collect her thoughts. Her anxiety gave way to amusement when the party planner began to shout, over the dryer's wind, the special ingredients to the various foods on the festive menu, which included kalua pork, poke, poi, lomi salmon, opihi, and white cake with haupia for the birthday dessert.

"It's fabulous!" she screamed when the air died and, grinning, Hannah started on her makeup. "Not too much now. Simple elegance is what we're aiming for, and that was you when you got here in your dusty old jeans and—" Hannah turned from the mirror above the low chest of drawers to face her. "Yes. Perfect. Now let me help you with this dress. It's no wonder they use this style so often for Hawaiian weddings— it's so elegant, even in plain old cotton like this. So plain with the simple ruffles at the shoulders to dress it up and yet it looks like a million bucks. Oh, yes. Don't you think so? You look lovely."

She turned back to the mirror and while she might not go as far as a million bucks, she didn't think Anna would be embarrassed to introduce her to her friends.

"Thank you. This is very nice." Then she made the mistake of asking, "Simple hoop earrings, too?"

Lyndsey sighed and forced a smile . . . though Hannah saw her roll her eyes as she turned toward the bed and opened the box lying on it. The room swamped with an exotic sweet floral smell as she pulled out a magnificent white-and-red lei and draped it over Hannah's shoulders.

"Wow."

"I know. White tuberose and tiny red rosebuds. I think I've outdone myself this time."

"Me, too." On Anna's party and on Hannah's *costume*. Granted, times were different than when she was sixteen, and of course the situation was entirely dissimilar, but throwing a party like this for Anna was beyond her wildest imaginings. "I appreciate it. All of it. Thank you."

"I'm not finished. This one's a special order." She made a little hoopla of coming up with a second, smaller flower box and extracting a solitary blood red hibiscus, which she tucked behind Hannah's right ear. They both looked in the mirror and nodded approval—it was like a Hawaiian tiara.

"Special order. You mean someone sent it to me? Like a hostess gift."

That Grady. . . .

Lyndsey grinned eloquently. "You only get a flower for behind your right ear for one reason. And a big, bright one like that is practically screaming it."

"What? Screaming what?"

"That you're single and ready for romance and marriage."

Her arm swung up to attack the flower but Lyndsey caught her wrist.

"Who sent it?"

Shaking the aggression out of Hannah's hand the woman reached in the small box and withdrew the card. "It says *Wear it. Love, Joe.* Is this someone who wants to be your boyfriend? Or is he a boyfriend who wants to talk marriage?"

"He's the pain in my ass who wants me to find someone and live happily ever after."

"Well, the way you look tonight that very well might happen. Now, I've got several more things to do so if you don't need me any longer I'm going to leave you. Come down any time in the next fifteen to twenty minutes. We serve fruit punch to the teens, but there's beer in the kitchen if you'd like. You look great. So relax and enjoy the party and . . . let me know if you need anything."

"Thank you. I will."

Lyndsey left, creating a vacuum of silence and stillness in the room that made Hannah incredibly nervous—like waiting for the other shoe to drop or like lighting the fuse and waiting for the explosion. You begin to wonder if the fuse fizzled out or if it was wired incorrectly; if the explosive got wet or if everything is fine and you simply need to be patient one or two seconds longer.

Anna would be the other shoe, the explosion . . . or the atomic meltdown if this wasn't something she wanted. With one last glance in the mirror, she hesitated and then freed the bloom from behind her ear. "Very subtle, Joe, but it's the last thing in the world I need right now."

She couldn't toss it in the trash—too pricey—so she'd float it in one of the table bowls in the front yard with the others, the cost of which she wouldn't think about.

"Daddy? Where are you?"

"I'm here, baby," Grady said, responding to the panic in

Lucy's voice—grabbing his keys and heading for his front door. Chest tight. Adrenaline pumping. "Where are you?"

"Anna's party. Why aren't you here?"

His steps slowed but his heart continued to race. "Oh. I thought I'd stop by later for some cake. I didn't want to put a damper on all the fun."

"No, I mean, why aren't you here with the other cops?"

"What other cops?"

"That new Deputy Jenx and Freddy Murphy."

"Don't call him Freddy, honey, he doesn't like it."

"Oh, yeah . . . well, shutting down Anna's party and arresting the neighbors and half the kids from the high school seems like a real Freddy thing to do, if you ask me."

"What's he doing?" Grady's staff consisted of ten full-time deputies and nine part-time. Fred Murphy was full-time, sensible, and trustworthy, which is why he'd partnered him with the new deputy—to show him around and teach him the ropes. "Are you okay?"

"No. I'm not okay. They're ruining Anna's party . . . not that it wasn't way weird to begin with, but Anna didn't want to hurt Hannah's feelings because you could tell she'd gone to a lot of trouble. They cooked a pig in the front yard and everything."

"They . . . Why?"

"Then Deputy Jenx said the torches were illegal and wanted to arrest Hannah, but the party lady said they were hers and that the Open Air Burning Guidelines for the Commonwealth of Virginia were being followed to the letter." An involuntary laugh. "She's a piece of work, Dad. The first time the cops came because someone complained about the noise so she went door-to-door inviting all the neighbors over for birthday cake. And they came. We were actually starting to have some fun. The Ripley kids started all the trouble and then the cops showed up again. It wasn't Cal's fault, I swear."

"Cal? Why are there Ripley kids there? Look, I'm right around the corner. Where are you now?"

"Across the street. Hannah said invite anyone who might want to come, and I guess they overheard us talking about it yesterday at the track meet or something because they showed up a couple hours ago, and at first it was okay because we didn't know half the people who showed up anyway but Biscuit said he thought they might have stuff in their cars. You know, like stuff to drink and pot maybe, because they started yelling and saying nasty things to the dancers and . . . Oh! There you are. I see you now."

Grady dragged his gaze from the mingling mob ahead of his cruiser to scan the other side of the street for his daughter. She waved and started walking toward him in a hurry, her slim young body graceful and . . . beautiful in fact, in the colorful sarong that wrapped around her and tied at the back of her neck. He endured a crimp in his heart at this sudden vision of things to come and swallowed the urge in him to command her to stop growing up.

She still talked to him via her cell phone. " . . . I couldn't tell if that guy pushed her first or just said something, but Cal jumped him and Hannah staggered backward . . . he was only trying to help her ask the Ripley kids to leave, but then she tripped on the hem of her dress and fell into one of the fat Hawaiian guys who was carving the pig; he was caught off guard and started tipping forward over the food, waving his big knife around at these two old ladies who showed up from down the block; they screamed, one ran off in one direction and the other one threw her plate of food up in the air, some of it landed on her face and I guess she couldn't see because she bumped into the fat Hawaiian guy again and he finally fell face-first into the middle of the food table and she sort of bounced off him and fell in the fish pond. She's screaming and then suddenly the table with the fat guy and all the food on it falls on the ground and he's yelling and swearing. This all takes about two seconds it seems like," she said to his face as she reached the vehicle and he got out to check her over, make sure she was in fact all right. They both flipped their phones closed and she went on. "Meanwhile, Cal's fighting the Ripley kid who came with friends, so Cal's friends had to step in, too and by the time the cops got here everything was such a mess . . . Anna covered her face and ran inside, up to her room. I think she was crying. I was going to go with her, but when I saw you weren't here . . ."

"It's good you called me, honey." He slipped an arm around her shoulder to comfort her and noted the chill on her skin—and, okay, the amount of skin exposed. "Want my jacket?"

"Mine's inside. I didn't get cold until I left all the fires and the people to call you. And it wasn't a half-bad party . . . well, pretty weird at first but once you got into it, you didn't have to pretend to be having fun anymore. Even Stacie Wymer and Lilliann Ness said they were having fun and they never have fun anywhere. So . . . so don't be too hard on Hannah, okay?"

He looked down at his daughter in surprise. "First off, why would I be hard on Hannah; and second, when did you start defending her?"

She shrugged. "I guess it isn't her fault she's Anna's aunt from Baltimore and, it's like Anna says, 'she's trying.'"

"Yes, she is," he said, planting a proud kiss on the top of her head. "Come on. Let's go see what's going on now."

Together they walked a hundred feet up the street to the back of the crowd. Unwilling to step in unless needed, he assessed the situation quickly. No blood anywhere—that's always a good sign and despite the fact that the James's front yard looked like a typhoon hit it and it was now a . . . a South Pacific disaster area, people were having animated discussions and chuckling among themselves; righting chairs and collecting bowls and plates—some were clearly a moving crew.

Deputies Murphy and Jenx had eight young men, a miserable-looking Cal included, handcuffed and sitting on the curb in two groups of five and three—Ripley kids and Turchen County kids, separating them to keep the peace. Teenagers and a few adults were wandering off to their cars to go home. Some were heading into the house to change their clothes or to get their jackets. Most stopped to speak to someone standing on the porch. An enormous blue and yellow macaw blocked his view of her, but he didn't need to see her to know who it was.

"Sheriff." Fred Murphy, looking confused and concerned, stepped away from the witnesses he was interviewing and came toward him. Lucy made a huffy noise and departed in the opposite direction—hopefully to find her clothes. "Sorry to bring you out on this—"

He stopped when Grady held up his hand. "Not here as the sheriff tonight, Fred. Just a dad . . . and a friend. You seem to have all the hard work done anyway." He motioned with his head to the teens on the curb.

"Yes, sir." Then seeming to recall who Cal was, he stammered. "I—I . . . He . . ."

"I understand, Fred. Treat him like you would anyone else."

"Nobody wants to press charges so I'm going to call their parents to come get them. Sometimes getting the parents out of bed and out here in the streets with their kids is more than just a wakeup call, if you know what I mean."

"I do. It's a good idea. And when all the others have left you can turn mine loose. Is he okay?"

Murphy glanced behind him at Cal, then turned his back more fully so no one could see what he was saying. "Little split on his lip. It's stopped bleeding already. But the guy in the red shirt and his pal in the Grateful Dead T-shirt there are going to remember the feel of his fist in their face for a good long while. I think the one has a broken nose. Ambulance is on its way to check out both of them. Story is Red Shirt said something to the little Benson girl, it's her party by the way . . . well, you know that. Anyway, your boy told him where to go and what to do when he got there and started moving the girl away when Red Shirt sucker-punched him. Then all hell broke loose, I hear. They said that big ass bird over there got upset and was dive bombing people for a while but I have this . . ." he looked at his notebook " . . . Lyndsey Makel, the caterer's word that it won't hurt anyone and it'll calm down when everyone else does . . . which I see it has." He watched the bird bobbing on the front porch railing. "The aunt's over there. She's not taking this too well."

So maybe this wasn't a bad thing after all, he thought, veering off track a little. He'd been wondering how to provoke Hannah's temper since she got here. She'd gone to a great deal of trouble on this party. Beyond the limits of any party he knew of for a teen . . . or an adult for that matter. He imagined she was seriously mad about this—fire-eatin', ass-chewin', head-bashin' mad.

One last glance at Cal caught the boy staring at him, shame-faced and worried. It had to be hell being a sheriff's kid. And Cal was no angel. He'd pushed and tested his limits like any other young man—harder a couple of times because he was the sheriff's son—but certainly not as often or as far as he could have. And part of that refrain, he knew, aside from Cal being a good person in general was in deference to him—to spare him the embarrassment and concern.

Before walking away from Deputy Murphy he scowled

over his shoulder at Cal, then winked at him and watched the tension drain from his posture. They could talk later.

He skirted tables and chairs and stood for a moment to watch two burly men load a palm tree on a tip dolly. Not something you saw everyday in Clearfield.

He nodded to people who spoke to him and patiently listened while the neighbors explained again what they'd seen and how the chaos had progressed to pandemonium. Several were elderly so he made sure the excitement hadn't been too much for them and asked if they needed help getting home.

"I understand you're the sheriff," said a small blond woman in a Hawaiian dress who stepped up to him with a small covered plate with two plastic forks taped to the top. "I'm Lyndsey Makel, events planner for Anytime Party and Catering. Hannah wanted me to save this for you when the crowd started to expand, in case you didn't make it in time: birthday cake for you and your mother.

"Now she's agreed to pay for any damages incurred that our insurance doesn't cover and between the two of us, we've decided we wouldn't know where to start pressing charges against any of the guests . . . I mean, these things happen from time to time . . . more often at the Punk Rock–Heavy Metal karaoke parties, that's true, but anywhere you have raging hormones—"

He showed her his palm to stop her and she stared at it as if she didn't recognize it. "I'm not here in an official capacity tonight. I'm the father of two of the guests and a friend of Anna's . . . and Hannah. I've come to see what I can do to help."

"Oh. Well, we retain a cleanup crew that will handle most of this—"

"I meant, I've come to see if there's anything I can do to make her feel better."

"Oh. That's nice. Anna's upstairs with a—"

"Hannah."

"Oh. Well, I doubt there's much you can do but . . . well, just don't get her started again, okay?"

"Started again?"

"She's very upset."

"Upset?" Once again he had visions of the fire-blue rage in a young girl's eyes as she slammed Josh Greenborn's face into the seat on the bus that long-ago afternoon. "She got violent?"

She frowned. "She said she might be violently ill, but once she started to cry she got over that."

"She cried?" He remembered seeing her cry once, too. He craned his neck to see around the support pillar on the front porch. He curled his toes inside his shoes to keep himself from flying up the steps and taking her into his arms.

Even wretched, she was the most beautiful woman he'd ever seen. Maybe because she was wretched and still smiling at guests and thanking them for coming on their way out of the house. But either way, for the second time that night, his chest filled with emotion and grew tight; adrenaline pumped through his veins and his muscles tensed for action. Yet where his path and actions had been crystal clear to him when his daughter called, this time he felt like a fish out of water, flopping and twisting around on the dock.

"Certainly not like I would have cried, God knows," the blonde went on. "But her eyes got misty, and when Anna ran off I thought she'd lose it for sure, but . . . I think she's holding out for all the guests to leave . . . so be careful."

"Yes, ma'am," he said as they turned away from each other. He spoke to a couple more citizens and then slowly but surely came to the bottom of the steps and looked up at her.

Stunning in the long red Hawaiian dress with the white-and-red lei, her skin smooth and pale, her healthy dark hair tucked behind one ear . . . it was her bare feet that did him in.

Hannah glanced down at him and while the fake but very convincing smile remained on her lips, the armor dropped from her eyes and she connected with her place in his soul as if she'd never been away—as if she instinctively knew she'd be safe there.

"Are you thinking of arresting me, too?" she asked, walking toward him like the goddess Laka or Pele or Hinakuluiau or one of those other goddesses with too many vowels in her name.

He shook his head—something stuck in his throat.

"Then don't speak to me at all. Don't tell me I screwed up." He opened his mouth to contradict her and she stuck her finger in his face—his mother being the only other woman allowed to do so without remark. "And don't try to make me feel better." She reined in her finger self-consciously. "I knew it the moment I saw Anna's face when she got here. I thought it was a little over the top, but Lyndsey assured me it was only a larger version of a small backyard celebration and not the equivalent of a Hawaiian circus that would embarrass and humiliate Anna in front of her friends. Not that it's Lyndsey's fault, at all. I take full responsibility. I gave her no guidelines, no . . . nothing. I just threw my checkbook at her and told her to throw a party and she did. She . . . she's been great . . . aside from the broken window out back and that poor woman who landed in the koi pool, which wasn't her fault either and . . . and the fight, of course, but how do you plan for those sorts of things?"

He glanced down at the thick lei of white and red flowers hanging around her neck and blinked twice as he realized the scent of it was filling his head, blurring his thoughts like smoke from a bonfire would distort his vision. Warm skin on skin, panting breath, power and passion—his mind spiraled.

"And Anna . . . God, she's such a great kid, Grady. So tough.

I would have jumped into that damn pig oven and died if it had been me, but she and Lucy both put on happy faces and tried to make the best of it to spare my feelings. Wholeheartedly, you know? They put on the sarongs, tried the hula lessons . . . ate *poke,* for God's sake." She bobbed her head a little, distracted. "Lucy's hair clashed a little with her pareo but she was great." She refocused; he tried to. "Just great. She's a great kid, Grady. Anna's so lucky to have her. When the fight broke out that stupid bird went berserk, and they were on the porch trying to calm it down and then everything went to hell in slow motion. The bird swooped by my head and I looked over at Anna, her eyes were huge. She was in complete shock"—Hannah sliced the air in front of her with her hands—"everyone was screaming at once—the guy in the food, the lady in the pool, the cops, the bird, Anna's friends, the neighbors . . ." She sighed, deflated. "She just covered her face and ran inside. And I haven't been able to bring myself to face her. How can I possibly apologize for all this? Me, of all people, inflicting this on her. I spent my whole life in this town miserable and ashamed and embarrassed and trying not to draw unwanted attention to myself so I wouldn't stand out like some sort of freak and—"

She stopped abruptly and scanned his face for answers; looked into his eyes for the friendship and support she needed.

"Speak," she said, lowering her gaze, waiting to be castigated. "Tell me what to do."

He pressed his lips together and tried to stop feeling sorry for himself—he regretted, more than he could say, having missed all the action. She needed him now and he wanted to give her the best answer he could.

"The sooner you face her, the sooner you can deal with it and move on. However," he said emphatically, "I can't believe it's going to be as bad as you say. Anna knows you'd never deliberately do anything to hurt her."

And when were *his* doubts on that subject going to abate?

Whenever his gut stopped telling him she was hiding something from him, he reflected, defending his suspicions. He didn't know what it was, couldn't even imagine, but it was there in her eyes like the dark side of a lighthouse beacon.

"You didn't see her face before she ran off. She looked ready to fall apart."

He nodded. He empathized. He hated it when the women in his life cried. It made him feel helpless . . . it made him want to make everything perfect for them. Even when he knew perfect didn't exist.

"Come on." He turned her toward the house, putting his arm around her shoulders but holding her as far away as it allowed to the avoid the fragrance of her and the flowers. "You'll feel better once you get it off your chest. I promise. And I don't think you'll need me, but I'll hang around in case you do. I've got your back, remember?"

Chapter Sixteen

Nodding silently, looking entirely inconsolable, she allowed him to lead her up one step to the next, across the porch, past a couple more guests who thanked her for the party, and into the house. Like a woman facing a French guillotine, she bravely took stair after stair to the second floor and stopped outside the closed door to Anna's room.

He reached out to tap on the door but Hannah grabbed his hand and held it as she leaned in closer and closer to the door to listen. After a moment he did the same . . . to listen and to breath her in again.

He couldn't hear what was being said, but the tone of both girls was weepy and one of them blew her nose; the other said something and the response was muffled with something.

Hannah looked up at him, her true blue eyes welling with tears. He hated it when the women in his life cried.

"Want me to take this one?" he whispered. "I can—"

"No." She straightened her shoulders and took a deep breath. He knew this Hannah—this brave, brave Hannah—and he admired her as much now as he did when he was seventeen. More, actually, knowing what he knew now. "I'll do it."

He stepped back as she rapped lightly at the door.

"Anna? It's Hannah. I . . . I don't know a word big enough or . . . or powerful enough to express to you how truly, truly—"

The door flew open and Anna, tears streaming down her face, flung herself into Hannah's arms, sobbing and gasping for air.

"Oh, God," Hannah muttered holding on tight with one arm and smoothing her hair with the other hand. "Anna, I'm so, so—"

"Aunt Hannah!" the girl wailed between racking sobs. "That was such a great party! Can we do it again next year?"

Shocked, Grady looked around the doorjamb for his daughter, who lay sprawled on the bed, eyes and nose red and puffy, laughing hysterically. He looked back at Hannah's stunned expression as she held her niece at arm's length to connect the tears to the laughter. She couldn't get it to sink in.

"Daddy, you should have been here," Lucy said. "Malcolm snatched off Mr. Mahoney's toupee."

This comment sent Anna into a fresh fit of laughter that made her knees so weak she wrapped her arms around Hannah's neck again.

"Who's Malcolm?" he asked.

"The macaw," she squealed, rolling into her own grand mal of delight.

He watched and waited and at last Hannah's eyes shifted to his, and when he smiled she finally let herself hope. And yet . . .

"I don't understand." She shuffled Anna back into her bedroom and Grady closed the door on the four of them. "What's so funny?"

The girls tried to sober up but would snort laughter out their noses and burst into giggles and hoots all over again. All it took was a word.

"Knife!"

"Table!"

"Fish!"

"Fire!"

"Duck!"

That one got Hannah's attention. "There was no duck out there."

"No," Lucy said tightly, fighting the hilarity. "You ducked. Malcolm swooped off the porch when Mrs. Yates screamed and fell in the water, you ducked and he snatched Mr. Mahoney's toupee right off his head and flew away with it."

"I couldn't stand it anymore." Anna wept with laughter. "I'm sorry I left you to deal with all those people alone but I thought I was going to wet my pants."

"You did wet your pants," Lucy reminded her and they fell helplessly, gleefully into each other's arms.

Their laughter caught like wildfire. Hannah released a reluctant chuckle and then a giggle and then a flat-out laugh as joyful as any he'd ever heard before.

"Did you see poor Lyndsey's face the first time the cops showed up?" She sat on the bed next to Anna. "I thought she was going to blow a fuse."

"I know. Her face got all red and her eyes were bugging out."

"Yeah, Dad." Lucy made room for him on the bed next to her. "You don't want to cross that one. She may look cute and bubbly and all that, but she can get really scary really fast."

He nodded, eyes wide. "I met her. I almost turned around and went home."

The women in his life started laughing again. He leaned back against the foot of the bed listening to more party details, wishing again he hadn't missed so much of it . . . though truth told, it seemed to him like this was the best part of the party anyway.

* * *

The next day, Sunday, dawned sunny and bright and sweet April warm. Aunt and niece faced each other over coffee and a banana-protein milk shake the next morning and decided they couldn't face the farm and all the work that still awaited them there. Hannah would be there all week and they deserved a day off.

They spent the morning slopping around in pajamas and sweats, reading the paper and giggling with friends about the party on their cell phones. Joe, like Anna, was hoping for a reenactment on her seventeenth birthday—and Hannah promised to see what she could do.

The crack in the back laundry-room window was indeed *not attractive.* But all other evidence of the party had been swept away and Lyndsey Makel, Party Planner Extraordinaire as they now called her, said there would be no charge for the koi Mrs. Yates squished when she fell in the pond, and the window would be entirely covered by their business insurance.

Still, after Anna left for church, Hannah called May and Don James to tell them and to apologize, profusely.

They laughed and said they'd already had several calls from neighbors, including Jim Mahoney who wanted his toupee back if anyone found it.

Sighing, Hannah terminated the link on her BlackBerry and held it against her top lip as she thought about people like the James's and . . . well, like most of the people at the party last night. Small-town people. She didn't know who had complained about the noise, but she'd sensed they'd all been happy to join the festivities, happy to wish Anna well.

They were Anna's people.

However, some of them she recognized as people who'd lived in Clearfield all their lives, who had lived there when she lived there; people she knew—if not personally at least by sight. Most had acknowledged that she was a child of Clearfield come home. And while they all knew about it now, part of her was grateful none mentioned the manner in which she'd spent that childhood. But another part of her—unfortunately the greater part—ranted and screamed, "Where were you? Why didn't you help us? How can you look me in the eye and pretend to be forgiven when you never said you were sorry? When you never lifted a finger . . ."

Why hadn't they been her people, too?

She stood and shook her arms and hands to loosen and release the venom building inside. These were the thoughts and feelings she'd gone to therapy for so long to dispel. The conclusion: She would never know or understand why no one helped her or her mother or poor little Ruth. Nor could she take responsibility for their inaction, she knew, though in low moments she suspected it was her basic unworthiness, her worthlessness. But as low as those moments became, her rage surged tenfold in response. She might not have been as sweet and lovable as some children but she was, ultimately, *a child*. Ruth was quiet and gentle and totally adorable and no one had come to help her, either.

Why? *Why?*

Dr. Fry had alluded to the possibility that her inability to make sense of the town's apparent apathy had damaged her capacity to trust; had warped her attitude toward personal relationships. She'd laughed. She'd scoffed. She'd said most people weren't worth her time to begin with . . . but she sensed he was right. How to rectify those flaws was still a bit of a mystery but simply being aware of them was sometimes helpful.

As for the citizens of Clearfield, her favorite explanation was that it was a different time. There were more laws now and a greater public consciousness of child and spousal abuse. But set on a scale with the pain and misery endured in her home all those years, it was a lightweight excuse.

Still, it was all she had. That and the conviction that being solely responsible for herself alone wasn't something she'd tolerate in or around her life ever again.

By Wednesday, Hannah saw that even the most insurmountable looking projects were surmountable with a lot of help and stick-to-itiveness.

The dealers and auctioneers had taken all they wanted; secondhand stores near and far were stuffed to the windowsills with leftover Benson paraphernalia. The recycling center in Charlottesville would, she was sure, be sorry to see the end of Cal's after-school deliveries.

It was a bright sunny day with the barest of breezes blowing the scent of spring through the air like expensive perfume.

With her track season in full swing, Anna went straight home to the James's after practice to start her homework and Hannah met her there at six thirty, or whenever she got tired, for dinner. Cal and Biscuit came faithfully to help her at the farm after school—on Grady's order she suspected, but hopefully with no resentment once she convinced them to let her pay by the hour (they did have a prom coming up). Her friends Sam and Jeremy Long came, too, their mother dropping them off to feed and water their cows and to help, and then picking them up in time for their own chores and homework and supper at home. Even Grady and his mother came from time to time to help when they could but . . . well, eventually there wasn't that much to do anymore.

So she was alone at the farmhouse that day, refusing to feel or acknowledge any qualms at being isolated there. The house was nearly empty now, so in light of the fact that they hadn't unearthed a single skeleton or glimpsed a solitary ghost, it was looking more and more ordinary all the time. More like an empty, rundown old farmhouse with dusty walls and floors and grimy windows . . . which she planned to sic her favorite teens on Saturday. Girls inside, boys outside, she decided, boosting every one she came to wide open.

With no drapes left, the sun filled every room in the house with cheery light—something that made her pause and wonder if there had ever been a Benson living there who might have appreciated such a thing, who took the time to enjoy the feel of the sun on their face. She smiled, closed her eyes, and let the warmth sink into her cheeks—if she wasn't the first, she didn't mind being the last this time.

As each room became emptied out—closets, furniture, rug, everything—she headed in to dust and sweep up the big chunks of debris and then went back to repeat her steps with her mother's canister vacuum and warm soap and water—sucking up cobwebs and dust bunnies the broom scattered and missed; scrubbing the very top shelf in the closet, the light fixtures and anything else that needed it. By the time she finished, the room looked old and faded but clean and tolerable.

She'd finished two of the upstairs bedrooms the day before and another that morning with a huge linen/storage closet. According to her chore list she still had her mother's room and Anna's; and the attic had been reported empty and ready for her down-and-dirty brand of housekeeping.

"Great, I'll take that one," Grady said on hearing this, as if keen to get the cobwebs in his hair. "First thing Saturday morning, it's mine."

But when he wouldn't meet her eyes, she knew it wasn't the project he wanted so much as he wanted to save her the memories, from looking back again on the story she'd told him.

Standing at the bottom of the attic steps, broom and bucket of water in her right hand, the vacuum and its tubing in the other, she smiled at the idea of him trying to save her from her own thoughts.

But the attic was on *her* list, ready for her, and she was on a schedule. She'd have the entire top two floors finished and out of the way *before* Saturday if she stuck to her schedule.

Grady. He was a good man. Always. But he didn't need to protect her—she couldn't afford to let him try for fear he'd come too close to the truth. Still, it was kind of him to make the effort.

So, what sort of insanity did the women in Clearfield share that none of them had persuaded Grady to marry again? Her smile drooped and her brow furrowed. Come to think of it— and she was a little surprised she hadn't before this—there had to be at least one woman in town he . . . associated with. Right? He was still a young man. He had needs . . . urges. Prostitution came to mind but there was the cop thing, and try as she might she simply couldn't picture him paying for sex. The abstinence thing got a disbelieving mumble as she started up the stairs, and that left the last two alternatives: do-it-yourself or friends with benefits—her own answers to the dilemma.

So who was his lady friend? She couldn't help speculating as she came to the top of the stairs and set her cleaning gear down.

She realized she hadn't been in the attic once since returning to Clearfield. She braced herself for a flood of emotion but barely a trickle got through. Maybe because it was empty now and someone had already opened the 18 x 24-inch windows on either end to let in fresh air. Perhaps because she'd come up voluntarily or because she was twenty years older now, hard to tell.

"Okay, then," she spoke out loud, feeling confident. Using the wireless headset to her BlackBerry, she turned up the music and took the broom to the rafters.

She liked music and her taste was diverse—Queen, Sarah McLachlan, Abba, Coldplay, Garth Brooks, Bach, Rogue Wave, Rod Stewart . . . more recently the Jonas Brothers, to have something else in common with Anna. The trouble was that no matter how hip or harmonious the tunes were, they couldn't occupy every corner of her mind, couldn't keep it from wandering off task. And since the passage to the past was bolted and off limits, that left her with only two directions to go . . .

So who was Grady's lady friend? Generation after generation of spiders lost their homes as she reviewed every instance of seeing Grady in public since she came back. She scanned each event mentally for any woman—not his mother, daughter, Anna, or herself—that he'd shown favor to or who had looked at him with longing. Surely, Anna or especially Lucy would have said something about a female friend he was partial to . . .

She sneezed, twice, and rocked her brain back on track.

Thinking about the present or the future didn't involve thinking about Grady. Except for how to avoid him. It was none of her business if he had some mystery woman—who likely lived in a nearby town, most likely Ripley—who he consorted with . . . probably every chance he got!

She gasped and stood statue still until she had her thoughts where they belonged.

The girls. They were excited about their coming weekend in the city, and so was she. They were leaving right after school Friday and they'd be in Baltimore by ten o'clock. The decorator promised to have Anna's room finished by then. Up early the next day for a surprise day of prom-dress shopping, dinner out, and maybe a play if Joe was able to get tickets for them at the last minute. If not, they could always take in a movie. Sunday morning they'd lounge around or do anything the girls chose, then start out around noon and get them back by six thirty or seven o'clock—Hannah loved a good plan, she genuinely did. And the only thing that could go wrong this time would be if they couldn't find dresses they—

She felt more than heard the attic door when it slammed shut. It reverberated and the flow of the breeze in that direction stopped. It startled her. But it would have startled anyone.

She turned off the vacuum and the music and listened for a moment to the silence. The silence—and the chirping of the birds outside. Stepping over the long tubing she went to stand at the top of the stairs and looked straight down at the door— no shadows at the bottom, nothing hiding.

She skipped down the steps to open the door and could feel herself melting like a warm stick of butter when it opened with barely a touch.

She let out one large nervous laugh and it echoed in the hall. Silly. Ridiculous. *But understandable,* she thought, deciding to be kind to her psyche. She roamed in dangerous territory today, but she was okay and she'd stay that way—for Anna, but mostly for herself.

Resolute, she set the attic door wide open again and spun on her heel to go back up the steps. Nearly to the top, reviewing what she had left to do, the door closed with a bang again; a sound so loud it could have been gunfire.

Caught off guard and off balance she slipped on the step, grabbed the left handrail as she bumped her head against the wall, turned and lowered herself to the stair second from the top, her heart beating wildly under her palm. She cursed as soon as she could breathe again.

"Fine. We leave the door closed, then." Shaking her head in resignation, she reached for the 2 x 4 handrail attached to the wall to haul herself up, reaching back with her other hand to push from the top step. That's when she came across the rough grooves on the lip of the stair and let her fingers slip over them like brail. She recognized the code.

Crouching and sitting again she traced the etching with her fingertip and smiled a little—though she wasn't sure why.

Dirty and dusty and old, the etching was barely visible but she remembered it, perfectly.

"Is it true, girl?" Mama was pale and bug-eyed when she opened her eyes, looking up at her from the kitchen floor where her daddy had left her. Her head pounding, she noticed the scarlet mark on her mama's left cheek that was clear evidence of a recent slap. Ruth sat on a chair in the corner, her knees drawn to her chest, her arms holding them tight—she looked like she was trying to make herself so small no one would see her.

The moment she recalled what had happened, her heart sank and dread like thick, black crude oil coursed through her veins.

Buzz Weims told her daddy he'd seen her kissing Grady at school.

"Is it true, Hannah? You been kissing the Steadman boy?"

"What?" Not *what* like she misunderstood, but *what* had gone wrong because they were always so careful—stealing kisses, brushing fingers, they'd become experts at speaking with their eyes; and she always rode the bus home terrified of being seen with him.

Yet in that suspended moment in time, those were her regrets. If she'd known she was going to get caught anyway she would have kissed him every chance she got, held his hand every second of the day and night, and told him all the secrets in her heart without fear or reservation. She loved Grady.

She was a fool. She should have known that it was only a matter of time before their secret came to light. Eighteen months had passed since that first ride in the bed of Grady's truck—she'd pushed her luck too far.

She struggled to her feet only to stagger from another blow to her left cheek that had her blinking through the stinging in her eyes as her mother shouted, "Do not lie to me. Is it true? Did you kiss him?"

"Yes, ma'am."

"Did you . . . he do anything else?"

Some things—like the mating of two souls—were sacred and private . . . and might hurt Grady if anyone else knew.

"No, ma'am. Nothing else," she said without compunction. "We hold hands, we kiss sometimes, mostly we talk."

"You sure? Nothing else?"

"No. Nothing."

"He can take you to a doctor. He can check. He will know."

She'd cross that bridge if she made it over this one. "Nothing else."

Perhaps wanting to believe more than actually be convinced, her mother sighed and stepped closer, put her hands on Hannah's shoulders, scanned her face with troubled eyes. There were always a few strands of hair that escaped her dark braid at the end of the day—tonight there were more than usual—and Mama smoothed them back in place with a shaky hand.

"He . . . he's gone after the boy. I doubt he'll do him any harm. Tell him to stay away, most-like." She glanced over at Ruth. "But I think it best if he don't see you first thing in the door. Neither one of you. You go to your room and stay there," she said to Ruth, who scrambled from her chair to obey. "Take a sandwich. And you," she said, her eyes filled with the hopelessness she felt for her eldest daughter. "I'll say I struck you, again, and sent you up there for the night with no food. I'll say you swore not to see the boy again." She hesitated. "You swear?"

If anything ever happened to Grady because of her . . . the decision was easy.

She nodded. "I swear."

Turning in haste to the refrigerator, her mother opened the crisper on the bottom and removed an apple that had seen better days and stuffed it into Hannah's hand.

"How could you have done such a stupid thing?" A rhetorical question that her mother didn't expect her to answer. She shook her head and motioned with her arm the direction in which to exit. There was nothing left to say . . . no point in making recriminations. It was all in God's hands now—God's and Karl Benson's.

And while she could easily confess to not understanding the ways of God at all, she understood her daddy better than anyone.

He was going to kill her . . . or get as close to it as he legally could, she determined, opening the attic door, stepping inside and closing it behind her like a trained mouse in a maze. She took each step slowly to the top and sat down to await her fate.

She played with the apple for a few minutes then set it aside. Her stomach was too tight to eat now. If she lived through the night she'd eat it in the morning or save it for supper if it looked like she'd be there the entire weekend. The most likely scenario, however, would be its becoming an unexpected treat for the mice.

If she lived through the night she'd run away, she decided—wanting to cry, wishing she could but feeling already dead inside. She'd go to Grady and they could run away together. If she lived and if she ran away, she'd never come back to this place. Never. Not for Mama. Not for Ruth. Not for anyone or anything. If she lived . . .

Inspired, she stood and blindly felt her way to the back of the attic for her emergency stash of a candle and matchbook and lit them. It was hard to tell if it was dark out yet or not—

the windows having long ago been buried in junk to prevent that very thing—but she found what she was looking for and let the candle burn as she returned to the top stair, stepped down twice, and sat again.

For the next however long she had, she used a flat-head screwdriver to scratch and gouge as she picked at and blew on her artwork, at what might be the only permanent evidence that she ever existed after tonight—her name dug into the lip of the top step of the attic in an old farmhouse in Virginia. It wasn't a national monument in her honor but that wasn't the point. That wasn't what she wanted; it wasn't what she deserved.

The point was that she lived. Period. Maybe not for very long but long enough to know real love—something lots of people never knew. Her parents, for instance. Grady taught her about love and trust. She hoped he'd come someday and see her name; that he'd remember her and that she loved him once.

The longer her daddy was gone, the more certain she became of her doom. It meant he was bottlenecked at a bar with Buzz Weims soothing his pride . . . fueling his rage. Still, she didn't pause in her work on the last *N* of her name when she heard his old truck rumble and crunch to its place in the drive outside the back door.

She brushed the last of the scrapings off the wood and used the candle to inspect her work. She heard a door slam closed and glass breaking as she traced it with her fingertips. She blew out the candle and hid it and the matchbook with the apple . . . then wondered why she wasn't trembling with fear. The tightness in her belly remained but it wasn't fear, she realized. She was angry.

"Hannah!" she heard him barking from the first floor. "Come down!"

Her fingers turned to fists. She was going to get the beating of her life for falling in love. He was going to try and ruin the one truly good thing to happen in her life—dirty its innocence, scar its beauty.

"Hannah!"

He was going to take Grady from her. Grady was going to feel responsible for getting her in trouble when he didn't do anything but make her happy.

"Hannah!"

The anger had free reign of her now. She wasn't going to make this easy on him. If her daddy wanted to beat her bad enough, he'd have to stagger up the steps to get her and fight her all the way back down. When he knocked her down, she'd get up again. When he punched her, she wouldn't cry. She'd do her best to stifle her screams to minimize his satisfaction— killing her was going to be a bothersome chore.

"Hannah!" His voice on the second floor, not far from the attic door, made her hammering heart frantic. She scooted up to the top step and pressed her fingers over the name she'd carved in the step. Her name. Hannah Benson . . .

Oh, yes—dirty and dusty and barely visible, she remembered it. She remembered, too, the attic door flying open and her daddy taking the steps two at a time despite his inebriation, grabbing her by her hair and dragging her down two flights of stairs. She recalled trying not to scream and failing; refusing to cry but doing it anyway. Eventually she fell and she couldn't get up again.

After that there was the blur of waking in the darkness, her cheek glued to the kitchen floor with dried blood. And running, running, and falling—coating herself in dirt and dried leaves—running till her lungs were on fire. The look of alarm and horror on Mrs. Steadman's face flooded her with shame . . .

and then the despair, like a giant tsunami, for having forgotten Grady's camping trip. Where else could she go? Who else could she turn to?

The attic door flew open and she gasped, startled.

Grady shrieked.

Chapter Seventeen

"What are you doing?" Hannah shouted even be-
fore she could breathe normally again, scrambling to her feet
and stomping down the steps, taking the offensive. "Trying to
scare me to death? Aren't cops supposed to identify themselves?
Fire two warning shots or something?"

"Are you okay? What happened? You're pale," he said,
backing up, as shaken as she.

"No shit!" She smacked his chest as she slipped by him into
the hall. "You just scared the crap out of me."

"I called your name. I called for you to come down. When
you didn't I . . . What were you doing up there anyway? I told
you I'd clean it on Saturday."

She whipped a rumpled piece of paper from her back pocket
and waved it at him. "It's on my list. See? Third bedroom.
Storage closet. Attic. Last two bedrooms, linen cupboard, and
Anna's track meet tomorrow. The basement on Friday. I'm
on a schedule. I need to get out of this place." He slid into
observant-cop mode; she could see it in his eyes. "I told you.
I have a business to run and getting this place ready to sell is
taking forever."

He studied her. "Are you sure that's all it is? You're sure you're okay?"

"Yes," she said on the tail-end of a calming sigh, realizing she sounded a little hysterical. "I'm fine. I just don't like surprises, is all. So, why are you here?"

A whole minute passed before he held up a paper bag of fast-food and a soft drink. "I knew you'd be out here alone and took a chance that you didn't pack a lunch for yourself."

Now that he mentioned it, and with the familiar scent of burger and fries wafting in her nose, she was starving.

"Okay, I forgive you." She grinned at him and reached for the food.

He snatched it away, smiling back. "It's beautiful out. Go clean up a little and we can have a picnic on the front steps."

Self-conscious of what she must look like she didn't argue, though she did pause at the top of the stairs to say, "By the way, Sheriff, you scream like a girl."

He turned on the steps to catch her teasing expression. "I was hoping you hadn't noticed."

"But I did."

He nodded and looked sheepish. "Then I'll rely on your discretion at election time."

"Or . . ."

"Or?" He looked like it never crossed his mind that he might not be able to count on her. "Or I'll send Lucy to live with you while I hunt for a new job."

The thought of it made her laugh out loud. But while she washed her hands and splashed water on her face, she mulled it over; and by the time she joined Grady on the porch, she was thinking quite differently.

"You know that isn't much of a threat," she said, walking across the porch and sitting down beside him, spreading her lunch out next to his. He looked askance. "Sending Lucy to live with us. Not anymore. I like Lucy. She grows on you like . . . like lichen. Not an ordinary fungus, mind you, but a complicated mix. Intricate and often exquisite. Interesting. Temperamental—vulnerable to environmental disturbances . . . like lichen. She's somebody very special, Grady, and I like her."

Holding his hamburger, feeling both humble and proud, he stared and listened to her remarkable description. Then he nodded to say she wasn't telling him anything new, glanced away and then back with an expression that told her he didn't need her approval but was glad to have it all the same.

"Just remember all that if she reacts badly to the environment in Baltimore this weekend. Are you sure you want to take them both this first time?"

"I think having Lucy there will make it easier on Anna. Don't you? She'll have someone to share it all with . . . and if Anna's unhappy, Lucy won't hesitate to tell me." She chuckled and took a bite of her burger. He still looked worried. "What is it?" she asked. "Is it a murder rate seven times the national average?"—He shook his head—"six times New York, three times L.A.? If I had to, I could probably find documentation of at least one kid who grew up in Baltimore in the last twenty years who's never heard the sound of an AK-47. Or even a handgun."

"Very funny." But thinking about it, he asked, "Have you? Heard gunfire?"

"No, I live in a nice quiet neighborhood." She paused. "Knives and stranglings mostly." She laughed at the droll look on his face. "Isn't where I live part of that background check you were doing on me? Didn't you check to see how many child molesters live on my block?"

She was half teasing and so was half surprised when he answered, "As a matter of fact I did. Did you?"

Her mouth dropped open. "There are pedophiles on my street?"

"I didn't say that. In fact, your background check is clean. You live in a nice middle-class neighborhood. Your neighbors trust you with their pets when they go on vacation. You've never even had a speeding ticket."

Her mouth went dry. This was no friendly burger break. It was an ambush, another interrogation that, stupid and naive, she hadn't expected. She thought he'd begun to trust her, that in these past few weeks she'd won over his suspicions and he'd stopped looking for cracks in her defenses.

Nibbling at her tasteless burger, she tried to chuckle. "You don't have to sound so disappointed."

Shaking his head, he put his sandwich down and wiped his mouth with a napkin, looking her straight in the eyes. "Believe me, I'm not disappointed. I'm . . . confused."

"Confused?" Appetite gone, she stopped pretending to eat. "About what?"

"You."

"Me?"

Nodding, his hazel-green eyes keen and astute, his charming dimples nowhere in sight, he studied her. Probed. Waited.

And the longer she had to gather her defenses, the shakier she felt. Soon she was obliged to go on the offense. "What do you find so confusing about me? The fact that I dug myself out of this hole or the fact that once I did I didn't come back for you? I explained why I couldn't come back and I said I was sorry. If you can't get over it, that's not my problem."

"That's not it and you know it." He wasn't pretending to eat anymore, either. "You're hiding something. I can feel it. Whatever it is, Hannah, I can help. I just want to help."

"You'd be better off helping someone who needs you. And that ain't me."

He shook his head. "I knew it when we spoke at the cemetery the day you arrived. I've been over it a thousand times in my mind—what am I missing? Then it hit me. If you started running that Friday night and never looked back, how'd you know your old man was dead? When I called I told you about your mother and Ruth. You already knew he was dead. How? You didn't ask me. And the first place you went when you got here was the cemetery. Why?"

"To make sure, okay? I went . . . I needed to make sure he was dead." A little truth. A little lie. "I figured I'd be the very last person anyone would call to care for Ruth's child, especially if he was still alive so I simply assumed he was dead. Then I began to imagine a dozen different ways he could still be alive and not involved with Anna so . . . so I called St. John's anonymously about Mama's passing—said I was distant relative. I said I couldn't get in touch with Karl to give him my condolences and the woman told me he'd been dead for twenty years but . . . well, I still needed to be sure. Part of my neurosis, I guess."

Grady listened to her story in silence, revealing nothing of his thoughts—which annoyed her more. "That clear everything up for you, Andy? Feel better? Frankly, I feel cheapened by the fact that you thought you could bribe me with a hamburger and fries. Next time you want to ask me stupid, suspicious questions bring something with a bigger price tag on it."

Furious, she stalked across the porch, flung open the screen door, walked inside, and slammed the door hard enough to make the dust on the floor bounce.

Sighing, leaning back against the door when she heard his cruiser start up, she let her chin hang to her chest and closed her eyes until her pulse slowed. Damn his cunning cop instincts and damn him for catching her off guard. How could she have been so careless? Well, she wouldn't let him throw her. Couldn't. His background check on her was clean and everyone else involved in that night was gone. He couldn't prove a thing.

But that knowledge was of no comfort at the moment because as the anger and fear drained away and her breathing slowed and the silence in the old house closed in around her, she heard a voice from deep inside—a familiar voice; the voice that told her to turn left instead of right, to stop instead of go; the voice that kept her alive. It told her to tell Grady the truth.

It wasn't as hard as she thought it would be to admit that she longed to tell him—to purge her soul and release the memories . . . to Grady. He would listen. He would care. He would accept her as he always had. She was as certain of that as she was that she didn't dare tell him.

There was too much at risk. Anna primarily. Hannah wasn't going to let anything interfere with the little family they were making together. She'd waited too long, wanted it too much to let the dead and buried past rise up to mar it.

Perhaps if Grady was just . . . Grady. But he wasn't. He was Sheriff Steadman with duties and obligations that he promised to fulfill. And worse than the thought of telling him and putting him in the position of denying her custody of Anna and sending her to jail was the contemplation of telling him and having him do nothing—because he still cared for her. It would be freeing herself of an ugly, festering secret and giving it to him to carry.

Well, she still cared, too, so either way telling him plainly would not do.

For the next few hours she let the music on her BlackBerry soothe the wild beast prowling around inside her. And it didn't hurt that she had a dozen other things to think about to push Grady's visit out of her mind—like returning an e-mail pertaining to a client's retirement plan, Anna's next track meet, and an American Academy of Financial Management Workshop she wanted to attend in September in New Orleans. Would it be better to take Anna out of school for a couple days so she could see the sights or leave her with Joe? She thought about setting aside money for this year's bonuses, which she planned to make a little nicer than previous years because of all the help she was getting at the office. And wasn't it nice that the last few reports from Joe put Jim Sauffle in a better light. And prom dresses! Good God, what did she know about prom dresses? That's what saleswomen were for, right? All she had to do was make sure they were . . . appropriate . . . whatever that was for a couple of sixteen-year-olds. She'd have to wing it.

Only slightly off schedule—Anna had a few things to finish up in her room, and Friday did find Hannah in the basement, *as planned,* knocking down the cobwebs and sweeping dirt off the walls but doing little more than pushing the grime around on the floor to no avail. Defeated, she went back upstairs to get the vacuum and a new bag. She was going to need some serious suck here and a new bag would take the old machine up to optimum performance.

There was a single electrical outlet installed at the same time as the solitary light fixture, and it was located directly below it.

Hannah plugged the vacuum in—then yelped and jumped back as sparks flew out at her.

Lots of sparks. For a second it fascinated her to stand and watch them catch on puffs and wisps of dust, burst into flame and then disappear. But suddenly it wasn't merely sparks. Flames curled like fingers around the electrical socket, upward on the dry wood beam behind it.

She reached for the vacuum cord and yanked the plug from the socket but it was too late. Fire scurried up the post to lick at the desiccated floorboards above.

Frantic, Hannah grabbed the damp towel she'd been wiping shelves with and used it to whip at the flames, which only sent them billowing. She doused the rag in the filthy water and tried it again. It served only to annoy the flames and make them burn faster, hotter . . . the basement filled with thick dark smoke as she tossed the last of her scrub water at it.

Popping her earbuds out as she ran—Alan Jackson's "Remember When" is not a firefighting tune—she leaped the steps two at a time, digging in her pocket for her phone as she went.

Halfway to safety through the back door, she recalled that she'd left her purse hanging on the newel post in the hall. She calculated that if the house went up like paper, she'd still have time to fetch her purse and escape via the front door. So she turned and went back into the kitchen, where thin gray smoke was chased by thicker dark smoke up the basement stairs. It billowed then crawled along the ceiling looking for an exit.

The caustic, mixed odor of wire, wood, and rubber burning attacked her nose and throat and she coughed as her eyes stung and watered. Her heart raced as she ran through the kitchen, past the basement door to the hallway beyond, her thoughts focused on snatching her purse and getting out the front door. Which is why she didn't immediately recognize the object hanging on the newel *over* her own purse. Bright red. Heavy-looking. Rectangular. Straps.

"*Oh, God! Anna!*" she screamed when the backpack finally registered. Panic like none she'd known for years and years reached out and squeezed her chest. Glancing at the smoke barreling down the hall toward her, she flew up the steps. "*Anna! Where are you? Anna! Fire!*"

On the second floor she flung open every door, looked in every room, all the while calling Anna's name. She checked the attic, astounded to see a thin haze of a smoke already forming in the rafters.

The acrid stench clawed at her throat and nose. She pulled her T-shirt up to cover them with little relief. There was none at all for her eyes, now streaming with tears—from smoke or fear was a toss-up—and she was too crazed at the moment to care. She screamed for Anna until she thought she might cough blood.

She stopped outside Anna's empty bedroom on the second floor and turned in a circle. What had she missed? Where could she be? Had she already succumbed to the smoke and lay unconscious somewhere?

"Oh please, God," she prayed, deciding to check each room on the second floor one more time before doing the same downstairs. "If You need to take someone today, take me. Please. Let her be okay." Then she prayed that God wouldn't mind that she never called on Him except in times of great need—as a last resort. Though technically, if He really existed, that freed Him up for other people's requests, didn't it? Joe never saw it that way. And being raised Catholic she knew that God was supposed to be everywhere everyday; in her life in everyway but . . . in her house growing up? "If You are out there, please . . . please, keep her safe. Anna!"

She started down the stairs to meet a thick black screen creeping up and realized the whole first floor was filled with it.

"Aunt Hannah?" Her knees went weak with the sound of Anna's voice and she grabbed at the wall and the banister to keep from falling. She took a deep breath and headed down toward her.

"Anna. Where are you? I'm coming down the stairs."

"Aunt Hannah? I'm here. I'm here."

From the first landing Hannah spied a dark figure through smoke so thick and black it might have been something tangible. Anna felt her way along the hall wall, chased by the sinister cloud to the base of the stairs. "Go! Outside. Go now, Anna. I'm coming. I'll be right behind you. Go!"

"What happened? What's burning?"

"Outside! *Now!*"

The door she'd closed against Grady two days ago swung open and late afternoon light cut briefly through the smoke before the top half filled with a new tributary of escaping black smoke. She grabbed both her purse and the backpack on her way out the door, certain that nothing else of value remained inside.

"Are you alone? Is Lucy here, too? Anyone else?" she asked, meeting Anna on the front porch, turning her and all but pushing her down the steps and away from the house. "Why are you here?"

"Teacher workday, early release. I told you Monday at dinner."

"Today's Friday! I don't have enough to think about? You couldn't remind me this morning?" She stuffed the phone she'd been holding in her hand all along back in her pocket for the moment.

"I did remind you. I told you I'd get Cal to drop me off here so I could finish cleaning out my room, and you said 'great.'"

"I did?" She stopped cold. Anna was safe. They were both safe. No doubt it was the clean fresh air washing up her nostrils and filling her lungs that made her feel suddenly euphoric. "You're a great kid, you know that? Reminding me of early release days and helping out and . . ." she glanced up at the black smoke-engulfing house— "Here, take my keys and drive my car down the lane a good safe distance while I get this stupid truck moving."

Anna had taken driver's ed. in school and had a learner's permit but hadn't had much behind-the-wheel practice yet— plus she wasn't allowed to drive alone for three more months. Still, in the face of fire . . .

They met on the gravel road beside the U-Haul some five

hundred feet or more downhill from the fire, sooty-faced and excited. Hannah had her BlackBerry in hand again—punched in 911 before she hesitated, and looked at Anna with joyful mischief in her heart.

"You know," she said, dragging out her words, "I haven't seen any real flames yet, have you?"

Confused at first, Anna was wonderfully quick to catch on. "No, I haven't."

"How do you know a house is really on fire if you don't see any flames?"

Anna looked at the black swell of smoke over the house. "Beats me."

"Maybe we should wait and make good and sure it's on fire before we call the fire department. We don't want them running out here for just a little smoke."

Anna grinned. "I think that's the way Gran would do it."

Hannah nodded. Anna knew Ellen Benson better than anyone; she'd take her word for it. "Okay, then let's sit back here and enjoy the show, shall we?"

Releasing the roll-up door on the U-Haul, they climbed inside and sat, swinging their legs; each lost in their own thoughts for the short time it took for something at the back of the house to explode.

"Whoa!" They both gave a nervous laugh.

"Houston, we have flame."

"Roger that." They watched flames like so many snake tongues striking out of the windows and door to savor the flavor of its meal. They could feel the heat of the fire on the wind. "Guess we better call now before someone else does."

They looked at each other and grimaced without concern when the sirens sounded in the distance—even before Hannah finished dialing.

"Hello? This is Hannah Benson. My mother's house is on

fire . . . No, no. There's no one in the house. Everyone's safe . . . No, no injuries. It's just the house . . . Thank you."

Not three minutes later the trucks—sirens blaring, lights flashing—pulled into the driveway.

First on the scene, the sheriff, who must have seen her from the corner of his eye as he sped by because he skidded to a halt, pulled to her side of the road, and backed up until he almost hit her as two fire engines flew by them toward the house.

Grady was the sort of pale that clashed with his county-khaki uniform—it made him look green and sickly. He marched around to the end of his cruiser and took Hannah by the upper arms, inspected her for wounds and burns, then barked, "Are you okay?"

"Yes. I'm fine. You—"

"Anna?"

"Yes, sir. I'm fine, too."

"What happened?"

"We decided to have a house fire. You didn't happen to bring any marshmallows did you?"

He literally staggered back as if someone had struck him. "What?"

"I said . . ."

"Don't say it again," he said, from behind clenched teeth. The blood sitting heavy in his chest since the moment he'd heard the dispatch, shot to his head; threatened to blow the top straight off. "Did you start this fire on purpose?"

"Of course, I didn't."

"What happened?" he asked again, determined to get a better answer.

"I plugged the vacuum into the socket in the basement and the place went up in smoke."

She slipped a sidelong glance at Anna and muttered, "We had to wait for flames."

Anna made a noise, covered her mouth with her whole hand, and coughed a couple of times while Hannah bowed her head to hide her grin from him.

"Are you on drugs?" He was at a total loss. What else could provoke this sort of behavior? He looked to Anna and back. "Have you been drinking? Do you know what you just did? There are men up there risking their lives to put out this fire you're enjoying so much."

"They don't have to." Looking up the road at the firefighters, the house a black skeleton in flames, he watched her sober. "We don't want it put out. Call them off or . . . or tell them to stand back and let it burn."

"Let it . . . So you did set it on purpose. You said you wanted to burn it down the first day you got here."

"Yes, I did. And so did Anna. And so did my mother. I bet there hasn't been a Benson woman who ever lived in that house who didn't want to burn it down. But I didn't do it on purpose."

She looked at him defiantly. Adding to that the nasty sarcasm and evasion she'd fed him at lunch the other day, he was ready to take her over his knee . . . or shake her or . . .

"You know I can arrest you, right? At the very least you need a demolition permit to burn a house down." While Hannah sputtered at this, he spoke into the microphone on his shoulder.

"Mike?"

"Yeah?" the fire chief came back promptly.

"Containment only. Let it burn."

"Will do. Not much choice."

By the time he turned back to Hannah, she was ready for him.

"Not if it started as an accident, Sheriff."

They caught him off guard, those gas-blue eyes, so hot and intense and . . . beautiful. He stared, desperate to hold on to his anger as he felt himself slipping into them, struggling not to get scorched. Not here, not now anyway.

Hundreds of feet from the house and he could feel the heat on his face, the breath of the fire blowing across his cheeks, the smoke stinging his eyes as Hannah's stare-down continued— the unstoppable force and the immovable object personified. With more control than he ever dreamed he could muster he took her arm, firm but gentle, and turned her away from him to break her spell. She shook out of his hold but let him lead her around the end of the truck to the front, away from Anna.

He inhaled sharp and angry when she turned to face him again, ready to do battle; taking that scrapper's stance that defined her so well.

They both kept their words low but fierce.

"Do not threaten me with jail, Grady. I'll bury you in lawyers and countersuits so fast it'll make your gold star spin."

"Well, that's terrifying, all right, but if I find out you've lied to me again, that this fire was no accident, I will be throwing your lovely ass in jail."

She gasped, incensed. "Leave my ass out of this. And who do you think you are, calling me a liar?"

"I am your worst nightmare, sweetheart. A man with a cage and a key." That worked. He had her attention now. He watched caution and fear creep in around the edges of her bravado. "A real cage downtown and a *sur*-real one right here in my hand."

"What's that supposed to mean?"

"It means you don't have the upper hand anymore with your mysteries and your secrets. It means I'm sick of giving you time to remember that you can trust me. It means I'm tired of waiting for you to tell me the truth— and without it, it means that Anna isn't going anywhere with you."

Instantly, he regretted his words and wanted to take them

back. The look of pain and fear and betrayal on her face was devastating. His frustration had taken him too far. But he'd dealt the cards and now they had to play the game—the pot was enormous. Anna's future. His, too, he realized. He could lose Hannah forever this time.

"But . . . you can't do that. She's my niece."

"I'm her legal guardian. It's in your mother's will."

"I'll contest it."

"Go ahead. I'll use every dime of Anna's share of this farm fighting back. You want that?"

"That's not fair."

He shrugged. "Of course, it is. You give me what I want; I give you what you want. I told you," he said, turning to go, smacking the hood of the truck with one hand—mostly to keep it from touching her stunned and tormented face. "I always fight fair."

Chapter Eighteen

That man could give lessons on being a stubborn, pigheaded, meddling, pompous, inflexible, pigheaded, chauvinistic, infuriating, power-inflated bully," she told Joe Sunday evening, seconds after the hostess left her at Joe's favorite table, in his favorite restaurant, and she'd plopped down in the chair across from him. "I did everything I could think of to get him to give in on this weekend. The girls are furious with him. I didn't tell them all of it, of course, but I did tell them that I'd been planning an extreme day of prom shopping and he'd nixed it—then I turned Lucy loose on him. Apparently, he didn't bat an eye. My sweet Anna tried, so you know how coldhearted he is if he can refuse her. I finally decided it was time to play *really* dirty. I called his mother. I asked her to have a talk with him."

She nodded her thanks to the waiter who poured sparkling water into her glass and stepped away. "She convinced him to let the girls go shopping with me and her, in Charlottesville next weekend, which is cutting it too close to prom; and it's where everyone else will be shopping for their dresses . . . but . . . well, I'll take what I can get."

She'd run out of steam and, at last, took note of the fact that Joe was staring at her.

"What?"

"Hello. How are you? I'm fine, too. You're looking very . . . alive tonight."

She grinned sheepishly. "I forgot to say hello." Not a question, yet he raised his bushy white brows in assent. "I'm sorry. But do you see how crazy he makes me?"

"I do. And the crazy color in your cheeks and that fire in your eyes . . . it becomes you."

"Fire pun intended?"

"Of course." He smiled at her fondly and she started to relax, as she always did in his company. She was safe with Joe, and as the heavy armor she wore behind the shields inside the thick protective walls all began to melt away, she realized how exhausting it was to maintain it all.

"It's good to be home. I've missed you."

His smile came jolly and his dark brown eyes twinkled, like always. This man was her anchor in a sea of confusion and doubt, like always.

"Joe, I'm so mad I could spit. I want to take him to court but that's likely to take the full two years that she has any real need for me. Once she's eighteen . . . plus, I wouldn't win. I'm her aunt but I don't have any experience with kids and Grady's . . . Grady. He always has been. He's one of those people, you know? The ones who always have all the right answers, to everything. How do I fight that?"

He took a fortifying sip of his wine before he answered. "Maybe you shouldn't."

"What?" Hurt overwhelmed surprise. "Give up on Anna?"

"No. Give him what he wants. All he's asking for is truth."

She glowered at him, mulish and petulant—a little like a thwarted child who wants everyone to do things her way. A time-to-time attitude he'd enjoyed and been proud to watch her develop in the years since he met her.

"*Bekl*," he murmured as he reached across the table for her hand. It was a Yiddish endearment said to a small child, but in moments when he was feeling particularly caring and in need of gentleness, he used it on her. The smooth, thin skin of his palm was warm and accepting . . . as always. "I am on your side, you know that. No matter what. I am so proud of the woman you have become." She smiled and remained silent as she could hear the but coming from a mile off. "I know some of your past. The stories still break my heart . . . those you've told me, but more, the ones you haven't."

"But I—"

"No." He squeezed her hand to stop her. "The stories are yours to tell or not. But I can tell that some are . . . not meant to be told. Maybe not yet. Maybe not ever. That's up to you. And if you ever wish to tell me, I will listen. But your past is in the past to me. It is not important to me. I care about what I have seen and felt and learned about you since I met you, which is nothing but good and kind and honorable. You are my friend. My daughter. I love you. But"— he emphasized each word by lightly bumping their clasped hands on the table—"it's important to your sheriff. He needs to put the past to rest as well. And I'm afraid that if you want Anna, you're going to have to tell him this truth he's asking to hear."

"He's imagining—"

"No." Again he squeezed her hand. "Do not pretend. You know it's there. I know it's there. He knows it's there and he's concerned for you . . . for the girl, too, I suspect. You must tell him."

"And if it costs me Anna . . . permanently?"

His bushy white brows almost touched when he frowned. "If that is the case, and the worst comes to be, then at the very least your heart will at last be free." And when he saw how little this consoled her, he smiled. "Although, I've never known anything but good to come from telling the truth."

There's a first time for everything, she thought to say, but she didn't want to be the one to burst Joe's delusional bubble. She gave him a considering nod and channeled their conversation to work and her new schedule since preparing the old farmhouse for sale was now moot.

She was happy to be able to cut his hours back. He would never complain, but he was beginning to look a little ragged around the edges.

And sitting across from him a short time later, watching him eat Italian with his usual gusto, she realized that telling Grady the truth was a can of worms that involved more than just her and Anna. It could tip over onto the insurance business Joe built from scratch—and the five other people who made their livelihoods there.

"You're not eating," Joe pointed out with his usual astuteness. "You don't like it. Is Marcos trying new recipes in the kitchen again, do you think?"

"No. The linguini is great. I'm not very hungry."

He studied her face, read it easily, as only a father could. "You're exhausted. You should go home. We can talk at the office tomorrow."

She shook her head and leaned back in her comfortable chair. "I'm going to sit here and watch you eat. It's very . . . normal and relaxing. And tomorrow I'll bring Chinese takeout over to your place for dinner. I can handle most things at the office by computer. In fact, I think for the next couple of months, until I bring Anna home, I'll cut back to half-weeks and spend long weekends in Clearfield. I can leave at lunchtime on Thursday to catch her track meets and spend Friday night and Saturday with her and leave about lunchtime on Sunday—

that's when she goes to mass anyway. And then phone calls all week . . . we should be fine and you can take up retirement again."

"So that's it. You have a plan and now you're done with me." He used a crust of bread to push pasta onto his fork and attempted to look forlorn. He missed it by a long shot.

She chuckled and took a sip of water. "Hardly. Not for a long, long time yet."

Fun makes time fly. Being busy makes time fly. Together, plus the dread of an upcoming confrontation, puts time in warp speed.

The weekend trip to Charlottesville with Janice Steadman and the girls was more fun than she'd ever had shopping before.

One quick jaunt through the large college town's downtown mall, with its quaint shops and rather unique boutiques, it soon became evident that—thanks to Grady's pigheadedness—their selection was limited. So they all piled back into Hannah's car; and while she drove them on to Richmond, a little further east of Clearfield than Charlottesville was north, Janice called Grady to inform him that Hannah was hijacking them to Nordstrom's. She smirked at the angry squawking leaking from Janice's cell phone, and when the dear lady flipped her phone closed, sighed, and said, "Oh my," Hannah laughed out loud.

"I think he's being silly now, and I told him so in no uncertain terms. Not taking the girls all the way to Baltimore is one thing—though I'm not completely clear on that either—but what difference does it make where we shop for the dresses . . . we're still so close to home?" Hannah shrugged and gave her a quick, ambiguous glance—she liked that his mother thought him nuts. "He said I'm to remind you that he has GPS tracking and to not push your luck."

Hannah rolled her eyes as if she found his threats boring, and then her gaze settled on the rearview mirror and her niece's keen blue eyes watching her with interest. She winked and Anna sent her a small but true smile.

She was careful to take Janice's lead in a price range appropriate for this stage of young female formal wear, and was grateful the dear lady was open to visiting some of the other more upscale stores in town if for nothing else than to get a feel for the trendier styles. She talked, of course, relentlessly but she was also an excellent source of motherly know-how in regard to hems and bustlines. A little conservative for Lucy's tastes, but that was okay with Hannah.

Eventually, they found a saleswoman eager to help them. The girls giggled and scooted off to the dressing rooms with handfuls of lovely dresses to try on.

Janice stood, clutching her handbag, her arms across her chest. She sighed and went silent for a moment, peacefully waiting . . . and Hannah looked at her. Really looked at her for the first time in . . . probably ever.

She was old, like Joe. Signs of fatigue were etched deeper in her face than earlier in the day and Hannah realized that, without complaint, she'd let herself be hauled all over the Piedmont region of Virginia looking for prom dresses—she had to be exhausted.

With the clerk's help Hannah found padded folding chairs and they settled in, making themselves comfortable for the fashion show to come.

"You're a good sport, Janice Steadman," Hannah said before turning her head to look at her. "In my book you are exactly what a mother ought to be and I think you're a remarkable woman."

Stunned silent and a bit confused, Janice stared back, her eyes old and watery behind big round glasses. "Thank you, dear. That's one of the nicest things anyone has ever said to me." She nodded. "I do my best." She took a deep breath and turned in her chair to face Hannah more head-on. "I usually do what I think is best but . . . I never should have tried to keep your secret that night. I should have dragged you into the house—you were so weak, it would have taken no effort at all. And then I should have called the police, and an ambulance. Calvin and I should have driven over to get your mother and sister and taken them to safety as well. If it weren't for me that night, the next night might have turned out so differently—"

"Janice." Hannah took her hands and held them, shook them a bit to get her to stop talking; to stop her from painting a picture that struck terror in her heart just thinking about it. Had Janice Steadman done anything differently—had Mama or Ruth or she done anything differently—Karl Benson might still be alive today. "Janice. Please." She used the scenario everyone believed to ease the old woman's mind. "My friend Joe is a very smart man and he says there's a reason that things happen the way they do—we might not see the pattern at first, he says, but eventually everything turns out the way it's meant to. What I asked you to do that night was unfair, but by keeping my secret you gave me enough time to hide. You saved my life. And probably Mama and Ruth's as well because if that night and the next hadn't happened exactly the way they did, he would have . . . eventually he would have killed one or all of us. You know that. So, thank you. Thank you for my life."

Weeping now, Janice threw her beefy arms around Hannah and pulled her tight against her big, soft bosom. She smiled and relaxed and faced a pang of jealousy for anyone who got such a hug on a regular basis. Mother-hugs were a precious thing that couldn't be bottled or boxed or given away by anyone with a cold heart.

As fashion shows went, the girls hit all the highs and lows gracefully and in good spirits, trying on a couple of dresses. *Just to see you in one before I die* or to answer a plea to *Just trust me on this one.* But in the end they picked two gowns that couldn't have been more in sync with the girls' personalities than if they'd been made by fairy godmothers.

Thirty minutes before the store closed for the night, Hannah hurried everyone off to lingerie with Janice while she settled the dresses and made a short phone call.

"Where the hell are you?"

"You know where we are. And I just sent the girls and your mother across the way to buy pajamas—on me—because we're spending the night here—also on me. Your mother, possibly the kindest woman I've ever known, is exhausted. Plus we still need shoes. I'll have Lucy call you back after we've checked in somewhere. And . . . and please don't say anything mean to her because we're having a wonderful time—save it for me when we get back tomorrow. That's all. Over and out."

She waited with a grimace on her face, phone in hand, holding her breath, for him to call her right back. And when he didn't she gave him a victorious nod, smirked, and dropped him into her purse—forgotten . . . . for the most part.

The salesclerk accompanied Hannah to the next department to get Janice's signature on the sales slip for Lucy's dress. The nightwear paid for, the four of them straggled out of the store with their feet and lower backs aching; minds numbed by too many choices; hearts light from a critical mission accomplished.

They watched a movie and ate room service in their pajamas, giggling and laughing—another one of those pure girl things so alien to Hannah, she had no idea it was a pure girl thing.

"This was a good idea." She leaned back against the pillows at the head of her bead and grinned at the girls sprawled at her feet. "Even if I do say so myself."

Janice nodded. "It's one of my all-time favorite things to

do. Shopping with the girls. That one"—she motioned to Lucy—"hates department store shopping, but there's a wonderful Goodwill here in town and Anna's a good shopper when her . . . well, when her Gran, your mama, would allow her to come with us." She laughed. "You know, I never thought of it before but maybe we should have swapped girls. Anna could have shopped with me and Lucy could have gone Goodwill Hunting, as she calls it, with Ellen. Bargain hunters, both of them. But I also have a group of gal-pals, ladies I've known for years and years, and we often get away from Clearfield for an overnight to shop." She took her voice down three octaves. "Mostly we like to eat and gossip, but I always manage to spend more money than I mean to."

"I love room service. No dishes." Lucy scratched her head through her bright blue hair and grinned.

"I can't believe the sheriff agreed to it since he sounded so angry this morning when we changed our minds about Charlottesville." The worried glance Anna sent her aunt asked what sort of bargain was struck; what price had Hannah agreed to?

"He didn't say a word when I called him from the store. Was he upset when you called him to tell him where we were, Lucy?"

"Nope. He said thanks for calling, sleep tight, and call again when we head for home tomorrow." She rolled off the bed and disappeared into the adjoining double room to use the restroom.

"See? A perfectly reasonable man." She grinned at Anna. "You don't find that too often."

"Oh no, indeed. My Calvin was an exceptionally patient man and Grady takes after him in that respect. I think it should be mandatory for his profession . . . especially when you hear about police brutality so often in the news now because it truly is a trying profession. I couldn't do it myself. The constant worry and stress . . . it's no wonder they snap, but truly that's not a good enough excuse. It just isn't. I know every time I see . . ."

Hannah was watching Anna as Anna paid polite attention to Janice. From the beginning, she'd been a fool to think she could gather up her niece, all legal and nice, and sneak out of town before anyone noticed anything wrong.

The first time she heard Grady's voice on the phone, she should have hung up. He was the only person in Clearfield who knew her well enough to know she was keeping secrets. And if she hadn't let him tell her about Anna, she never would have known or cared about what she was missing.

But she knew now . . . and he knew . . . and what would Anna think when she knew?

Her heart winced at the thought of disappointing her—and there were so many ways of doing just that that she closed her eyes to disconnect from the confusion in her head and to once again avoid having to make the decision between telling or remaining silent; truth or myth; the possibility of losing Anna or losing her for sure.

She was aware of the comforter from the bed being draped across her shoulders.

"Good night, Aunt Hannah," Anna said softly. "Good night, Mrs. Steadman. Thanks for a great day." Anna's whisper seemed to come from far away.

"Good night, dear." A pause, another whisper. "Anna?"

"Yes, ma'am?"

"Do you know why the sheriff's so angry with your aunt?"

"Not really. They had a big fight the day of the fire . . . sort of about the fire, but not. I mean, I don't think that's what they were actually fighting about. They were only using it as an excuse to fight . . . but it was about something else . . . if that makes any sense."

"It makes a lot of sense when two stubborn people come together."

TWO stubborn people? Hannah tried to open her eyes but they wouldn't budge.

"Do you think they're in love?"

No!

"Dear, I think they've always been in love. Haven't you noticed the way they look at each other?"

Janice, get your eyes checked!

"I have but I thought . . . well, I thought it was because of, you know, before, when they were young. Like they're best friends."

"They are, dear. The very best and truest of friends—that's what love is."

Oh, right!

Hannah strained to hear Anna's response to this but heard nothing.

She thought about jumping out of bed and scolding Janice for feeding that kind of trash to Anna but . . . well, she was tired and she didn't want to say anything she might regret later. She'd sleep on it and think of the right things to say to Janice in the morning. She'd be careful of the way she looked at Grady from now on, too—she suspected she'd have no problem glaring at him a great deal of the time—and she'd put Anna's silly notions to rest as well.

Besides, if she and Grady were the best and truest of friends, if he truly cared, why was he threatening to deny her custody of Anna? Why was he insisting that she dredge up the past and tell him a secret that involved no one still alive except her?

No, the only thing Janice had right was that *Grady* was stubborn—as a rock.

* * *

It drizzled on prom night. Not a lot. Just enough to make the pavement wet and to send the young people dashing for their cars—the girls holding their pretty party dresses up off the ground and their young men chasing with open umbrellas. Giggling and laughing, happy to be free of their pesky adults—ignoring their cameras and the repeated last-minute instructions to be careful, to drive defensively, to call if they get into any sort of trouble or if they were going to be later than expected or if they decide to go for breakfast or . . .

Hannah wrapped herself in a shawl and curled up on the swing on the James's front porch, one bare foot up snug beneath her thigh, the other on the railing to rock her gently. The light of the television flickered from the window on the other side of the steps. Don and May kept the sound on low so all Hannah heard were the noises of the night—crickets and frogs, an owl from somewhere, a car now and then.

She was having what she'd come to identify as a *mother moment*. Actually, they came in various lengths of time in which her heart swelled full to the point of bursting with emotions like amazement and satisfaction and overwhelming luck that somewhere in her past she'd done one thing right . . . or that the stars had aligned in some special way on the day of her birth . . . or that whatever magic had been performed on her had allowed her to have Anna in her life.

And if she was subject to these things like a sweet stinging soreness what must real mothers, birth mothers, feel about their children? And her own mother?

Hannah sighed and pulled the shawl closer. It was obvious that Ellen had loved Anna. Anna wouldn't be Anna if she hadn't grown up feeling the affection she needed to be able to identify it as love, and to pass it on to her friends . . . pass it *back* to her grandmother.

She must have loved Ruth, as well, turning her life around

to raise her alone, taking in her daughter, nursing her until she died.

Hannah sat in the shadows of the James's front porch twisting her mind through the past for one precious memory of her mother saying *I love you* or *I'm proud of you.*

In fact, she didn't realize she had company until a car door slammed.

"I see I missed it." Grady stood halfway up the walk with his hands in the pockets of his windbreaker, his shoulders drooping in defeat. "As Sheriff, I get paid the big bucks and have most evenings off. Unless, of course, I especially want that evening off, then something invariably happens that I have to get involved in because I'm the one who gets paid the bucks, you see."

"That sounds about right to me. Lucky for you, though, you have a mother who took more pictures of the kids than I did. You'll have a digital blow-by-blow account of our little pre-prom party when you get home."

"Is that your way of telling me to leave?"

Was it? "No, of course not." He'd already started walking toward her. "Come up and I'll tell you all about it. Want a beer? I mean, can you have one . . . if you want one? Are you off duty yet?"

He chuckled and settled himself beside her on the swing. His shoulders took up considerable space and his feet on the floor threw her swing rhythm off. She pulled her other leg onto the cushion and sat sideways, facing him, the dim light from the James's TV at his back—he extended his right arm along the back of the swing, angled his big body at her, and started a gentle back-and-forth motion.

It was . . . cozy. Or it might have been under different circumstances.

"I am done for the night but no beer for me, thanks. I just

want to unwind for a minute and then I'll head home. I'm beat." She couldn't see his face in the shadows, but she could hear the fatigue in his voice.

"Bad night?"

"No." He sounded surprised. "A good night. Just a long day."

"Anything you want to talk about?"

He shrugged and tipped his head. "A couple of my deputies got called out on a domestic dispute . . . a neighbor heard screaming and called it in. My guys went in to arrest whoever *wasn't* screaming and walked into a sweet little meth lab . . . methamphetamines."

She nodded. "I watch TV."

"Then you know there's nothing new about them renting rural farmhouses like your mom's, where no one can see them, or even houses inside small communities like Clearfield for a few months. People might be watching, but they buy their supplies and sell their product out of town so no one gets too suspicious. They make as much as they can for as long as they can before they start getting antsy and move on.

"Turns out the couple's not married, of course, and I don't think they were the only ones involved in the operation." He traced the curve of her neck with the side of his index finger—she pulled away but not before her body shivered with warm tingles. "Whoever they were working with is, in all probability, long gone now; but when we ran these two through the system, we found they both had warrants out in Maryland, Ohio, and northern Virginia so, since I don't have the budget for a proper bomb squad, we took a vote and decided to dump the whole thing on the Feds."

"They were making bombs, too?"

"No. They did have quite an arsenal of guns that I was . . . am grateful we didn't walk in on, but no bombs."

"Bomb squad?"

"Oh, right. Sorry." His hand on the swing back moved again; she braced herself but he didn't touch her. She hated being so tuned in to his every movement—it made her jumpy. "Meth labs. They're extremely combustible. Sneeze in one and it can blow up in your face. You need to be really greedy, really desperate for money or really, really stupid to work in one."

"I thought local cops hated the FBI."

"Depends on the cops and the FBI guys. They're good to have around when you need them and they're a pain in the butt when you don't. Aside from being able to handle the meth lab better, they also have more resources for dealing with our perps. Since they're wanted in three states, that automatically makes it a federal case and they'll end up going to a federal prison. Or, and this is more likely to happen, they'll try to turn these two for the names of bigger fish. Remember these are the stupid ones sitting in the combustible meth lab. Someone much higher up on the food chain thinks these two are disposable, and let's face it—there's no point in filling the jails with disposable people."

"Disposable people." Like her. People mothers throw away. People who wander the streets, wash up in gas station restrooms, and beg for food or money. People other people stare at. Lost people. Angry, sad, and sick people. Like her . . . no, like she once was, could still be but for the compassionate hand of Joe Levitz.

Sensing her thoughts, he lowered his voice. "You know as well as anyone that people cling to the hands that are offered to them, whether those hands are good for them or not. You were lucky. But you also made choices, Hannah. Your old man's hands were bad and you ran from them. Joe's hands were good and you stayed. So do you have exceptional survival skills or is there something burning inside you that refuses to allow *anyone* to make you a . . . ah, lesser person, be it a punching bag or a meth-lab chemist?" He took a breath. "The two we locked up tonight are not disposable people. Not to me anyway . . . that's not what my job is about. But they did make their choices."

"Would you like to see the pictures I took of the kids?" She didn't care if he thought the subject change was too abrupt or if it made him suspicious. He clearly thought making choices was a black-or-white thing; that people couldn't ever be pushed or forced into doing something they wouldn't ordinarily do. If he was right, then she was a monster . . . and he'd never let a monster have Anna. More, a monster didn't deserve Anna. He had to be wrong. She chose to believe he was wrong.

"I would." He leaned back and watched while she removed her BlackBerry from her pocket. "Did the Walkers make it over?"

She nodded. "I've met Principal Walker a couple of times at the high school, but Biscuit's mother is charming. I love the way she calls him, *Darlin' Bobby*, with that thick Georgia accent. I could sit and listen to her talk all night. Here. Push with your finger for the next shot, like this."

"She's beautiful."

Hannah nodded her agreement, craning her neck to look over Grady's arm at a picture of Anna in long, flowing lamé chiffon with deep Caribbean charmeuse trim and spaghetti straps—a tall, cool, lovely drink of water. And in the next shots a thirsty-looking Cal gave her flowers for her wrist, gazed down into her adoring eyes with a smile on his lips, and stood dutifully beside her for his grandmother's camera.

Grady released a soft, resigned puff of air through his nose and Hannah pressed her lips together—neither of them feeling the need to comment. They both saw it . . . the young, intense affection blooming between Anna and Cal. They saw it and they both knew the futility of trying to stop it . . . and the inevitable heartache that would follow. He passed his finger across the screen and sucked in air this time.

"Isn't she darling?" She tried to see his expression in the dark as he stared down at a shot of Lucy in a short black halter dress of platinum sequin jersey that sparkled like the billion stars in a night sky every time she moved. Her hose were dark, and on her feet she wore a pair of life-threatening bright red patent leather platform pumps that elevated the top of her head to Biscuit's chin. "We were so surprised when she picked that dress. It didn't look a thing like her the day we tried it on at the store. Your mother kept saying 'It's too ordinary, we'll end up bringing it back,' but Lucy insisted. She had a vision." She chuckled. "Those god-awful shoes and her hair change the whole picture. She's a genius with her hair."

She'd pitched her hair back to one side of the crown and tied it with a shiny red bow that peeked out here and there below pale blond hair tipped in black and platinum . . . well, fairy dust for all anyone knew. She shimmered head to toe like something magical . . . even the light in her eyes was enchanting, if the expression on Biscuit's face was any indication.

Grady said nothing.

"Don't you like it?"

"What, that she's all grown up and going to proms? Hell, no. I hate it." He scanned a couple more pictures and finally gave in. "She looks excited. Happy."

"She was."

"Looks like I need to have a little talk with our friend, Darlin' Bobby, here. What? What's that smile for?"

"I don't know much about parenting, but I do know a little about girls—and Biscuit isn't the one you need to have the talk with. He knows she's young and he calls her jailbait to her face. Plus he's a thinker. He isn't going to do anything to ruin his friendship with Cal or make you angry. Anything more than kissing would be her idea and she'd have to push him pretty hard before he gave in—even then he'd more likely run in the other direction for a while. He isn't stupid. He definitely might kiss her, though, but . . ."

"What?"

"She needs to be kissed. I hope Cal kisses Anna. It's important to girls their age to be kissed by someone special."

"You're speaking from experience?"

Her smile was small and reminiscent as she nodded. "You know I am."

"But wasn't that what got you into trouble that night? Kissing me? Spending time with me? Seeing me behind his back?"

"God, no. Well, yes, technically. But you were just the match that lit that particular fuse. I hope you haven't been feeling guilty all these years because kissing me . . . loving me back then . . . you saved my life. You *gave* me life." She started to speak, closed her mouth, and then started over. "Growing up in a house like that you think, at first, that everyone lives like you and that the fear and the pain are normal so you try to accept it; you push it to the back of your mind and try to ignore it. But then you go to school or to church and you quickly see that you're very different from everyone else. You see in their eyes that they haven't been to the places you have. The other kids don't respond to subtle changes in the teacher's voice or automatically flinch when someone nearby swings their arms in the air. They speak with loud voices, talk back, and scrape their chairs across the floor. They laugh . . . with their mouths open. You wait for someone to twist their arm or pull their hair or lock them in a closet, but no one ever does.

"So then you realize you've been living in hell, that it's not normal, it's not the way all the other kids live, and then you begin to wonder, well, why me? And you begin to hope that maybe if someone knew they'd change things at your house. So you let the teacher see your bruises and she's shocked and sends you to the nurse, who is also appalled and calls your parents—who tell the nurse you fell off the bike you don't own or down the cellar steps or out of a tree and you're sent back to class. And guess what happens when you get home? Your daddy twists your arm so hard it breaks and they take you to the emergency room, and two days later when you still can't hold a pencil because your arm is so swollen, and you think, you hope, the doctor will scold them and tell them not to hurt you anymore, but the doctor gets a different lie and . . ."

She sighed. "Eventually, you learn to accept that your life is the way it is. You don't understand why or what you've done to deserve it but you can't change it because the harder you try the worse it gets. You begin to think that you are as stupid as he says you are because you just can't figure out why the women in your family are so unlovable. Sure we were ugly and worthless but . . . But don't you see that you changed all that for me?"

He shook his head. "I was so self-absorbed. All I thought about was how you made me feel, how I loved being around you, how amazing you were and I was the only one who knew, the only one you *let* know. *I* was the special one. I look back now and see it all so clearly. I hear the things people used to whisper, the things I ignored because I thought they were just gossiping and being mean—things I didn't want to know, I think, because of how it would have changed things between us. I knew you were afraid of him. I knew he was strict. I thought the worst of it would be him grounding you and maybe he'd call and yell at my parents or something. I never would have put you in that kind of danger if I'd taken the time to see the truth."

"I know." She pulled the shawl tight, a defensive maneuver because what she had to say next crossed some mine-infested terrain. "I thought you were another mean trick at first—someone like you wanting to spend time with someone like me. But you were so persistent and gentle and patient . . . I fell in love with you like that." She snapped her fingers.

"Like that?" He snapped his fingers, too. "I seem to recall it taking months and months."

She grinned. "It took that long to learn to let myself trust you; to decide that maybe I *was* someone you could love; that I was someone worth loving." She bowed her head. "And that's what he tried to beat back out of me that night. He could see I was different, that you'd changed me. Every time I picked myself up off the floor, he'd look into my eyes and knock me down again. He saw it and I did nothing to hide it."

"What happened that night, Hannah? Tell me all of it." His voice came from a distance. She scrambled to bring her mind back to the present.

She shook her head. She wasn't going to discuss those details again. "The point I'm trying to make is that if you hadn't made me believe I was someone . . . well, *someone,* I never would have run away that night, or any other night for that matter. Mama, Ruth, and I would have stayed in that house with him for as long as we lived." *Careful! Careful!* "I mean, who knows how much more Mama would have taken? So, um . . . what was my point? Oh. Right. So you see how important kisses can be?" His fingers grazed the back of her neck. "For young people."

"For all people," he murmured, his hand coming to rest on her nape. "Hannah—"

"Grady." It didn't sound like don't-touch-me. "Grady, please. We're different people now. We've changed."

He didn't speak at first but she could feel him studying her face by the light of the James's TV. He swallowed and caressed the side of her neck with his thumb; slid his hand below her ear and did the same to her cheek . . . and then her lower lip. "I admit we've changed. People do. And I like, very much, all the changes you've made." He leaned forward and gave her a brief, soft kiss. "But, you're wrong about one thing. We're not so very different than we were before." He released a sad sigh. His voice was weary. "You're still full of secrets and I'm still waiting for you to trust me."

His disappointment in her was like a piece of wicker furniture she could pick up and drag around the porch—were she so inclined. Instead, she left it sitting, prominent and out of place, as she watched him walk away, blinking back tears and trying to ignore the tight, painful, twisting sensation in her chest and abdomen.

Chapter Nineteen

The frequent April showers brought the May flowers the old adage promised. Clearfield rotated into its green season. Daffodils and tulips gave way to lilacs, dogwoods, and bleeding hearts—and then evening primrose, iris, and poppies. Time, like a giant steamroller, was unstoppable. Days disappeared, week after week, until the end of Anna's school year was only days away.

Grady was either busy or avoiding her; she hadn't seen him since the night of the prom.

Hannah continued to straddle the line between the life she was building for Anna and herself in Baltimore and the life she was trying to bury, finally and forever, in Clearfield.

She hired an excavation crew to dig out and fill in the hole left by the fire and to tumble down two of the three outbuildings. She'd planned to send the barn the same way, but let the realtor talk her out of it—he thought it picturesque.

When back in Baltimore, she'd spend as much time as she could at the office. Going home meant standing in the doorway of the room newly decorated for Anna and wondering if the girl would ever see it. Too much time to think and worry.

She read—*Moby-Dick,* and a mind-blistering book on U.S. government and economics, hoping she wouldn't appear too stupid next year when she and Anna talked about school. Grady would give in and she wanted to be prepared.

He *would* give in.

She never missed a track meet on Thursdays, but Fridays—when Anna ran for practice and her own enjoyment—were more fun. She'd gotten proficient at hearing the tiny little noises she made early in the morning before her weekend runs—the faint beep of her alarm, the light brush of wood on wood as she opened and closed her drawers, barefooted tiptoeing outside her room, and a few minutes later the front door closing softly as she left. More than a few times Hannah would leap from bed to watch her warm up and stretch her muscles in the front yard, always dazzled by her innate elegance . . . amazed by the way she looked so relaxed and comfortable in her skin.

Anna did well at the regional track meet. She came in second in both the 1600- and 3200-meter events, but broke her personal best, in both, by several seconds once again. She was delighted.

And still, with all Hannah had done, all she was doing and all she had yet to do, Grady's ultimatum loomed about her like a tight-fitting coffin—confining her, suffocating her . . . terrifying her. Because no matter how often she told herself that he was bluffing, that it was too unlike him to be so callous, that he would never keep her and Anna apart—there was always the chance that he might. Add to that a distant, niggling hint of a notion that perhaps he should, that she'd never deserved to be so happy in the first place, and the coffin grew tighter.

The Bensons were invited to sit with the Steadmans to watch Cal and Biscuit graduate the last Saturday before school let out for the summer. Hannah and Grady maintained a strained, casual air that didn't dampen the festivities. Likely, it would have taken a great deal more than his feelings for her to subdue his happiness. He appeared so proud of Cal that the only change in his expression throughout was the size of his smile—big and bigger. And after the ceremony while the graduates milled among the spectators, Hannah watched with envy as father and son hugged without hesitation.

Glancing around, she saw that most of the parents and grandparents hugged their children the same way—with abandon. No way could she picture Karl or Ellen hugging her with anything resembling affection but she recalled—vividly—not wanting either of them or anyone else to touch her at all . . . .

"Aack!" Her short gasp for air echoed in the night beyond the gazebo. Her heart went wild. She struggled for her freedom.

"Shhhh." She recognized the whispering voice against her neck. "Jeeze. You are the jumpiest girl I ever met."

"Then don't sneak up on me."

"I like the way it makes your heart race." Grady slid his hand the short distance from her upper arm to her breast above her heart. They were both comfortable with and excited by the move. "It's the only way I can feel it since you won't let me touch you under your clothes."

"That's not true. You said you could feel it when you kiss me."

"Oh. Yeah." She laughed. He was teasing her. He often teased her about having sex but he never pushed her.

They talked about it sometimes. He'd done it. And when she'd asked with whom, he wouldn't say and, for some reason, that had pleased her. It had taken months of gentle patience before she stopped cringing every time he touched her, months almost forgotten now that she was so comfortable in his embrace. He said he loved kissing her. Kissing her made him feel invincible. *Invincible!* And sex would happen when they were both ready. No need to hurry, he said. Though . . . well, some-times they got so worked up kissing that she wanted to climb all over him, consume him, bore into him like a giant Body Snatcher and even then she wasn't sure it would be enough to satisfy the hunger in her. Her skin craved his touch. At times like that, with his arousal pressed hard and tight against her—the mystery of it something that she both feared and delighted in—she knew no greater sense of loss than when he pulled away from her and kept his distance.

Lost and yearning to be touched, by him alone . . .

"Will I see you later, then?"

"What?" Grady stood in front of her, knees bent to be eye-to-eye with her.

"Will I see you at the house later? I have to stop by the of-fice for a few minutes, but I shouldn't be long."

"Yes. I'll be there. Wouldn't miss it."

"Are you all right?"

"Yes, of course. I forgot my sunglasses. The light's giving me a little headache."

"Take something for it." He turned to walk away.

"I will." She watched him grab Biscuit by the back of the neck and shake him fondly; he also got a pleased clap on the upper arm as the Sheriff said something to the Walkers and all four of them laughed. She followed his wake through the crowd. By the time she made it to the young man's side, though, Grady was long gone and the Walkers had been claimed by an-other set of parents.

"Congratulations."

"Thanks. How lame was it?"

"Not at all. It was . . . way awesome." She grinned at Biscuit.

"At least you didn't say *bitchin'*."

She scoffed. "I wouldn't have said that when it *was* cool."

He nodded and tipped his head to one side. "So, I see you and the sheriff are putting on a civil front."

"A . . . why wouldn't we?"

"Rumor has it that since the last day of school is Tuesday, that on Wednesday when you try to take Anna to Baltimore, the sheriff is going to put up roadblocks and arrest you for kidnapping."

"Rumor or Lucy?"

Biscuit shrugged. "Same thing."

"Roadblocks, huh?"

"Well, the other scenario is a high-speed chase halfway to Baltimore, but I don't think you or the sheriff would put Anna through that."

"Thank you for that." She sighed. "I thought Lucy was starting to like me a little."

"She does. You haven't heard the rest of it."

"Do I want to?"

"At the roadblock you break down and cry and tell the sheriff whatever it is he needs to hear; you guys make out; you get married and live happily ever after so she and Anna can be like real sisters then."

"What. Here in Clearfield? Yeah, that's going to happen. And you shouldn't encourage her fantasies." She bumped her shoulder to his upper arm. "They just make reality harder to live with." His parents called to him. Hannah waved and smiled at them. "Will I see you before Wednesday?"

"Sure." He started walking away and spoke over his shoulder. "If not, I'll see you at the roadblock."

"Very funny."

The postgraduation get-together at the Steadmans' was very nice, but she was indeed working on a headache. When the sheriff arrived and continued to treat her with polite indifference—

with a sad, disenchanted expression in his eyes—it escalated to an all-out-throbber and she decided to excuse herself.

"Oh, my." Janice fretted. "Well, stay in the house out of the sun and rest awhile. Let me get you some Tylenol or would you rather have Advil. I have both, but I have no idea what difference it makes if you take one or the other, they both seem to work on headaches."

"Thank you, Janice, but I've already taken some. I think I need to go home and sleep it off. That usually works best for me."

"You have a lot of headaches, do you?" Grady asked, walking up behind her through the open patio door. He made it sound like headaches equaled a guilty conscience.

She turned and spoke quickly. "No. I mean, no more than anyone else. Hardly ever, in fact. Rarely." Somehow she made not having headaches a sign of guilt. "But I did want to congratulate you, both of you, actually. Cal's a great kid, a fine young man. I know you're very proud of him."

Grady nodded his thanks, disappeared into the kitchen for more ice cream and beer, and left the way he'd come in without a second glance at her. Janice, of course, was more gracious.

"Cal reminds me so much of his father, who was very much like his own father. I believe the Steadman men have a very special gene that's passed down from generation to generation . . . like those silly dimples."

Hannah laughed. "Your husband had them, too?"

"Oh my, yes. I can't tell you how many arguments I lost to that smile over the years."

"I can believe it." She went silent for a moment, remembering . . . and when she glanced back at Janice, she could see that the older woman knew where her thoughts had gone.

"I've tried talking to him, Hannah. He's just so stubborn,

I could shake him sometimes. The whole town thinks he's in the wrong."

"The whole town?" That didn't seem likely.

"Everyone I've talked to. They don't want Anna to leave, but they all know she's better off with family."

"Even me?"

"Of course, dear. Who else is there?" She reached out and touched Hannah's arm. "But, you know, you had faith in him once. I believe you can again."

On impulse, without hesitation, she leaned in and hugged the old woman. And with abandon Janice hugged her right back.

More than anything she wanted to believe Janice, but the circumstances *were* different. She couldn't look to him for safety and comfort as she had in the past. Their lives had taken them in different directions. She'd broken the law and he'd sworn to uphold it. Even if he wanted to help her, he couldn't. Not anymore.

Damn her! Grady hotly flipped another burger on the barbeque and tried not to think of the stress he'd seen in Hannah's face— the dark circles under her eyes, the hollow in her cheeks. One look at her and he'd known she wasn't sleeping or eating . . . and that it was his fault.

"Shame on you," his mother hissed angrily at his left elbow.

"What now, Mother?" he snapped back softly. She'd been harping at him for weeks about this mess with Hannah. Rotten thing was: It wouldn't make him half so angry if at least part of him didn't agree with her.

"You know what—and if you hurry you can catch up with her and tell her what a fool you've been and that you're sorry."

He took a deep breath. He was tempted, powerfully. Then he sighed and shook his head.

"I can't. She's keeping something from me."

"How do you know?"

"Because she did it before. When we were kids. I thought it was her distrust of people in general I was fighting but it wasn't. She was hiding what was happening to her at home. From everyone, but from me specifically. And she's doing the same thing now. She's hiding something from me."

"But how do you know you need to know what it is? That's what I want to know. Maybe it's personal. Maybe it's none of your business—not anyone's business but hers."

He went back to flipping the burgers, ignoring his mother until she wandered off to mingle with their guests, sick with the feeling that she was right. He reached for a few hot dogs to add to the grill and stood holding them unopened for what felt like hours as he fought the urge to do exactly what she'd told him to do—go after Hannah. Only the soul-deep conviction that *everything* about Hannah was his business held him in place. Presumptuous, he knew, but he couldn't help it. More than anything he wanted—no, needed—just once, *just one damn time* for her to trust him. Just once.

His chest closed in around his heart, squeezing, and he cursed again. She did trust him. Once. Twenty years ago. She'd let him love her, loved him back; and when she'd needed him most he'd been camping, for God's sake! But he would have been there. He *would* have. He would have done anything he could to help her.

Okay, so he wanted a second chance. And he still didn't think he was asking for too much.

He tossed eight dogs on the grill and admitted this was all personal stuff. It shouldn't have anything to do with Anna's custody. Not legally. Except the cop in him sensed trouble—Hannah's secret was big and painful; it was hurting her, he wanted to help.

This time he wanted her to walk away from Clearfield a free woman—no pain, no fear, no ghosts. He owed her that much. And Anna was the only leverage he had.

Traditionally the graduating seniors were allowed to stay out all night and celebrate with their friends, but Janice had warned Hannah to hold firm to Anna's curfew. She was a "firm believer that nothing good ever happens after midnight," and as Hannah lay half awake, listening for Cal's truck to pull up outside her window, she was hard pressed to think of an exception.

Cinderella's clothes disintegrated at midnight. Visitations from spirits, ghosts, demons, and devils are most common after midnight. She once had her right baby toe smashed at a Black Friday Midnight Madness Sale—it hurt long after Christmas. Fevers often peak at midnight—she'd heard that somewhere. *Midnight at the Oasis . . . Midnight at the Oasis . . . Midnight at the Oasis . . .* Ah God, the tune was stuck in her head now. Clearly it was after midnight.

She stuffed her head under her pillow to block out the song but it kept coming. She rolled over on her back and lay, spread-eagle, in her pajamas and stared at the ceiling.

Slowly, like ooze, Grady, Anna, the truth—the consequences of telling and not telling—filled her mind again. She couldn't win. No matter what she did there was no right or good way out that didn't weigh heavily on her future.

At last Cal's truck rumbled down the street and stopped in front of the house. The engine died. When no car door slammed she got up to make sure it was Cal bringing Anna home. She stood mystified for several minutes wondering what could be wrong. Why didn't they get out?

"Oh!" She covered the second half of the word and the giggle that followed with her hand and scrambled back to bed; pushed her face in the pillow and screamed with glee.

"Yes, yes, yes," she whispered in the dark, folding her arms beneath her head.

Kissing or talking, Anna would remember these few minutes after midnight as pure magic. And Hannah refused to be the skeptical, insipid, thirty-six-year-old woman to forecast no future for the young lovers. Not in this day and age. Not if it was a true love. Not if their love was anything like. . . .

Well, circumstances and times were different for her and Grady, weren't they?

Hannah stood up, straightened her sheets, plumped her pillows and laid back down on her right side, her favorite side, looking for sleep. It eluded her most of the night.

Morning came. Anna ran, came home and showered, went to Sunday Mass with May and Don James, and brought her back a homemade sticky bun from the CCD Bake Sale after church—and it barely registered through the foggy haze inside Hannah's head.

"Are you okay?"

"Sure, sweetie. I just didn't sleep very well last night." She tried to muster up some perky. "How about you? Did you have fun last night? Anything you want to share?"

"We had a great time." She started to walk away then turned back. "And thanks. For not waiting up to make sure I got home on time. I mean, I did, but Gran always stayed up and watched TV and it made her tired in church the next day and . . ."

"And it didn't feel like she genuinely trusted you?"

"Yeah, sometimes." Anna shrugged.

"She was probably more worried than distrustful, don't you think?" Hannah felt big inside for giving her mother the benefit of the doubt, but was it worry or distrust last night that kept her company while waiting for Anna to come home? Neither, she decided. She simply hadn't been able to sleep.

"Probably. But thanks anyway."

She said, "You're welcome," but it was another misdirection of the truth, a lie.

It was beginning to feel as if that's all she could do anymore . . . lie.

She went out for a sluggish walk, came back an hour later and tried to settle down with a book while Anna studied for her last biology final the next day.

"What?" She looked up to catch Anna staring at her, a frown creasing her brow.

The girl shrugged and shook her head. "Nothing. Is that my copy of *The Crucible*? I thought I packed it."

"You may have. This is May's copy. I missed a lot of these books when I went to high school. I'm trying to catch up with you."

They discussed the dangers and madness of a group mentality and how important it is to think for oneself and to make one's own decisions. A perfunctory conversation that was quick to wear itself out . . . and yet Anna's brow remained clouded.

"What is it, Anna? Seriously. You look worried about something. Talk to me."

"You are still planning to take me with you to Baltimore on Wednesday, right?"

"Right."

"What about Sheriff Steadman?"

"I think he wants to stay here in Clearfield, for one thing. For another, I don't think–"

"No. I meant, what about what he said? Did you talk to him? Did he say it was okay for you to take me?"

"Lucy, Lucy." She sighed. It didn't matter. "I don't need his okay. I'm your aunt."

"But you do. He's my legal guardian until you adopt me and he can—"

"He won't keep us apart. He's not a cruel man. He's bluffing. He thinks I have some deep dark secret that he's trying to sweat out of me, but once he realizes I have nothing to tell him he's going to look like an idiot for making such a fuss."

"Really?"

"Yes. Really." Anna nodded, gave her a small smile, looked away but continued to knit her brow. "Anna! Stop it. You're fretting about nothing."

"I know. I'm sorry. I can't help it. Lucy says the sheriff told Cal to start boxing up his bedroom because once he leaves for college, I'll be moving into it. They're going to section off a space in the garage for him when he visits. I don't want him staying in the garage when he comes home. He'll hate me."

"He won't hate you. He could never hate you; he's crazy about you." There was no enthusiasm to her reassurances . . . she was in far too great a need of her own bolstering. "And the Sheriff only told him to pack his things up because he knew it would get back to me. He's taking this too far . . . making a mountain out of a molehill."

"So there is something to tell?"

"No."

"A mole's hill worth?"

"No." It was annoying and hurtful that Anna was doubtful despite the fact that there was a mountain to tell. She began to wonder if *I have a secret* was tattooed on her forehead. She put her fingers there and rubbed for a moment. "No. Nothing."

Anna nodded and gave her an awkward guilty/forgive-me expression that she couldn't refuse . . . though she also didn't deserve it.

Anna went back to doing her homework and Hannah stared at the same page of *The Crucible* until the words blurred and disappeared.

Less than four months they'd known each other and already she was feeding Anna boldfaced lies. The very foundation of their relationship was a lie. Anna thought her some sort of hero for running away. What would she think if she knew the truth?

Her one regret with Joe was not telling him the entire truth. But it had been easy—an act of self-preservation in fact—to separate her life with him and her life *before* him with a thick black curtain of memory loss.

But she was no longer a child and she wasn't struggling to survive anymore. She was an adult who knew about accepting responsibility for her actions . . . and who planned to teach Anna to do the same.

Christ. That made her a coward and a hypocrite—and their foundation doubly weak.

Maybe Anna was better off with Grady.

The thought made her nauseous with fear and hot along the sides of her neck with anger. It finally occurred to her that she was waiting for one of Joe's miracles and she wished she'd taken them more seriously.

Grady flipped through the Benson murder file once again trying to read it with a fresh eye. It was always the same. And aside from the fact that Hannah had run hard and far and had *not* gone back to the house the night before as everyone had surmised, it was as clear and accurate as he remembered it.

He tossed the folder on his desk and pick up the background check required by the state as part of the child welfare petition for custody of a minor. Nothing suspicious—unless Hannah thought her four years of therapy would count against her. And frankly, knowing even a fraction of what she'd been through, he would have been more concerned if she hadn't had any.

He sighed and tossed that file on the desk with the other, then went to stand at the window, his eyes naturally gravitating to the gazebo on the low knoll. Maybe his mother was right. Maybe whatever Hannah was keeping from him was none of his business. Or at the very least something he had no right to pry out of her by force. Maybe if he could simply let go of it, apologize to her for being a jerk and show her he did indeed trust her, that he believed in her, that he loved her more now than he ever had before—all of which was true—well, then perhaps someday she'd share her secret with him.

Could he handle that? Having faith in someone who didn't completely trust him?

For the long haul? Truthfully? He didn't know, not for sure.

But at the moment, in regard to Anna, he had complete faith in Hannah. And first thing tomorrow he'd take the petition papers over for her to sign. He would say he was sorry and tell her he wouldn't stand in her way with Anna.

That was the best he could do. For now.

She moaned at the first faint scream, knowing even in sleep what was to come as the next one slashed and tore at her. She groaned and automatically turned away as the shrill cries came one after the other like a lunatic's lullaby. Over and over, the shrieking *would not* stop. Her hands shook violently. She covered her ears with them.

"Oh, God," she whimpered. "Please, please stop."

Another squeal of pain ripped through the night and she started to cry. "Ruthie. Shhh. Ruthie, please. I can't. Mama, I'm sorry. I can't do it."

Something wet on her face. She touched it with her hands. Blood. Sticky, dripping from her fingers. Everywhere she looked. So much blood.

She woke with a start, hyperventilating and wet with sweat. The room was unfamiliar at first but gradually the James's second guestroom came into focus and the blood and the tormented cries began to fade.

A kind, gentle numbness settled through Hannah, releasing

her body and soul from the pain . . . if only for a little while. A trick she'd learned in her youth and had all but forgotten in recent years. A trick that prevented her from stepping off the edge of madness time and time again. A trick that gave her time to pull herself together again—collect her physical strength, renew her spirit, assemble her thoughts . . .

Her eyes popped open and it was as if all the instructions had changed from Chinese to English. She knew what to do. She even knew why.

She scrambled into jeans and a sweater but her thoughts were already ten steps ahead of her. She was quite likely making the biggest mistake of her life, but it felt so completely right that she tried not to think about it too much.

Leaving a note on the refrigerator door for Anna, she carried her shoes out the front door, danced across the lawn wet with rain to her car, and got in—she was in a hurry. Fearing her resolve would slip away, she started the car and pulled away from the curb.

She was a coward at heart, most people were, and that was all right. If there were no cowards, heroes wouldn't be a big deal. Not that she was expecting any sort of medal or trophy for what she was about to do, but there had to be some sort of satisfaction from doing the right thing that heroes could always point to and say "See? That was the right thing to do"—even if they were pointing from behind prison bars.

Her thoughts raced and her heart pounded; she felt like she was running down the street to The Sheriff's Office.

It was all about Anna. The questions, the answers, all of it. Anna. The moment Grady told her, *"Ruth had a daughter. And she needs you,"* it became all about Anna. Hannah's life spiraled inside out. Literally. Her feelings, her secrets, her memories, everything she'd kept inside for so long was now on the outside for everyone, for Anna, to see and feel . . . and judge. And the moment she met Anna, and experienced love at first sight, she knew she wasn't playing solitaire anymore. Running away, fighting to stay alive and making a safe, productive life for herself all took on a new purpose; made it all more significant than simply surviving.

This was an Anna thing . . . which made it a mother thing. It had to be. It was the sort of sacrifice a mother would make for her child's welfare. She was sure of it.

Parking in front of the County Sheriff's Office she slipped her feet into her sneakers and got out of the car, propping one foot at a time on the bumper to tie them. Not wanting to appear crazed at all, she took several slow deep breaths, checked her hair in the side mirror, and gave herself an encouraging smile. "It's the right thing to do."

Inside the station was a small waiting area in front of a glassed-in counter. On the other side of the main desk there were a dozen smaller desks with computers and chairs and stacks of files; a hall that led further back in the building to the cells and private offices and interrogation rooms and to the rear entrance where the officers parked their cars and booked the people they arrested.

Two deputies sat at the desks, typing industriously while they talked about a baseball game. They both looked up when Hannah walked in but only one stepped forward to offer assistance.

"How can I help you tonight?" He gave her a pleasant smile.

Hannah took another deep breath. "Could you wake up Sheriff Steadman, please. I'd like to report a murder."

Chapter Twenty

Truth be told, there weren't that many murders committed in Turchen County.

An accident now and again, naturally, but murder? Not so much.

Come to think of it, the last murder they had was what many people believed for years was a double homicide, out at the old Benson place.

Funny how Grady could get a call at four in the morning, hear something garbled about a woman and a murder, and wake up instantly thinking of her, isn't it?

Funny how he regretted every ounce of pressure he'd put on her the last few weeks when he saw the pallor of her skin and the stress in the lines of her face as she sat wedged between a weary woman waiting to bail out her drunk husband and a furious father counting the seconds for his son, the sleeping huffer in back, to wake up enough for his ride back to rehab. Hannah's posture was resigned; her eyes downcast for the few seconds it took her to sense him staring at her.

He saw resolve but no fire in the true-blue of her eyes. He tried to smile reassurance, but his lips barely curled and remained closed. He froze in place on the other side of the glass. If he moved he could start an avalanche of truth and emotion he might not like.

Unfortunately, *she* moved and the earth beneath his feet began to shift and slide. They took slow deliberate steps toward each other and met at the open gate at the end of the front desk.

"Hi." She looked over his shoulder for a moment then back at his face. "Don't expect me to apologize for waking you up. If I can't sleep, you don't get to either."

"Fair enough." He nodded and reached out to open the gate for her; stood to one side to let her pass. She looked back for directions. "Left and then left again— Mike?" His deputy looked up. "Could you round us up a couple cups of coffee, please?" He mouthed, *"fresh,"* indicating he knew what kind of crap coffee they drank all night to stay awake and he wanted what they all called "morning or daylight coffee," which you could actually stir with a spoon if you wanted to.

He caught up with Hannah as she stood in the doorway of his office.

"Please, come in, get comfortable. I've got—"

"This isn't an interrogation room. Shouldn't I go in an interrogation room?"

"We don't interrogate people who are voluntarily reporting a crime. I've got coffee coming so go ahead and sit and we'll get started with some of the paperwork—"

"But I committed the crime. I don't want you to be nice to me or treat me any differently than you would any other killer. I should be in an interrogation room." She looked out his office window, at the wide-open view it had of Main Street and across the way at the park and gazebo. Her gaze met his and he knew her head was as full of memories as his was sometimes— of the two of them huddled close to stay warm at night in the gazebo; learning and practicing their kissing techniques in the gazebo; declaring their love for each other for the first time . . . in the gazebo. "Really. I should be in an interrogation room."

He stared at her for a good long minute trying to wrap his brain around the words *crime* and *killer* and attach them to Hannah. They weren't sticking.

"Sit." He turned on the overhead light and immediately turned it off again. It glared. This wasn't an interrogation. He turned on his desk lamp and filled his office with a soft, glowing ambiance more conducive to a confession. "I'll be right back."

By the time he came back with a small handheld tape recorder, the coffee had arrived and Deputy Martin asked if she wanted anything in hers. She shook her head no and held onto the cup like a lifeline. "I'm going to tape our conversation, Hannah, so Deputy Martin can get back to work."

"Maybe he should stay. To keep you honest."

"Me?"

"I don't want any favors from you, Grady. I don't want you doing anything that might jeopardize your future. You're the sheriff. You have to put me in jail like you would anyone else. Promise me."

He opened his mouth to tell her it wasn't up to him who went to jail and who didn't, but he knew that wasn't what she wanted to hear.

"I promise . . . in front of Deputy Martin here, that if you've done something illegal I'll put you in jail for it. How's that?"

She nodded, leaned back in her chair, got as comfortable as she could, and took a sip of coffee. He tipped his head to Mike to leave the room and stepped behind his desk. Reaching out, he snapped on the recorder, announced the date, time, and their names and asked her, "Are you giving this confession of your own free will?"

"Yes."

"Has anyone threatened you?"

She gave him a pointed look and pursed her lips, then muttered, "No."

"Then start at the beginning, Hannah."

He watched the quick intelligence in her eyes glaze over with recollection and caught himself holding his breath. After straightening the corners of three files on his desk he picked up a paper clip and tried to look calm and casual and patient when he was anything but. When she did speak it startled him.

"We had the nicest, warmest Indian summer that year, remember? That's why you and Mark and your friend Billy wanted to go camping that weekend—you weren't sure when you'd get another chance to go. And . . . and you were torn because you knew I'd be alone after work that Friday night, so I practically had to beg you to go, remember?"

"I do."

"And we said goodbye at school. You gave me a quick kiss before I got on the bus, then ran off. That might have been my last memory of you . . . your back as you jogged away from me." She smiled. "But you turned before you got to your truck and threw me a big kiss." She swept her arm out wide then settled it back at her side. "That was the last time I saw you. That's what I've always remembered about you . . . that kiss, and your . . . stupid smile and the way you looked so happy that day."

"I was happy. I had you and—"

She held up her hand to stop him. "A friend of my daddy, a drinking buddy, Buzz Weims, was parked in the parking lot waiting for his daughter. I didn't see him but . . . he saw us. I've always wondered if it was the first or second or third thing he told my daddy at the bar that night: 'I had to pick my daughter up at the high school today and take her over to the dentist. Oh, by the way, I saw your girl, Hannah, kissing Grady Steadman in the parking lot. My little sweetie didn't have one single cavity.'" She shook her head. "By the time he came around the corner to pick me up, he couldn't see straight. He almost hit me with the truck. He drove up on the sidewalk and stopped three inches from the bench." She glanced out the window but the bench she referred to was further up the street. "I . . . I still don't think he was trying to kill me then; he never would have done it so quickly, for one thing, and for another it was a Friday night, a payday. He'd want his money first." She started to shake her head slowly. "And I never would have gotten into that truck with him if I'd known that he knew about us. Oh, I knew he was angry. Immediately. I could feel it pouring off him like the heat from Mama's oven, so I didn't say anything. I tried to be very quiet and very small so maybe he'd forget about me. But when we got home and I started to get out he told me to stay. He . . . he relieved himself, there beside the truck, then came around to my side and opened the door. He grabbed my braid and pulled me out of the truck, threw me to the ground and called me a 'whoring slut'."

"Jesus." Grady felt nauseous and numb at once; certain he didn't want to listen to any more and equally as certain he was obligated to—and not because he was sheriff. He was responsible for what happened at the Benson house all those years ago. If he'd left Hannah alone . . . If he hadn't won her trust or kissed her in the parking lot or gone off and left her alone with that animal . . . If . . .

"He said if I wanted to act like a bitch in heat he'd help me, and then he used my hair like a leash and dragged me into the house. I kept asking him what he was talking about, what was wrong . . . deep down I already knew, I think, but it wasn't until he explained it all to Mama, saying it was a 'like mother, like daughter' thing that I realized how much he knew. I was afraid for you, so when he wanted me to admit I'd been kissing you I said no, Mr. Weims was wrong, I'd been kissing someone else, but he didn't believe me. I . . . I told him I was in love. He wanted me to promise to stop seeing you but I wouldn't. I told him no. Again and again, I told him no. He knocked me out.

"When I came around he was gone—after you, Mama said. I completely forgot about your camping trip, that you weren't home. He . . . We didn't think he'd put his hands on you—not his style. Not in public. Mama was unusually optimistic that night. I think she thought we'd seen the worst of it, but I knew better. She sent me to the attic hoping that out of sight out of mind would somehow work on him. But I knew he was going to beat me to death."

She swallowed, her mouth dry enough to distract her thoughts and remind her of the coffee in her hands. Barely lukewarm now, she drank several big gulps and set the half-empty cup on her side of his desk.

"He gave it a good try when he finally got home." She went silent for a moment. "Eventually I woke up in the dark. Alone."

He watched in silence, his chest tight and his stomach in a painful knot. He'd arrested a few men who thought it was okay to pound on their wives, even a woman who "accidentally" stabbed her husband three times in the leg, but he'd always been grateful he hadn't had to deal with any child abusers. The mentality of someone who could hurt a kid was beyond him. He couldn't understand it so all it did was make him angry.

"In the dark my face was stiff and tight and twice its normal size." Her voice was dull and weary. "I couldn't move at first. I thought . . . I thought that I was paralyzed. But everything hurt so bad. I couldn't see out of my left eye. There were cuts inside my mouth, my teeth were all there but they were loose. I could taste blood. I wanted to die. Just lie there and die. But it was so dark and the house was so quiet I began to worry that maybe he'd gone after you, again. I was confused, disoriented. I couldn't imagine where Mama and Ruth were or why they left me on the kitchen floor like that unless he'd taken them with him. Ruth or Mama always came when they could, to help me. We helped each other. Always.

"I finally pulled myself up to the sink. My right ankle kept giving out and I remembered Daddy stomping on it. I rinsed the blood out of my mouth, but when I put my cold, wet hand on my face it stung like hell." She stopped and looked straight at him. "I knew your parents would take care of you, protect you, but I was still frantic with worry—for you, for me . . . for Ruth and Mama. I don't remember how I got to your house. I kept thinking I'd be safe with you. Your mother probably told you more than I remember of what happened next. I heard her tell me you wouldn't be back until the next afternoon and then I remembered—and all I could think about was where could I hide until then?

"I didn't know where else to go. I *had* nowhere else to go. So I went home. The next thing I remember is being in our barn. My ankle hurt so bad I was crying and I didn't even realize it. I took a quick chance on the light, hoping no one in the house would see it, and wiped my right eye clear to take a look at my ankle. It was red and black and the size of a cantaloupe." She raised her right leg and used her hands around her ankle to show him. "I guess I must have fallen down a hundred times staggering back and forth between our houses that night because along with all the bruises Daddy gave me were cuts and scratches." She gave a soft awkward laugh, then grew sober again. "I was a mess." She took a deep breath. "I turned the light out. I was so afraid he'd find me. The only place I could hope to hide in the barn was up in the loft, but there was no way I could climb the ladder with my ankle. I got lucky, though, and found hay bales stacked well enough that I could pull myself up on them until I could reach out and drag myself up. It was close to dawn. There was a dark blue light filtering in through the cracks. I crawled to the front of the barn and found a place to peek out. Daddy's truck was parked where he left it the night before. It didn't look like anyone was up yet but I watched—with my one good eye—for as long as I could. It took a while before I realized I wasn't blind in my left eye, it was simply swollen shut.

"Routine stuff at our house." She reached out for her coffee cup, drank it dry, and set it back on his desk. She uncrossed and crossed her legs, shifting her weight in the chair. "When I was too tired to hurt anymore or to worry about being caught or to care about anything really, I covered myself in hay to get warm and fell asleep.

"Sometimes it feels like I never woke up. I hear his voice in my dreams calling me, but I don't know if he actually went looking for me or if I dreamt it. And at first I didn't know if I was dreaming the screams or if they were real, you know? I was in so much pain that sometimes I thought the screams were mine and I'd put my hands over my mouth but I could still hear them.

"I . . . I told you that Daddy didn't hit Ruth, that he . . . I think he was molesting her, though she never said so. But she hadn't gone down in the cellar for a couple of years . . . I hadn't heard her scream . . . I didn't recognize it, at first. My mama's screams, I knew, and I could hear him yelling all the way out in the barn. He thought they knew where I was, that they'd hidden me from him."

She was talking so fast now she had to stop to take a breath. "I thought it was a dream. I've had that same dream over and over ever since. Mama crying out and Ruthie's screams." She closed her eyes. Tears slipped down her cheeks from the corner of each one. "It went on and on and on while I listened, too

314 Mary Kay McComas

weak and in too much pain to help them. But then I opened my eyes. I saw Ruth sprawled in the doorway to the hall. She had a split lip and a cut on her forehead. There was blood everywhere. On her little face and dress. Mama came up beside me. I'd never seen her so bad. There were whole chunks of hair missing from her head and those horrible marks around her throat from where he choked her, but she was looking and acting more afraid of me than she was of him. She reached out, like this . . ." Hannah opened her eyes and showed him trembling fingers. "And that's when I looked down . . . and saw Daddy on the floor . . . and saw the fry pan I hit him in the head with in my hand." Another deep jagged breath. "Mama took the pan from me by the handle and . . . and she said she'd lie for me, that she'd take the blame. But I'm the one who killed him."

The silence that followed her declaration made it seem unfinished somehow, like there was a great deal more to the story that she wasn't telling. They stared at each other across the desk until she cleared her throat and asked, "What?"

"Is that all?"

"Isn't that enough?"

He'd read the police reports. He'd seen the crime scene photos. There was more to the story.

"Did your mother say anything else to you?"

She'd been so forthcoming with the rest of the story that her sudden reluctance was telling. This was the deepest, darkest part of her secret—this hurt the worst, affected her most.

She'd tell him. He sensed that she'd come to get everything off her chest once and for all. He listened to himself breathing while he waited for her to speak. How she'd survived that house with her mind and soul and her heart intact, he couldn't guess. His gaze roamed over her face and slender form with gentle appreciation. She looked like a flesh-and-blood woman to him—a smart, kindhearted, funny, wonderful woman. Who knew mere humans could walk out the front gates of hell and then thrive?

She looked out his office window into a long-ago kitchen where her sister and father lay on the linoleum bleeding—dazed both then and now.

A grimace crossed her face and the right side of her body cringed protectively.

"What, Hannah?"

"Mama. She takes the fry pan from my hands and raised it over her head. She's going to hit me with it but then . . ." she winced and covered her right ear with her hand, " . . . she starts screaming at me. She tells me to get out of her house. She says my blood is tainted by his. I'm a violent soul. I killed him. That makes me as evil as he is and now I'll go to jail. I'll rot in prison. Someone, me I guess, I say, But . . . he was going to kill us. Not *you*, she says, not this time. He was after her and Ruth, looking for me, but it wasn't self-defense for me. And no one will believe I was there with them because there was no fresh blood on me. They'll know I came back to kill him—murder him. I have to go. She'll take the blame for killing him; she's my mama and she owes me that much, but I'm not to ask her for anything more. Ever. She wants me to go and never come back." The sorrow and defeat in her eyes when they gravitated around to meet his was crushing. "So that's what I did."

He studied her for a long minute. "That's it then? That's all?"

"Jesus, Grady, I just confessed to killing my own father. What more do you want?"

He almost grinned. There she was, his scrapper. *That's* how she'd survived in that house, she was a fighter. He stood and walked to the other side of the desk—to be closer to her but also to nonverbally let her know the worst was over and he was there for her. "Well, for starters I'd like to know why you gave in, why you decided to come in and tell me all this."

"Anna." She sighed. "Mostly. I don't want to spend the rest of our lives lying to her. Everything I say to her should be the truth. Ruth told her I was a hero for running away . . . and I think there's a part of her that thinks I'm a jerk for not coming back for Ruth when I got on my feet. I want her to know the truth. And Mama . . . Anna has no idea who that woman was when I left here because I have no idea who they're talking about now. She's like Jekyll and Hyde . . . Hyde when I left and then Dr. Jekyll. She raised Anna very differently than she raised me. Thank God."

"I would imagine that getting out from under your father's fist your mother simply reverted to the woman she was meant to be in the first place. Maybe. She did change a lot. I didn't recognize her when I first came back to town."

She nodded and went silent for a moment. "I'm glad . . . I guess . . . you know, that she found a way to become happy with her life. We have that in common, at least. That we survived and made better lives for ourselves."

Grady loved that her expressions were so easy for him to read now. He watched the dawning of awareness light her features. She'd confessed to murder—*her* better life was no more.

"And if Mama straightened herself out to set a good example for Anna, then I feel like I should, too." She stood, faced him, and put her wrists out ready for cuffing. "If I'm never able to teach her anything else maybe I can show her that I loved her enough to tell the truth and to take responsibility for my actions. That's something good parents teach their kids, isn't it? Taking responsibility?" She dropped her hands abruptly. "And you are going to take care of her for me, aren't you? Raise her with Lucy? She'll have plenty of money after the farm sells and

I have savings I won't be using. Promise me, Grady." He shook his head. "Grady! Please."

"Hannah. Sit down. Please. You may be finished, but I'm not. I have a couple more questions."

"Oh." She sank back into the chair. "Sorry. I've never been arrested before and I want to get it over with. But maybe I shouldn't be so eager, huh? Go ahead."

Now that the story was out she was calm talking about it, relaxed with the fact that she'd killed her own father. "Did you ever think your mother might be wrong? That you could have claimed self-defense or temporary insanity from what he'd put you through the night before?"

"Not at first, no. I believed her completely. It was years before I even wondered if maybe . . . you know, after watching TV and reading newspapers. But I was scared. Once I even considered going to a lawyer and asking, you know, because they have attorney-client privilege . . . but aren't they also obligated to report a crime if they know one's been committed?" He nodded. "I guess they could have defended me then, but I'd also covered up and withheld the information for so long that I figured that even if I somehow got off for killing him I'd still go to jail for keeping quiet. Right?"

He shrugged. "Theoretically. But probably not."

She thought for a moment. "I also thought I'd have to be sorry I did it, like show remorse for my crime? But I was never sorry. Killing him was the best thing I ever did for me and my family. The only regret I have is that it's going to keep Anna and me apart."

He folded his arms across his chest and stretched his legs out in front of him. "Something in your story doesn't add up for me."

"What?"

"You haven't mentioned how many times you hit him."

"How many–" He could tell she was rewinding the film in her head to come up with a plausible number. "Once? I think, just the once. The pan was heavy. Really heavy. And I was in bad shape. I could barely hold it off the floor when Mama took it from me. I don't remember how I got from the barn to the house . . . or deciding to kill him but. . . ."

"Okay, answer me this: When you left the house, when you ran, could you still recognize your father's face?"

"What?"

"Hannah, honey, I'm trying to avoid showing you the crime scene photos. Tell me if your father's face was . . . intact when you left."

She jerked a slow nod, her expression wary. In a soft voice, she muttered, "Show me."

"You don't want to see."

"Please."

Reluctant to leave her side, he went back to his chair and opened the bottom drawer of his desk to remove a thin file folder. Clutching it close to his chest, to keep as many of the memories of that night inside and unseen, he combed through the pictures until he found the least gruesome shot of Karl Benson's corpse.

Glancing up at Hannah again he saw that she'd steeled herself for whatever was about to come but he still hesitated.

"You don't need to do this. I believe that you only hit him once."

"Show me."

Reaching across the desk he laid out one 8 x 10 photo of a large body in a pool of blood on an old linoleum floor with a mash of meaty pulp where his head should have been. Hannah leaned forward, took half a glance and squeezed her eyes shut. He flipped the photo over and brought it back to his side of the desk.

"You stopped him, Hannah, but she killed him. Just like she always said."

When she opened her eyes, they were brimming with tears and pain. "She . . . All this time . . . She let me think, all this time, that I killed him. She . . . she could have looked for me . . . she knew I wasn't dead. She could have looked for me sooner and told me. Even if she didn't want me back, she could have told me. She should have." She was full out crying now and it was tearing him apart. He knew the recorder was still on but he hadn't put a tape in it anyway. He couldn't sit in his chair and pretend to be professional any longer. He scooped her into his arms, held her close, and let her cry. "Why couldn't she love me, too?"

He didn't know what to say—he didn't understand it any better than she did.

Chapter Twenty-one

 September 9, 2007

Dear Hannah,

If you are reading this I have gone to meet my Maker. Even as I write I am hoping and praying that I have already found the strength in my soul to contact you and the courage and humility in my heart to apologize for the way I have treated you.

Many times I have started this letter and many times I have failed. I have been a coward all my life, something you will never have to lower your pride to admit.

After I sent you away that night Karl started making noises and moving across the floor. I was terrified that he'd come around and blame me for what you'd done. I hit him in the head with the pan again. But once I started I could not stop. Not until I realized I was hitting something soft not hard anymore.

I couldn't believe what I'd done, how coldly evil I was and what a relief it was that he was gone. I couldn't confess to Father Paul or beg God's forgiveness for some time because I felt no remorse. Still I knew I would go to hell and be there with Karl forever if I didn't. So I went to Father Paul and we talked.

He taught me so much, Hannah. He showed me what an ignorant woman I was. He called it unenlightened but it was ignorance. I was a stupid and fearful woman. He showed me how hurtful it can be in so many different ways. He gave me books to read and I learned to drive so I could go to a special doctor in Charlottesville. I tried to get Ruth to go but she did not like him. She did not like men at all.

Mostly I learned about you though, Hannah. All the times you stood between me and Karl, when I believed it was the evil in your blood rising up to meet his, it was you defending me, like a Guardian Angel. And I should have been the one defending you. You and Ruth both. I know that now. I know you were defending us that night and that I was wrong to condemn you and send you away.

I know now. But it was many months before I learned that the evil in Karl was not in his blood but had been put there by someone else. His own daddy is my guess. And for all those months I let the police look for your body even though I knew you weren't dead. By the time I realized the mistake I had made I was too ashamed and embarrassed to admit it. To the police, but most of all to you. I allowed everyone, including your sister and my priest to believe Karl had done something to you.

I write this letter because I am still a coward. Because I need to beg your forgiveness and I am afraid you won't give it. Not because you are not able to forgive because God and I have seen you do it often enough, but because I do not deserve it.

I have tried to make up for my sins with Anna. I have

given her the love I have always felt for you but was too weak and afraid to show you. But I am certain that I will never sit with my Lord God until you are able to find it in your heart to forgive me. I pray someday you can.

Your loving mama

It was the ninth day of an August heat wave in Baltimore. Fuses were short and tempers were exploding all over town. Newscasts were full of reports of road rage, elderly victims with heat prostration, and power outages that kept the circle revolving—like a dog chasing its tail.

At Benson Insurance & Investments where the power didn't waver and the AC blew like a nor'easter in January, one particular temper had been simmering—and boiling over from time to time—since early June.

"You fired Jim?" Joe's voice on the phone didn't sound as disapproving as much as surprised.

"I asked him to leave, yes. I told him I'd give him a good reference and help in any way I could, but I'm sick of him drooling down my neck and expecting me to make him a partner. I hate that sense of entitlement some men have. I mean, what makes them think everything has to be their way solely because they're men? What happened to give and take and compromise and stuff like that? Give a little, get a lot, you know?"

"Are we still talking about Jim Sauffle?"

Were they?

She hadn't heard directly from Grady in almost two and a half months.

The morning she and Anna left, the Steadmans and Biscuit joined Don and May James to wave them off. With the car packed up, with barely enough room left over for driver and niece, they were being passed from one person to the next for hugs, and Grady . . . cheated. He kissed her—like she was going off to war.

The kids made embarrassing noises and the other adults smiled and looked at one another like it didn't surprise them at all.

And all he said was, "I'll see you soon."

She was halfway home before she'd collected enough thoughts in her head again for a proper response. "How soon?" It took her the rest of the trip to realize he was talking about driving the U-Haul up for her—eventually.

Since then, he hadn't called once. Not even to see how Anna was settling in. Though, to be fair, the girls had been Skype-ing practically all day everyday and he'd peeked in over Lucy's shoulder several times to say hello to Anna—but he never passed a message on for her. And she missed him. More than she thought she would.

Well, she'd learned to live without him once before, she could do it again.

Their relationship had been doomed from the very beginning. It wasn't meant to be. The people of Clearfield needed Grady and he would never fail them—she admired that about him. And unfortunately, while she'd put many of her ghosts to rest in Clearfield, she simply couldn't live there again. Plus she had responsibilities of her own, employees who were counting on her . . . and there was Joe.

Still, she was going to miss Grady. The quick intelligence in his green-hazel eyes, that wonderfully stupid smile that warmed her like the coals of a campfire . . . that strange magic in him that spoke to her heart and soothed the mistrust in her soul.

"Hello?"

"What. Oh. What did you say, Joe?" She rubbed at the tense dull throb across her forehead. "Sorry."

"Are we still talking about Jim Sauffle?"

"Um. I don't remember. How was Anna's practice? Did you go to watch again today?"

"I did. And I'm glad she doesn't mind because I very much enjoy watching her."

"She's beautiful, isn't she?"

"She is, indeed, very graceful. And her new coach waved me down to the track. He says she's very talented and in just the few weeks she's been with his team she's improved and now runs in the upper five percent. She's very much self-motivated and he has great hopes for her."

"Was she there? Did she hear all this?"

"I told her after." He chuckled. "She blushed."

"Tell me you're not falling in love with her, too, Joe."

"I can't. Next to you I think she's one of the finest young women I've ever known."

Hannah wasn't altogether sure how or what she felt about her mother these days—except that she'd done a good job of making up for her sins with Anna.

Her legacy to Anna was not that of the beaten and down-trodden but that of a resilient spirit determined to live in peace and of a woman aching to love and nurture and protect the family she was always meant to have.

Anna had, at first, been hurt to think Hannah preferred going to jail than staying with her but once the lies and night-mares were explained, the importance of truth between them discussed and the promise to be there for each other made and sealed with a hug, Anna recovered.

Anna forgave easily and she loved her for it.

Hannah tried to forgive her mother. She did. Some days she was more successful than others—if she used every ounce of understanding and empathy she could muster. On those other days, she couldn't quite make it and the pain and resentment and anger came anew. But she kept trying.

"She reminds me a great deal of you, you know."

She frowned. "Right. I'm graceful. I can't hold a pencil and answer the phone at the same time. And I'm not sweet. I'm tired and grumpy—"

"I've noticed."

"Sorry. I heard this guy on the radio today saying it was the barometric pressure pressing . . . or not pressing on our brains when the weather is like this that makes some people cranky, but who knows? Hopefully, it won't last much longer and I'll be back to my old happy self."

"I'll look forward to it."

She laughed. "You know you *could* argue with me and tell me you hadn't noticed how crabby I've been."

"I've never lied to you before, why would I start now?"

"You wouldn't. And I depend on you for that. So, did you call to tell me about Anna's practice or did you want me to bring takeout when I swing by to pick her up?"

"Yes. Anna. I told you she had a good run."

"Yes, you did."

"I did." Silence. "But I don't need food tonight. I'm going out with friends. Later."

"Okay. That's great. Which friends? I can pick Anna up early if you want."

"No, no. It's a late dinner."

"With who?"

"Ah. They're new friends. Well, old friends, new in town. Tell me what are you planning to do about Jim?"

Hannah leaned back in her chair and began to wonder if Joe's medications had lost their shelf life. "I don't know. Hire someone to replace him, I guess. I might promote one of the junior analysts. Ken Lyman. I like him. He's sharp. What did you think of him when you were here?"

"He and young Jack would both do well, I think, with—"

"Dammit." A noise in the outer office sparked her temper and sent her blood pressure soaring. "Joe, I have to go. Tell Anna I'll be there soon."

"Is something wrong?"

"One of the idiots who works for me forgot to lock the front door like I asked, and now some other idiot has walked in. Why would you have to explain to someone that when most of the lights in a building are out for the night, it means we're not open for business? How tough is that to figure out?" She paused before opening her office door. "I'll be there soon."

She put her BlackBerry in her suit-jacket pocket and worked at twisting her face into something that looked professionally friendly but please-come-back-tomorrow-ish. Halfway down the hall, murder and mayhem occurred to her so she slowed her pace, taking softer steps. She took her phone back out of her pocket and dialed in 911, keeping her thumb on Send as she peered around the corner.

She gasped, dropped her precious phone, and the intruder turned to face her.

"Hi."

Her lips moved but nothing came out—so she nodded.

"I have this whole speech prepared." Grady's voice came low and cautious. "You're supposed to be excited and ask me what I'm doing here. Maybe you could fake it?"

She laughed. She didn't need to fake anything. "What are you doing here?"

"I missed you."

She sighed. God, he was handsome and wonderful and . . .

"This is where you say you missed me, too."

Hannah nodded. "I do. I did. I've missed you, too. A lot."

"Good." He took two steps toward her. "Now all you have to do is admit that you love me as much as I love you—and don't try to deny it." Two more steps. "I can see it in your eyes . . . I can hear it in your voice. I feel it, as sure as I've been of anything in my life." One last step and he reached out to brush the backs of his fingers down her cheek. "You got away from me once and it tore me apart. It changed me forever. I can't let you get away from me again, Hannah. I need you in my life. I love you."

It was, hands down, the best speech she'd ever heard. Much better than the ones she'd dreamed up for him over the years.

"And this is where you say——"

"I love you, too?"

"For starters."

She bowed her head; took in and let out a deep breath. "Grady, I . . ." She looked up and caught his expression changing from hopeful to confused—as if she'd stabbed him in the chest and ripped out his heart for no reason. She framed his face with both her hands to make the look of pain go away. "I do love you, Grady. I've always loved you. I've never loved anyone else but you. But . . ."

"But what?"

She looked to his shirtfront for the right words. There weren't any. "Well, I know love is supposed to conquer all things but . . ."

"Just say it."

"I cannot live in Clearfield. I know you have responsibilities and a job you like there——"

"That's it? That's your big objection? That's why you've been pushing me away?"

"That and I thought I was a murderer. And I was sure that when you found out you'd have to throw me in jail. So there was no point in giving you any hope."

He took her by the upper arms and pulled her close, wrapping first one arm and then the other around her tight.

"Man, you're stubborn."

"Well, you're annoying." She didn't make it sound like a bad thing.

"You're frustrating."

"So are you."

He leaned back and took her face in his hands.

"You're also very beautiful."

"So are you," she whispered as his lips brushed against hers. She went up on her toes to press her mouth to his. He nipped at her lips to punctuate the rest of his speech.

"Here's the deal— Your friend Joe and I, we've been plotting against you . . . for weeks. No, hold still—and listen. He called you to make sure you'd still be in the office so we could talk alone, since Anna lives with you—and because Lucy and I just moved into his guest rooms."

"You what?" No more kissing, but he wouldn't let go of her face.

"Shhhh. It's temporary. We weren't sure how long it would take me to convince you to let us move in with you." He grinned. "You told me once that you felt cheapened by the fact that I thought I could bribe you with a hamburger and fries. You said next time I wanted to ask you a potentially incriminating question to bring something with a bigger price tag on it."

The cold air on her right cheek startled her when he removed his left hand to fish in his pocket and withdraw a princess-cut diamond ring. She barely glanced at it, she was so distracted by the rare uncertainty in his eyes. *Uncertainty* in someone like him—who would have thought it possible?

He took her left hand in his right. "So the potentially incriminating question is this: Will you marry me, Hannah Benson? Will you let me stay with you for the rest of my life? Promise to let me love you forever?"

Smiling, she nodded. "Yes. I promise."

A brief glance down and he slipped the ring on her third finger, saying, "I'd have come sooner but I wanted to line up a job first. I gave notice and quit my old one three weeks ago."

"You . . . you're going to be the sheriff here?"

"Nah. Too much work. Too boring. I don't know anything about Baltimore except that it's where you are and where I need to be, so the captain up here said he'd put me on a beat for a while. Later I can patrol if I want. I prefer that, being with people. Someday, I think I may take the detective's test."

"And Janice and Cal?"

"Clearfield is her home, all her friends are there and we'll go back and forth. Cal's off to college in a few days."

A powerful ache broke loose in her chest, constricting her throat and blurring her thoughts. She leaned in, wrapped her arms around his chest, and listened to the steady thumping of his heart against her cheek. An ache so perfect and so fearsome that it could only be love.

"I can't believe you did all this for me."

He gave her a quick, affectionate hug then pulled away so she could see him grinning with that outrageous smile of his. "Hannah, don't you know yet? You're one of *those* people. One whose strength and love make the world a better, brighter place to live. I'd do anything for you."

A⁺

AUTHOR
INSIGHTS,
EXTRAS, &
MORE...

FROM

MARY
KAY
McCOMAS

AND

Wm

WILLIAM MORROW

Behind the Book

It took me five years to write *What Happened to Hannah*. Not because it was a particularly complicated story to write. Not because I didn't care about the characters or know where I wanted the story to go. And not necessarily because I'm a super slow writer—I'm slow but I'm not *super* slow. No, the only excuse I can give for it taking so long is: stuff happens.

My last novel, *Necessary Changes,* was published in 2001. The solid little fan base I'd acquired while writing twenty-one short contemporary Loveswepts for Bantam Books assumed that it was my swan song, my last hurrah, the last thing I'd ever write. I thought so, too. After all, writing was not my first career . . . or my second. It was my third career and I'd been at for thirteen years. I was not a one-book-wonder and I considered my body of works to be, if not exceptional, at least above average. I was satisfied.

However, and without regard to my fans and I, my agent wasn't buying it. She refused to let me quit: What do you mean you're out of ideas? Why don't you *try* writing something and send it to me? It doesn't have to be a romance, write about your dogs. Explain to me, once more, why you can't write? How about we set a little deadline for you? Did I tell you, I have you on speed dial now? Call me back and we'll brainstorm, okay? When can I count on seeing something from you? Have you forgotten that I know where you live? She was relentless.

Finally, knowing how much I loved writing *Necessary Changes*—a historical chronicle of sorts—she came to me with the news that a well known publisher was starting a new line specializing in sagas, stories stretching over a period of time.

Well. Okay. Now, she was talkin'.

I am what some call a seat-of-the-pants writer. I often don't have more than a kernel of an idea to start a story with. This time the seed was a story that happens over time; a story with a past and a present. I'm not kidding. It was that vague at first.

But as every writer will tell you, the best way to write any story is to sit your bottom down in front of the computer and write it. And so I did, in late 2004.

Grady came to me first. He was . . . an M&M, rich milk chocolate in a hard candy shell. Firm and sturdy on the outside; soft and sweet inside. I wanted Hannah to have a tougher shell—because of something in her past perhaps—and while she might be just as sweet and mushy inside, she was different; she wouldn't simply melt in the mouth, she needed to be chewed . . . she was a Tootsie Pop. Unfortunately, the only commonality between my two characters was that they were both candy and what I needed for a really good story was some *meat*.

And that's about as far as I got in 2005 before Nora Roberts, a friend of mine, came to my professional rescue. She asked if I'd like to contribute a short story to a paranormal anthology she was planning as J. D. Robb. Well, duh. So, I put aside Hannah and Grady and spent the next several months writing "Mellow Lemon Yellow" for *Bump in the Night,* published in 2006.

But I went right straight back to my novel after that. I'd

been mulling on it while I wrote the novella, you see, and my characters now had histories. He was all-American country boy; popular at school, solid family; healthy and innocent. Her life was all-American as well but on the other end of the spectrum. She was a social outcast, her family was a festering nightmare, and her life was anything but healthy. Yet where their lives touched from time to time. . . .

That's as far as I got before I was offered a spot in another J. D. Robb anthology. And everyone knows that an offer in the hand is worth more than a story in the bush so I happily put aside my novel in 2006 to write another novella for 2007.

When I got back to Hannah and Grady they'd both grown up, had lives that didn't include each other, and had now met again. Storytelling dictates that the situation must be stressful so I added a single-parent family for Grady and a niece for Hannah that she knew nothing about but must now take custody of . . . *after* I wrote another short story for 2008.

Unfortunately, or fortunately, depending on your point of view, I wasn't asked to do another novella until 2009 for a 2010 release date. That left me with almost a whole year to work on my book. I gave it a working title of *The Legacy* and sent the first half off to my agent to read. Denise Marcil and I have worked together for twenty-four years and she always asks me the same thing: What's your character's motivation? And in my head I always reply: to get to the end of the story.

In truth, I sent this part and then that part of the story, then this revised part and that rewritten part to Denise so often that year she was quoting passages to me over the phone with her next set of suggestions such as: Can you enhance the drama here or try making that more compelling? or See if you can flesh out that character a little more.

And then suddenly, finally, it was done. In late 2009 I sent the final copy to Denise and then the truly hard work began. She had to sell it.

Which she did, of course.

Avon bought it as part of a two-book contract. I am presently working on *Something About Sophie*—and I don't have five years to finish it. I'm looking forward to seeing it on shelves in 2013.

I hope you enjoy Hannah's story. Clearly she's a character that kept drawing me back, again and again, to tell her tale.

Mary Kay McComas

Discussion Topics for Book Clubs

1. How do the children impact Hannah? Do you think they help Hannah deal with her own childhood? Which one was your favorite?

2. Do you think Hannah feels love and resentment toward her mother in equal parts? Or one more than the other? Are her emotions understandable? As an adult, after years of therapy and an educated awareness of the dynamics of her family, do you feel her reactions to her present situation appropriate?

3. What was your favorite scene and why?

4. Were you able to find any symbolism in the story? For example: Hannah purging her memories and emotions while purging her childhood home.

5. Hannah clearly grew and changed during the story. What about Grady? What adjustments did he make in his thinking? How did Hannah's return to Clearfield alter him?

6. Love isn't something to be wasted or ignored. When Hannah and Anna finally moved back to Baltimore, Hannah was testy, short tempered, and missing Grady. Do you think she might have eventually conquered her feelings and moved back to Clearfield to be with him if he hadn't come to her?

7. There's a little storyteller in everyone. If you could re-write any part of Hannah's story what would it be? And how would you tell it?

Kathleen Branigan

Mary Kay McComas

MARY KAY McCOMAS was dyslexic as a child, so becoming a writer was way down on the list of things she dreamed of doing someday. In fact, she earned a Bachelor of Science degree in nursing, worked in ICU-CCU for ten years, traveled a little, got married, had four children under the age of six, and *then* started writing. That was twenty-five years ago and now she can't imagine not writing. To date she's written twenty-one short contemporary romances, five novellas, and *What Happened to Hannah* is her second novel. She was born in Spokane, Washington, and now lives in a small town in the beautiful Shenandoah Valley of Virginia with her husband, three dogs, a cat, and her children nearby.